Blood
&
Chocolate

Blood & Chocolate

a novel by

Mark Zero

A GIANT BOOK

First Giant Publishing Edition June 2006

© 2006 by Mark Zero

This book is a work of fiction. Any resemblance to actual events or to any persons living or dead is purely coincidental.

All rights reserved under International and Pan-American Copyright Conventions. Published in the United States of America by Giant Publishing, Tucson, Arizona.

Library of Congress Control Number: 2006928638

ISBN-10: 1-933975-00-8
ISBN-13: 978-1-933975-00-9

10 9 8 7 6 5 4 3 2 1

Front cover photograph by Eugene Atget. Used by arrangement with the Bibliotheque nationale de France.

www.giantpublishing.com

Contents

Jeremiah's Pipe Smoke	1
Marnie Hawthorne Writes a Letter to her Husband	8
Skinny Dipping	12
A Fateful Interview	19
A Subtle Shift	44
The Exquisite Longing of Regret	58
Here and Now	73
An Illicit invitation	92
Arguments and Omissions	101
Shave and a Haircut	113
How the Past Repeats Itself	134
How We Know What We Know	155
Toffee in the Blood	163
A Crossroads	178
Old Affairs, New Desires	198
An Equal and Opposite Reaction	222
A Loss of Equanimity	239
One Predictable Consequence	250
Claims Against the Will	258
Kate Benjamin Writes a Letter to Jon Ridgely	272
The Apple Orchard	276
No Good Reason	285
The Ghost of Calvin Hawthorne	293
The End of the Season	303
A Farewell	310
A Shot in the Dark	319
Nothing More to Say	331
The New Head of Hawthorne Enterprises	336
Another Farewell	348
The Living and the Dead	354
How the Doubts Lingered	362
Marnie Hawthorne Writes a Letter to Her Husband	368

1

Jeremiah's Pipe Smoke

Thick and blue and bittersweet with a nutty pungence mingling the acrid and the saccharine in equal parts, the smoke from Jeremiah Grayson's bulbous amber pipe clung to his body like an aura. It was unclear which people objected to more: his constant smoking or the attitude it represented.

Jeremiah had fought in the second world war and had stayed in Europe until 1951—three years after his army discharge. He had acquired foreign tastes and peculiar habits during his time abroad, which he clung to in spite of the passing years: he listened to dissonant cool jazz and bebop, snacked on tinned mussels and vinegar fries and ordered his tobacco from the same tiny shop in Brussels that he'd discovered in the forties. Though he had run a quiet, respectable barber shop just off of Templeton's town square for half a century, his unusual tastes and watchful manner made people regard him with suspicion, as if his next move might prove alarming.

Jeremiah enjoyed this reputation, though he thought he did little to encourage it. Every day, he sidled into the Blue Cup for breakfast at seven o'clock, lingered over his copy of the St. Louis *Post-Dispatch* (another quietly insurrectionary activity, since everyone else was content with the Templeton *Constitution*), and then walked down Cross Street to his shop. He ate lunch at Bertram's at one. He walked home promptly at five-thirty. His unremarkable routine had remained the same day in and day out for decades, but it wasn't his routine that aroused the concern of his fellow citizens—it was his demeanor. They felt that he simply wasn't like them in some fundamental but ill-defined way, and it was this lack of definition that disturbed them.

Today, Jeremiah's pipe smoke preceded him up the hill from his barber shop toward the Square. It was a muggy September afternoon and downtown traffic was as brisk as it could be in a town of seven thousand people. Jeremiah passed Jean's Jewelry Store just shy of the Square, waved in at Jean as he always did, and crossed the street toward the Old Courthouse.

The Old Courthouse functioned symbolically as Lawford County's seat, but inside no cases were tried and no permits issued: the county's judges performed their duties at the newer court complex on the western edge of town. The Old Courthouse was now little more than a hall of records filled with yellowing documents from the time before computers; its maroon-red bricks were covered with an invisible but tangible grime, the ignominy of failure. Built in 1874, with a genuine Civil War cannon defending each of its corners and an attractively imperious clock tower (each of whose four clocks showed a different time), the Courthouse had fallen victim to incessant perfunctory use, then decay, and finally to the idea of progress that demanded ever more utilitarian architecture. In 1976, the year America had gloried in its past, the historic Courthouse had been replaced by a pair of long, flat, peach-colored buildings on the outskirts of town.

Jeremiah sat down on a bench on the north side of the Courthouse, beneath an ancient walnut tree, and re-lit his pipe. His old nose could no longer smell the blooming roses in the bed along the sidewalk. He sat for a few moments, puffing contentedly, watching a squirrel watch him, before he replaced his lighter in the pocket of his barber's vest, stood up again and continued slowly across the Square.

The jangling bells above the door announced his entrance

into Bertram's Drug Store, and he shivered in the dry, artificially cool air. He walked past aisles of craft supplies, household staples and bric-a-brac, to an awkward assortment of dining tables and plastic chairs. The luncheonette was chattering with small children and their gossiping mothers. Jeremiah weaved through them and pulled a stool up to the soda fountain.

Smoke gathered above him as he studied the menu, which hadn't changed in twenty years. Sharon Kazee, Bertram's manager, stalked over and glared at him, until he chuckled his thick, throaty, smoker's laugh and slipped the pipe into his pocket.

"If I see that pipe in here one more time, I'm going to ban you forever," Sharon said, with no trace of mirth.

"But what would you do without my five dollars every day?"

"Thrive." Sharon wiped the counter with a damp rag. "You want the usual?"

Jeremiah's usual was a cheesesteak, potato salad, a pickle, and black coffee, none of which he could taste. He hated the racket of Bertram's and the sentimental merchandise they sold, but he came every day for Sharon's sensible middle-aged bulk and the swing music she played on the sound system. He liked to stare through the picture windows at farm trucks wheeling around the Square and people taking packages into the post office.

Sharon went to start his order, and Jeremiah sneaked a last surreptitious puff on his pipe before it completely lost its flame. He put it quickly back in his pocket as Sharon rounded the corner with his coffee. The smoke lingered in the air.

"You're worse than my kids. Really. I don't understand the pleasure you take in flaunting that nasty thing."

Jeremiah sipped his coffee, content with their customary confrontation. He was lonely, and even stale conflicts with predictable ends were more satisfying than common public niceness.

As he sat thinking fondly of Sharon's surliness, he noticed a change in the lunch room's air. He looked around and saw that the eyes of his fellow diners were suddenly fixed on him, and he stared back, uncertain. He tried to catch the eye of Connie Carter, sitting with her two rambunctious sons, but her gaze was directed somewhere just beyond him. He heard a voice behind him, a ringingly clear female voice with a faint accent, possibly Irish, just light enough to be unplaceable.

"Excuse me, ma'am?" the voice said. "Could you tell me what that is you're cooking?"

Jeremiah turned and saw, standing a few feet away from him, a woman he was certain he had never seen before but whose features seemed nevertheless familiar. She was in her late twenties, with coarse blonde hair that hung to her shoulders in loose curls. The roundness of her cheeks emphasized her equally round blue eyes, which were as bright as a welder's arc and shot through with tiny, pale golden streaks. She had thin lips and a delicate jaw, and her furrowed brow made her look appealingly helpless.

Sharon came around the soda fountain. Sweat ran into the folds of her neck, and she wiped her hands on her apron. "It's a cheesesteak," said Sharon. Her voice was hard.

"I don't mean to bother you," the blonde woman continued. "It's just, there's a peculiar smell in the air I can't quite place. You're not baking anything, are you?"

"No." She continued to stare at the woman aggressively.

"Or brewing some kind of herbal tea?"

"No."

"Oh." The woman shifted her weight from one foot to the other and bit her lower lip. "Well. All right, sorry to bother you."

Sharon scowled and steamed back to her grill.

"What does it smell like?" Jeremiah asked. The blonde woman turned to him, and he felt the brightness in her eyes light up his own.

She made little circles in the air with both hands, as if conjuring the scent. "Sort of… like almonds. Burnt almonds."

"Almonds?"

"I don't know. It's such a familiar smell, but I can't put my finger on it. But… no matter." She moved as if to go, and Jeremiah cleared his throat.

"Like amaretto," he said. "Like hickory nuts and whiskey and oak." The blonde woman looked at him quizzically. Jeremiah reached into his vest pocket, drew out his pipe and offered her the yellowed bowl. She held the pipe below her chin and breathed deeply, closing her eyes. When she opened them again, she smiled at Jeremiah.

"I'm surprised I didn't recognize it at once, but with all the other smells in here…" She shrugged. "It reminds me of my father's tobacco."

"It's Belgian," Jeremiah said.

"You're joking."

"It's the house blend of a tobacconist in Brussels."

"My father's favorite tobacco was made in Brussels! He used to go there for his job."

"It's from a shop called Bjarne's. I discovered it during the war."

"Well." She handed Jeremiah's pipe back and put her hands on her hips. "You just never know, do you?"

"That's right," Jeremiah said. "You never know."

"Thank you."

She adjusted the strap of her small black handbag and walked out of the luncheonette toward the other side of Bertram's. Jeremiah unconsciously put his pipe back in his mouth and stared after her, trying to remember where he recognized her from. When he finally realized who the woman was, his blood ran cold.

Sharon set a plate down at his elbow. "Stop drooling, you old letch, and put that damn pipe away."

"That was Marnie Hawthorne, wasn't it?"

"Of course, who'd you think?"

"She's as beautiful as her grandmother was."

"Stop making a fool of yourself and eat your lunch."

Jeremiah picked up his fork and looked at Sharon silently, until she walked off shaking her head. Then he spun around on his stool and continued tracing the movements of Marnie Hawthorne with his eyes.

From a distance, Marnie could easily have been mistaken for her own grandmother, and it surprised Jeremiah that he had taken so long to recognize her. He had assumed that Dorothy Hawthorne's death had put an end to the fiasco of fifty years before, but now he saw that, to the contrary, her death had brought a living ghost of that past to Templeton, and it walked among them. Marnie Hawthorne's face, the casual elegance of her walk, her simple presence seemed a sign that the transgressions of the Hawthornes, that his own transgressions, remained unforgiven.

The legacy of the Hawthornes, which had survived for years in Templeton in the form of half-believed stories and bad jokes, in the form of the brooding Hawthorne Mansion, which conveyed a feeling of desperation and corruption even now—the legacy of the Hawthornes was strolling casually through Bertram's Drug Store. Jeremiah watched Marnie make her purchases, put her sunglasses on and walk out onto the Square, gracefully, easily, apparently oblivious of the animosity she inspired all around her.

2

MARNIE HAWTHORNE WRITES A LETTER TO HER HUSBAND

Dear Graham,

My second day in Templeton and I've already become maudlin and melodramatic, after the fashion of the town. My reputation—which I had no idea even existed—has preceded me, and the people here either hate or resent me. Of course, no one considers what a shock all of this is to me.

After a night at the dreadful Templeton Country Inn, I'm finally ensconced in my grandmother's mansion, which is creaky and gothic in a made-for-television sort of way. I can't tell if my grandmother was truly mad or just liked playing at being mad, or perhaps playing at being mad is its own form of madness. There's a Miss Havisham quality to the decadence, and there are stacks of detritus everywhere you look. It might be better to burn the place down than sort through it all. Given Grandma Dorothy's eccentricities, though, there are probably stock certificates worth millions stuffed under a pile of *Life* Magazines in the parlor. It's quite a disaster and makes me worry, first, that I'll never be able to organize it, and, second, that rats are lurking in all the corners.

The only clean room in the whole house is on the third floor—Grandma Dorothy's bedroom—and I can only imagine that some unfortunate brow-beaten caregiver has been forced to clean every square inch of it with toothbrushes and lemon juice every day for years, since there's nary a mote of dust. I know from Alexandra Bergren—that's the executor of the will—that my grandmother never left the house the last few years of her life. The doctors made house calls. Her groceries were delivered. I guess she sat up there in her room, high above everything, doing god-knows-what as her mansion crumbled around her.

In contrast to the dilapidation of the house, the grounds are well-tended and cheerful. Clearly, someone besides my grandmother has had a hand in the upkeep. I took a walk around the property this afternoon: there are about thirty acres attached to the mansion, with box hedges and flower gardens and fountains, and an amazingly gnarled old apple orchard. You'd love it, but I'm sure you'd have a thing or two to tell the gardener about complementary perennials, or whatever you green-thumbs get so excited about. It's idyllic and orderly, like those snobbish manor gardens you're so fond of, and someone obviously wants to keep it quiet and exclusive: I believe it's the only private property in the whole town set off by fences. The gardens here just flow into one another, and I'm sure the barriers around this estate have only fueled gossip about the crazy Hawthornes.

Day after tomorrow, I'll meet with Alexandra in the nearby town of Hutsonville to go over the details of the inheritance. There are already some challenges to the will and a lien on the toffee factory. Though I'm the only direct descendant, there are other family members here—second cousins and great-aunts by marriage twice removed or some such nonsense—and they feel irate about being left out. I haven't met them yet, but I expect it will be unpleasant when I do. They have a lot at stake in their hatred of me.

The funny thing about all of this, really, is that I know so little about my family here, about the family business and so on, that I can only feel perplexed and lost—I'm happy that we're inheriting the money, but, curiously enough, it seems to have little to do with us. As you know, my parents never gave me any reason to pursue relationships with the Hawthorne side of the family, and that part of my father's past just seemed closed. All I know is that my father didn't talk to his own mother for the last thirty years of his life, and now we're millionaires.

All of this will be sorted out in due time. My cavalier attitude will win no points with the natives, but I simply don't feel connected to any of it. Everyone here harbors secret feelings about my family, and I don't know enough about the grudges and resentments to be offended by them, which must intensify my aloof appearance. People look at me with loathing in their eyes.

I found a general store today and bought some sketch paper and colored pencils, so if you find poorly realized drawings enclosed, you'll know that I've been sketching as a kind of therapy. I haven't taken a deep breath in Templeton yet, but the idea of sitting in the town square and trying to capture its quaintness appeals to me.

Templeton is a very picturesque place. The main square is almost too storybook, with a courthouse right in the middle and rose beds and nook shops all around. If only the people weren't so nasty. . . but then, how could you have such idealized quaintness without a meanness underneath?

Now I must root around my grandmother's cupboards for her secret stash of liquor—it seems inevitable, doesn't it, that a mad shut-in would at least be a tippler? Hopefully, with her wealth, she'll have stockpiled a decent vodka, though martini fixings seem too much to hope for.

I miss you, and I feel strange and disoriented, like a shipwreck survivor washed ashore to some heathen village. . . Well. . . I told you I've become melodramatic since my arrival. I'm now a character in someone else's soap opera. A fabulously wealthy character! With fabulously wealthy emotions!

Finish up as soon as you can and come join me, so you can assume your rightful part in the drama. There's nothing sadder than a lonely soap opera actress reading dialogues to herself.

Much love for you, my dear,

Marnie

3

SKINNY DIPPING

Just after midnight, the full moon a diaphanous circle of light oscillating on the dark water's surface: Marble Lake, between Templeton and Prairieville off of County Road 11, hidden in a copse of sycamores, red elms and shingle oaks. The fetid smell of mud and decaying plants. A trickling, unnamed stream feeding the lake from the copse. Cattails and lush green grass along the banks. A rickety pier extending into the water.

On the pier: two sets of clothes, a blanket, towels, a half-empty bottle of red wine. In the lake: a naked woman, splashing, laughing: Kate Benjamin. In the water beneath her, a naked man—Jon Ridgely—gripping her ankles, trying to pull her under.

Kate kicked and spluttered and tried to get free. After a few moments of slippery struggle, Jon let go of her ankles and swam away beneath her. Kate stopped splashing and waited for him to resurface. When he didn't, she spun around and squinted across the dark surface of the lake.

She became silent, treading with slow, easy movements, scanning the ripples for a nose, a hollow reed. A bullfrog croaked. A breeze rustled leaves high in the trees.

"Jon?"

The trees circling the lake seemed dense with foreboding, and she was just at the edge of genuine worry when something brushed her foot, and then, in a heartbeat, Jon had her by the legs and yanked her toward the bottom. She flailed at the water and screamed, gasped for air, then went under, engulfed by liquid darkness, her face wrapped in her own long hair.

Kate allowed Jon to take her down, down, down; she closed her eyes tight. The water felt cool and otherworldly against her skin, swathing her in ether, and with the wine floating through her brain and her heart pounding in her ears, she felt utterly alive. Still farther beneath the surface, till she wondered how Jon could hold his breath so long and swim so hard.

At last, he let go and she achieved a momentary stillness, suspended under the water; then she paddled herself still farther toward the bottom of the lake, until the spaces behind her nose and eyes became dense with pressure and her lungs seemed about to explode. Her arms felt weak, and she tried to enjoy the sensation of panic that crept over her.

She allowed herself to float slowly upward, fighting the impulse to swim with all her might toward the moonlit surface. She imagined bursting out of the water and frantically swallowing great, clean mouthfuls of fresh air, but she did not give herself this satisfaction: instead, she slowed her ascent by paddling her hands. As her lungs screamed for air, she opened her eyes and calmly blinked at the turbid blackness around her. Her eyes teared, but her tears washed away in the murk.

By the time she reached the surface, she was gasping and panting. Her limbs felt sodden. Her head felt light. The moonlight on the water blinded her, it seemed so clear and bright. She laughed and smacked the surface of the water with her hands.

"Jon?"

Nothing stirred on the surface of the water for a long moment, until she felt his arm around her waist and she went under again. Jon's hands grabbed at her sides and shoulders, then his lips found hers and they were locked in a cold, tight, breathless kiss. They rolled over involuntarily and bobbed to the surface.

She disentangled herself and swam toward shore. She was a much better swimmer and reached the edge of the moldering pier first. She grabbed at a rotting plank and pulled herself out of the water, then flopped down on her towel, happily exhausted. She lay on her back and let the stars dance and reel overhead until Jon emerged and wilted down beside her, smiling, breathless.

"You're going to drown yourself one day," she said, and laughed. "And me with you."

Jon reached for the wine and took a swig, then handed it to Kate, who shook her head no but sat up and drank anyway. She closed her eyes and felt the wine's harsh cheapness coating her teeth and throat. Heat flushed through her chest. She laughed again, for no reason, and lay back down.

Jon Ridgely and Kate Benjamin had known each other since kindergarten, had graduated in the same class from Templeton High School. They had rarely seen each other socially during their school years: Jon had played on the football team and read Mark Twain; Kate had been a mathlete who liked solving recreational logic problems, whose hero was Marie Curie. After they went off to separate colleges—she to Wellesley and he to the University of Illinois—neither had thought about the other for nearly a decade, until they had both returned to Templeton in their late twenties, Kate to help manage her family's seed business and Jon because he had no other ideas. They had met by chance one afternoon at Ploughman's Grill and suddenly, as if they had been complete strangers, had begun dating and falling in love. That was four years ago.

Jon laid his palm between Kate's breasts. Barely visible, decayed brown bits of plants from the lake clung here and there to their bodies. He leaned over her as a light breeze caressed them, and they shivered through a full, wet kiss.

Kate got to her knees and began drying her hair and arms

with a towel. Jon propped himself up on his elbow and drank more wine, watching her.

"You're going to be hungover for your interview tomorrow," she said.

Jon worked part-time as a reporter for the Templeton *Constitution*. Like every member of the *Constitution*'s staff, Jon also had another part-time job—in his case, as a waiter at Ploughman's Grill—because there simply wasn't enough news in Lawford County to keep a full-time staff of reporters occupied. But lately, since Dorothy Hawthorne's death, everyone was working overtime, with a renewed sense of purpose. Tomorrow morning, Jon's assignment was to interview Dorothy's heir, Marnie Hawthorne.

"I love your hair wet," he said, caressing a thick strand of Kate's hair away from her face. "It makes your skin look ghostly."

Kate unfurled their blanket and stretched luxuriously across it. Her tall, slender body glowed pale in the radiance of the moon. Jon kissed the gentle curve where her belly met her hip. She shivered and giggled and ran her fingers through his hair, pulling him toward her.

Kate loved the narrow triangle of Jon's waist and hips, how simultaneously delicate of feature and sturdy of build his body was, how unaware he was of his beauty. Jon was smaller than she was: shorter by two inches, with finer bones and facial features, but he was more compact and muscular, and she felt safe and confident beside him. She ran her hand over his broad chest, down to his stomach, and let her fingers linger between his legs.

"You know what I want, don't you?"

He regarded her with a mixture of fondness and lust. "I'd be guessing."

She leaned close to him and touched her cheek to his. The

stubbly hair of men's faces fascinated Kate, and she particularly liked the coarse hedgerow of Jon's unshaven jaw. She whispered, "I saw your guitar in the truck."

"My guitar?" he exclaimed. "That's what you want?" Kate rubbed her cheek against Jon's scratchy face. "In that case," he said, "there's something I want, too."

"Is it something I can guess?"

Jon guided his hips between Kate's legs. He cupped her breast in his hand and kissed her with his mouth open, and they lay in each other's arms, kissing and writhing in slow motion, as water slapped against their little jetty and swayed the cattails nearby. The cool breeze shushed through the tall grass near the path, whispering of the coming of autumn. Gradually, the sounds of their own sighs and moans filled their ears, so that the croaking of the bullfrogs and the chirping of crickets and the occasional flopping of fish in the lake receded into the distance.

The rickety dock groaned and swayed as their movements graduated from slow arousal to easy violence. They smelled the heady, fecund reek of the lake all around them, and the odor and the discomfort of their makeshift bed heightened their pleasure, in each other, in the clarity of the night, in their solitude. All around them, for miles, there was only dark forest, cultivated fields and rolling, moon-dappled meadows. They took their time making love and found the gestures they had made a thousand times before a little strange, a little new and exciting.

* * * * *

They wrapped themselves in their blanket and lay passing the bottle of red wine back and forth, staring up at the moon. The night seemed late.

"So," Kate said. "I think we had a bargain."

Jon nuzzled his nose into Kate's neck. "A bargain?" he said sleepily.

"I told you what I wanted."

Jon lifted his head. "You can't want a show, still? At this hour?"

She shrugged her shoulders and nodded in the direction of his truck. "You know you want to."

He grinned sheepishly and kissed her. He trotted down the pier to the shore. He loved Kate for her easy thoughtfulness, for so affectionately giving him an opportunity to show off his guitar playing, which they both knew was bad. Always seemingly effortlessly, she made Jon feel good about himself.

The moist earth squished between Jon's toes, and the grass tickled his legs. He followed the narrow, overgrown path through the trees to the gravel road, grabbed his guitar from the back of his pickup and trotted back to the lake.

"A song, a song," Kate said in a tone of feigned boredom, as Jon sat down next to her.

He strummed a few hesitant chords, then plucked the G-string and fiddled with the tuner. "Okay," he said. "By popular demand," and he launched into a halting version of "Side by Side."

Kate lay back and closed her eyes. She knew that he learned old pop standards just to please her, and for that reason it did please her. He had a sweet, ingenuous singing voice that made up for his labored playing. "Don't know what's coming tomorrow," he sang. "It may be trouble and sorrow/ but we'll travel the road/ sharin' the load/ side by side." He finished that song and played "Blue Moon," followed by a jokey version of "Besame Mucho" that made Kate laugh.

"Thank you," she said. "My silly songbird."

Jon set his guitar aside and kissed her. "Would you like to

come home with me tonight?" he whispered.

"I would. I warn you, though, that I have to be in the field at the crack of dawn tomorrow."

"I'll go back to sleep when you leave."

Instead of dressing and scuttling their midnight picnic, however, Kate and Jon stretched out against each other and pulled their blanket close around them and let the sound of the water soothe them into forgetfulness, enjoying the gentle lullaby of each other's breath.

"My silly songbird."

4

A Fateful Interview

After Jon had graduated from the University of Illinois with a degree in American Literature, he had moved to Chicago and worked as an editor at a specialty magazine called *Gumshoe*. *Gumshoe* featured hard-boiled detective stories and accounts of true crime—not the setting he'd imagined when he was reading Ralph Waldo Emerson and Herman Melville in college. After five long years of editing other people's noir clichés, he had searched for other work but found his skills in demand only for writing internet-ready text (which he found distasteful), crafting pithy advertising copy (which bored him) or stringing hard news for the daily papers (which didn't pay enough). Ultimately, disgusted by Chicago's high cost of living, he had returned to Templeton to save money, regroup and decide what to do next.

Jon was the *Constitution*'s lead reporter on the Hawthorne story, and his articles so far had taken two forms: straight news about Hawthorne business holdings and the legal repercussions of Dorothy's controversial will; and human interest stories about the Hawthornes' rise to prominence. Everyone in Templeton knew the outline of Hawthorne family history by heart, but Dorothy had been a recluse for years and the Hawthornes hadn't played an active role in the community for decades, so the *Constitution*'s editor thought it wise to review the family's rags-to-riches past. Since Dorothy's death, every edition of the paper had sold out, and everyone argued endlessly over the details of the stories.

People disagreed about both the substance and the implications of Jon's articles, despite the fact that many of the events were well-documented by witnesses and victims. There was, for example, the fact that the Hawthorne family patriarch, Henry, inventor of the world-famous Hawthorne Toffee Bar, had immolated himself on the steps of the Old Courthouse one summer night in 1953, leaving behind no note or explanation. There were the odd circumstances of Dorothy's marriage to Robert Meese, who died mysteriously at the Hawthorne Mansion: the police had labeled the death accidental, though no one believed it was an accident. There was the strange disappearance of Calvin Hawthorne, Henry's only son and Dorothy's brother—Calvin had vanished without a trace in 1971 and was never heard from again. And then there was Dorothy herself, who, in her later years, had surrendered the daily operations of Hawthorne Toffee to business managers and secluded herself in her mansion, apparently never setting foot outside the house for the last ten years of her life. The Hawthorne family's oddities ranked second only to their economic influence in the life of Templeton, and the *Constitution*'s stories were supplemented all over town by gossipy variations and postscripts.

In addition to prurient, sensationalist rumors about the Hawthornes, the townsfolk indulged in speculations of a more practical nature arising from Dorothy's death: who would inherit the Hawthorne Toffee Factory, Templeton's leading employer? Would jobs remain secure? What about the extensive Hawthorne holdings in the county, the oil wells and farm land and commercial property? Would they be sold or partitioned? And what about all that money accumulated over the years, rumored to be in the tens if not the hundreds of millions of dollars?

The gossiping and speculation had taken a nasty turn

when the *Constitution* had revealed that Dorothy's will named just one heir, her granddaughter, a stranger to the town who had lived her whole life not only outside of Templeton but overseas. Dorothy Hawthorne had relatives all over the county, from the Longmores in Stoy to the Fullers and Meeses in Prairieville: none of these distant relations had laid eyes on her in years, but people were still appalled that Dorothy could pass over her own Lawford County blood for a complete stranger, no matter that the stranger was technically her next of kin. To the town, this development simply proved Dorothy's madness and continued the long line of shocking and inscrutable Hawthorne behavior.

In Jon's mind, the built-in antagonism of Marnie Hawthorne's relationship to the town put considerable pressure on his interview, the shape and tone of which would help determine Templeton's first real impression of her. She could make progress toward détente simply by appearing sensible or she could sully her reputation irreparably, and Jon would have as much to do with determining the perception of Marnie Hawthorne as she would. It was the first day in months that he had felt a sense of purpose.

For the occasion, Jon took his one good suit out of mothballs: a black double-breasted coat, tailored black pants and a yellow silk tie, with a crisply starched shirt so white that it practically consumed the colors around it. He walked around his small apartment several times, trying to feel comfortable and natural—he had worn the suit only half a dozen times in the four years he had been back in Templeton, and he felt transparently clownish in it. He studied his reflection in the mirror and realized with a shock how much of his former self he had forgotten: he had traded the easy cosmopolitan confidence he had developed in Chicago for small-town comforts and dead-end jobs. He sighed deeply. A story of this magnitude came along once in a lifetime in Templeton, but it was a daily occurrence in a real city, and he suddenly saw how aimless and self-satisfied he had become. He checked his tie for the last time, had a final sip of coffee and grabbed his satchel with its journalistic props—pens, notepad, camera and microcassette recorder.

Jon's apartment was a small room above Fendick's Glass and Windshield Repair on Cross Street, a block away from Deerfield Park. He trotted down the steps along the outside of his building, smiled at his landlady, who was polishing a mirror inside the shop, and headed across the park. He would walk to the Hawthorne Mansion—he didn't want Marnie Hawthorne's first impression of him to be his rusted-out truck or his clunky old motorcycle—and he would take an inconspicuous route through Deerfield Park, to avoid the hungry eyes of scandalmongers. People were bound to see him dressed up "in his Sunday best" for the interview, which would invite mockery later on.

Deerfield Park had been one of Jon's favorite haunts since childhood. A gigantic bronze doe stood at the park's entrance, inviting you toward the charcoal barbecues, jungle gym sets and Frisbee golf course beyond. The park hosted most of Templeton's community events in summertime, from Little League games to Shriners' picnics and the county fair. The park's centerpiece was a public pool, from which Jon could hear the squealing and screaming of children.

He crossed the baseball diamonds to the wooden footbridge over Big Creek. Big Creek and its cousin Little Creek eventually became tributaries of the roiling Wabash River on the Indiana border, but here they babbled peacefully, tiny streams marking languid paths through Templeton. Deerfield Park ended at the creek, and Jon found himself on Sycamore Avenue heading through a neighborhood of small aluminum-sided houses toward Main Street.

The morning was muggy and close, and he began to sweat. He removed his suit coat and slung it over his shoulder.

He thought about the ghost stories surrounding the gloomy Hawthorne Mansion that he remembered from childhood, that every generation of Templeton's children grew up hearing. Enchanted creatures lived in the gardens. Dorothy fed twisted little people mincemeat pies on full moon nights. Captured boys and girls lived in chains in the cellar. As a kindergartner, Jon had once had a nightmare of sneaking onto the Hawthorne estate and being discovered by a fearsome man-eating giant. He ran from the giant down a cobblestone street, tripping over and over again on the stones, as the slobbering ogre came closer and closer, eager to devour him. He still remembered that dream more vividly than many things that had actually happened to him: such was the power that the Hawthorne Mansion and old Dorothy had over his and the whole town's imagination.

Jon turned on Main Street, walked past the First Bank of Templeton and crossed Big Creek again as it passed through a culvert and washed into a gully. He crossed Main Street into a district of immaculate two-story houses, the dwellings of Templeton's most successful oil barons.

Oil had been discovered in Templeton at the beginning of the Great Depression, and it was the main reason for the town's unusual opulence. During the 1930s, when most American farm towns were suffering privation and decay, Templeton had been undergoing an oil boom—the entire town was almost constantly employed in the construction of private wells, or at the Marathon Refinery, or with the shipping and supplying businesses that grew up around them. Due to the influx of workers, farmers had markets for their crops and employed a healthy number of field hands, and during the winters the field hands built houses and public works for their thriving neighbors. For these reasons, Templeton—even seventy years after the boom—retained a vitality and luster that other small towns lacked. There was still local money here and it had been invested in the town.

It was also for these reasons that a successful international business like Hawthorne Enterprises could arise in such a tiny, out of the way place. It was during the period of Templeton's oil boom that Henry Hawthorne's toffee business first grew beyond the confectionary shop he had opened on the town square: as traffic to and from Templeton increased through the oil business, people carried Hawthorne Toffee Bars away to other towns, and Hawthorne's fame spread, until he was selling and shipping candy to other towns himself. During an economic depression, when few people had the heart or the capital to invest in new businesses, Hawthorne Toffee had found few competitors for the region's sweet tooth.

Jon followed Argus to Poplar Street, the very heart of this impressive district. Unlike the aluminum-sided single-story crackerboxes on the south side of Templeton, these houses were expansive and elaborate, built of stone masonry and brick, their walls covered with ivy, their porches decked with rocking chairs, swinging benches and flower pots. Instead of clear-cutting the land (the usual practice in Illinois), the owners had built their houses in among the black jack oak, sycamore, wild plum and crabapple trees, so that a lush canopy of leaves provided almost constant shade from the warm summer sun, and red-winged blackbirds feasted on ripened fruit in the shadows. Every yard was large and rolling and severely mown, with trellises lush with flowering vines and sandboxes for the children. Robins tittered and flitted overhead as Jon strolled down the street, and the occasional caw of a crow livened the morning air. Somewhere in the distance, someone was operating a gas-powered weed trimmer.

Jon fanned himself and mopped his brow with his handkerchief. He felt a contradictory mix of emotions: on the one hand, he felt calm, occupying the professional equanimity he had learned as a magazine editor; on the other hand, the idea of interrogating the last remaining Hawthorne titillated him. Templeton was just a little town, he knew, but it was his town, and for generations the Hawthornes had been the only family that really mattered here. Besides, though the town was little, the money was big, and what wasn't intriguing about truckloads of money?

On top of everything else, Marnie Hawthorne was rumored to be elegant and beautiful, and for the first time in four years, Jon had the feeling that something extraordinary was happening, something to break up the comfortable lassitude he had settled into. He put his suit coat back on and stood momentarily still outside the open gates of the Hawthorne estate before walking up the long gravel drive.

At the very end of Poplar, like the king at the head of the table, the Hawthorne Estate presided over the neighborhood. The most noticeable difference between the Hawthorne property and its neighbors was the preternatural darkness hovering over it. The landscaping up and down Poplar Street was verdant and profuse, with sunshine peaking through the leaves, dappling the walks with cheerful patterns; but along the Hawthorne driveway, the foliage was abnormally dense and tangled. It was perpetual evening. No squirrels skittered among the thick shrubberies. No birds called.

Jon's footsteps crunching the gravel were now the only sounds. He rounded a bend in the drive, and the mansion loomed.

The Hawthorne Mansion was ponderous and difficult to look at without a sense of unease. It was three stories high, with countless balconies and alcoves, and medieval-looking stone figurines perched on the corners. Despite the preponderance of picture windows, it gave the impression of a dark, elaborately masked insane asylum, and the dingy paint peeling from colonnades and porticos made it seem desolate and forlorn. Jon couldn't decide which was more oppressive: the building's actual, grandiose decrepitude or the moral opacity behind it.

A white sedan was parked at the mansion's doorstep, and Jon walked behind it and read the license plate bracket, which advertised a rental company in St. Louis. He approached the mansion's intricately carved wooden door, which was ten feet high and broad enough for three people walking abreast. He clanged the heavy brass knocker several times, the thudding of which died instantly on the air.

He waited. He clanged again, then stepped off the porch and leaned around a shrub to peer through the French windows. The house was dark inside, and he could see only his own reflection. He knocked yet again, and when no one appeared, he sat down on the porch steps.

He fished in his satchel for the harmonica he had been carrying everywhere for the last few weeks. Since he couldn't master any one instrument, he had decided to achieve technical proficiency on a wide variety of them and develop a party act based on the range of his undistinguished talent: such were the meager ambitions he pursued in Templeton, so far from the dream he had once entertained of becoming another George Plimpton. He played guitar, banjo, bongos and the fiddle, and now he was building a repertoire of harmonica tunes. He played a slow, drawn-out rendition of "I've Been Working on the Railroad," which sounded mournful in that setting.

As he was bending the final notes of the song into a blues, Jon heard a latch click and the heavy creaking of hinges behind him. He stood up, and a woman with honey-blonde hair emerged from the mansion. Jon's heart tightened.

She wore a green, short-sleeved silk cardigan so light and sheer that it followed every contour of her shoulders, breasts and waist; simple, white Capri pants; and brown leather sandals. There was a gold anklet on her left ankle, a gold bracelet on her right wrist, and a plain gold band on her left ring finger. She smiled, and Jon noticed that one of her bottom teeth had grown in front of the tooth next to it, pushing its neighbor slightly to the side.

"You must be Jon Ridgely?"

"Yes. Marnie Hawthorne?"

Jon dropped his harmonica into his satchel and shook Marnie's hand, which was fine and smooth, obviously unaccustomed to labor.

"I hope I haven't kept you waiting," she said. Jon was charmed by her light, lilting accent. "I've had three visitors so far, and they've all had to pound and scream before I've heard them."

"No trouble," he said. "It does seem like a house this large would have more than just this knocker." He immediately regretted the clumsiness and banality of this remark.

"Perhaps I'll install a harmonica in the door, and people can summon me with folk tunes." Marnie smiled again. "Please come in."

Jon followed her into the mansion. She stepped aside to close the door and he walked through the ghost of her perfume, which was as subtle and insinuating as her accent.

They were in a long, vaulted entry hall. A baroque chandelier high overhead provided the only light—despite the morning's bright sunshine and the long row of windows Jon had seen from the outside, no natural light filtered into the foyer. There was a heavy black table on one side of the hall and a black secretary's desk on the other; beyond these were open arches leading to darkened rooms. At the end of the hall was a long, broad, red-carpeted staircase leading up into the gloom.

"Right this way," said Marnie. "I thought we could talk on the back porch, where the mood is somewhat lighter. You can see that the house is in a certain amount of disarray."

Marnie led Jon through a large, musty parlor, which held high-backed red leather chairs and bookcases filled with thick, leather-bound books. Victorian lamps sat on end tables and breakfronts. Jon imagined that, even if every light in the room had been turned on, darkness would still have predominated. The Persian rugs beneath their feet were worn and the patterns difficult to make out, and all along the baseboards were messy stacks of yellowing newspapers and magazines.

Beyond the parlor was a windowless alcove with empty metal wine racks and glass-doored cupboards. This storeroom opened onto an enormous kitchen, which smelled strongly of disinfectant, as if it had just been cleaned. Three doors led in three different directions from the kitchen, and Marnie hesitated before choosing one.

"I still don't know my way around the house," she said over her shoulder. "It's a labyrinth—I keep finding new nooks and crannies."

Jon was puzzled by the naturalness with which she addressed him, as if he were nothing more than a casual visitor and not a reporter from the newspaper that had been publishing garish accounts of her family's past.

They came to a screened-in veranda that looked out onto a bright, well-kept garden. Jon couldn't have been more surprised: before him were neat rows of blooming shrubberies and flowerbeds. White ornamental-gravel paths wound through the flowers and converged at a marble fountain, where water burbled cheerily down the sides of a statue of Cupid shooting his bow and arrow. The fountain figured prominently in Hawthorne lore—it was where Robert Meese, Dorothy's husband, had met his drunken end. The death had been classified accidental, but more than one person suspected that Henry had murdered Robert and that his guilt over the murder had precipitated Henry's own suicide.

Bordering the garden on all sides were tall box hedges, into which arches had been cut and wooden gates installed. It seemed as if they had passed through a magic portal from the murky gloom of the mansion to an alternate estate filled with hope and cheer. Even Robert Meese's death seemed genuinely part of the past in this merrily ordered garden, whereas every moment of Hawthorne history clung darkly to the mansion. Jon wondered how the two tempers could coexist within a few feet of each other.

Marnie directed him to a seat at a round glass table on the veranda and sat down opposite him. The table offered a vase of fresh-cut white roses, a pitcher of blood red liquid and two glasses. Jon took a pad and pen and his microcassette recorder from his satchel.

"May I offer you a glass of champagne punch?" Marnie said.

"Champagne punch?"

"It's a fine morning for it—it cuts the mugginess." Marnie smiled, and Jon found himself wanting to agree with everything she said. In the garden, bees buzzed and hummingbirds flitted between blooms.

"I think my editor would be unhappy to find me drinking on the job," Jon said.

"So those old movies about tough, hard-drinking reporters—they're just old movies?" She said this in a winning, jocund way, but Jon felt genuine mockery underneath. A jab and a feint. She poured herself a glass of punch.

"And the movies about dizzy blonde heiresses?" he countered. "Are those just old movies as well?"

Marnie poured a second glass of champagne punch and pushed it toward him. "I guess we shouldn't mistake movies for real life, should we?"

Under Marnie's gaze, Jon felt transparent and uncouth, a small-town bumpkin. He tried to compose himself in a more offhanded, self-possessed way, to match the casual energy of his subject.

"Do you mind if I record the interview?" he said.

"Not at all. Just tell me when you want to start."

"How about now?" He pushed the record button and the cassette machine clicked lightly as the tape unwound in its cartridge.

"All right. Before you ask me any questions," Marnie said, "I want to tell you why I granted this interview. It seemed that your paper was going to report every detail of my grandmother's passing and the legal disputes surrounding it, whether I had anything to say about it or not, so I thought I might as well have something to say about it. Mainly, I want to say this: I know a lot of people have a lot at stake in Hawthorne Toffee, and I don't want anyone to be concerned that I'll disrupt their livelihoods. I've been advised not to say anything specific about legal matters, but I understand that people are anxious, and I'd like to say that, insofar as I can, I sympathize with the concern that my grandmother's death has caused. So, that's my statement."

"You want people to know that you sympathize with them?"

"That's right. I don't know how this is all going to play out—who will end up controlling the toffee company, the other assets, and so on—but there will obviously be a change in ownership of Hawthorne Enterprises, and I want to clear the air and say that I'm interested in the continuity of my family's business." She sipped her punch. "I know that Hawthorne Toffee is the major employer here, and I can understand why people might feel worried, so I want to assure everyone that, if it's up to me, everything will remain more or less the same. It may not be up to me, but there seems to be a lot of speculation in the air, so I'd like my position to be known."

Jon scribbled her statement into his notebook. "When you say you can't discuss the legal matters, does that mean that you won't answer questions concerning your relatives in Lawford County?"

"You could try me, but I can't comment about their claims until the courts are through settling the will. You obviously know that the will is being contested."

"Have you been advised about the time frame in which disputes will be resolved?"

"Everyone has their own solicitors—I'm sure you know who they are—and they'll work according to the schedule of the court." She shrugged. "The probate period is six months, but who knows how long the disputes might last? They could be resolved quickly or dragged out, it's anybody's guess." Marnie's eyes captured and concentrated the sunlight, making everything she said about these prosaic legal matters seem sunny and bright. "I assume," Marnie continued, "that you knew I couldn't discuss the finer points of the estate or the business right now, so. . . What did you want to ask me?"

Jon had come more in his role as entertainment columnist than news reporter—he was here to do an exposé about the last of the eccentric Hawthornes, and he had prepared a series of discreetly prying questions about Marnie's personal life. He felt above the town gossips, since his curiosity was sanctioned by the newspaper, but he had already printed racy stories about Henry Hawthorne's auto-da-fe, Calvin Hawthorne's unexplained disappearance and Robert Meese's mysterious death, and he suddenly saw that, from Marnie's perspective, he couldn't avoid being implicated in the muckraking. In Jon's imagination, without the fact of Marnie Hawthorne in the flesh to consider, his role had seemed harmless, even salubrious, a fact-based antidote to the wild rumors about everything from Dorothy's sex life to the secret recipe for Hawthorne Toffee. Yet, sitting in front of the personable, actual Marnie Hawthorne, he hesitated to ask anything anyone might want to know. He suddenly wanted to protect her—from himself! He couldn't take his eyes off of her and didn't want to, and the wheedling questions he had carefully rehearsed became tawdry and repugnant to him.

Marnie sipped her champagne punch and waited while Jon digressed into these private deliberations. She looked at him with a steady, shrewd expression, until he put his pen down and reached for the glass of champagne punch in front of him.

"I promise I won't tell your boss," Marnie stage-whispered, raising her own glass in a toast. Jon met Marnie's curious eyes and listened to the water splashing down Cupid's statue in the garden fountain. He felt juvenile and incapable. Finally, she said, "I don't mean to tell you your job, Mr. Ridgely, but it's only an interview if you ask me questions."

"Right," he said. He cleared his throat and straightened his notebook, sat up in his chair, tried to pull himself together. "You'll notice by the nature of the questions I'm going to ask that our crack staff has learned nothing about your life, so I hope you won't mind if I concentrate initially on your biography."

"Fire away."

"Actually, I want to say something else, before I ask you any questions, and I hope I won't offend you."

"I hope so to."

"We requested this interview because your grandmother was a recluse and everyone considered her mad, and you surely know that people are mystified that she chose you as her heir. What people really want is to find out who you are and what light you can shed on the perceived strangeness of your family. I'm telling you this up front because our subscribers are probably more interested in the skeletons in your closet than in your plans for Hawthorne Enterprises. But I wanted to let you know that this won't be a sensationalized article, and my paper isn't a gossip sheet."

"I appreciate your candor, Mr. Ridgely. And I've read the *Constitution*, so I know what kind of paper it is."

She said this blankly, without equivocation, but Jon still sensed the irony in her voice. But then, how could anyone with any sense read the *Constitution*'s folksy coverage of rural trivia and talk about it with a straight face? He trusted that she did know what kind of paper the *Constitution* was, and it embarrassed him.

"But why do you think I granted this interview?" Marnie continued. "I knew you'd be interested in my personal life—no one here knows me. I thought it might help if you all knew I was just a normal person and that this whole situation surprised me as much as anyone. It disturbs me to see the suspicion in everyone's eyes, everywhere I go, so of course I want to talk about my personal life. And I don't know anything about the business yet. I'd like to clear the air a bit, so I can buy groceries without everyone staring at me like I'm a circus sideshow."

"Okay. Let's do that, then."

Jon knew that there was no reason for all this prefacing and explaining. He felt like the boy he had been in his childhood dreams of the Hawthorne Mansion, when he had stumbled onto an occult and threatening world from which he couldn't escape. Only this, he reminded himself, was not a dream, he was no longer a child, and the Hawthorne in front of him was no terrifying ogre. He sipped his champagne punch.

"Let's start with something simple," he said. "Where do you live?"

"In Kensington, London, with my husband Graham."

Jon jotted this tidbit in his notebook. "How long have you been married?" Jon looked past the wedding ring on Marnie's finger to her delicate wrist and freckled arm with its fine, light blonde hair. He thought of Kate, who, at that moment, was probably hard at work hoeing weeds between rows of snap beans on her parents' farm.

"I've been married two years. I met Graham through my job—I'm a graphic designer at a small record company, and Graham is a recording engineer."

Jon was enthralled by the hard brightness in Marnie's eyes. "So you make posters and that sort of thing?"

"The whole gamut of promotional materials, though I don't do much of the actual artwork or photography. I'm the conceptual person. The company I work for specializes in symphonic music, so they'll record, say, an orchestra doing something by Saint-Saens, and I'll come up with the design for the packaging and the point-of-purchase displays and so on. Then, I'll oversee the production of the material from layout to manufacture. It's more a management job than anything else—the symphonic market is fairly staid, though it does require a certain amount of visual flair, just thinking in terms of mood and shapes and colors."

"What's the name of the company?" Jon congratulated himself on ignoring his growing infatuation and asking respectable if completely tedious questions.

"Bartel—it's a subsidiary of Parlophone. Technically, my

job is 'Art Director,' though that seems somewhat inflated. I am good at it—I'm not given to false modesty—it's just that 'Art Director' has always struck me as needlessly self-important."

Jon noticed the effects of the champagne punch in his jotted notes, whose letters were giddier and larger than usual. He had entered the first stage of tipsiness, in which everything seemed fabulous and buoyant. He shifted his gaze from his notebook to the glass table, through which he lingered on the curve of Marnie's hips.

"And you ended up in Europe because of your father's occupation as a diplomat? You see, we got that far, at least."

Jon knew that Marnie's father, Ronald, had been an attaché in the State Department, working with the European Community in Belgium. Marnie's father and mother had died ten years before in an automobile accident.

"Right," she said. "My father worked in Paris and Brussels, but he sent me to an American High School in London, and I eventually settled in London permanently."

Jon took up his glass of punch again and stared at a pair of blackbirds hopping near the garden hedge. "Your father must have been really passionate about his politics. I mean, to leave behind such a lucrative business career with Hawthorne Enterprises."

Marnie raised a single eyebrow. "That's a very roundabout way of asking why my father left Templeton, Mr. Ridgely," she said flintily. "You said you weren't a gossip columnist."

Jon was taken aback by the abrupt shift in Marnie's tone, and he realized with a start that Marnie was not as casual about this interview as her demeanor had suggested. "You're right, I apologize. So, why did your father leave Templeton?"

"It's just as gossipy if you ask it directly."

"I'm sorry, I thought you wanted to talk about your personal life."

"But that's not my personal life," Marnie said.

"I'm not sure I agree. I mean, your father's choices certainly have some influence over why you're sitting here now."

"So you're not a gossip columnist, but you are a psychologist?"

Jon looked at Marnie for the first time without falling into the thrall of her beauty. He observed that the brightness in her eyes was a shield hiding something darker, that the open expression on her face was also an open question. Whereas her earlier comments had caught him off guard with their perceptiveness and decorum, this accusation seemed excessively defensive.

"Again, I apologize," he said. "I guess I didn't understand the boundaries you were setting. I'll try to confine my questions—"

"No, it's all right." Marnie sighed, took up the pitcher of punch and refilled both of their glasses. As she set the pitcher down, she froze for a moment, seemed to decide something and then sat back in her chair, her composure restored.

"To answer your question," she said. "You surely know already that my father and grandmother had a terrific falling-out, that he left Templeton and never spoke with anyone here again. That seems to be common knowledge, since complete strangers have implied things about it to my face. But I can't answer for his motives, since I don't know them myself. I don't know."

"Perhaps I could ask you just one other question about your father?" Jon said apologetically. "About his work?"

"Yes, of course," Marnie bowed her head slightly in an attitude of contrition.

"We discovered that your father was employed by the State Department diplomatic corps, but we were unable to learn in what capacity. Could you tell me what he did?"

"He was fairly low-level—he worked in the area of trade regulations, reviewing treaty language and working out the wording of commercial policy abstracts. He had a facility with language, but he was just a functionary, which is what he wanted to be. It's sexier to call him a diplomat."

At the word "sexier," Jon looked up from his notes and studied Marnie's face to see if there had been any flirtation in it, but he detected none. Despite his glimpse of a less composed Marnie Hawthorne—or perhaps because of it—he found himself more enchanted by her than ever, and he noticed for the first time how translucent her skin was. The champagne made him feel winning and magnetic.

"You mentioned earlier," he said, "that you were as surprised by this situation as everyone else. What did you mean by that?" He drank some more punch, and he saw that his glass was half-empty once again.

"Put yourself in my shoes. I've never known much about the family business, or about my family here in Templeton at all. I'm my grandmother's only direct descendant, so, from a legal standpoint, it isn't unusual that I should inherit something, but the fact that I'm the only one named in the will confounds me as much as anyone."

"So you're not the gold-digger everyone seems to think you are?"

"Thank you, no. My grandmother never gave me anything before and I never expected a penny from her now."

"Mm-hm." Jon held up his finger for her to wait a moment while he caught up on his notes. Absently, he emptied his glass and was startled by how his head swam. The sun was higher and warmer than seemed possible and he wondered what had happened to the time. It felt like only a few minutes since he had arrived, but the champagne punch was quickly disappearing.

"Since you've never set foot in town," he said, struggling to suppress the effects of the alcohol on his speech, "I'd be interested in getting your impressions of Templeton. Aside from the fact that everyone thinks you're a circus sideshow."

Marnie did not answer for a moment. Her eyes sparkled defensively, and it seemed to Jon that she was tipsy, too.

"Are you making fun of me?" she said.

"I'm sorry?"

"Circus sideshow?"

"Those were your words."

"Ah, yes." Marnie guffawed and waved her hand. "Silly. That was hyperbole, Mr. Ridgely, though people are very apprehensive here, just in general. I feel as if everyone were always watching me, you know, waiting for something, but I suppose that's understandable given my position. The town itself, though, just physically, I find lovely—except for the Marathon Refinery. That seems like an Expressionist nightmare. Otherwise, Templeton looks like a charming nineteenth-century hamlet, and I'm sorry I haven't been here before."

"The refinery," Jon said, "is so ugly that it sometimes becomes beautiful. When they burn off gas from the release valves, the whole plant lights up like an industrial birthday cake, and people take evening picnics to Deerfield Park to watch the flames."

"Is that safe?"

"It's controlled burn-off. Of course, sometimes there's an actual explosion, and people do die in those, but rarely. I suppose it's like living next to a volcano, where you become accustomed to the occasional drama, and you accept the risks for the rewards."

The more inebriated Jon became, the more his gaze lingered on Marnie's neck and breasts. He imagined how the skin of her cheeks would feel against his fingertips, the shimmery coarseness of her ringleted hair brushing the back of his hand. As he imagined unbuttoning her silk cardigan, blood rushed into his cheeks and thighs and he felt exposed. He felt guilty about Kate—he had never been so infatuated with another woman since they'd been together. Anyway, he told himself, he already had enough material to write the article he had been assigned—it was just a personality profile—so perhaps it was time to go, before he said something foolish or offensive.

It was the mystique of the Hawthornes, he told himself—there was something about them that made people do and want unusual things, but what caused it, exactly? He wondered why Marnie had served champagne at a newspaper interview, and why he had drunk it at all. He never drank on the job, or in the morning, and now he was feeling drunk beyond the amount of alcohol he had consumed. Could she have spiked it? She was a Hawthorne, after all.

He looked at his cassette recorder and saw from the progress of the tape that he had been there a little under an hour, but it seemed simultaneously much longer and much shorter. He felt completely out of balance, as if he were uncertain what either he or Marnie might do next, and yet, nothing at all was happening. They were just sitting on a veranda on a beautiful summer morning, talking.

"I guess that concludes the interview," he said abruptly. He switched off his tape recorder.

"So that's it, then? Just like that?" She lifted her glass and took a sip. "It seemed to be going so well." Again, an undertone of mockery.

"Well, there's still the matter of pictures. My editor says that stories sell ads but pictures sell copies. Would you mind posing for a few photographs?"

"I'd be pleased," Marnie said. She pushed her chair back

and stood up in one fluid motion, seemingly unaffected by the champagne. "How would you like me?"

For the briefest moment, the sexual quality of the question emerged in Marnie's look, but then it disappeared so that Jon wondered if he had imagined it. He stood up and found his legs relatively solid, and the drunken exaltation of their interview stayed at the table with their empty glasses.

"How about in the garden? A couple of shots among the roses, and maybe by the fountain?"

Marnie agreed, and Jon retrieved his camera and followed her through the veranda's screen door. The sun was shining brightly, and a blue jay fluttered in front of them and then screeched and flapped away. The whole garden was alive with bickering cardinals and sparrows.

Jon photographed Marnie posing beside a pink rose bush; then sitting at the edge of the fountain, with Cupid peering over her shoulder; then against one of the wooden gates cut into the box hedge. As he viewed her through his lens, he took the opportunity to ogle her unabashedly on the pretense of getting just the right shot, making minute and unnecessary alterations in her posture, in the position of her hands, in the direction of her gaze. He studied her from a variety of angles, and he was painfully aware of how obviously he was objectifying her, in more than merely photographic ways, and moreover that she was not stopping him from doing so. He had shot half a dozen pictures before she protested.

"Just how many photographs of me does the *Constitution* plan to run?"

"Only one," Jon said. "But I'm not the best photographer, so I like to cover my bases."

"So." She fixed him with a hard look that seemed a little put on. "You're a bad photographer, an apologetic journalist and I've heard you play harmonica. Is there anything you're good at, Mr. Ridgely?"

Jon considered her tone and demeanor. If she was being playful, she was taking liberties, since they were not friends and she had no call to use such a familiar tone. He couldn't decide if she was flirting with him now or mocking him so openly that it seemed like flirtation. Perhaps she was just angry at him for leering at her. His embarrassment complicated his impressions, and there seemed no way to determine the truth.

"My greatest talent," he said, replacing the cap on his camera lens, "is that I don't care."

They followed one of the white gravel paths toward the house. Marnie stopped to snap a red rose from its stem.

"That seems less a talent than an unfortunate disposition."

"Only someone with a great deal of luck and money would call not caring an unfortunate disposition. Truly not caring, like truly not thinking or not wanting, is an art to be cultivated."

"And how many of those arts have you cultivated, Mr. Ridgely?" She brushed her cheek with the rose she had just plucked.

They reached the veranda and passed through the screen door. Jon put the camera back into his satchel and slung it over his shoulder.

"Do you care that so many people here view you with hostility?" he asked. Marnie didn't answer. "Sometimes it doesn't pay to care, especially about things you can't control. And it almost never pays to want."

"If you never want," Marnie said, "then you never get what you want."

"On the contrary, if you never want, you always get what you want. That's why not wanting is such an art." The conversation suddenly wearied him, and he did not know what to make of Marnie's change in attitude. "Thank you for your time," he said. "I promise I'll include your original statement in my article—about not disrupting your family's business or costing people their livelihoods."

"I look forward to reading it," she said. She smiled at him, a warm smile that bore no traces of their interview.

She led him through the gloomy mansion to the front hall. They shook hands politely, and then she showed him out and closed the door behind him with a thud that struck Jon as unmistakably final.

He looked at his watch. Barely more than an hour had passed since he had stood there before. He walked slowly down the long, dark gravel drive to Poplar Street, where nothing at all had changed.

5

A Subtle Shift

Kate Benjamin stood in her parent's triticale field outside Honey Creek Township, mopping her brow with her shirt sleeve. The triticale—a green grass grown mostly for cattle feed—stood eight feet tall and blocked the afternoon breeze that might otherwise have cooled her. The rustling of the plants' tassels sounded like petticoats sweeping across a ballroom floor.

She had finished hoeing weeds between rows and now she was trooping up and down each line, tagging the most robust plants, which would be harvested and used as seed plants for the next generation. With each generation, irregular plants with unwanted characteristics were weeded out and hearty plants were retained and propagated, so that, over a number of years, perfectly predictable and regular plants could be produced. The seeds culled from these predictable crops would then be sold to commercial farmers, who would grow fields full of feed grasses to sell at market.

This generation of triticale was the twenty-first of a variety Kate's father had been breeding since his days as an agriculture professor at Southern Illinois University. Mr. Benjamin had retired early from teaching and moved to Templeton in order to pursue his favorite plant breeding projects full-time: he produced hybrids of feed grasses, beans and peppers, and then patented his novel varieties. His plots were quite small, since he grew crops experimentally rather than commercially—he and his wife had tended their fields by themselves for years, until he'd had a heart attack four years ago. Now Kate and her mother worked the fields while her father negotiated sales with seed companies.

Before returning to the family business, Kate had been working as a medical researcher at Boston University, in a study of HIV-related vaccines. It had been a dull, repetitive occupation whose day-to-day joylessness had overwhelmed the nobility of the project's eventual goal—a cure for AIDS. Her work station at BU had been a tiny windowless cubicle in a cramped lab that she'd shared with four other researchers, and she had spent three years there in mole-like claustrophobia, hating the stark fluorescent lights and arid chemical smells. She had been happy to return to Templeton, to work outdoors for a change, to help her mother and father in what was becoming an increasingly difficult business.

After tagging individual plants, Kate recorded their row number and location in a log book, so they could be separated later from their less desirable neighbors. After the selected plants were culled and their seeds retained, the unsuitable individuals would either be plowed under, to serve as mulch for the soil, or harvested for the Benjamins' own dinner table. It was an old-fashioned method of breeding plants, one that Kate knew would probably die with her parents and their contemporaries: farming had long since become a major international business, dominated by chemical firms who didn't so much breed plants as engineer them.

These days, it was common for genetic engineers at large agrichemical firms such as Cargill and Monsanto to alter the DNA of existing plants, splicing in various characteristics and eliminating others in laboratory procedures far removed from the fields. This process allowed geneticists to give crops traits that they could never acquire naturally. For example, a corn variety with resistance to Banks Grass Mites could be analyzed to determine which gene provided such resistance; then, that gene could be spliced from the corn DNA into the DNA of another plant entirely, such as a variety of wheat; the wheat would then acquire the corn's resistance to the pest.

Other beneficial traits, such as disease immunity, could be transferred from one crop to the next as well; but more dubious crossings might also take place, and DNA could even be spliced from animals into plants, confusing the gene pool. The cold resistance genes of flounder had been spliced into Roma tomatoes, making the tomatoes less susceptible to frost. The gene that produced the luminescence in fireflies had been isolated and spliced into snap beans, so the beans would glow in the dark—making night-time harvesting possible. Though many of these procedures sounded like science fiction, they were real and already dominated the commercial seed market: more than a third of the food that Americans consumed contained some kind of genetically modified ingredient. Food was becoming just another artificial product of industrial mechanization, and the long-term impact of such a system on the natural world—and therefore on the human world—was far from certain.

Kate believed that her parents' insistence on developing new plant varieties in the traditional way was both noble and doomed. Since she was a romantic, this combination appealed to her. When her mother finally retired or her father died, she would give up plant breeding, but for the moment she was happy marching up and down the rows of her father's crops, developing thick calluses on her hands, exercising in the humid summer air. The work was hard, but she loved to smell the loamy darkness of the soil beneath her feet and the sweeter, thinner scent of the beans and feed grasses in the air.

Kate finished marking the triticale and walked down the tractor path to where her mother was marking popping beans, a pet project—her mother had developed a variety of pinto beans that popped like popcorn when subjected to heat. Mrs. Benjamin was resting on her knees in the dirt, her clipboard by her side, her hat pulled all the way down to her eyebrows, looking at her thigh-high greens.

"How's it coming?" Kate said.

"About finished. You?"

"I'm done, so whenever you want to go… I'm supposed to meet Jon at Ploughman's, so I guess I'll start packing up."

"You're not having supper with us? Your father will be disappointed."

"Why?"

"He wanted to talk about the Welsh contract." Some Welsh farmers had agreed to buy a variety of Mr. Benjamin's triticale, and their paperwork had arrived the day before.

"It's a standard agreement," Kate said. "I can tell him everything I know about it before I shower."

They gathered their hoes, spades, rakes and clipboards together and trundled them into their pickup truck. Kate drove slowly along the edge of the field toward the dirt track that led to County Road 8.

The Benjamins' twenty-acre plot sloped acutely toward the road. Because of the incline of the land here, this stretch of field was awkward for the heavy machinery of a big commercial farm, and the Mathers, whose vast corn fields surrounded them, had sold it to Mr. Benjamin for a bargain. As an experimental plot, it was perfect: it could be worked by hand or with the Benjamins' tiny Massey-Ferguson tractor, and it could be watered using the stream that trickled between oak trees near the dirt road.

The Mathers' corn stalks swayed invitingly in the breeze, sporting burnished brown tassels—a sign that the harvest was near. Kate stared at the endless corn, feeling grimy and tired.

She took Squirrel Hill Lane, a back way around Templeton to her parents' house. They lived in a ramshackle nineteenth century farmhouse, whose adjoining fields were owned and managed by the First Bank of Templeton. Kate's parents had bought the house at auction, after the previous owners had gone bankrupt, but they had not been able to afford the considerable acreage attached to it. They were living on a farm they didn't till and working a small patch of land four miles away—a common situation for family farmers in the age of industrial agriculture.

They pulled into their gravel driveway, past the pair of mockernut hickory trees guarding the front yard. At the end of the drive was a hulking garage that held irrigators, combine attachments and other old farm equipment. They unloaded their truck, then walked to the back porch and took off their dirty boots.

"Daddy, we're home!" Kate said, as they stepped into the kitchen.

"In here," Mr. Benjamin called from the living room.

Her father was lying on the sofa, reading the latest issue of *Feedstuffs* magazine. Kate kissed his forehead.

"Mom said you wanted to talk about the Welsh contract?"

"I just want to make sure we're not being ripped off, the way those Canadians stole our peppers last year."

"They only changed those two clauses, about ancillary markets and seed preservation," Kate said. "I don't think they're trying to pull anything."

"Maybe we should get Harmond to look at it."

"He never helps us, Daddy. He's the one who reviewed the contract with Stauffer's, and we ended up losing money anyway. Plus, he charges seventy-five dollars every time we call, whether he does anything or not."

"Let's get the contract out after dinner," Mr. Benjamin said, "and we can read the fine print together."

"Tomorrow, Daddy. I'm going into Templeton."

Mr. Benjamin snorted. "Jon? You should tell Jon he can come out to see us more often. I'm sure your mother would set an extra plate."

"Any time," Mrs. Benjamin shouted from the kitchen.

"He has to work at Ploughman's tonight. We're just having a quick bite at the beginning of his shift. All right?"

"Then you can come back and look at the contract after you eat."

"No, Daddy, I'm going to the Flying Pig to read a book. Let's do it tomorrow, okay?" Kate rubbed her father's arm. "I'm going up to shower."

She ran upstairs. Though Kate loved her parents, she sometimes hated being the focus of their lives. After four years of living with them, she still had to negotiate for free time—her father did little these days but obsess about his projects and watch television, and he would have been overjoyed to have Kate sit with him every evening and listen to his rants about the sorry state of modern farming.

Kate stripped off her dirty clothes and threw them to her bedroom floor. The top story of the house was entirely hers, like a spacious walkup apartment. She grabbed the towel draped across the corner of her dresser and walked, flat-footed and fatigued, down the hall to her bathroom.

* * * * *

Ploughman's Grill had been built in the 1920s and was still family-owned. It stood just west of the town square, down the hill from Bertram's Drug Store.

Tawny ceiling lamps hung in diamond patterns around

Ploughman's dining room, dripping yellow light onto the customers below. The booth seats were plush, faded cardinal red and contrasted sharply with the midnight blue of the walls. The smell of grease and old smoke, the residue of thousands of hamburgers, catfish fillets and fried potatoes, lent the place an air of comfort and solidity, suggesting continuity with generations past.

Kate sat down at a window booth with a view of Main Street. Martina, the nineteen-year-old waitress who always worked the evening shift, brought her a glass of sweet tea with a splash of orange juice, her usual order.

"Jon's still at the *Constitution*," Martina said. "He called to say he'd be a few minutes late."

Kate thanked her. It was too early for the dinner crowd, but there were a few elderly men in shirt sleeves sitting at the lunch counter, smoking aimlessly or reading the paper. An old doo-wop group was crooning four-part harmonies over the stereo speakers, and Kate felt a wave of affection for Ploughman's. She sipped her tea and felt content.

A few minutes later, Jon came loping down Main Street, his hair tousled in eighteen directions at once, a sign that he had been working frantically on an article. He swept into the restaurant, banged the door behind him and flung himself into Kate's booth.

He apologized for being late, and Kate remembered what a compromise he had seemed when they had first started seeing each other: how strange it had been, after staying away from Templeton for so many years, to return and suddenly start dating a local man she had known since kindergarten. It had felt too clichéd to be real—the long-lost childhood romance—and Jon himself had seemed more convenient than truly suitable, like the first struggling salmon that had made it upstream into Kate's mating pool. But the longer she had been with him, the more he had grown on her, until the floppy, animated hand gestures he used when he spoke and his bedtime idiosyncrasies had become endearing, and she could hardly imagine a future without him.

Martina came back with a lemon seltzer for Jon and took their orders. When Martina left, Kate reached across the table and took Jon's hand.

"How was your day?"

"Good. Strange. I just finished writing my interview with Marnie Hawthorne—it'll come out tomorrow. Maude was so happy with it, she's splashing it across the center truck." Maude was the *Constitution*'s editor-in-chief.

"So? Is Marnie as crazy as the rest of the Hawthornes?"

"Maybe," Jon said. "There's something unusual about her, that's for sure. Maybe it's just because she's foreign—or, almost foreign, anyway—but there's something really different about her frame of reference. I've talked to the Longmores in Stoy, and the Meeses, and they're all just bitter. They want Old Dorothy's money and that's the end of it. But Marnie seems a lot more. . . playful. . . about the whole situation."

"Playful?" Kate found this choice of words strangely irritating. "It hardly seems right to be playful when your grandmother's just died."

"But Marnie never knew her grandmother, and she did just inherit a whole lot of money, which might make you a little more good-humored than usual. I don't know. Maybe she's just as crazy as Dorothy was, but she seemed different from the rest of the family. The ones I've interviewed, anyway. Really different." He selected a plastic straw from the dispenser on the table and inserted it into his seltzer. "How was your day?"

As Kate told him about the prospects for this generation of triticale, green peppers and beans, she monitored him, watched him glance out the window at the setting sun, tried to discern a substantial reason for the foreboding she suddenly felt about Marnie Hawthorne, but she found none. He seemed his usual self.

"Where did you interview her?" she asked, when her account of her own day had finished.

"Believe it or not, up at the mansion."

"And you made it out alive?"

"I guess those stories about Dorothy eating babies weren't true after all. Though, you never know. . . the inside of that house really is creepy." Martina arrived with their food. "Come to think of it," Jon continued, "there's clearly something wrong with that place. You get this feeling of desperation just walking through the house. It's like an actual presence."

"You talking about the old Hawthorne place?" Martina asked.

Jon nodded. "I was just there."

"Leonard went up there one night about a year ago. He saw a candle moving from one room to another. Just one candle, floating through the rooms, and then all of a sudden there were two candles in the same room." She said this evil-eyed, as if it were proof of something extraordinary. "And then they went in opposite directions all through the house."

"So Old Dorothy liked candles," said Jon. "So what?"

"Old Dorothy and someone else!"

"She had a live-in maid. That Clark girl from Honey Creek."

"Who, by the way, never says one word about the Hawthornes."

"Dorothy paid her to keep her mouth shut!"

"But what were they doing walking around after midnight with candles?" Martina persisted. "They've got electricity."

"I don't know. What was your brother doing spying on them in the middle of the night?"

"That's not the point, Jon. Tell me that sneaking around your own house after midnight by candlelight is normal."

"I'm not saying the Hawthornes are normal—that just doesn't sound like evidence of anything, that's all."

"They say she used to pay high school guys to come up and have sex with her. Can you imagine?" Martina made a sour face. "A seventy-five year old woman!"

"But you can never find any of the guys. Who are these guys?"

"Maybe Dorothy paid them to keep their mouths shut."

Jon shoveled a forkful of mashed potatoes into his mouth. Martina rolled her eyes and went off to wait on another table.

"But Marnie Hawthorne herself seemed playful?" Kate said. Something about Jon's choice of this word really bothered her. Had Jon been playful with Marnie Hawthorne?

"It *is* a pretty absurd position. You've never met your eccentric grandmother, and all of a sudden you're living in her creepy house and you're worth millions of dollars and everyone hates you. She just has a sense of humor about it, a sense of the ironies of her situation."

Jon's tone sent a weak electrical current through Kate's breastbone, and she finally realized why she was so irritated. He was defending Marnie Hawthorne, first from Martina and now from her. "All I'm saying is that playfulness seems strange," Kate said, "when so many people's lives depend on what happens to the toffee plant."

"I know. That's what makes Marnie so interesting. I mean, she's remarkable because of the situation she finds herself in, by itself. The fairy tale aspects of it, you know? But if she were like Dorothy's other relatives, she'd just be another sniping, disagreeable moneygrubber, which isn't all that intriguing. But she struck me as very open and. . . I don't know. . . bright."

Kate stared at the cars creeping down Main Street as Jon

continued to eat hungrily. The Crew Cuts' "Sh-Boom" came on the sound system, but the nonsense of the chorus did nothing to dispel Kate's misgivings.

"Did you tell me that Marnie Hawthorne was married," she said, "or did I read that somewhere?"

"Probably both. If you read it anywhere, it was in one of my articles."

"Did you meet her husband?"

"No. He's still in England."

As they had been talking, dinner customers had been trickling into Ploughman's, and Martina was moving faster around the restaurant and eyeing first the clock above the cash register and then Jon. Now, a family of six came through the doors, and Jon pushed his plate aside.

"Looks like all the regulars are coming at once," he said. "I'm sorry."

"That's all right."

"Let me seat these people and get their drinks, and I'll come back."

"No, don't worry about it," Kate said. "I guess I'm finished."

"But you haven't even touched your food."

"I'm not really hungry. Besides, I want to go to the Pig and read my book."

He leaned over and kissed Kate on the mouth. "Let me at least wrap your sandwich."

He stacked their dirty plates and carried them through the swinging doors into Ploughman's kitchen. He came back a few moments later wearing his apron, carrying his order pad in one hand and her sandwich in the other. Kate made a point of kissing him again on the mouth.

"I'd be curious to meet this Marnie Hawthorne sometime," she said.

"You probably will. The fight over the estate is just getting started, so she'll be around for a while."

This news did not encourage Kate, though she couldn't understand why she was so sensitive all of a sudden. She told herself she was just tired from working in the field all day, and that she was probably hungrier than she thought, and that she had heard too many rumors about how beautiful and cunning Marnie Hawthorne was. It was all just nothing.

"Should we get together later?" Jon asked.

"If you want to come out to the house, that'd be great. I'll probably be asleep by the time you get there, though—mom and I need to be in the fields early again tomorrow."

"I won't bother you, then. Take your cell phone tomorrow, though, and I'll call you later in the morning." He walked her to the door, then picked up a water pitcher from the counter and went to fill the customers' glasses.

Kate stepped out onto Main Street. A large hazy sun was perched just above the horizon, and the humid air was still warm. She looked at the sky and tried to find evidence of the rain supposedly heading their way, but the few clouds were puffy, white and harmless.

She crossed the street, got into her car and drove the few blocks to the Flying Pig, a Seattle-style café in a building that had once been a cobbler's. The Pig had opened earlier in the summer—the espresso and biscotti craze that had swept the nation fifteen years earlier had finally found its way to Templeton, and Kate was glad to have someplace to go in the evenings that wasn't dominated by farmers, housewives and children.

She selected a patio table under the front awning and opened the book she had brought along, but she couldn't focus on the words. After a while, she just stared past it at the setting sun.

It's stupid to spend two seconds in a row thinking about

Marnie Hawthorne, she told herself. She hadn't felt the least bit insecure with Jon for years—she couldn't recall the last time they'd even had an argument—and yet, she felt a lump in her stomach when she remembered the unsettling tone in Jon's voice.

Andrea, the Flying Pig's owner, came out and greeted Kate warmly, and they made small talk about the weather and the gossip floating around town. Mostly, they discussed the Hawthorne Toffee drama, and Kate quietly acquiesced to Andrea's version of events, which had all the Hawthornes mad as hatters and Marnie already paying off the mayor for special favors.

When she was alone again, Kate picked up her book and stared at the same page for an hour. The darkness of the evening grew around her as she rehashed Jon's remarks about the Hawthorne heiress, all of which, on the surface, seemed perfectly innocuous.

6

The Exquisite Longing of Regret

Just after eleven o'clock at night, Jeremiah Grayson poured himself another tumbler of white rum in the tiny, sepia-colored kitchen of his cottage on Lincoln Street. He had not drunk alcohol in many years, but since Dorothy's death, he found himself incapable of passing an evening without it. He replaced the bottle in the cupboard and shuffled into his cramped living room, where musty armchairs and nicked end tables competed with an antique hi-fi for space. Above the record player, framed black-and-white photographs of long-dead friends stared down at him.

He withdrew a Wardell Gray album from the record cabinet and set it spinning on the turntable. Light hissing and popping and then the hard bop of "Twisted" filled the room. He eased himself into his favorite chair and sat with closed eyes and open mouth, feeling the saxophonist's deftly hesitant single notes as solitary aches in his own heart.

He was replaying the few simple words Marnie Hawthorne had said to him in Bertram's Drug Store, amazed at how closely she resembled her grandmother. He was reliving the shock of discovery, the moment when he had at last recognized Marnie, when he had first seen Dorothy. It was yesterday, it was sixty years ago, it was now, in this living room, where his portrait of Dorothy stared at him from the wall.

With his eyes still closed, he found his pipe and tobacco pouch on the table next to him, refilled the bowl and lit it. Soon, a wreath of thick blue smoke swirled around his head and hovered like a nimbus over the floor lamp.

His love affair with Dorothy had begun the instant he'd set eyes on her in 1942. It had ended eleven years later, on the night Dorothy's father Henry had set himself on fire on the steps of the Old Courthouse. Jeremiah had witnessed Henry's suicide but had been too mortified and confused to stop it. The memory of Henry striking the match, of his gasoline-soaked hair and clothes licking into flames, of Henry's guttural cries and wild flailing and final toppling down the steps did not haunt Jeremiah half so much as the icy and superior look Dorothy had given him when she had confessed the truth about her other lover. Even the blood on Jeremiah's own hands had faded faster than the memory of that look.

He took a long drink of rum. There was something exquisite in this solitary descent into drunkenness, revisiting the muddled longing half a century past, finding that the object of his desire had not quite passed from the earth. She still inhabited the form of a beautiful woman with Dorothy's face and Dorothy's name: Marnie Hawthorne, whose blood was Dorothy's blood.

He tried to conjure through Marnie the mad rush of desire he had felt sixty years before for Dorothy, but he found that the erotic compulsions he recalled so clearly in his mind had contracted into wistfulness in his body, into a vague but pervasive feeling of despair. He had been handsome, winning, powerful; he remembered the pleasure of romantic discovery, the single-mindedness of love; but now he thought of romance only as naïveté. He was a modern-day cartographer looking at medieval maps of the New World. He wished to believe in those flawed maps again, to remember the innocence and danger of unexplored territory—to look into Marnie's eyes and find some trace of Dorothy as he used to see her.

* * * * *

Dorothy Hawthorne was eighteen years old the first time Jeremiah saw her, and the Hawthorne family was already preeminent in Lawford County. The Hawthorne Mansion was still lively and bright. The newly-built Hawthorne Toffee Plant, though not yet fully mechanized, produced chocolates at a prodigious rate, and Henry's coffers were filling faster than he could empty them. His early days as a novice confectioner seemed like another lifetime.

Henry had opened Hawthorne's Confections in a storefront on Templeton's town square in June 1911. At the time, as a twenty-three year old man, his only ambition had been to establish a reputable business, to prove that making candy was a legitimate enterprise and not the effeminate evasion of hard labor that his brothers considered it.

The idea for the confectionery had been Henry's grandmother's: in his youth, Henry had loved spending time with her in the kitchen, and he had stolen all of her baking secrets so adroitly that he was soon making pies and sweets to rival her own. His brothers teased him cruelly and his father pretended not to see how proficient his "womanly" skills became, but Henry gradually began experimenting on his own and he developed his own methods and secrets. Even his brothers would never refuse one of Henry's sweets, and eventually the entire Hawthorne clan understood that Henry was too talented a baker to continue milking cows on the family dairy farm. With money borrowed against his grandmother's land, Henry opened Hawthorne's Confections in the shadow of the Courthouse.

He offered tartlettes, hard candies, chocolates, shortbreads and cream sodas, and he became known for the dependable quality of his cordials. Though his first few years were hardly triumphs, he made enough money to repay his startup loan. His brothers, in the moments when they could contain their contempt, expressed jealous admiration that he had established a real business in town and escaped the constant backaches of the farm.

Henry lived in an apartment above his shop, and though he worked as hard as any other shopkeeper during the day, he found it difficult to sleep at night. As he was turning in, he would think of a new flavor of cordials or a more efficient method of setting hard candy, and he would go down to his shop in his bed clothes and experiment. In this way, after many pedestrian successes and inconspicuous failures, he hit upon the recipe for his chocolate-covered toffee bar.

At first, the toffee bar was just another of the novelty features he would rotate onto his shelves every few weeks. But people asked for it so often that he started making it as part of his daily routine, and it quickly became his most popular candy. Henry was proud of this success, but he thought no more of the toffee than his other sweets, never imagining that it would eventually make him one of the wealthiest men in Illinois. In fact, he was much more pleased with another of his inventions—a process for setting custard that took him months to perfect—but that process died with Henry Hawthorne, and the Hawthorne Toffee Bar, a mere flash of inspiration late one evening, became known the world over.

In the early 1920s, Henry's business expanded. He hired employees and opened a second shop on the north side of town, and the second shop was soon as busy as the first; and Hawthorne's Confections was not the only thing in Henry's life that flourished. He met and married Charisse Rutherford from Flat Rock, and they bought a house near Deerfield Park.

Henry was happy in his marriage and overjoyed when he and Charisse had a son named Calvin, in 1923, and a daughter named Dorothy, in 1924. He worked at Hawthorne Confections as little as possible and spent every free moment at home with his wife and children, on whom he doted with unqualified enthusiasm. After several years of such domestic bliss, Henry and Charisse supposed they would be even happier with a third child, and it was this supposition that, in unexpected ways, made Hawthorne Enterprises into an international candy concern.

In 1928, Charisse became pregnant with a third child. Henry's breast swelled with pride, since he had no inkling that Charisse would die while giving birth to this child: a son who would follow his mother to the grave after only a few days of life.

Charisse's death and the death of her unnamed son devastated Henry. His hair, which had been thick and black, turned white and limp almost overnight and he stopped going to work. He lost enthusiasm for Calvin and Dorothy, often leaving them at the family dairy farm while he disappeared into the woods with a jug of bootleg gin, and he found it impossible to manufacture candies—products of whimsy and celebration. He lost all interest in the business and left his employees to tend his two shops.

At this point, the Hawthorne legacy might easily have reverted to ordinariness. But at this critical moment, the world was plunged into an economic depression and, almost simultaneously, oil was discovered in Lawford County. The constellation of these seemingly unrelated events—the death of Charisse Hawthorne, the discovery of oil in Templeton and the onset of the Great Depression—had a fantastic effect on the fortunes of Henry Hawthorne.

The Hawthorne dairy farm failed in the Depression and, for a few years, the family struggled to put food on the table. Only Henry's confectionery, which continued to prosper in spite of his voracious thirst for gin, kept the Hawthornes solvent. Henry saw through his alcoholic haze that his family's only hope of avoiding the bread lines was toffee and bonbons, and he sobered himself up and returned to the daily operation of his shops.

* * * * *

Jeremiah finished his glass of rum as Wardell Gray's "A Sinner Kissed An Angel" moaned from the hi-fi. He stared at the melting ice in the bottom of his glass, and through the glass at the long distant past rising through the rum to meet him.

The first time Jeremiah had seen Dorothy Hawthorne, at the opening of the Jefferson Street Theater in January 1942, she was wearing a mink half-coat over an ankle-length black evening gown, as glamorous as a movie star at her own premiere. Her long blonde hair was twisted into a French braid and her high cheeks were rosy in the frosty night air. After her father's speech dedicating the theater, she cut a ceremonial red ribbon hanging across the entrance and then joined her brother and father in inviting everyone inside, free of charge, courtesy of the ever-expanding Hawthorne Candy Corporation. The movie that night, the first motion picture ever shown in Templeton, was a forgettable Ingrid Bergman film called "Adam Had Four Sons," but that opening ceremony and the sight of Dorothy Hawthorne hugging herself against the cold changed Jeremiah forever.

The Jefferson Street Theater, Templeton's first and only indoor movie house, had been commissioned and built by the Hawthorne Candy Corporation as a way for Henry not only to increase his standing in the community but to appease his daughter, who complained bitterly that there was nothing for her to do in Templeton. Henry refused to let Dorothy work and deemed it improper for girls to go to college. He considered most of the boys in Templeton unsuitable for her, but he would not allow her to travel, so there was no chance that she would meet anyone else. There was nothing for her to do but dally with oil painting or lawn tennis or horseback riding, hobbies that Henry considered sufficiently patrician for an heiress.

People attributed Henry's special strictness with Dorothy to the grief he suffered over his wife's death. He could not bear to give Dorothy up to another man, the theory went, because he needed a substitute for Charisse who could also act as a scapegoat for her loss. Henry was building monuments to his dead wife all over town—the mechanized toffee factory, the new housing subdivision near the factory, the public library that he had donated to the county—while he punished his daughter for no obvious reason. In his son Calvin's social life, he took no special interest at all. During the day, Henry was a severe taskmaster as he taught Calvin the toffee business, but at night his son was free to do as he pleased, and Calvin was known to be profligate. Not so Dorothy: Henry showed her no affection, but he nevertheless guarded her like a secret family recipe.

He was not entirely insensible, however, to his daughter's constant complaining: Dorothy had finally convinced him that solitary aristocratic distractions did not suit her, so in a grand concession he offered her an activity more popular and social. However, the Jefferson Street Theater promised no relief from Dorothy's loneliness and boredom: as the theater opened, the United States was sending troops off to the Pacific and Europe, so even the potentially suitable boys who might have escorted Dorothy to the movies were enlisting in the army and leaving town.

Jeremiah had stood at the back of the crowd for the theater's dedication. At the time, he was living in Eaton, twelve miles away, and had made the long journey into Templeton especially to see his first motion picture. But the excitement of the movie paled next to his first glimpse of Dorothy, and during the show he spent more time gawking at her than watching the screen. The larger-than-life projections of Ingrid Bergman held no allure next to the forthright beauty and presence of Dorothy Hawthorne, and he was encouraged that, whenever Dorothy caught him staring at her, she looked back invitingly, with no hint of bashfulness. He took this attention personally, unaware that she did this with every man who showed her any interest.

Immediately following that first movie, the Hawthornes hosted a social at their confection shop on the Square. The shop was crowded to overflowing, and despite the fact that Jeremiah was just a farm boy with no social standing, he quietly made his way through the prominent families and businessmen toward Dorothy's table. The crowd chattered excitedly about the film. Dorothy was surrounded by fawning older men, and Jeremiah sipped his cream soda and eavesdropped: he was charmed by her demure deportment and beauty, and he began to scheme for her love. Like every infatuated man, Jeremiah imagined that if he could spend but a few minutes alone with her, she would see how different he was from all the others and return his feelings in kind. He was struck most by her burbling laughter, which suggested not just the girlish pleasure on its surface but something quiet and profound underneath—the gift of order.

* * * * *

As Jeremiah poured himself another glass of iced rum nearly sixty years later, he could still hear that laughter, and he heard the echo of it ringing in Marnie Hawthorne's voice.

For the better part of fifty years, he had occupied a mood of reflectiveness and regret about his involvement with the Hawthornes, but this mood had been sharpened to a fine point by Dorothy's death and Marnie's arrival. He wished he could communicate in some way with Marnie; more to the point, he wished she would communicate something to him, but he couldn't articulate what. He wanted to recapture the purity of feeling that he had lost when he'd learned of Dorothy's true romantic feelings; or he wanted to erase his knowledge of Dorothy's reclusive final years, as she withered in her mansion, alone with the secret that shut her off from every other member of society. He didn't know what he wanted.

He removed Dorothy's portrait from his living room wall and sat in his easy chair with it, slowly running his thumb around the oval frame. In it, Dorothy looked off to the right, inviting the viewer to stare at her without the confrontation of meeting her eyes. She wore a blue v-necked dress, white eighteen-button gloves, pearl teardrop earrings and a pearl necklace. Her hair fell behind her and was straight except for a few fine strands that curled in front of her ears.

This photograph had practically supplanted Jeremiah's actual memories of Dorothy. He hadn't seen her in person in the ten years prior to her death, and much of the drama of their relationship had faded into the background of this simple portrait. Before Marnie's arrival, Jeremiah's memories alternated between remorse and fondness for those nights so long before, when he had courted Dorothy—in the days before their ultimately adulterous and murderous affair.

* * * * *

As the oil trade swept through Templeton in the 1930s, men from all over the Midwest arrived to find jobs, and these

"Oil Johnnies" sent Hawthorne Bars to their loved ones. From Minnesota and Nebraska to Pennsylvania and Georgia, Hawthorne's fame slowly spread, and people began writing Henry directly to request boxes of chocolate: the idea of selling the toffee to dime stores and soda fountains around the region not so much suggested itself as forced itself upon him.

As one of the few chocolateers with enough money to expand his business during the Depression, Henry met few obstacles to growth; when merchants saw how quickly his toffees sold, they were almost as eager as Henry himself to assist in the expansion of Hawthorne Enterprises. Throughout the 1930s and '40s, Hawthorne Toffee spread like a celebrity rumor, until around-the-clock production in Henry's two stores could not keep up with demand. He incorporated, expanded his production facilities and personally worked twenty-hour days. The unlikelihood of this fantastic success persuaded Henry of its inevitability, and it helped him find a fatalistic purpose in his wife's premature death. He set increasingly grandiose sales goals and surrounded his children with the gaudy trappings of wealth—he came to imagine a Rockefelleresque empire built on a foundation of chocolate.

For Dorothy, however, her family's increasing prosperity meant only isolation, as not only her mother but now her father disappeared from her. She was given over to nannies and tutors, and her activities were reported in rigorous detail to her father, so that his absence was not compensated by a corresponding freedom. She became claustrophobic and resentful, and it was this general dissatisfaction that made her receptive to the letter Jeremiah wrote two days after the opening of the Jefferson Street Theater.

In his letter, Jeremiah compared Dorothy favorably to Ingrid Bergman. He spent an entire page of tiny, cramped writing describing with lavish praise the minutest details of Dorothy's evening dress. The letter ended with a flourish of poetry stolen from Keats, which Dorothy recognized and found amusing.

Dorothy could not conjure a memory of Jeremiah from that evening, but his potential charms captivated her less than his letter's inappropriateness. Not only was the letter brash and presumptuous, but Dorothy's father would certainly consider Jeremiah Grayson of Eaton a poor match, and he would prohibit Jeremiah from even looking at his daughter, much less courting her. Most of Dorothy's potential suitors in Templeton had already been examined and dismissed, so that Jeremiah's letter came at just the right moment and traced just the right fault lines to succeed.

Dorothy replied immediately, with a reserved note asking that Jeremiah send a photograph and propose a rendezvous. She decided not to broach the subject with her father, but instead, right from the beginning, to have a clandestine romance, in order to relieve her boredom. While everyone else talked about the war, Dorothy could stare out the window and pine for her rustic Romeo.

Jeremiah's photograph arrived and she found him passably good-looking—with a thin face and hollow cheeks, but a keen stare—and Dorothy was unaccountably attracted to the shape of his eyebrows: fine, unobtrusive curves of black hair perfectly shaping his eyes. She agreed to meet him at the Dog and Suds Soda Shop.

On the designated afternoon, a frigid January day in 1942, sleet was falling. Jeremiah drove down the muddy road from Eaton to Route 44, through fallow fields and winter-stripped sycamore groves. Despite the freezing temperatures and the faulty heater in his father's truck, Jeremiah still managed a palm-dampening sweat, the enjoyable anguish that Dorothy always inspired.

He arrived early, hoping to relax his nerves with a quick

root beer. He leapt from his truck and ran through the rain, dashed inside and then stood for a moment at the entrance, dripping onto the welcome mat. The Dog and Suds was nearly empty, but Dorothy was already there, staring at Jeremiah from a corner booth with the same rosy-cheeked freshness he had admired at the theater. There was a steaming cup on the table before her.

His heart pounded. He removed his wet hat and lingered for a long, strange moment at the entrance.

The Dog and Suds, to Jeremiah's mind, was not an ideal place for a first date. It was a cheap grill with kitschy decorations, near enough to the Marathon Refinery that you could see the burn-off towers and occasionally catch a whiff of unrefined petroleum. It was a block away from the railroad switching station, so that whistling trains would clatter by, suspending conversation. But it had been Dorothy's choice and that made it more than acceptable.

Jeremiah approached Dorothy's table and accepted her invitation to sit down. Though her hair was tousled and her clothes limp from the rain, she looked as alluring as she had in glamorous evening wear.

"Thank you for your letter," she said.

"Thank you for meeting me."

A gust of wind blew rain against the window, and a waitress arrived to take their orders. Dorothy demurred, saying that she was satisfied with hot cocoa. Taking this as a cue, Jeremiah requested only coffee, and Dorothy and the waitress exchanged a meaningful look. Jeremiah blushed: he was being evaluated by more than one stranger.

A long, awkward silence followed, as Jeremiah and Dorothy looked at each other and then looked away. Jeremiah knew that Dorothy was waiting for something to happen, that he had to make it happen, but he could think of nothing to say except banal small talk or grandiloquent reveries, neither of which seemed appropriate.

His coffee arrived and the waitress left a ticket on the table. He sipped the coffee, and, as he did so, the ordinariness of the act relaxed his mind and he once again regained the sure knowledge of fate that had brought him to Dorothy. He smiled, a warm, inviting, confident smile. "I want to tell you a story," he said. "About Abraham Lincoln's hat."

* * * * *

Jeremiah sat alone in his living room nearly sixty years later, growing blind drunk on rum. He could not remember what had possessed him to tell Dorothy the story of his great-grandfather Renick and Abraham Lincoln. Renick Grayson had homesteaded eighty acres of land in Southern Illinois in the early 1800s. He had built an inn, a stagecoach stop on the route from Vincennes to Carbondale which eventually became the hub of the Township of Eaton. In 1830, Abraham Lincoln and his family had passed through Eaton and had stayed at the Grayson Inn, and Mr. Lincoln had left behind a bowler hat. Renick had kept the hat for himself and thought nothing of it until Abraham Lincoln became first a local politician and then the president, at which point the hat, by then well-worn and battered, became a family heirloom. Jeremiah still owned it.

In telling that story to Dorothy, Jeremiah had somehow dispelled her doubts and settled his own nerves, and they spent the rest of that frigid afternoon chatting and winning each other over, until at five o'clock they parted and agreed to meet again. Jeremiah immediately scrawled another letter, more impertinent than the last, and a pattern of charged meetings and increasingly romantic correspondence was established. Jeremiah and Dorothy formed a bond of mutual secrets, silences and faith, a bond that was stronger for its clandestine nature and that, by the time Dorothy's father discovered it, was already too strong to sever with simple prohibitions.

* * * * *

The diamond needle on Jeremiah's turntable skipped on the silent inner circle of the record. Jeremiah sat and stared at his portrait of Dorothy, unable to rouse himself from his alcoholic miasma. He looked at his own portrait hanging on the wall opposite him—the picture of himself as an army private, taken just before he shipped out to Europe. He imagined, as he had imagined all these years, that if he hadn't been drafted into the war he would have married Dorothy Hawthorne, and the nastiness of his rivalry with Dorothy's eventual husband, Robert Meese, would simply never have happened; that his conflicts with Dorothy's brother Calvin would never have happened; that, perhaps, Henry would not have killed himself. But those things were also a matter of fate: if his courtship of Dorothy had been preordained, then everything that followed from it must also have been destined, including Robert Meese's death, the circumstances of which Jeremiah had never revealed to anyone.

Jeremiah wished Dorothy had not gone mad. He wished he had not killed Robert Meese. He wished Marnie Hawthorne, in all the freshness of her youthful beauty, were there in his living room with him.

He drank rum straight from the bottle. In Marnie, he thought, the Hawthorne legacy might either be restored to respectability or reach its final nadir, the end that destiny had prepared for them. He struggled out of his chair and switched off the record player. Just as Henry Hawthorne had found no answers for his misery in bathtub gin, Jeremiah knew that he would find no answers in white rum. He thought there might be some answers, though, in the coming battle over Dorothy's will, in the decisions of Dorothy's heir.

He stumbled into his bedroom and set his bottle on the nightstand. He fell immediately to sleep and, despite his stupor, dreamed vivid dreams of Dorothy.

7

Here and Now

The sky above the Hawthorne Mansion was gunmetal gray and a cool, fragrant dampness filled the air, as if it were already raining nearby. Marnie glanced at the coming storm from Dorothy's bedroom window as she slipped into a pair of pumps. She was running late for her meeting with Alexandra Bergren, the executor of her grandmother's will.

She rushed out of the bedroom, onto the creepy landing, where two ancient hutches filled with porcelain dolls waited. The hutches were positioned on either side of the hall, so it was impossible to enter any room on the third floor without an audience of tiny, implacable observers. The doll collection disturbed Marnie—permanently smiling faces staring wide-eyed through thin glass panes, their incorruptible happiness a token of her grandmother's dementia.

She descended the stairs, snatched her jacket from the coat rack near the front door and stepped outside. A copy of the Templeton *Constitution* lay on the front porch. She opened it and found a small picture of herself in the upper left hand corner of the front page, above the paper's masthead, with instructions to turn to page six for her story. On page six, she found a handwritten note from Jon scrawled along the margins of his article, which occupied the paper's entire center spread.

"Marnie," Jon had scribbled. "I trust that you won't regret this interview. Please call me at 544-7238 (*Constitution* headquarters) or 546-1177 (my home) with any questions or concerns. Or, if you'd prefer, you can stop by Ploughman's Grill on Main Street this evening, and I'll treat you to dinner to compensate you for your pains, and we can discuss the article or anything else on your mind. Yours, Jon Ridgely."

Marnie couldn't decide if Jon's invitation was completely ingenuous or a clumsy request for a date. She recognized that his note was a common enough courtesy, and yet he was asking her to dinner and the invitation unexpectedly intrigued her. There was something engaging about Jon Ridgely, a tantalizing, forthright loneliness that solicited no pity, and this quality enlivened him in her memory. She recalled what an attractive figure he had cut in his black suit.

There was a dreamlike quality to everything that had happened since her grandmother's death, as if she had become a character in someone else's play, and she wondered if Jon might be part of that drama. Looking up at her grandmother's mansion—at her own mansion—she felt that recent events simply had nothing to do with her real life. For the first time since she had been married, she allowed a physical attraction to another man to slip out of her mind and into her body, just to see what might happen, and she found that the loneliness she sensed in Jon corresponded to a loneliness of her own that she hadn't previously recognized.

She got into her car, tossed the newspaper onto the passenger seat and drove off down Poplar. She would reserve judgment until she had read the article, but it seemed clear that she would speak with Jon again, because he was the reporter covering the inheritance, and if this fact allowed her to test certain feelings that her grandmother's death had inspired, then so be it. She and Graham were individuals, she reasoned, and even married couples were never meant to share every feeling and experience.

She followed her street map to Main Street. Marnie had

spoken with Alexandra by phone several times, but this would be their first face to face meeting. In addition to discussing the terms of probate and other technicalities, the executor had promised to give Marnie a packet of "manuscripts" her grandmother had left her, and Marnie hoped that these manuscripts would tell her why Dorothy Hawthorne had left her entire fortune to Marnie alone.

She soon came to Ploughman's Grill and slowed, thinking of Jon, but the restaurant was dark inside and she passed it too quickly to see anything. She continued through the Square and past Grayson's Downtown Barbers, where Jeremiah was standing outside looking pensively at the sky.

Down the hill past the Square, there were several fast food restaurants, a funeral home, the county library and then a bank. Traffic was moving at twenty-five miles an hour, which, Marnie noted, was five miles an hour below the speed limit, and she felt antsy and irritated. She crossed the railroad tracks, drove by the Dog and Suds and then left Templeton's city limits. On the very outskirts of town, she passed the cemetery, a Super K-Mart and the Marathon Oil Refinery.

Marathon was a massive expanse of hundred-foot-tall smokestacks, metal towers, fat round storage tanks and gray buildings, with so many flashing red lights that it looked like a grotesque Christmas display. The sweet heavy smell of gas filled the air. As Marnie left the refinery behind, Main Street became the slightly wider Route 44 and the countryside opened into a rolling prairie. The chemical sweetness in the air persisted long after the refinery had disappeared from Marnie's rearview mirror.

About three miles outside of Templeton, she came to Gordon Junction, where Route 44 met Route 1, another blacktopped country road. She turned north and sped through several miles of wheat and soybean fields, which were dotted with black oil pumps bobbing up and down like giant mechanical cranes.

Marnie quickly reached the outskirts of Hutsonville. On the phone, Alexandra had described the drive as if it were a day trip through the wilderness, but she had arrived within half an hour of walking out her front door, and she wondered at the provincial mentality that could consider Hutsonville far removed from Templeton. A light drizzle began to fall, and the air became white with moisture.

Hutsonville resembled Templeton in many ways, from its grid layout to the crouching stodginess of its houses and the doughy faces of the people on the streets. Its size was about the same, but certain differences were also obvious at a glance: Hutsonville's roads were pocked with holes, the public buildings needed paint and the sidewalks were cracked and weed-choked. Marnie recognized by comparison what a prosperous little idyll Templeton really was.

Alexandra Bergren's law office nestled into a row of shops designed to look like log cabins. Rather than giving this strip mall an air of homespun sincerity, however, the roughhewn beams and warped wooden walkways seemed comical, like a giant Lincoln Log construction. It was self-parody, and Marnie wondered how Ms. Bergren had become the executor of an important estate like her grandmother's.

She parked her car, stepped out into the light rain and closed her eyes to enjoy the fine drizzle against her face and neck. She climbed the steps onto the covered walkway. A man wearing a baby blue suit and a wide navy tie stood loitering in front of the Burnside Insurance Agency, and he stepped aside for her unnecessarily.

"Hello," the man said lasciviously, through his ill-trimmed mustache.

"Hello!" Marnie exclaimed brightly, to keep from laughing.

Under the absurd man's watchful eye, she located Alexandra's office. She went inside and found a small reception area, whose walls were wood-paneled and whose carpet was an ugly beige, badly in need of cleaning. A kindly, doe-eyed woman with a helmet of iron-gray hair sat at a brown metal desk, poring over some papers. The woman wore a peeved expression, which did not change as she looked up to greet Marnie.

"No problem at all," she said, as if Marnie had apologized for something. "I'm Alexandra." Alexandra rose and offered Marnie her hand. "Let me finish this and I'll be right with you."

Marnie sat down in an uncomfortable chair opposite Alexandra and shivered—the air conditioning was turned on high and the office was freezing cold. There were no computers or copiers or other technology one might expect to find in a law office, just an old, manual, upright typewriter on the desk at Alexandra's elbow.

After a few minutes, Ms. Bergren set her file aside and invited Marnie into an inner office. The carpet here was less worn but still needed cleaning, and the law books along the wall were dusty, their bindings cracked and worn. Ms. Bergren's dress resembled the fashion of her office: functional and unpleasant, as if no attention had been paid to it in years. She sat down behind her desk and Marnie occupied another uncomfortable chair across from her.

"How was your drive over?"

"Good."

"Did you have any trouble finding the office?"

"None at all. Your directions were very clear."

"Nasty weather, though, isn't it?"

"I rather enjoy it."

"I suppose it's good for the farmers. My lawn will be impossible to mow this weekend, though. It gets so out of control this time of year." Alexandra opened a drawer in her desk. She withdrew three manila envelopes, which bulged to bursting. "Have you found any good restaurants in Templeton?"

"I haven't eaten out since I've been here. I'm subsisting on the toffee they send from the plant."

"Well, Joe's Italian is good, if you want a nice meal, and Ploughman's has good burgers. And there's an Asian restaurant called Betty's Chinese Food and Catering, if you like that kind of thing. Of course, they're not actually Chinese, but I understand it's as good as the real deal."

"I'll keep them in mind." Marnie wondered how long this small talk would continue before Alexandra came around to the matter at hand.

"There's also a pizza place called Monical's that my kids just love. I wish they'd open a Monical's here in Hutsonville. They have another one in Champaign, but a lot of good that does me." Alexandra opened a file folder and handed Marnie a sheaf of papers. Without missing a beat, she launched into a discussion of the Hawthorne estate, as if it held exactly the same weight in her mind as Monical's Pizza.

"I'm sure you've seen these before," Alexandra said. "They're copies of the probate documents and notices from Lawford County Superior Court, and then there's the will itself, which I know you have a copy of."

"I've seen the will, but not these others."

"Oh. Well, as I said, those are copies, so you can keep them. Basically, Josephine Longmore and Susan Meese have filed liens against your grandmother's house and the toffee factory, Mack Fuller has a lien against most of the acreage your grandmother owned around Prairieville and Mt. Carmel, including the oil wells, and there are several other claims against her stock holdings, and so on. I'll answer whatever questions

I can for you, but I'd have your own lawyer go over any details you don't understand. Or have you done that already?"

Marnie shook her head no. "I don't have anyone yet, not locally. As you know, I've been talking to the solicitor my husband and I use in London, but he's not very familiar with American law. I've been dragging my feet on that count."

"Probably isn't super-urgent, but I wouldn't put it off, either." She slid her rolling chair over to a bookcase, where she retrieved a single sheet of paper from a neat stack. "Here's another copy of the lawyer list I sent you the other day."

"You sent me a list? Where to? I haven't received any mail since I arrived in Illinois."

Alexandra's face corkscrewed into a tight little frown centering on her nose. Her eyes narrowed, her brow furrowed, her mouth pursed and wrinkled, as if all of her features were trying to scrunch themselves into her nostrils. She brought her hand up to her face and rested her chin in her palm. Then, just as suddenly, she brought her hand down and her face returned to normal.

"Ah, yes, the mail to your grandmother's residence would have been stopped," she said. "So you haven't seen any of the documents the court has sent you?"

"Well, I assume they're still going to my London address, but as I said, I haven't received a thing since I arrived here."

"Mm-hm. If I were you," Alexandra said, "I'd get a post office box in town. You don't want the delay of shipping that stuff twice internationally, and it's going to be an incredible rigmarole to get the post office to deliver mail to your grandmother's house, since everybody knows you're not the legal occupant."

"But you just said that you'd sent me mail. Did you send it to my London address or to my grandmother's, then?"

"Your grandmother's, and a lot of good it did, too. I should have thought of that. Besides, I know the postmaster in Templeton and he's good friends with Josephine Longmore, so he won't exactly speed things along. I'm sure you've noticed that certain people in Templeton are predisposed against you. Anyway, this list I've given you is my own directory of lawyers, ones I refer people to. They're all good, but I've put them in descending order of quality, so the top ones are better."

Alexandra's carelessness disconcerted Marnie. She looked at the list without reading the names. She had put off retaining counsel because she was unsure how involved a process the lawsuits and counter-suits might be, and she wanted to reserve the option of hiring someone from a reputable firm in Chicago, rather than letting her fate rest with some two-bit litigator from the hinterlands. As she glanced through the probate documents, she saw that the claims against the will were numerous and complicated, so she would certainly need expert advice.

"What did you mean when you said I'm not the legal occupant of my grandmother's house? That's not what you told me when you sent me the keys." Marnie had received two complete sets of keys to the Hawthorne Mansion before she had left London. "Your letter implied that the burden of proof would fall on claimants against the estate rather than on me, since I was named specifically in the will."

"True," Alexandra said. "But you're not legally entitled to property or money or things of that nature until the claims are resolved and the probate period is over. Until the will is executed, in other words."

"Are you saying I'm staying in my grandmother's house illegally?"

"Well, not illegally, but extralegally."

"Then why on earth did you send me the keys?"

"Frankly, as the executor of the will, I can fudge things here and there. If I decide to give you the keys, then you have the keys—it's that simple. A judge can order you to give them up and move out, but that's a whole separate legal process and nobody's filed any motions like that, for the moment. They usually think it's just too much trouble. Anyway, I have a certain amount of wiggle room, because I actually have possession of all the keys and lock combinations and documents, and everyone else just has claims."

Marnie shivered under the air conditioning. Her rain-dampened clothes clung uncomfortably to her body, making her feel shrunken and tight, and her wet hair against her neck sent a shudder of goose flesh all over her.

"Would you mind turning the thermostat up a little?" she said.

Alexandra looked at Marnie uncomprehendingly for several seconds, as if no one had ever asked her this before and she couldn't be sure what the words meant. Then she said, "Not at all," and walked into the next room to adjust the air conditioning. The blower kicked off, and Alexandra returned to her seat.

"Hot flashes," she said. "Some days, I'm just hot and uncomfortable all day, in creeping waves. You know?"

Marnie decided not to comment on the executor's hot flashes. "So why did you give me the keys? Why fudge things on my account? You've gone out of your way to help me in certain respects, and I've given you no cause." Alexandra had given Marnie plenty of free guidance over the phone, mainly about the social climate in Templeton and the Hawthorne family's position in the town.

"In all honesty," Alexandra said, "I don't like the Fullers and Meeses very much, so I did it partially to spite them. If you mention that to anyone, I'll deny it, of course. Also, your uncle, Calvin Hawthorne—I guess he'd be your great-uncle, your Grandma Dorothy's brother—he gave my father a job once when he was down on his luck, and that helped put me through law school, so I feel that the Hawthornes should have their wishes respected over and above the wishes of the extended family. I'll give you the benefit of the doubt every time. Again, I'll deny that if asked, though technically it doesn't matter what I do, as long as I don't violate the law."

"Which you haven't done?"

"Which I haven't done."

The telephone in the reception area rang and Alexandra excused herself. Marnie noticed that there was no telephone in Alexandra's private office, nor was there a fax machine or any electronic equipment of any kind. Even the standard niceties that one might expect from any office—such as wall hangings or a coffee pot or windows—were absent, so that the room seemed to Marnie less like a law office than a portable trailer attachment.

Alexandra finished her telephone call—about a Caroline Emmons jewelry party she would be attending—and returned to Marnie. The helmet of gray hair atop her head bobbed and bounded.

"Now," Alexandra said. "These things I can give you. It's possible that a judge will order you to return them, but they're just personal papers, letters and whatnot—they're of no monetary value and no one has mentioned them in their claims. I'm sure that's just an oversight, but that's country lawyers for you. In any event, I'm not really supposed to give you these, but I'm devoted to seeing Dorothy's wishes carried out, and I doubt anyone else will notice." She pushed the three bulging manila envelopes across the desk at Marnie. "Here are certificates of receipt for you to sign. They list all of the items individually, so you might want to double-check the list before you sign it, to make sure everything's actually there. I prepared the documents myself and I've double-checked them, but once you sign for it, you're legally in possession of whatever you sign for, whether it's in there or not."

Marnie felt extremely uncomfortable with this transaction, but her curiosity got the better of her discretion. She opened one of the envelopes and emptied some of its contents onto the desk. A jumble of yellowing papers spilled out, and as she turned over the first little envelope that came to hand, her heart raced: it was addressed from her own father to her grandmother, postmarked May 20, 1971. She squeezed the envelope between her fingers and found a letter still in it. She picked up another: this one from Robert Meese to her grandmother, dated 1945. She began sorting them faster, with increasing eagerness and excitement, finding letters from Robert Meese, Jeremiah Grayson, Calvin Hawthorne, Josephine Longmore, and Henry Hawthorne. There was a second letter from her own father. They were in no order and were mixed up with curiosities such as hand-drawn maps, pressed dried roses and pages torn out of books.

In spite of her eagerness to read the letters, Marnie deliberately examined each item and checked it off against Alexandra's list, a tedious process that took more than thirty minutes, during which she fretted about the possibility that she was violating the law and might muck up the will. But, she supposed, she could hardly be held accountable for not knowing probate law—that was the executor's responsibility.

While Marnie sorted the papers, Alexandra made small talk about the County Fair, the Super K-Mart that had just opened in Hutsonville, her pet Lhasa Apso, a movie she had seen on television and the prospects for the harvest, until Marnie could hardly bear her prattle. She finished going through the list, signed the receipts and then put all of the items back in the manila envelopes, in a fit of increasing pique.

"You might want to stop by the County Court when you

get back to Templeton," Alexandra said. "Actually, I should have told you this the minute you got to town, but I didn't think of it. Go to the post office and get a mailbox and then go to the court and give them your box address. I'm sure they're sending all your paperwork to London, so whatever's been sent is on its way and your husband will have to send it back. The court dates on some of these hearings have already been set and they'll notify you of everything by mail, so it's important to get that information as quickly as possible." Marnie said that she would see to it. "Now," Alexandra went on, "are there any other questions you want to ask while you're here?"

Marnie had had a whole catalog of questions for Alexandra earlier in the morning, but they suddenly seemed trivial compared to the bundle of letters she had just received. More than that, she didn't trust Ms. Bergren's legal expertise and figured she should save her questions for real legal counsel. She thanked Alexandra for her help, apologized that all of her questions had slipped her mind and asked if she might call later if anything occurred to her.

"Certainly," Alexandra said. "But again, I can't act as your attorney. I can only answer general inquiries."

Marnie thanked her, gathered up the materials Alexandra had given her and followed the executor to the outside door, where they parted politely. The man in the blue suit was still standing in front of the insurance agency, and he watched her all the way to her car.

In contrast to the freezing cold office, the misting rain now felt positively warm against her skin. She hunched her shoulders and clutched her grandmother's papers to her chest to protect them against the drizzle.

Now, in spite of Alexandra's rather dubious handling of the will, she felt that she was making some progress. She set the manila envelopes carefully down in the passenger's seat, on top of the newspaper featuring her interview, and headed back to Templeton.

* * * * *

By the time Marnie reached Gordon Junction again, the skies had opened in earnest and the rain was falling so hard she couldn't see ten feet in front of her. Lightning flashed and thunder clapped almost simultaneously overhead. She flipped on her headlights and slowed the car, but the road markings were still difficult to make out, and the raindrops ricocheting up off the pavement seemed as fierce as the ones plummeting from the sky. She nearly missed the turn onto Route 44—she saw the junction late, braked late and fishtailed as she made the turn too fast.

Her windshield fogged, and she rolled down the driver's side window a crack and turned on the defroster. Water was already pooling in the fields, the earth unprepared to hold such a sudden rush of water after the morning's saturating drizzle.

The squall forced her to drive slower and slower, and the slower she drove, the more the crashing of the rain, the whipping of her windshield wipers and the monochromatic gray of the stormy landscape lulled her into reverie. The very violence of the storm seemed paradoxically insulating and comforting. Unconsciously, as she stared out at the sloggy meadows, Marnie stopped paying attention to the road and her mind wandered into a daydream about the transformative power of rain. It seemed that everything in Illinois was changing not just by the day but by the moment, and the climate here was as inconsistent as her own feelings. As she began to feel the countryside itself as an extension of her private fate, she glimpsed something looming at the edge of her vision, a mass of silver on the road coalescing out of the grayness.

Her heart skipped. All at once the silver mass became the grill of an oncoming semi truck. In the wrong lane! The truck's horn blared.

Marnie cranked her steering wheel hard right and her wheels darted and skidded off the road. The car slid sideways as the truck swerved away and a blast of air buffeted her. She hit something in her path and the car was airborne. Her wheels crashed down and the car lurched, still skidding sideways, as the truck's horn blared away into the distance. The car teetered as if it might roll over and then, without warning, it skipped and righted itself. Her sidelong momentum came to a halt so suddenly that her neck snapped to the side, sending a jet of pain down her back.

The car rolled forward a few feet, into the meadow at the side of the road, before stopping completely. The truck's horn continued to bellow into the distance.

The slap of windshield wipers and the drumming of rain gave a rhythmic shape to Marnie's frantic breathing. Her eyes were frozen wide open: she had to instruct them to blink. She shifted into park, eased her foot off the brake pedal (which she didn't even remember using) and switched off the wipers.

She listened to the din of raindrops and stared at the meadow, the reality of which now hit her with unexpected force. The wildflowers, the variegated greens of the grasses, the stand of black willows and blue beech trees bordering the field in the gray wash of rain—it all suddenly seemed less the picturesque backdrop of a quaint pastoral tale and more like real grasses and real wildflowers and real trees. Her trembling hands registered the texture and curves of the plastic around the steering wheel, and she burst into tears and sobbed uncontrollably.

* * * * *

When she finally regained her composure, Marnie's first thought was that she had lodged in the sodden mud. She checked her rearview mirror: the road was nearly obscured by driving rain, and she saw the deep brown marks her tires had cut into the soil. She shifted into reverse and tapped on the accelerator: the car crept slowly backward, and she breathed a sigh of relief. She maneuvered onto the gravel near the pavement, and there she decided to wait until the worst of the storm blew over. She saw no need to play chicken with speeding trucks. Thunder boomed, and she switched on her hazard lights.

Her neck felt tight and uncomfortable, and she wondered if she had pulled a muscle or suffered whiplash in the confusion. The fact that she had nearly been smashed sidelong into this real countryside gave it new depth and substance and she felt less like the theatrical character she had been playing and more like frail flesh and blood.

The three packets she had received from Alexandra now seemed graver and more substantial. She reached into an envelope and pulled out a letter to her Grandma Dorothy from Robert Meese—Marnie's own grandfather, about whom she knew nothing.

Her Grandfather Robert had apparently been left-handed: his thin handwriting was seismographic, tracing jagged, nearly illegible lines across the page. Marnie couldn't decide if it was the superficial appearance of his old-fashioned script or just her trembling hands that gave her an unexpected pang of regret, but she felt too addled and emotional to make sense of the words on the page. She set the letter aside.

She fished around in the passel of papers. The scraps and envelopes and torn pages were so jumbled and discontinuous that she decided it would be better to wait to read them until she could sort them by date and person, so that she might have some idea of the progress of events—if any story at all could be uncovered.

A car passed slowly on the road, its lights on and windshield wipers whipping frantically as it rolled toward Templeton. Marnie sighed.

Her eyes fell on the copy of the *Constitution* that Jon had left for her, and despite the fact that the article inside was about her, it seemed to have less to do with her than her grandmother's private letters. She felt calmer just thinking about it, and she spread the paper open across the steering wheel. The typeset words on the page became sensible, lacking the weird emotional charge of her dead relatives' quirky writing.

The *Constitution* had given her the star treatment—her story covered two whole pages with no advertisements, and included four photographs. She was embarrassed by how vampy and mischievous she appeared in the photos: she had let Jon's flattery affect her, and she imagined the gossipy women at the IGA Supermarket seeing them and confirming their nastiest notions about her.

Jon's writing was keen and elegant, and the portrait he painted was sympathetic to a fault. Jon himself came off as an engaging raconteur. In a couple of instances, he had arranged her quotes in false order, but these liberties made her seem more winning, so that the article nearly convinced her of her own charm. As she read the account a second time, it seemed as if Marnie Hawthorne were someone else, that the article told of a meeting that she had not even attended.

She remembered what a blurry uncertainty their interview had seemed even in the moment, and she wondered which was closer to the real Jon Ridgely: the vacillating interviewer she had met or the urbane storyteller he became in his article. The truth was probably somewhere in-between, but she was impressed by the refined tone of his writing and how plainly likable she seemed in his depiction.

She stared at the sheets of rain falling around her. In retrospect, serving champagne punch had been a bad idea, and she wondered why she had done such a thing. She had become entirely too enamored of her own composure, of the character she had been playing.

"What is the matter with me?" she said aloud.

Her claim in the article that she was concerned about the plight of the Hawthorne workers was simply a trait of her heiress character. In reality, she felt no connection whatsoever to the Hawthorne Toffee employees or what might befall them as a result of her grandmother's death.

Seeing this account of herself in print, in this town's actual newspaper, convinced her, more than the barreling truck had, of the irrefutable gravity of her position, and she realized that her aplomb would not do. It was all undeniably serious, and with a sudden grasp of what everyone else had considered obvious all along, she recognized that she was about to inherit millions and millions of real dollars, that she needn't play an heiress because she actually was one. The fact that she had never cared about money dulled the impact of this epiphany, but she suddenly understood the power of her position in a new way.

She thought about her grandmother's wealth and supposed derangement, and for the first time she perceived that everything she did from now on would affect literally hundreds if not thousands of people.

The wealth and madness of her own blood were after all hers, and she felt not so much frightened as fallen. She started her car again, guided it back onto Route 44 and drove slowly toward Templeton, her hazard lights flashing.

8

An Illicit Invitation

Jon stood sheltering under the eaves of the Hawthorne Mansion's portico. He wore a voluminous black poncho and floppy sou'wester hat. Beneath his poncho, he was carrying a ukulele, which, in the half-hour he'd been standing there, had become a source of embarrassment. He was frequently caught in this trap since he had returned from Chicago, unsure how seriously to take himself in any of his roles in Templeton and therefore unsure how seriously to present himself. The longer he waited there, the more foolish he felt: the idea of singing the song he had written for Marnie now struck him as asinine. Still, he couldn't bring himself to walk away with dignity and pretend he had never come.

It was bad enough that he was betraying Kate by being there, by writing a song for another woman. He felt guilty and paranoid that he would be found out, but Marnie had compelled him to come—her walk, the thick ringlets of blonde hair grazing her neck, her inscrutable smile. He wasn't sure exactly what he wanted from her. She would likely leave Templeton the moment her grandmother's will was executed, and she was married, anyway, but she was the first breath of life he had breathed in a long time, the first challenge. Through her, he imagined once again a larger life for himself, and the failures that had brought him back to Templeton seemed distant and inconsequential. He believed that telling the Hawthorne story—such a peculiar family saga that even people beyond Templeton might want to read it—could provide him an avenue back into serious journalism; but more than that, he imagined that Marnie herself represented an entirely different kind of life, one that he had once dreamed of.

There was nothing necessarily sexual about his attraction to Marnie, he told himself. Perhaps they could meet occasionally for a cup of coffee and it would be beneficial for both of them—a way for him to recapture a lost piece of himself, a way for her to acquaint herself with Templeton from the inside out. Jon knew that such an arrangement, no matter how superficially platonic, would be a betrayal of Kate, and the idea that Marnie would be interested in pursuing a polite friendship for his benefit seemed unlikely. Jon could therefore construe his presence at the Hawthorne Mansion as nothing more than folly.

He had just convinced himself to leave when Marnie's white rental car entered the driveway. Her headlights made a momentary rainbow in the sheet of water cascading down in front of the alcove. When she pulled up and saw Jon at her door, her eyes narrowed.

Jon thought of Kate and panicked, and then Marnie got out of the car and he could think of nothing but her. She clutched a bundle wrapped tightly in a jacket, and she dashed through the rain and leapt through the wall of water falling onto the porch. She let out a little yelp as the water plunged down her neck, and then she was standing beside him, and between the yelp and her wet hair and the shaky vulnerability in her big blue eyes, Jon knew that he no longer had a choice in the matter.

"Mr. Ridgely?" Marnie said, shouting above the splashing water.

"Ms. Hawthorne."

"What can I do for you?"

"I'd like to speak with you, if you have a moment."

"Is it about your article?"

"Yes. No. That is, not really. Well, yes."

Marnie opened the door and Jon followed her across the threshold. The mansion's entry hall breathed a clammy, chilly staleness. Marnie closed the door behind him, leaving them to face one another through murky shadows. A puddle formed immediately at Jon's feet, where his poncho was shedding water.

"I assume this is important, if it warrants loitering on my doorstep in the rain." Marnie unwrapped her bundle and set some manila envelopes and a passel of papers on the secretary's desk. She wiped her wet hands on her hips. "You have my cell number, don't you?"

"I do, but it's rather confidential, what I have to say, so I wanted to do it in person."

"Very well. Oh, forgive my manners," she said, noticing with alarm the puddle Jon was making on the hardwood floor. "May I take your coat?"

Jon made a flourish with his right hand as he removed his hat and poncho, sweeping the ukulele behind his back. Marnie gave him an odd look, as he twisted strangely in front of her. She hung his wet things on the coat rack behind the door, and it wasn't until she turned to face him again that she got a full-on look at the instrument.

"I hope you'll pardon my ukulele," he said, feeling incongruously crushed.

"I hope you won't do anything with it that requires pardoning." She crossed her arms and gave him a steady, bemused look. "Yesterday it was a harmonica, today a ukulele. Do you always carry a little musical instrument with you, Mr. Ridgely?"

"I'd like to live in a world where people spontaneously break into song." He took up the ukulele and accompanied himself through half a verse of "Raindrops Keep Fallin' on My Head." "See?"

Marnie arched her eyebrow. "Mr. Ridgely, the last time you were here, you said that your greatest talent was that you didn't care. I underestimated the power of that talent."

"That's actually why I wanted to see you."

"How so?"

"May I speak frankly, Ms. Hawthorne?"

"I invite you to."

"About my article... Have you had a chance to read it?"

"I did read it," Marnie said. "And I want to thank you for it. It was quite good."

"Thank you."

"And flattering."

"Yes, well, that's why I wanted to speak to you. You could probably tell by the article that I enjoyed our interview."

"To be frank with *you*, Mr. Ridgely, I hardly know what to think of our interview, much less your enjoyment of it."

Jon shook water off of his ukulele and wiped his brow with his shirt sleeve. "I'm trying to think of a simple way of saying this—that is, a way of saying it that won't seem inappropriate—"

"Mr. Ridgely, you're standing in my hallway unannounced, dripping wet with a ukulele. You'd be hard-pressed to compound the impropriety."

"I could ask you for a towel," he said. "That would at least remove one of the offenses."

"I'm sorry," Marnie said. "I foolishly thought you might be brief. Allow me to get you a towel." She walked toward the kitchen.

"Thank you."

She stopped and turned. "May I offer you a cup of tea?"

"Thank you," he said, taken aback by this sudden shift.

He followed her through the kitchen to a breakfast nook, where Marnie directed him to a stool. She lit the fire under a kettle of water on the stove.

"I'll just be a moment," she said.

She exited through a side door and Jon set his ukulele in an inconspicuous place at his feet. A dark hallway led away from the breakfast nook, and this hall was dominated by a single heavy armoire, the shelves of which were crammed with newspapers and magazines. Jon got up to examine them. They were recent, and they were all Asian or Filipino. A stuffed raven, mounted in an aggressive posture, sat atop the armoire, its wings spread and its beak thrust forward. Jon stared up at the bird, wondering why a mad shut-in like Dorothy would collect Asian newspapers. He paged through them, looking for a mailing address label, but there was none: they hadn't come through the mail. He made a mental note to ask Maude at the *Constitution* who in town might deliver foreign papers.

Footsteps announced Marnie's return, and Jon hurried back to his seat. She had dried her hair, which had turned frizzy, and pulled it back with a pair of matching butterfly clips; and she had changed out of her wet blouse into a stretchy, baby blue rayon shirt. She handed Jon a towel just as the kettle whistled.

"Earl Gray?" she asked, as Jon stood to dry himself.

"Fine."

"Milk and sugar?"

"Thank you."

Marnie prepared two cups of tea. "I've been living on tea and toffee," she said. "Every day, the Hawthorne plant sends over an enormous bag of irregulars—you know, the bars that are misshapen and not fit for sale?"

"I'm extremely familiar with Hawthorne irregulars," he said.

Marnie shot him a glance. "Are you?" She brought the cups to the breakfast bar, then took a seat opposite Jon.

"When you reach the fourth grade in Templeton," he said, "you go on a field trip to the Hawthorne plant, and at the end of it you get a big bag of irregular candy. Also, on Halloween, the plant doles them out by the wagonload. Did you know that Templeton has more dentists per capita than any other town in Illinois? One of the ancillary Hawthorne industries."

"Perhaps you could write an exposé."

"It's an open secret." He sipped his tea.

"So," Marnie said. "What did you want to see me about?"

"I came because I'd like to invite you to dinner."

"I believe you've already invited me to dinner, Mr. Ridgely. In your note this morning."

"Yes. Well, no. That is, I offered to treat you to dinner at the restaurant where I work. When I'm not chasing news, I'm a server at Ploughman's. That offer is still good, by the way. But now, I'd like to invite you to dine with me."

Marnie sat back and folded her arms. "You're asking me out on a date?"

"No, not a date. You're a married woman."

"I'm aware of my marital status, Mr. Ridgely. So you're inviting me to dinner under the auspices of your newspaper?"

"No, I'm acting on my own."

"Then this conversation has nothing to do with the article you wrote."

"It has everything to do with the article I wrote. Or, not the article exactly, but our interview."

Jon felt at a loss: he might claim to be working on a separate account of the Hawthorne family, perhaps for a book, but that idea had barely formulated itself in his own mind; he certainly couldn't ask Marnie to dinner because of her personal charms without becoming plainly impertinent. His invitation had forced them into an impasse.

"What if I invited you to dinner under the auspices of the *Constitution*?"

"For what purpose?"

"I'd like to do a follow-up interview. My editor wants to run another feature about you for our Sunday edition."

"Two features in one week? That seems excessive."

"Since your grandmother died, we've run a story about your family, or toffee, or Hawthorne Enterprises, every single day. This morning's paper, with your interview in it, sold out before nine o'clock." Jon ran his fingers through his hair. "You're very appealing to our readers, Ms. Hawthorne."

"When the *Constitution* buys dinner for its interview subjects," Marnie said, "where does it usually take them?"

"Since we're the main daily paper for the entire county, we have expense accounts all over. In this case, I'd suggest Nellie's in Palestine. It's rustic, a kind of hunter's inn. Venison, buffalo steaks, potato pies. Local delicacies."

"I didn't know Lawford County had its own cuisine."

"There are lots of surprises here, if you're willing to explore them."

The air between them had become thick with calculation and ambivalence. Jon cleared his throat and started making a case for the innocence of a working dinner, but Marnie cut him off.

"If you want the story for Sunday, I suppose you'll need to do the interview fairly soon."

"How about tomorrow night? We could meet there at eight o'clock."

"At Nellie's? In Palestine?"

"I'll draw you a map."

Marnie stood up to get pen and paper, and the strangeness between them multiplied. Neither looked at the other as she handed Jon her sketch pad and a charcoal gray pencil, and he drew a map from the Hawthorne Mansion to the restaurant. He pushed the map across the breakfast bar and then stood up beside her, his shirt sleeve just touching her shoulder.

"Thank you for your time," he said, which seemed stilted and ridiculous.

"Thank you for stopping by."

Jon stepped away from the breakfast nook. He brushed Marnie's shoulder with his chest as he squeezed unnecessarily close around her—her hair smelled like apples. She followed him through the kitchen and the pantry, with its empty wine racks, through the parlor, to the entrance hall.

Jon retrieved his hat and poncho from the coat rack and put them on, and it was only then that he remembered his ukulele resting on the floor in the breakfast nook. He decided against mentioning it, for fear that the tension would collapse and Marnie would think better of seeing him again. He held out his hand, and Marnie shook it with neither warmth nor resistance.

"I'll see you tomorrow night, then?" he said.

She looked at his shoes and shook her head yes, her hand still clasped in his. When she finally met his eyes, her look was unreadable—Jon could not tell what she had decided. He opened the door and stepped out. Before he had a chance to turn and look at her again, Marnie had closed the door behind him.

Rain was still falling lightly. Jon walked down the driveway and rounded the hedge onto Poplar Street. For the second time this week, he was leaving the Hawthorne Mansion changed, in ways that were becoming increasingly risky and material.

He quickened his pace, looking only at the wet sidewalk directly in front of his feet. He felt eyes watching him from every house, from behind every door and picture window he passed, and, for the first time in his relationship with Kate, he invented some convenient lies. His guilt was matched only by his conviction that he simply had no choice—he had to meet Marnie for dinner, he had to see her again.

A small voice told him that he could go to Kate right then, that he could go home, get into his truck and find her, wherever she was; that he could miss his appointment with Marnie tomorrow night; that he could take Kate to dinner instead. But this voice was matched by a more persuasive one that told him it was already too late. He removed his hat and turned his eyes up to the sky, and as he did so the rain fell harder.

Is it already too late? he asked himself. He looked back at the Hawthorne estate, which, like an impenetrably black cloud, hovered ill-naturedly at the end of the street.

9

Arguments and Omissions

The rain that morning forced Kate and her mother to abandon their work in the fields, so they returned to their house and stowed their wet gear in the garage. They tromped into the kitchen and shed their dripping coats and muddy boots. "There's going to be trouble," Mr. Benjamin called from the living room.

"Why?"

Kate found her father sitting on the sofa in his usual position, reading the Templeton *Constitution*. He peered at her over his reading glasses.

"This spread in the newspaper by your boy—when Susan Meese sees it, she'll scream bloody murder."

"What does it say?" Kate swooped toward her father, snatched the paper out of his hands and plopped down beside him.

"You know how Susan hated Dorothy," he said. "And now with the ruckus about this will... It sounds like Marnie Hawthorne's cut from the same cloth as her grandmother."

"Susan Meese is always complaining about something," Mrs. Benjamin said from the kitchen. She busied herself fixing a pot of coffee. "Remember when the Prairieville city council offered to replace her septic tank for free, and she fought them for a year because she didn't want to pay city sewage?"

A gust of wind blew rain against the living room windows. They heard the faint rumbling of thunder in the distance toward Stoy.

"But this is about real money, not some piddling sewage bill," Kate's father said. "We'll never hear the end of it."

Kate opened the paper to Jon's article and examined the pictures of Marnie Hawthorne. The first thing she noticed was not Marnie herself, but the perspectives the photographs had been taken from—they were anything but the bland, badly framed, poorly cropped head shots that usually appeared in the *Constitution*. The four pictures in this spread had been taken from a variety of different angles, with some care to position the subject (in one shot, a statue of Cupid peered over Marnie's shoulder). The photos were set at jaunty angles to the text and bordered with bold lines, a technique usually reserved for Templeton High School's Homecoming Royalty. The text itself was bordered by a thin black line adorned with gray starbursts, and this graphic touch was also a striking departure: only during the County Fair or Fourth of July would the layout editor go to such lengths to highlight an article. The effect was so striking that it almost looked like an advertisement for Marnie Hawthorne, and Kate felt the effect of these stylistic embellishments as a cold emptiness in her stomach.

"How do the beans look today?" her father asked. When no one answered, he poked Kate in the arm. "How do the beans look?"

"Fine, Daddy. Ask Mom."

While her parents discussed how sodden and weedy their field was becoming, Kate read Jon's article with a growing sense of disquiet. It was written with a cunning hyperbole that flattered its subject without making particular claims about her graces. There were no exaggerating adjectives or sensational statements, just a general impression of winsomeness, and Kate was reminded of the care and style with which Jon had once written all of his articles, a care she hadn't noticed for many months.

"I think I'll go into town," she said.

Her mother snorted. "It's pouring rain, honey. Have a cup of coffee with us."

"No, I'm going into town." She stood up and folded the copy of the *Constitution* under her arm. "Do you need anything from the store?"

Her parents looked at her as if she were crazy. "The coffee's almost ready," her mother said. "You know, you're just asking for it if you go gallivanting around on a day like today."

"Mom, seriously, I won't be struck by lightning." Kate gave her mother a hug. She slipped into a pair of sandals lying next to the kitchen door. "I'll pick up some doughnuts on the way back."

"But why can't you wait till it clears up?"

"I want to talk to Jon."

"Call him on the phone."

"I'm going now, Mom."

"I don't understand what's so urgent. Remember what happened to Edgar Washington?"

"Mom, you never even knew Edgar Washington, and that was thirty years ago in Muncie, Indiana. The storm isn't that bad." She waved goodbye and stepped out into the rain.

In fact, the rain was falling in torrents. Kate sprinted to her father's truck, turned the key in the ignition and pulled onto the single-lane blacktop of Harvey Road.

She normally loved the way the green stalks of sweet corn swayed and swooshed in the wind—the Conway field to her left was alive with manic undulations, as the corn rippled and heaved like a bright green sea—but she took no pleasure in it now. She drove as fast as she dared toward Route 44.

She had nothing at all to suspect, she told herself: Dorothy Hawthorne had died, Jon had been assigned to interview her heir. He had said some flattering things about Marnie Hawthorne in a nice profile of her. That was all—it wasn't as if Kate had caught him kissing her. This thought caused Kate's pulse to quicken.

"Stupid," she said out loud.

Kate hated her intuition, the more so at this moment because it was so reliable and she couldn't believe what it was telling her. She trusted Jon. As she came to Route 44, she decided to stop at the IGA and buy some flowers for him on the way to his apartment. But her intuition would not be silenced by her resolution, and she felt her alarm growing second by second.

* * * * *

Kate parked in front of Fendick's Glass and Mirror and went racing up the outside stairs to Jon's apartment, bouquet of flowers in hand; but he didn't answer his door. Though she had a key, she suddenly felt strange about entering his apartment, so she returned to her father's truck and called him on her cell phone, but he didn't pick up. She drove around the Square a few times, looking in at Ploughman's to see if he might be there covering someone else's shift; then she stopped at the *Constitution* offices, but Jon was nowhere to be found. Moreover, his truck was parked outside his apartment, where it usually was, and his motorcycle was on its center stand next to the back wall of Fendick's. If he had gone anywhere, he had walked—in the pouring rain.

Vexed, Kate went to the Blue Cup Café, two blocks away on Cross Street, where she could watch the outside of Jon's apartment. She sat at a window table nursing a cup of burnt coffee, and every fifteen minutes or so she dialed Jon's number.

Finally, the rain slackened and stopped, and Kate walked back to Fendick's. She felt alternately angry, foolish, and offended, and she asked herself why she shouldn't just drive up to the Hawthorne Mansion and put these fears to rest—but doing so seemed to cross a boundary of sanity. She mounted the stairs to the landing and resolved that, whatever the truth of the matter, she wasn't going to waste any more time feeling unwelcome at her own boyfriend's apartment. She unlocked the door and went in.

Jon's large main room was sparsely furnished, with a queen-sized bed along one wall, a brown recliner next to it and a small wooden desk with a rollaway chair. He had no pictures or posters of any kind, and the walls were painted stark white. There were nine-pane windows in the center of each outside wall, so that daylight streamed in all day from one direction or another. The apartment was immaculately clean and tidy except for the clutter of books—there were piles of books on the floor, under the desk, beside the chairs, peeking out from under the bed, but even these were aligned in neat stacks.

Beyond this main room was a small kitchen with an ancient, two-burner gas stove, a refrigerator and a few cupboards. A heavy brown curtain separated the kitchen from the bathroom.

Kate laid her flowers on Jon's desk and strolled around the entire apartment, touching every piece of furniture. She lingered in the kitchen to stare out the open window over the sink. A sparrow fluttered from branch to branch in the elm tree outside, and she spent a calming minute watching it.

The air in Jon's apartment was muggy from the rain, and the morning was growing warm, so Kate closed the kitchen window and turned on the air conditioner: the vent in the ceiling soon huffed cold, dry air. She slumped down in Jon's recliner and felt aimless and distracted. She hated being in limbo, and she hated herself for being suspicious.

He's just at the library, she thought. He's eating at Bertram's.

He's shopping at Super K-Mart.

She heard footsteps coming up the stairs outside, and she caught her breath. She felt guilty for being there, for spying on Jon, and she was angry that she was jealous. She picked up her flowers and stood to meet him, trying to wipe away her turmoil and embarrassment with a smile. As Jon opened his screen door, Kate pulled the inside door open and thrust the bouquet of flowers forward. "Welcome home!"

"Ah!!" Jon jumped, caught his heel on the threshold and fell backwards. The black poncho he was holding flew into the air. He plopped to the landing on his rear end and banged his head on the railing.

"Oh my God." Kate dropped the flowers and knelt by his side. "Are you all right?"

"Fine," he said defensively. He checked the back of his head for blood. "I wasn't using my head today anyway." He got to one knee. "What are you doing here?" It was not a welcoming tone.

"I came to surprise you."

"Mission accomplished." He pointed to the flowers lying dashed on the landing. "What's the occasion?"

"No occasion. We got rained out of the fields, so I decided to come by and tell you I love you." She gathered the flowers, gave them to Jon and kissed him. "I thought we could laze around together and drink tea and read books."

"Sounds nice," Jon said, without feeling.

"Actually, it may be sunny this afternoon after all, so we could play Frisbee in the park."

"That sounds nice, too."

Kate kissed him again and then picked up his poncho and helped him to his feet. "Where have you been?" she asked, trying to seem nonchalant. She led him into his apartment, then went into the bathroom to drape his wet slicker over the shower rod.

"Nowhere," he said. "Just went for a walk in the rain."

"Down along Big Creek?"

"No. Just around town. Nowhere in particular." He walked past her into the kitchen and ran water into a glass.

"I read your article this morning."

"Yeah? What did you think?"

"I think Maude thinks Marnie Hawthorne just got elected Homecoming Queen."

"Quite a splash, wasn't it?" He put the bouquet in the glass of water and set it on the kitchen window sill. "That's one thing about Maude—she knows which side her bread is buttered on."

"Do you?"

Jon turned to face Kate. "Meaning what?"

A note of anger crept into her voice. "Pandering to the crowd, is that what you're doing?"

"What are you talking about?"

"That story you wrote, Jon, those pictures. Not exactly the style you used when you wrote about Susan Meese or Josephine Longmore."

"No, because they're tired, greedy old hags."

"Susan Meese is only fifty-six years old."

"Doesn't mean she's not an old hag."

"So Marnie Hawthorne isn't tired or old, so you write her up like a movie star?"

"Where is this coming from? There's nothing wrong with that article."

"No, how could there be?"

"Look, I don't write one way for every story. I have no idea how a story's going to look. I just tailor it to fit the information, and this was a feature interview, so it was written in a more—I don't know—whimsical style."

Kate was losing patience with Jon's use of jovial adjectives to describe all things Marnie Hawthorne: playful, good-humored, whimsical.

"So when you interviewed Josephine Longmore, that was a news interview and not a feature interview, and that's why you used a more straightforward news style to describe that old hag?"

"That isn't fair." Jon threw his hands up. "When I interviewed Josephine, it was about the lien she'd filed against the toffee plant. Besides, you're forgetting all of those historical pieces I wrote about the whole Hawthorne family—Calvin and Henry and everyone. Those weren't exactly landmarks of journalism—they were fluff pieces, just like this one."

They stared at each other. Kate folded her arms across her chest.

"I thought you came to surprise me and tell me you loved me," Jon said.

"Don't do that. I'm just upset."

"By that stupid article?"

"It wasn't a stupid article. It was a very good article, and I know what it means when you take the care to write a good article."

"That I'm doing my job?" He unfolded Kate's arms, embraced her and stroked the back of her head. He spoke softly in her ear. "It's just the Hawthornes, you know. It's affecting everybody. And to tell you the truth, I can't remember the last time I had something truly interesting to write about, or even to think about." This last qualification made Kate stiffen. "Remember my article about Robert Meese's death? That was pretty good. I took just as much care with that one. And the one about Old Henry setting himself on fire."

"No, but those pictures. . ."

"Of Marnie? They were just photographs. You should see

the garden out behind the mansion. It's so elaborate and beautiful, I guess I got carried away, or maybe the light was just right, or. . . I don't know."

Kate was growing more and more annoyed, because he was refusing to acknowledge what was bothering her. He was shaping their argument into the conversation he wanted to have. She knew from experience that she could not let him get away with dumbing the issues down or changing the focus of the discussion, or his viewpoint would seem increasingly sound and she would seem less and less sensible and her concerns would be argued away. She hated arguing with Jon.

"You didn't take four different pictures of Josephine Longmore," she said.

"Actually, I did," Jon countered, "but Maude only printed one."

"Because Josephine Longmore is a hag, so they couldn't possibly print four photos of her? And Marnie Hawthorne is just so pretty?"

"You know what Maude always says—pictures sell papers."

"Pictures of pretty girls, right?" Kate sighed and wilted in Jon's arms. Now she remembered why they hadn't fought for so long: Jon was impossible. "Why do you make me spell everything out? Why can't you grant me one thing?"

"I don't understand what you're so upset about. You come all the way over here to give me flowers and tell me you love me and then you attack me for some stupid article I wrote."

"You know you're proud of that article. It's a lit match in a gas can. Everybody in the county is talking about it by now."

Jon released Kate, and she drooped down into his recliner. He remained standing, looming over her.

"All right," he said. "I *am* happy with the way it turned out, and I'm happy that Maude splashed it across the center truck.

Which makes it all the more puzzling that you're attacking me for it."

"Why didn't you call me this morning?" Kate asked. "You said you were going to call me."

"I was going to as soon as I got home, but you were already here."

Kate sighed again. Jon was going to force her to say out loud that she was jealous so that he could make light of it. But didn't she want him to make light of it? she asked herself. Didn't she want him to dismiss her fears and take her in his arms and tell her how much he loved her and that their relationship was not boring at all, that it had not become routine and predictable? That Marnie Hawthorne was an attractive novelty, but novelty paled in comparison to the deep love and trust and friendship they shared?

She looked at Jon's sensuous lips, his brackish green eyes, and tried to find some sympathy in his expression. But there was only a vague hardness, a challenge. She felt jumbled up inside, but what if everything he said was true, what if he hadn't thought twice about Marnie Hawthorne and she was just chasing phantoms?

"You know what we should do?" he said. He kneeled down next to the recliner, so that he was looking up at her. "We should go to the drive-in tonight. We should take a vacation today. Do you have to go back to the field?"

"No," Kate said hopefully.

"I've already filed a story at the paper, and I'm off from Ploughman's. Why don't we just spend a lazy day together, like you said? We can go play Frisbee, and then come back here and I'll make lunch, and we can just lie around and read or do nothing. And tonight, if the weather clears, we can get a pizza from Monical's and take it to the drive-in and sit on lawn chairs in the back of my truck, and it'll be a nice day. How does that sound?"

"Do you know what's playing?" she said, trying to hide how relieved, thankful and simultaneously maddened to the point of tears she felt. She wished Jon could just once volunteer a kind word to reassure her without making her jump through hoops first, but she was glad for this peace offering. She decided that maybe he hadn't said anything to reassure her because her jealousy had mystified him and he simply hadn't known how to respond. She caressed his cheek.

"I have no idea what's playing," he said. He rubbed his cheek against her palm and kissed her hand. "A schlocky double-feature, if we're lucky."

"You really irritate me sometimes," she said.

"Not really." He ran his hands up and down her thighs, from her knees to her hips and back, quickly at first, and then more slowly and sensually, holding her gaze.

"No, really."

"I've just never known you to be jealous," he said.

"I've never known you to be interested in other women."

"You wanna fight some more?"

"Yeah, I do."

She sat up in the chair and took Jon by his elbows. They held one another's gaze, searchingly, for what felt like a very long time, and then Kate kissed him and did not stop kissing him until they stood up together and slid gently down into his bed.

10

SHAVE AND A HAIRCUT

Grayson's Downtown Barbers occupied a sliver of space between Jean's Jewelry Store and Main Street Realty, just east of the Square. It had three barber chairs, a shoe shine bench and a row of padded metal chairs along one wall, where farmers would congregate to chat about the bushel price of corn or the Indianapolis 500. The aroma of Jeremiah's pipe tobacco blended with the pungent smells of aftershave and medicated lotion, which hung in the air despite the ceiling fan that spun languidly day and night. The mint green paint on the walls showed the unmistakable graying of pipe smoke, and the black-and-white checkered floor tiles around the barber chairs had been worn dull by Jeremiah's shuffling feet as he circled and snipped and swept.

Despite Jeremiah's aloof reputation, his barber shop still functioned, in the usual manner of small town barber shops, as a combination men's club and community center, where information, wisdom, gossip and lies were manufactured, mixed up and passed along. Here, one could still provoke an argument about the Marshall Plan or the House Un-American Activities Committee, and the Farmer's Almanac was sworn by almost as often as the Bible. During the summer, a small transistor radio on the shoe shine bench broadcast Cardinals and Cubs baseball games, and the men would sit comparing current players to bygone stars.

Although barbering had been in his family—Jeremiah's Uncle Skip had owned this shop before him—Jeremiah never imagined in his youth that he'd become a barber. His only ambition had been to continue his father's dairy farm, but after he'd met Dorothy Hawthorne, both the farm life and the barber shop had seemed too lowly. Henry Hawthorne would never let such a humble workman marry his daughter, so Jeremiah had cast about for a more urbane profession, something that might suit the husband of a wealthy beauty.

In Eaton and Templeton, there were only labor jobs and jack-of-all-trades work. Farther out in the county, there were oil jobs and construction and the cheese factory. There was only one thing he could think to do that might impress Henry, and the army had thought of it long before Jeremiah had. When his draft notice came in 1942, he jumped at the chance to win Henry's respect and Dorothy's hand in marriage.

Jeremiah dreamed of becoming a war hero, but during his time in the service he found no grenades to jump on, no squad of Gerries to single-handedly outfox. He never saw real combat. He had served in a supply unit, transporting heavy equipment and repairing roads in the wake of the fighting, and nothing he did was glorified in newsreels.

When the war ended, Jeremiah learned that Robert Meese had married Dorothy back in Templeton, and he despaired. Robert had striking good looks and the Meeses had oil money, and he feared that, if he returned to Illinois and the drudgery of milking cows in Eaton, he would never be able to stand it. So, rather than face his unrequited love, Jeremiah simply stayed in Europe after the war.

He landed a carpentry job in Brussels, where the shortage of men gave him many chances to forget about Templeton. He learned French, discovered jazz and had a series of affairs with women from all different walks of life, and he fell out of contact with his old friends and family. But Jeremiah never found contentment in his new life.

As months turned to years, he pined more and more for home, and Dorothy never escaped his mind. One spring day in 1951, a red tulip in a windowbox reminded him with inexplicable force of his faraway love, and he quit his job on the spot, gave notice to his landlord and hopped aboard an ocean liner to America, returning suddenly and unlooked-for to his home town.

In the meantime, while Jeremiah had been living aimlessly in Brussels, his parents had sold their land and retired to a small house in Stoy. When he finally returned home after years in exile, he returned to nothing—no farm, no work and no chance to win Dorothy Hawthorne. Lonely and out of sorts, he malingered around his Uncle Skip's barber shop, moping and mooning. After a few months, he started helping his uncle open and close the shop, just for something to do, and the feeling of the business—the rhythm of the day, shooting the breeze with the regulars—seemed the most natural thing in the world to Jeremiah, so he eventually learned how to cut hair himself.

He found that he had a touch for barbering, an effortless symmetry in his imagination, and the old-timers liked how delicately he shaved their faces. He was soon manning one of the barber chairs full-time, building a reputation among his own stable of regular customers. It happened with such ease that he didn't question it, especially since, around this time, he began his illicit affair with Dorothy.

Dorothy had married Robert Meese without love or enthusiasm: Robert had been her father's choice. After their marriage, Dorothy regretted her father's wealth more and more—it seemed to offer only limitations and compromises. When Jeremiah had taken a chance and written to her one drunken night, after he had closed his uncle's shop—a florid, ostentatious letter, just like the ones he'd written in the old days—Dorothy jumped at the chance to renew their affair. It promised her the passion she was missing in her marriage and gave her a new opportunity to defy her father. With the seeming inevitability of doing the only thing they could imagine, Dorothy and Jeremiah became lovers.

Meanwhile, Jeremiah's Uncle Skip proposed that they become partners, and Dorothy secretly gave him the sum necessary to buy into the barber shop. From that moment on, Jeremiah had been a full-fledged, full-service barber: in roundabout and unpredictable ways, Dorothy had made him everything he was.

* * * * *

After a busy morning, Jeremiah was sweeping his tiled floor, feeling rheumy. The morning gossip had consisted entirely of the profile of Marnie Hawthorne in the previous day's *Constitution*, and Jeremiah had been aggrieved by his inability to confide in anyone about the Hawthorne affair. After many decades of silence about the Hawthornes, everyone was talking about Dorothy again and Marnie, and Jeremiah longed to confess what he had seen and done, to unburden himself of the secrets he had been carrying for so long. But there was no one to tell.

Most of the people who had known Dorothy and Calvin and Robert Meese in their youth had died, and the younger people, Jeremiah felt, would hardly understand the tale he could tell. Their imaginations had become lurid with the confessions they heard every day on television, and Jeremiah doubted they would recognize the significance of what he might say, the difference between his story and every other tale of thwarted love and shame. Besides, everyone was more interested in Dorothy's granddaughter and what she would do with the Hawthorne money, what romantic imbroglios she might be involved in. The article in the paper was so flattering in such a sneaky way that people even suspected Jon Ridgely of having an affair with her.

Just as well, Jeremiah thought. He was fairly sure that he could still be prosecuted for the death of Robert Meese. And yet he longed to tell someone, and this longing dredged the channels of his memory, disturbing the old passions, making them rise to the surface.

Jeremiah finished sweeping and sat down in the barber's chair next to the window. He withdrew his pipe and a lighter from his vest. He sucked fire into his tobacco and puffed contemplatively as traffic passed on Main Street.

* * * * *

Jeremiah should not have been there that night. He should not have witnessed the ugly argument between Dorothy and Robert Meese in the Hawthorne garden, much less have confronted Robert by the fountain. He had confused his dates: he was supposed to have met Dorothy the next night, when Robert would have been with Calvin and Henry in Chicago for a candymakers' convention.

When Robert was away, Jeremiah would sneak onto the Hawthorne estate by circuitous routes, under the cover of night, and he and Dorothy would indulge their illicit desires in the mansion. When Robert was not away, Jeremiah and Dorothy would meet for afternoon trysts in the apple orchard: Dorothy had outfitted the gardener's shack there as a lover's retreat, with a twin bed and a lock on the door that only she and Jeremiah had the key to. Sometimes, at midnight, Dorothy would leave Robert in their marriage bed and slip out to the gardener's shack, and she and Jeremiah would make love and share momentary confidences.

Jeremiah would leave notes for Dorothy in their little shack, drop off a bottle of wine, a tin of sweets, a letter. The daring required to venture into this garden retreat and the impossibility of truly hiding his visits from the town made their affair seem alive with passion and necessity.

However, it was unusual for Jeremiah to venture so close to the mansion itself when Robert might be there. On that fateful midsummer's night in 1952, when Robert's life had ended, Jeremiah should never have been within shouting distance of the garden. The moment he heard Robert's voice, he should have turned and fled. That he had been there at all was an accident, a confusion of dates; that he had heard the hoarseness of Robert's angry speech was an accident; that Robert had tumbled unconscious into the fountain was an accident, nevermind that Jeremiah had pushed him. It was all an accident.

* * * * *

Jeremiah was strolling across the western pasture of the Hawthorne property, walking by the light of a nearly full moon from the apple orchard to the mansion—there were several acres of open fields around the manicured gardens near the house. Pale wildflowers dotted the field and glowed in the moonlight, and as he walked, he stooped to pick some for Dorothy, until he had a small bouquet of ragged blossoms. He leapt easily over the nameless stream that ran through the middle of the property, and on this night he felt no traces of jealousy or envy or guilt, as he often did crossing the estate. The air was still and humid and Jeremiah was content just to be meeting Dorothy, to forget about the larger impossibilities of their affair.

As he approached the first row of box hedges, he heard a man's voice raking across the night, a voice that he recognized as Robert's shouting in an oscillating stream of anger. The shouting continued just at the edge of his hearing, changing pitch, growing softer and then suddenly louder with no answering voice, so that Jeremiah could not quite make out the meaning of the words. He ran toward it.

He was disappointed that Robert was there at all, that he would not be able to make love to Dorothy, but he was alarmed at the vehemence of Robert's tone. The garden's first hedge stood well above his head, and he tiptoed along it until he reached a wooden gate. He knelt down to peer through the opening at the path beyond.

Robert's voice came louder and fiercer. Jeremiah slipped through the gate and slunk forward, clinging to the shadows of the hedges. He now heard clearly that Robert was angry about something Calvin had done: he was shouting that Calvin had no right, and Calvin should be strung up, but his words were slurred and his speech rambling. Jeremiah followed the meandering path to an outer rose garden. Here, the lanes around the rose bushes were laid with crushed white gravel, which glowed bright in the moonlight. He crept along the loamy soil at the edge of the path to avoid broadcasting his footsteps.

Past the outer rose garden, he entered a pergola—a vine-covered arbor that sheltered the path—and this arbor ended in another wooden gate, which opened onto the fountain with the statue of Cupid. He moved forward as stealthily as he could, still unconsciously holding the bouquet of wildflowers he had picked on the way. He stared through the slats in the gate and saw that Robert was with Dorothy, and he was now yelling an almost incoherent stream of drunken insults. They were standing on the opposite side of the fountain from Jeremiah, their figures partially obscured by Cupid and the water splashing around the winged god's delicately rounded limbs.

Robert was wagging his finger at Dorothy, pausing occasionally to drink from a bottle he held in his left hand. Dorothy, in a shimmering white shift, stood facing Robert with her arms crossed and her lips pursed.

* * * * *

As Jeremiah sat smoking in his barber chair fifty years later, he could see Dorothy in his mind's eye as clearly as if she were standing before him. He had never intended to open the gate from the arbor to the fountain that night, had never intended to come between Robert and Dorothy. But as he watched the arguing couple from the shadows, as Dorothy became ever more sullen and unresponsive to her husband's tirade and as Robert finished his bottle, their dispute suddenly escalated and Jeremiah was forced to intervene.

* * * * *

Dorothy pointed her finger at Robert and narrowed her eyes in hate and said something that Jeremiah couldn't make out, with a look so venomous that Jeremiah himself was taken aback. Robert froze and Dorothy's mouth dropped open, as if she herself were startled by what she had said. For a long moment, the splashing of the fountain was the only sound.

Jeremiah was so absorbed in the scene, as he peered through the gate, that the whole world seemed to exist there in the garden, holding its breath. He could see Dorothy's expression turn slowly from shock back to insolence. Her face grew bold and she said something else, low and provocative. At this, Robert lifted his bottle and hurled it viciously at Dorothy.

She flung up her arms, too late, and the bottle struck her on the right side of the head. She screamed and fell backwards.

Jeremiah's heart leapt into his throat. He dropped his flowers and flicked the gate latch open and rushed forward.

Robert stood over Dorothy as she curled into herself on the ground. He brought his leg back to kick her, but he spied Jeremiah running around the fountain and whirled to defend himself. Jeremiah tackled him, and all three of them lay sprawled in the neatly-trimmed grass.

Jeremiah jumped up and pinned Robert, but Robert was quick and strong and he wriggled free. Both men were soon on their feet again, tangled in each other's arms and legs, their fists landing awkward body blows. Jeremiah shouted obscenities as they tussled—he was no longer sure what he was saying or doing, but he was possessed by the desperate, sinking certainty that, no matter how this fight ended, his secret affair with Dorothy was over and nothing could ever be the same again. He felt his future disappear a little with every punch to Robert's ribs, with every elbow he took to the mouth, and his anger became boundless.

Robert pulled Jeremiah's shirt up over his head and Jeremiah flailed against him. He heard Robert grunting with his blows and felt the grunts in Robert's chest as their bodies mashed together. He became disoriented by the pulling and tugging and gouging, until he was no longer sure which direction the gate lay or where Dorothy was. His knee banged against Robert's knee, and they both buckled and lost their balance and Jeremiah was tumbling forward.

Robert seemed to disappear before him. Jeremiah heard a plonk and then he was tumbling into something hard. He was splashing into water. He was flailing under water. He was choking water into his lungs.

He was alone, face down in the fountain. He couldn't find his bearings. He thrashed his arms down and pushed himself to the surface. He gasped for air.

He was crouching gawkily on his knees—his wind had

been knocked out and his chest felt concave. He clinched into himself. Robert was in front of him in the fountain, facing away from him, struggling to stand up. Jeremiah lunged at Robert and caught him square in the hip with his shoulder. Robert lurched and his forehead smacked Cupid's bow with the full force of Jeremiah's weight. He crumpled into the agitated waters of the fountain.

Jeremiah coughed violently and choked and spat, trying to breathe fresh air into his lungs. He sat up on his knees and looked at Robert, but with the agitation of the water, the dark shadows of Cupid mottling the pool's moonlit surface, it was not immediately apparent that Robert was no longer moving.

Dorothy rushed to the edge of the fountain. Jeremiah could not move. He could not hear the splashing of the water or Dorothy's cries. He could not feel the heaviness of the water in his clothes or the droplets streaming into his eyes. Dorothy stood above Robert's body, pulling at his shirt to bring his head out of the water, shouting at Jeremiah to help her, but Jeremiah could not move. He could not take his eyes off of Robert as the darkness around his head registered in Jeremiah's mind as blood, as a great dark cloud of blood. Dorothy stepped into the fountain and cradled Robert's head and turned him on his side.

She reached out and smacked Jeremiah hard in the face and the sound came back to his ears and the feeling came back to his skin. As he returned to his senses, he could do nothing but cough uncontrollably. When he could breathe again, he helped Dorothy lift Robert out of the fountain, then he collapsed against it and his convulsions continued.

* * * * *

It had been an accident. He had never intended to hurt

Robert Meese. Robert, Jeremiah felt, had brought his death upon himself by attacking his own wife, which, he also felt sure, Robert had never intended to do. He had lost control.

Jeremiah emptied the ashen contents of his pipe into a waste paper basket near the door to his barber shop. He stood up, walked to the back of the shop and refilled the pipe from a pouch that he kept near the sink. He re-lit it and then went back to the barber chair and stared at the serene late September day outside.

Life had gone on after Robert Meese. Life was going on after Dorothy Hawthorne. A kind of life.

As he reflected on that night at the fountain, Jeremiah felt increasingly bilious. This was not life, this sallow wasting away. This was simply the scrap that Dorothy had left him, a scrap of Robert Meese's death that Jeremiah had made into a life. He bit down hard on his pipe until his jaw hurt, and then he leaned over to spit into the waste paper basket. He looked into the plastic bag lining the metal receptacle, and he saw something disturbing.

In the ash from his own tobacco, he perceived a pattern—the shape of Henry Hawthorne's face in tiny cinders and char. He could not look away. It was like the children's game of finding shapes in clouds, but unbidden: Henry's ashen face stared up at him from the waste can, seeming satisfied and vain, and Jeremiah could not make the pattern go away once he had seen it, could not find the random scatter of ash that should have been there. He felt Henry cackling, speaking in unintelligible but tantalizing whispers. The shop seemed to darken and shrink into the disturbing pattern beneath Jeremiah's gaze.

He tried to spit on it but couldn't. He closed his eyes, but even without seeing Henry's face, he felt it in his imagination, felt the weight of Dorothy's betrayals lifted by the exhilaration of Henry's whispered invitations. Yes, why had he never seen it before? Henry's suicide. . . Robert's death. . . Henry and Robert had both been spared years of torment by moments of simple violence.

Jeremiah considered what might have happened if he had lost that fight with Robert, if he himself had been killed that night. Nothing, Henry whispered in his ear. Nothing would have happened—he would simply have stopped knowing, and that would not have been so bad. Instead, he was left with something infinitely more complicated, a heart petrified by Dorothy's contempt, slowly cracking from the inside, until the whole marbled statue of himself threatened to split open and crumble. Every man who had ever been intimate with Dorothy had come to an evil end. Jeremiah had done Robert Meese a favor.

He opened his eyes and looked into the waste can. He could not find Henry's face there any more: his discarded ashes had reverted to burned tobacco lying scattered in the trash. The apparition had vanished as suddenly as it had appeared, and the whole shop seemed lighter. Jeremiah felt exhausted, and at just that moment Jon Ridgely appeared in the barber shop window.

Jon waved a greeting. He pushed open the door and the tiny brass bell above the entrance jangled, in a tone that sounded tinny and faraway to Jeremiah's ears.

Jeremiah stood up. "Well," he said. He felt angry now at something he couldn't name, and his own voice seemed unreal. "If it isn't the man of the hour."

"Good morning, Jeremiah."

He set his pipe on the counter. "People can't get enough of that story you wrote," he said, trying to steady himself with an everyday tone.

"What, about the Hershey offer?"

"Hershey offer?"

"Which story do you mean?"

"About Marnie Hawthorne."

"Oh. So I guess you haven't seen today's paper yet."

"Nobody cares about the Hershey offer, son, whatever it is. Hershey has been trying to buy Hawthorne Toffee for years, and if it didn't happen in 1971, it's not going to happen now."

Jon sat down in the barber chair, and Jeremiah retrieved a red and white striped cape from a hook on the wall and tied it around Jon's neck. "A lot's changed since 1971," Jon said.

"Nothing's changed." The conversation was bringing Jeremiah back to himself, but he couldn't shake the odd feeling that had come over him, the vision of Henry, and now it was compounded by his agitation about Jon's article.

"Sure it has. All the main Hawthornes are gone, and why would Marnie turn down such a lucrative deal?"

"Marnie won't sell. She has no reason to."

"Do you realize how much they're offering?"

Jeremiah scoffed. "Anyway, nobody cares about Hershey. They're all talking about Marnie."

"I guess you're right," Jon said. "That's all anybody cares about."

He said this dismissively, as if he were above it all because he cared about the Hershey offer, because he knew more about the Hawthornes than his readers. His tone suggested that Jon was in the center of the Hawthorne controversy because he was reporting on it, and this irritated Jeremiah no end. He liked Jon, had been cutting his hair since Jon was in elementary school; but he knew that Jon did not really understand the Hawthornes and would never have written an article glorifying Marnie if he did.

"The usual?" Jeremiah asked.

"And a shave, today, too, I think. I can never shave my own face the way you can."

"No, your perspective's no good."

Jeremiah sprayed Jon's hair with water from a plastic bottle and began cutting automatically. Jeremiah had spent the previous evening looking at Marnie's pictures in the paper, reading Jon's article, drinking himself to sleep once again on iced rum, and he knew that this young man's pride could be dangerous, both to Jon himself and to those around him. Jon was stirring a hornet's nest.

"You know, those pictures you took look like Dorothy," Jeremiah said. "It's uncanny."

"Maybe. I guess they look a little alike, around the nose and eyes."

"A little?"

"We've been running pictures of Dorothy Hawthorne for two weeks, and not one of them looks like Marnie."

"Not if you're blind, they don't." Jeremiah tilted Jon's head forward as he clipped the hair around his neck. "I've seen them both in the flesh. When was the last time you saw Dorothy Hawthorne?"

Jon did not answer. Jeremiah spent another minute measuring and clipping Jon's hair in silence.

"Actually, I've been wondering," Jon finally said, "if I could ask you a few questions about the Hawthornes."

"Go ahead."

"I mean, not casual questions." Jeremiah stopped snipping and held his scissors at Jon's ear. "I'm wondering if I could interview you sometime, for an article."

"Why would you want to interview me for an article about the Hawthornes?"

"Isn't it true that you dated Dorothy?"

Jeremiah picked up his pipe. He came around the chair to face Jon. Although he had been longing to speak to someone about Dorothy, telling his story to the *Constitution* struck him as the worst possible idea. He had no desire to explain himself in that way, to every household in Lawford County, to some judge at an inquest after the district attorney decided to prosecute.

"Who says I dated Dorothy?"

"People. It's not true?"

Jeremiah searched Jon's expression and found a look in Jon's eyes that he had never seen before, a look that he knew in other people as guile. He had always known Jon to be an open book, but this expression hid ulterior motives.

"Are you interviewing me now?"

"No, I came for a shave and a haircut. I'm just asking if you'd be willing to do an interview sometime."

Jeremiah walked back around the chair, set his pipe down and resumed cutting Jon's hair. "Sure."

"Great."

Jeremiah considered what Jon might know, and, upon reflection, he recognized a hardness in Jon's voice, a guarded flintiness that was also very unlike him. He wondered if Jon might already have discovered something incriminating. But how?

"You mind if I ask *you* a few questions?" Jeremiah said.

"Not at all."

"What can you tell me about Robert Meese?"

"Dorothy's husband? He was a farm boy whose parents discovered oil on their land, and they got rich and stopped farming. He married Dorothy and moved into the mansion, and they were married for about six years before he got drunk one night and fell. Hit his head and died. I guess he and Dorothy fought all the time, according to what people say. That's the Reader's Digest version, anyway. Dorothy never married again."

"And how do you know all that?"

"Interviews I've done. *Constitution* archives."

Jeremiah handed Jon a mirror and Jon inspected his hair. He nodded approval and gave the mirror back to Jeremiah.

Jeremiah retrieved a hot, damp towel from a warmer below the counter. He wrapped the towel carefully around Jon's face, leaving his nose and eyes uncovered, and then turned back to the counter and dolloped shaving cream into a ceramic mug.

"Do you believe the Reader's Digest version?" Jeremiah asked. He coughed phlegmatically and paused to wipe his lips with a handkerchief.

With his face wrapped in the towel, Jon did not answer, and the question hung in the air. Jeremiah took a leather strop from its hook on the wall and sharpened his straight razor on it, slowly and methodically, the blade producing a thick, wet cuffing every time he dragged it along the hide. He caught a glimpse of himself—though mirrors lined one entire wall of the barber shop, Jeremiah had long since stopped looking into them, and his reflection unnerved him now. His eyes seemed unnaturally wide and glassy and he didn't recognize his own expression. He thought of Henry staring up at him from the ash and seemed to see Henry's eyes staring out of the mirror into his own. He returned the strop to its hook, set the razor aside and pressed the towel against Jon's cheeks with both hands. Finally, he removed the towel and tossed it into a hamper, resolutely avoiding looking into the mirror.

Jon cleared his throat. "Lots of people think Henry killed Robert, and Dorothy just covered for him with that story about falling—but that's only because they're looking for an explanation for Henry's suicide. Henry had no motive to murder Robert and, you know, lots of people get drunk and fall down. If you're fighting a lot and troubled and unlucky, well. . . maybe bad things just happen to you."

Jeremiah picked up the ceramic mug of cream and a brush

and lathered Jon's face. "And what about Henry's suicide?"

"That happened nearly a year later," Jon said. "Nobody seems to know anything about it, except that it happened. There was no note, no clear motive. They say grief over his wife's death, or guilt because he killed his son-in-law, but it's all speculation. You have any theories?"

Jeremiah motioned for him to stop talking. He brushed shaving cream across Jon's mouth and then dabbed the line of his lips clear with a towel. He set the mug aside and shaved Jon's cheek.

"Doesn't it strike you as interesting," Jeremiah said, "that Robert and Henry died within a year of each other, and that Calvin, who apparently never had any interest in Hawthorne Toffee, was suddenly in charge of the whole works?"

"It's interesting, but where are the motives? There are witnesses who saw Henry set himself on fire, so Calvin obviously didn't do that. And Calvin was next in line for the money anyway, not Robert, so Calvin wouldn't have needed to kill Robert to inherit. Besides, Calvin already had more money than he could spend, whether he was in charge of the company or not, and he didn't want to be, from what I've learned." Jon held up his hand for Jeremiah to stop shaving him. He turned to look Jeremiah in the eye. "Are you telling me something? Do you have some information you want to give me for the *Constitution*?"

"I'm not telling you anything. I'm just asking a question."

They held each other's gaze for a long moment before Jon turned around again and sat back in his chair. Jeremiah scraped the flat of the razor across Jon's neck.

"If you know something you want to tell me, Jeremiah, just tell me, because I'm not smart enough to figure it out. Not like this."

Jeremiah didn't like the tone in Jon's voice. He let the edge of his blade linger on Jon's neck, with just a little too much pressure. "I thought you didn't come here for an interview," he said.

"I didn't. You said you wanted to ask me questions, but your questions are all leading, and they're not leading me anywhere I can see."

Jeremiah relaxed his grip on the razor and took a deep breath. He moved to Jon's chin, concentrating intently now on his work, refusing to meet Jon's gaze. The gentle whir of the ceiling fan became louder in the silence, adding its rhythm to the metrical motions of Jeremiah's hands—the plonk of the blade dunking into the mug, the clank of metal against ceramic, the splish of water droplets as he cleaned and wiped the blade. He slowly transferred the medicinal-smelling white lather and dark black whiskers from Jon's face into the mug, trying to forget about his own wild eyes in the mirror and how angry he suddenly was at Jon.

When he had finished, Jeremiah wiped away the remaining cream and wrapped another hot towel around Jon's face. He strolled to the end of the room and emptied the cup with Jon's whiskers into a sink basin, and the whiskers unexpectedly formed a pattern in the sink, the shape of a face contorted with laughter. Jeremiah stared at the face in horror, and it stared back.

He ran the tap to wash it away, but it lingered in his mind, and he attempted to suppress the effects of this unwonted vision with exact, economical movements. He removed the second towel from Jon's face and threw it into the hamper.

"You don't think it's peculiar," Jeremiah said, "that Henry Hawthorne killed himself around the same time Robert Meese died. But what about Calvin's disappearance? Isn't it funny that Calvin vanished into thin air at the very moment Dorothy's son Ronald left Templeton, forever? Or that Dorothy holed up in that mansion twenty years later, never to show her face again at the same moment Ronald died in a car crash? Why all this death and seclusion? Why these outbursts of violence and retreat?"

"I have no idea. If these things were clear, we'd all know by now."

Jeremiah shook aftershave into his palm. He rubbed his hands together and then slapped Jon's face, harder than necessary. Jon took a bracing breath to relieve the sting and glared at Jeremiah, who untied the red and white cape around Jon's neck and swept it away with a practiced flourish. He brushed the hair briskly off of Jon's neck and ears and set his tools back in their places on the counter. Jeremiah took up his pipe, relit it and sat down in the bank of seats opposite the barber chairs.

"Why do you want to talk to me about my relationship with Dorothy? What do you know about it?"

"Nothing. That's why I want to talk to you. To see if you know anything about the mystery woman everybody remembers and nobody knew. People saw her at the toffee plant or the market ten, twenty years ago, but the only people who have any opinions about her are the ones who knew her thirty or forty years ago, and they don't think highly of her. I figured, since you dated her, you might have some insight. You might see her more favorably."

"The same way you think more favorably of her granddaughter than everyone else does?"

"I'm not sure I see the connection."

Jeremiah sucked on his pipe. "Are you in love with Marnie Hawthorne?"

"No," Jon said. "Why do you ask that?"

"Because I'm in love with Marnie Hawthorne." He puffed smoke between them and squinted through it. "She's Dorothy all over again."

"She does have a certain. . . charm."

"A certain. . . charm!" Jeremiah mocked. "You wear her charm like a badge."

"What do you mean?"

"What do you know about the Hawthornes? I mean, what do you really know?"

Jon did not answer. They looked at one another disputatiously.

"They're shrewd," Jeremiah said, "sharp-witted, ruthless. And they all end in violence or madness."

"Ruthless?"

"And they're charming, aren't they? They're fascinating and dangerous in a way that doesn't seem dangerous at all. They make you do things you don't want to do, and it's difficult to take your eyes off of them. Especially if it's your job to watch their every move, isn't that right? If it's your job?"

Jon stood up. "What are you saying?"

"I'm saying you should consider what you do carefully."

"Because?"

"Look at yourself, Jon. Marnie's etched in your face like a cheap woodcut. When you fall in love with the Hawthornes, people see it in your eyes. I see it in yours." He paused portentously. "The Hawthornes are not to be trifled with."

Jon said nothing, standing motionless before Jeremiah. Finally, he looked down, pulled his wallet out of his pocket and proffered some bills.

"It's on me, kid."

Jon put the bills back in his wallet. He turned, opened the door and disappeared down the street.

Jeremiah put his head in his hands and sighed. This, he thought, cannot go on.

11

How The Past Repeats Itself

Marnie sat drinking tea at the head of the enormous oaken table in her grandmother's gloomy formal dining room. She had spent the entire afternoon reading the letters and memorabilia that Alexandra Bergren had given her; now, at five in the evening, a million tiny motes of dust caught the sunlight as it filtered through the grime of the French windows. The room seemed swathed in gauze, unnaturally still, and the table's tarnished silver candelabra cast a long shadow onto the antique breakfront in the corner. The grandfather clock behind Marnie ticked and tocked slowly, too slowly it seemed to Marnie, so that the measuring of each second took a little longer than a second and the room lost time moment by moment, falling implacably behind the rest of the world, as it had been doing for more than fifty years.

Along the dining room walls, in front of the breakfront, around the sideboard, on either side of the grandfather clock, yellowing porcelain dolls stared at Marnie with their blank painted eyes. These dolls turned up everywhere in her grandmother's house, expensive sentimental collectibles that seemed to have been Dorothy's constant companions in her later years, a maddening, unwavering chorus of approbation.

Marnie had stacked the letters in neat piles on the table, cross-referencing them according to their authors and addressees and arranging them chronologically. Almost all of them were addressed to Dorothy, though a few were letters that Dorothy had written and never sent. Marnie had read each one several times, and some of them she had returned to again and again, if not to read them a tenth time then to feel the brittleness of the paper in her hands, to trace the lines of their script, to try to make the words they carried real. She would pace around the table, picking up a letter and then putting it down, moving to another pile, going between Calvin and Dorothy or Calvin and Jeremiah Grayson, across twenty or thirty years in a single movement, her feelings confused a little more each time she rediscovered the secret at the heart of her family's disintegration. When she felt out of her depth, she would return to the head of the table and drink tea and stare at the porcelain dolls, or she would wander the halls of her grandmother's mansion, studying the elaborate decrepitude of one dim room after another, scaring herself with mementos of her grandmother's horrified life.

Through the letters, the tale of the Hawthornes had become clearer and the reasons behind the violence and madness of her family more obvious. Her grandmother's reclusiveness, the state of her grandmother's house, the irreparable falling-out between her father and grandmother all acquired their reasons. At the same time, the story became more mysterious than ever, since the reasons behind these things were difficult to fathom.

The longest and most telling letters were the two Marnie's father had written to his mother, one postmarked from Templeton in 1971 and the other postmarked from Washington, D.C. a few weeks later—after Ronald had left Illinois for good. In these letters, Ronald accused Dorothy and Calvin, daughter and son to Henry Hawthorne, brother and sister and heirs to the Hawthorne Toffee fortune, of being lovers.

Marnie's father's letters were outraged and hurt, written in flailing, revolted despair—Ronald simply had not been able to comprehend that his own mother might be having sex with her brother. He seemed to think that their "unholy affair," as he called it, had begun shortly after Ronald's own father, Robert Meese, had died in the fountain behind the Hawthorne Mansion, when Ronald himself was just a baby. Curiously, he was almost as horrified that his mother had kept this sexual perversion a secret for so many years as he was by the simple fact of it. He expressed utter outrage that his mother had been sleeping with his uncle right there in his own house, in the house of his childhood, and he called Dorothy a monster and said he was revolted by her motherly caresses. But Ronald's letters asked so many questions and grasped at so many uncertainties that Marnie was unsure how much of his speculation to believe, and it was unclear how he had discovered their affair.

Marnie was convinced, however, that the accusation of Dorothy's and Calvin's incestuous love was true, because her Grandma Dorothy defended their relationship in a letter to Ronald that she had never mailed. Read in this light, many of Calvin's letters to Dorothy, while not openly romantic, bore the mark of a lover's hand, from their care in describing mundane events to their recollections of times the two had spent together at the mansion. The details of Calvin's letters did not express a filial kind of concern—there was something more sly and insinuating about his sentiments than a brother's should be, comments about Dorothy's appearance and characteristics that made Marnie queasy. And yet, she could not help returning to these letters especially and sensing a glamour in them, the thrill of breaking the oldest taboo. Their affair, Marnie imagined, was like a scab: not quite whole skin but not quite an open wound either, an imitation of health that tantalized and begged to be touched, but, in being touched over and over again, refused to heal. It was romantic love imitated and consummated but starkly forbidden, and therefore satisfying in its prohibition the way simple romance could never be.

She took her cup and saucer into the kitchen. She turned the fire on under the kettle and stared out the window, past the veranda toward the statue of Cupid burbling water into the fountain. It had gradually become clear to Marnie what this love affair had done to her father, what this irreparable break with his own mother had meant to him and now to her. She had learned more about her father in this one afternoon than she had known through the many years he was alive. His bitterness and sadness, the galling weight of the loss that he carried with him and refused to discuss now had a shape in Marnie's imagination, and the formerly mysterious finality of his break with the Hawthorne side of her family became plain.

The teapot whistled. Marnie threw her dregs into the sink, selected a new tea bag from the package and poured the water. She spooned in sugar and added milk until the tea became muddy. She moved automatically, as if in a trance.

During her breaks from reading the letters, as Marnie explored the interior of the mansion, its dilapidation became sensical, repellent and fascinating, and Marnie felt for the first time that she knew a secret worth being a secret. She looked into every disorderly closet and disheveled bedroom, wandered the empty basement with its hulking gray furnace, sat in the rocking chair in the immaculate cleanliness of the third-story bedroom that her grandmother had occupied last and felt an enticing kinship with Dorothy, a sympathy for her grandmother's desperation. Marnie's sympathy both comforted and disturbed her. She almost felt that she understood her grandmother better than she did her father.

She took her tea and wandered into the entry hall and up the main staircase. Somewhere, in this self-abnegating murk and clutter, she hoped to find the missing pieces of the puzzle that had partially been solved by the letters—why Calvin had suddenly disappeared after Ronald had discovered the affair, what had happened to Calvin, who had been declared legally dead in 1978 but whose body was never found; why her Great-Grandfather Henry had chosen to kill himself and why he had found such a ghastly way of doing it; and exactly how Jeremiah Grayson fit into the puzzle.

Jeremiah's letters were the most perplexing of the group. They started in 1942 and ended in 1978. Initially, they were straightforward love notes, but they became allusive and coy and threatening as time went on. It seemed to Marnie that Jeremiah and her grandmother had had a very long affair, which had started before Dorothy had married her Grandfather Robert, continued during that marriage and lasted for some time after Robert's death. How Jeremiah fit in with Calvin she couldn't tell, nor could she discern whether or not Jeremiah knew about her grandmother's incestuous affair. Jeremiah's letters alluded to things Marnie didn't recognize and seemed as pleading and defenseless at times as they were aggressive and demanding at others. There were a few letters from Dorothy to Jeremiah that had never been mailed, but these, too, were written in a shorthand code of allusions that Marnie couldn't decipher.

The one overriding impression that Marnie took away from these letters was a vivid portrait of her grandmother's black, contradictory character. She had been a morose, guilt-ridden sexual libertine for whom no carnal boundaries existed, who was simultaneously ashamed and proud of her amorous affairs and took a paradoxical delight in her brother Calvin's sexual profligacy and the jealous torments it caused her. The tone of Dorothy's unmailed letters to her son Ronald, to Calvin and Jeremiah was of an imploded Victorian morality, filled with vituperation, vicious self-doubt and bathetic declarations of love.

Marnie supposed that Dorothy had bequeathed the entire

Hawthorne fortune to her either as a posthumous apology to her own son or as a way to further flout the expectations of her family. In any event, the inheritance seemed now like a consequence of her grandmother's secret erotic life, or an extension of Dorothy's furtive and unrequited sexual feelings—perhaps for her own son. These thoughts frightened Marnie, because they carried dark and inchoate implications about her own sexuality.

These people and events no longer felt separate from her, the way the Hawthorne family had always seemed in the past, and she felt previously incoherent emotions distilling and concentrating inside her, into forbidden ideas that she had never explored before and thought better of looking closely at now. She could see that her father's straight-arrow morality had been a reaction against her grandmother's perversions, and this fact cast her own blithe moral attitude in a different light. She had always figured that her live-and-let-live sensibility had simply balanced her father's stern, self-righteous uprightness, but she now wondered how much of her grandmother's unorthodox disposition she had inherited and how much of it she was participating in, just by occupying this creepy house.

Marnie leaned her forearms against the banister of the second floor landing and peered at the hallway below. She took a sip of tea and felt the weight of the gloom around her, and it seemed sexual and terrifying.

She felt no inclination to call her husband Graham. Day by day, her loneliness for her husband was being replaced by a more insular feeling—a feeling that her extraordinary inheritance had been intended for her alone. She had not spoken with Graham for almost three days, an unprecedented silence, a time in which nothing had happened but many things had been revealed and many other things were changing. Normally, she told Graham every detail of her days, no matter how trivial, but as she read the court documents and the revelations of her grandmother's secret loves—the desperate accounts of suicide and adultery—she felt inclined to keep it all to herself.

She looked around the faded rococo decorations of the foyer and wondered how much the pervasive bleakness of this place was affecting her. Sometimes she felt like running out of the house, jumping into her car and driving with the greatest possible speed to St. Louis, to a bright hotel room where she could bathe and rest in all the simple trappings of normal life, and she could call Graham in London and tell him how crisp the bacon had been and how weak the tea and what laughable thing she had done with her hair. But at other times she felt drawn deeper into her grandmother's house, her grandmother's seclusion, and she imagined what it would be like to take up residence here as the Mistress of Hawthorne Toffee and do just as she pleased with whomever she pleased, whenever and for however long it suited her.

Graham would finish work on the orchestral suite he was recording soon enough, and he planned to join her in Templeton directly afterwards. In the meantime, Marnie wanted to keep these secrets to herself, though for what purpose she couldn't say.

She finished her second cup of tea on the landing and returned to the kitchen. As an emotional purgative, she scrubbed the kitchen compulsively every day and it smelled comfortingly of lemon cleaner. She selected a piece of irregular toffee from the Hawthorne bag on the counter and munched it inattentively.

Cleaning the kitchen, drinking tea, downing vodka martinis: these methods were losing their capacity to distract. Since visiting Alexandra, Marnie had completely lost her detachment. She wanted solace, but she felt that the comfort her husband offered was now inadequate. She didn't need his sympathy or camaraderie—she needed something else, something she couldn't name, and this inability to name what she needed disconcerted her almost as much as her grandmother's black heart did.

Without realizing consciously that she had finished the first piece, she reached for another Hawthorne Toffee irregular and thought of the dinner engagement she had made with Jon Ridgely. The idea of meeting him appealed to her deeply, in her body, in a way that words could only adulterate, and she felt that wordless desire as the same desire for consolation that she could not name.

She knew it would betray Graham to meet Jon, yet her sense of honor felt untouched, as if it were a matter somehow separate from her marriage; the appeal of Jon Ridgely did not feel exactly sexual, yet it awakened in her a slow-motion tremor that was altogether tantalizing. Something was happening to her, some change that she felt incapable of understanding, yet she felt more like herself now than she had at any time since she had left London. She was confused, but she was calm at the center of the confusion, as if she occupied the eye of the storm of her grandmother's death, and as long as she stayed there, as long as she moved in just the right way at just the right pace, the eye would remain open in front of her. Part of Marnie recognized that this idea was patently absurd—that nothing good could come from following in the footsteps of a perverted old woman—but she felt calm and circumspect nevertheless.

She felt more poise than doubt, more confidence than responsibility. Her spirits were keen and open, and though she had no idea what to think about her family's past, she sensed possibilities that had nothing to do with the fortune that was about to be hers, possibilities whose meanings she could not interpret and whose limits she could not detect.

* * * * *

Evening's lingering pink light had just disappeared from the western sky, and Marnie's headlights shone on empty blacktop. Following Jon's hand-drawn map, she drove east on Route 44 past Gordon Junction, where she had previously turned north to go to Hutsonville; now, she sped straight on into an ever darker stretch of country road, dominated on both sides by ivy-covered forest.

She had the road completely to herself for miles at a time. A few twinkling lights appeared now and then on either side, shining through the picture windows of homes tucked into alder groves, until the green and white Palestine sign ("Oldest Town In Illinois") marked the sudden development of right angle grid streets and brick shopfronts on either side of the road. She slowed her car. A few other cars joined her on Palestine's Main Street, driving leisurely for a block or two before turning onto sleepy residential roads.

Palestine was a village of three thousand people, and Marnie drove all the way through it. She found Nellie's Restaurant exactly where Jon's map said it should be, on a crumbling asphalt side street in front of an open field.

Nellie's was the ground floor of a two-story home and Marnie judged, by the residential character of the street, that the dirt parking lot had once been the lawn of Nellie's house. Three other cars occupied the lot, and she parked farthest away from the building, near the field, in which an unseen oil pump was clanking and chuffing away in the night.

She stepped out of her car and breathed in the damp, warm evening air. The rhythmic metallic grinding of the pump served as a clunky metronome to the syncopated chirps of crickets nearby and the sporadic shouting of children a few doors down. The other houses along this street were single-story, aluminum-sided, with porch lights illuminating low concrete stoops.

A firefly lit up right in front of Marnie, then wafted away toward the field. Butterflies fluttered in her stomach: she knew that she should not have come. She wasn't sure what she was doing here, and the unreturned messages from Graham on her cell phone chastised her—but here she was, drawn by irresistible force to Jon Ridgely, whose attractiveness she felt growing within her.

Her whole body felt clammy as she walked up Nellie's front steps. She took a deep breath at the door, withdrew a compact from her shoulder bag and checked her face under the white light of the exposed bulb on the porch. Beyond the fear in her eyes, she thought she looked fabulous. The heat and humidity were doing wonders for the curl in her hair, and the color of her jacket—a deep crimson Chanel knockoff—brought out a healthy blush in her cheeks. She told herself that it was only dinner, that the Templeton *Constitution* was paying the tab as proof of the dinner's commercial nature, and that she had many easy justifications for coming here.

The rationalization for being there that made the most sense was also the one closest to the truth. Jon Ridgely had been following her family and its history for some time, and it was possible that he had information that would fill in the blanks left by the letters Marnie had read. By coming here, Marnie told herself, she might learn as much in an hour as she could from weeks of snooping in her grandmother's house.

She pushed against Nellie's door and went in. She was greeted by the slippery, throaty smell of broiling fat.

There was a short counter holding a cash register to her left. The small dining room opened to her right. Photographs of hunters with their bounty hung in heavy wooden frames all around the room. A mounted twelve-point buck's head presided above the fireplace on the far wall. The floor was brown linoleum tile and the tables were round presswood, with yellow plastic chairs pushed in around them.

A Johnny Cash song keeled softly through tinny speakers near the fireplace. A pair of middle-aged couples looked up as Marnie walked in, but, unlike the people in Templeton, they quickly looked away and returned to their meals. One silver-haired man with a beer belly gave her a long stare, but Marnie couldn't tell if he recognized her from the paper or was just ogling.

Jon was not there. The hostess, a birdlike redheaded woman with skeletal arms and a drawn face, bustled through the swinging door from the kitchen and greeted Marnie. She told her to choose any table, and Marnie sat near the fireplace and looked into the glassy left eye of the dead buck gazing down at her.

The hostess brought a menu, a set of flatware wrapped in a paper napkin and a plastic tumbler of ice water. Marnie told her that she was expecting someone else and ordered a glass of red wine. The hostess flitted back through the swinging door.

Marnie perused the menu: true to Jon's word, Nellie's specialized in venison, frogs' legs, rabbit and elk, and there were buffalo steaks and ostrich burgers as well, along with roasted corn cobs, vegetable kabobs and something called "Hobo's Pot Luck." The hostess returned with Marnie's wine, called her "dear" and wiped her bony fingers on her dirty white apron.

The wine was too sweet and fruity, and as she drank it Marnie felt lost in the restaurant's tattiness. She was considerably overdressed. The other diners wore everyday clothes—the men in blue jeans and cotton work shirts, the women in frumpy blouses and polyester slacks—and Marnie hid her demurely blushed and lipsticked face behind the menu. She felt her conspicuousness as a rebuke against this rendezvous, and she noticed that the discussions of the patrons near her were overloud and stilted, counterfeit conversations made to hide glances and nods in her direction.

She looked at her watch and felt a crushing need to talk to someone in a familiar way. A car pulled up outside and stopped near the building. The engine chugged to a halt, and a heavy door slammed. Nellie's front door opened and Jon came in.

He wore nutmeg-colored linen slacks that looked brand new, and a summery cream-colored sport shirt. It seemed to Marnie that he'd had a haircut since the last time she'd seen him, and his appearance filled her with satisfaction. She had not expected to feel pleasure in seeing him, and it frightened her and made her want to say something high-handed.

The hostess appeared almost immediately, while the dull thudding of the front door still echoed across the room. "Sorry I'm late," Jon said. "Hello, Nellie. Do you have the table I reserved?"

"Sure, Jon." Nellie turned to Marnie. "You should have told me who you were with. I would have taken you right to your table." Nellie motioned with her head.

The eyes of the other patrons were on them as Nellie led Jon and Marnie across the dining room to a door near the cash register. They walked through it to a smaller room, this one lit by a dim electric chandelier, and Marnie knew then, irreducibly, that this dinner was indefensible, that she was spending a large sum of her husband's trust in this cheap restaurant. The heads of a wide variety of game animals festooned the walls, and the floor was covered with dark brown shag carpeting. It seemed to be a conference area, with a bulky table in the center and a smaller table beneath the lone window.

Nellie led them to the smaller table and placed their silverware and menus in front of them. The window was bracketed by brown, masculine curtains. The owner said she would return for their orders and then departed through a different door, toward the back of the building. The music from the tinny radio in the main dining room did not reach here: except for the metallic screeching of the oil pump outside, the room was heavy and silent.

"Our conversation might require a certain amount of discretion," Jon said, "so I took the liberty of reserving the Stag Room."

"Stag Room?"

"The Palestine Elks Lodge uses it for meetings. Stag elks."

"I notice that you don't have your cassette recorder this time," Marnie said. "Are you planning to remember everything I say?"

Jon blushed. "I thought we could have dinner off the record, before we do another proper interview. If that's all right. My things are in my truck, if you want me to get them."

Marnie took a drink of red wine and noted that, the last time she had sat down with Jon, she had also been drinking and the results of that meeting had been mixed. She swirled the wine in her glass and imagined a photograph of the two of them, at their dinner tryst in Palestine, appearing on the front page of the Templeton *Constitution*.

"Everything I do here seems to be on the record," she said, "whether I mean it to be or not. I don't see why this dinner should be any different."

"Well, you have my word that, at least until there's a tape recorder in front of you, whatever we do or say in this room will remain in this room." Jon fixed her with a significant look that made her feel angry. "Between us."

"Until Nellie mentions it to her hairdresser in the morning."

"I've sworn her to secrecy," he said. "She owes me."

"Owes you? So that's how these things are done?"

"These things?" Jon put on an innocent look, as if baffled by Marnie's implication. "As I said, Ms. Hawthorne, I appreciate your position as a married woman and—"

"No, you don't." Her irritation grew. "Let's be frank for a moment, Mr. Ridgely. Let's really be frank."

Nellie burst through the door and Marnie hid her agitation by wiping her lips with her napkin. Their hostess set a tumbler of ice water in front of Jon and asked for Jon's drink order. He requested a glass of the wine Marnie was drinking. Nellie studiously avoided eye contact, chirping fast questions and answers.

When she left, Marnie and Jon sat in strained silence. Marnie fidgeted with her napkin and the air grew thicker with expectation. The longer they were silent, the more pregnant the tension became, and Marnie felt unpleasantly giddy, as if air bubbles were bobbing toward the surface of her chest. A dense thicket of marital vigilance and inertia surrounded her, preventing her from moving toward Jon openly, with plain speech, but she found it impossible, as an alternative, to entertain Jon's winking repartee, impossible to look past the fact that they had both come to this restaurant to begin an affair. It seemed ridiculous to pretend otherwise and suddenly quite grave.

They still had not spoken when Nellie returned with Jon's wine. Marnie looked into the blackness of the night through the window, and Jon told Nellie to come back in a few minutes for their order. Marnie realized that anyone passing by could see them—she stood up and reached across the table to close the curtains. As she did so, she brushed Jon's shoulder, and this simple touch softened her anger, and she sat down again feeling less solemn.

"I notice you don't have a musical instrument," she said.

"No tape recorder, no harmonica—I do seem ill prepared, don't I?" Jon looked at Marnie puckishly over the lip of his wine glass. "I was certainly unprepared for how elegant you look."

"You didn't find me elegant before?"

She watched the light dance in Jon's eyes. His face looked bright and eager, especially in this dour setting, against the comically grim backdrop of deer and elk heads on the walls. His facial features were fine and symmetrical, with a gently downturned mouth and a high brow that made him seem almost feminine—so different from Graham's dense, coarse bulk. Jon was more slight and lissome but nevertheless gave an impression of predatory energy. His eyes were covetous and mischievous, and once Marnie really engaged them, she found it difficult to look away.

"Elegant is the least of what I find you," he said. "But you surely know the effect you have on people."

"The impression I make here is somewhat different from the one I make in London," Marnie said. They sat captured in each other's eyes, until Nellie returned with her order pad raised defensively, in embarrassment.

Marnie suggested that Jon order for both of them, since she couldn't tell the difference between an elk steak and a bear liver. He ordered frogs' legs in mushroom sauce for himself and venison for Marnie, with potatoes and Hobo's Pot Luck. Nellie said that her husband Jack had just come back with a whole mess of fresh frogs that day, and Marnie's stomach turned.

Noticing her sour face, Jon said, "You've surely had escargot, haven't you? Or caviar? Think of frogs in those terms—an exotic delicacy."

Nellie darted out of the room.

The very mention of dead frogs had deflated the sexual energy between them, and Marnie decided that, before doing something she might regret, she should at least attempt to make this a productive dinner, devoted to something other than self-conscious infidelities. "May I ask you a question," she said, "concerning my family? About what you've found out through your reporting?"

"Of course."

"What do you know about Jeremiah Grayson?"

"I know he isn't part of your family."

Marnie shot him an irritated look and waited.

"Well," Jon said, "I know that he dated your grandmother before she married Robert Meese, but that's about it, as far as his involvement with the Hawthornes goes. It's funny you should mention him—I just spoke with him this afternoon about arranging an interview."

"You mean he's still alive?"

"Still alive? He's my barber."

Marnie's mouth involuntarily formed an "O." She couldn't believe that the Jeremiah Grayson whose old letters she had been reading all day was still alive, which meant that she could see him and question him personally about what he knew and what he'd done.

"What kind of man is he?"

"An outsider, of sorts. By his own choice. People like him all right, everybody likes his barber shop. But people don't know how to take him sometimes."

"Where is his shop? In Templeton?"

"You need a new bob?"

"Seriously."

"Just off the Square. Follow the pipe smoke."

"Pipe smoke?" Marnie remembered the bald old man she had met at Bertram's, just after she had arrived in town.

"He's always smoking this fancy amber pipe—it's the first thing anybody'll mention when you ask about him. It's a kind of signature."

The fact that Marnie had met her grandmother's lover randomly, fifty years after the fact, made her flush with heat. It seemed to infuse her every movement in Templeton with new meaning. It felt, all at once, as if she were living a small part of her grandmother's life over, constructing meaning from her grandmother's blueprint, down to the people she was meeting, and this idea thrilled her.

She looked at Jon now as if his presence across the table meant something more than confusion, as if her attraction to him had a reason and Jon's connection to Jeremiah were a revelation of her personal fate. It wasn't Jon *per se* that had attracted her, it was a piece of her grandmother that she wanted, a part of that vicious old soul that had haunted Templeton as much in life as in death, a part she might experience through Jon. Marnie wanted to be kissed with the same wrecked and morbid anguish that filled her grandmother's mansion, to make love to someone furtively, angrily, frantically, knowing that to do so meant to step outside all normal bounds of decency and good sense. She wanted Jon to take her down into the feeling she'd had while reading her grandmother's letters, so she could capture it in her body and hold it in her mind and understand in a new way who she was and what it meant to violate the rules that confined everyone else.

She remembered the look in Jeremiah Grayson's eyes when she had seen him at the drug store that day, the astonished, heartstricken look that she'd paid no attention to at the time but that struck her now with force. She felt a connection between Jon and Jeremiah, a connection through herself to her grandmother and to something boggy in her soul. She thought of her grandmother making love to her own brother and found it gripping and repulsive, and she wanted to make love to Jon with the same gloomy abandon.

"Are you all right?" Jon said.

Marnie brought her hand slowly to her mouth, feeling the thickness of the moment, the ponderous movement of time as heavy as the torpid air. It was luxuriant, this feeling, for its reek of decay and the moldering brine of sex that Marnie fancied she could actually smell rising from the ugly carpet.

She pushed her chair back slowly, keeping her eyes locked on Jon's, as his expression turned to doubt. She moved around the table like an animal in a dream and put one hand lightly on Jon's chest and one hand against his right cheek and kissed him with her mouth open.

She felt jets of adrenaline shooting through her arms and down her legs, and their mouths moved against each other with a sensation of pleasure that oozed through her whole body. It was a bottomless quagmire of a kiss that lasted she didn't know how long, but when she stood up again she felt powerful. Jon's face was flushed and guilty, as guilty as Marnie thought she herself should feel but didn't. She felt daring and self-possessed, and she wanted to have Jon right there beneath the frightened eyes of the dead animals on the wall.

"Are you ready?" she said. Jon looked a question at her. She took her handbag off the arm of her chair and slung it over her shoulder.

A door opened, and they turned to find Nellie in the doorway staring at them, two plates brimming with musky game meat in her hands. "Let's go," Marnie said. She walked out without saying another word. She heard Jon apologize to Nellie and tell her to charge everything to the *Constitution*'s account.

In the parking lot, in the muggy night air, Marnie felt giddy and tingling and perfectly at home in her newly unfaithful body. She noticed a lubriciousness in the pumping and grinding of the oil rig behind the restaurant, and the whole night seemed alive and fertile. Jon banged the door as he followed her out.

"Let's take my car," she said.

"Where?"

She grabbed the sides of his head and pulled his mouth toward hers. As they kissed, Marnie was aware of eyes watching her from the windows of Nellie's dining room, but she no longer cared—she wanted only to grasp this feeling of connection to her grandmother and her larger destiny, whatever it was.

She broke their kiss, found the car keys in her purse and punched a button on the key fob. The car unlocked with a flash of signal lights and she opened the driver side door. Jon hesitated only a moment before he slid into the passenger seat.

Marnie pulled out of the dirt lot, drove through Palestine and back to Route 44, running her fingers through Jon's hair, inviting him to touch her and stroke her and kiss her. They kissed and swerved through the thick country night, toward Templeton and Marnie's grandmother's mansion, and Marnie wallowed in the melancholy thrill of her freedom.

12

How We Know What We Know

Kate stood in the grass behind the Case dealership in Prairieville, squinting through the mid-day sun at the beech trees that marked the edge of the property. Beyond the beeches, a soybean field was beginning to turn.

This was Kate's favorite time of year, when the colors of the land changed day by day, almost hour by hour, first as the crops signaled their ripening toward harvest—wheat burnishing from golden to russet brown, corn tassels turning tan, soybean leaves yellowing before they dropped to the ground—and then as the trees withdrew their sap, oozing into themselves to survive the coming winter—the willow leaves turning from bright green to pale yellow, sugar maples waxing scarlet and orange, and the sweet gums moving through sunny yellows, blood reds and finally to a deep, satisfying bronze before their leaves lit to the earth. It was a season of abundance and sadness, when the full burgeoning of life anticipated the imminent death of the harvest and the bitter cold that would follow. Even the stray uncultivated plants were spectacular at this time of year, vagrant sunflowers in untended ravines with their black and yellow faces turned toward the sky, lonely chicory plants blooming periwinkle along gravel roads, all bursting and beautiful, clinging to the cusp of life and death.

"They're gonna run out of burgers," Kate's father called from the shop floor.

Kate reluctantly walked back into the bay of the giant steel building, past a black-and-red Case Axial-Flow 2388 combine that sat preening and shining in the sun. Some forty farmers were standing around in overalls and cotton shirts, chewing the fat, arguing about which farms were going up for auction and whether Lasso or Aatrex was a better herbicide. A black propane grill was smoking, and a man from the Case parts department stood behind it, flipping hamburgers. Beside him, a metal bin filled with ice brimmed with aluminum cans of soda and beer. Terry Wexler, the Case salesman, sat at a table full of pamphlets and brochures that extolled the virtues of his equipment.

Wexler wore a short-sleeved white shirt and a clip-on tie, and his face fell whenever he wasn't smiling expansively. For more than a decade, farmers had been buying used rather than brand new equipment, as their neighbors were either squeezed out of business by large corporate farms or fell to the downward spiral of government subsidy programs and bank loans. It made far more sense for those farmers who survived to buy their failing competitors' repossessed equipment on the cheap, and this trend spelled doom for smalltime salesmen like Wexler. To make matters worse, farmers in this area were traditionally loyal to John Deere, so that Wexler was plowing uphill in every direction.

Today's gathering was officially a Case IH seminar, which meant that farmers traded an hour or so of their time for a free lunch, while the Case people pitched their new products. Mostly, the farmers used the opportunity to rib each other and trade intelligence about the coming harvest.

Kate's father came as an agitator. Since his days at Southern Illinois University, he couldn't see a gathering of farmers without standing on his soapbox and preaching the Benjamin gospel: non-herbicidal farming, multiple crop plantings, fallow rotations and non-genetically engineered hybrids. Most of the farmers thought Kate's father a crank who knew a lot of intellectual things about farming but whose days as a professor had robbed him of the common sense that a real farmer needed. The Benjamins were the only ones in the whole county still planting triticale, and they were the only ones here at the Case seminar with fewer than five hundred acres. The fact that Mr. Benjamin had come to preach against the very combine that Case was exhibiting, a machine so huge and expensive that a small family farmer couldn't afford the down payment, was a source of amusement to the other farmers: Professor Benjamin was the seminar's comic relief, and when they called him Professor, it was with a wry glint in their eyes.

Kate's father genuinely missed the company of his fellow farmers, especially now that he wasn't able to work his own fields, but Kate didn't understand why he subjected himself to their mockery. She knew his arguments would never make the least impression on these obstinate herbicidal maniacs with their five generations of horse sense, and they thought her father less than a man because his wife and daughter worked his tiny farm for him. She hated these gatherings, but she came as moral support for her father.

She smiled at him as she slipped past, through the sea of plaid work shirts and feed caps to the barbecue grill. She got a hamburger, a bag of chips and a soda without meeting anyone's eyes. No one tried to talk to her until she came to the Case pamphlet table, where Terry Wexler made his lonely vigil. The farmers politely browsed his literature and asked questions about machine wear and parts before they got their free lunch; but Terry didn't like to push and no one was in a mood to buy, so he sat there for much of the time as alone as Kate felt.

"Have a seat," he said, as Kate strolled up. Kate sat in an empty lawn chair beside him and set her lunch on top of the pamphlets on the table. "Your father about done with that old Massey of his?"

"Even if he were, I don't think you have anything small enough for us." She motioned to the new combine Wexler was pushing. "You could barely turn that beast around in our field."

"I could show you some of our international models. We sell small tractors in Africa, yet."

"Well, you know my dad." Kate waved dismissively, putting an end to this line of inquiry.

Both Kate and Wexler soon realized that Kate was scaring farmers away from the table. They were reluctant enough to talk to Wexler, since they knew they didn't want his wares, but with Kate there they would never approach.

Kate had acquired a reputation as a feminist firebrand, though she did as much as she could to make polite conversation and not rise to their offhanded insults. She liked working on her parents' farm and she liked living near her old friends in Templeton, but she hated the farming community and nothing she could do would make her fit in. She was simply not one of them.

"Looks like the weather's clearing up," Wexler said nervously.

Kate's cell phone rang and her heart leapt. She excused herself and jogged out of the building into the grass. She flipped the phone open and answered it.

When her mother's voice piped in her ear, her heart sank. Mrs. Benjamin was calling to remind Kate that they needed to get back to the field, and what was her father doing flapping his gums for so long? Kate assured her that they would be back soon and hung up. She felt like crying.

She hadn't spoken with Jon in a day and a half. He was never at home when she called, he hadn't returned her messages and she could never catch him at the *Constitution*. He had had the last two days off from Ploughman's, but Kate had left messages there anyway, knowing that he often ate there on off days. She had been so busy in the field during the day and so exhausted at night that she hadn't driven into Templeton to see him—and she was becoming afraid to do that now, anyway.

Despite Jon's reassurances, Kate knew in her secret heart that he had a dangerous crush on Marnie Hawthorne, and she could feel herself slipping away. She told herself, quite logically, that it had been just thirty-six hours since they had seen one another last, since they had made love and then snuggled together like teenagers in the back of Jon's pickup at the drive-in, but logical proofs meant nothing to Kate's heart or guts. Nevermind the improbability of Jon's actually having a relationship with Marnie Hawthorne: he was pursuing her, and that meant he was replacing Kate. She was losing him, suddenly, unexpectedly, probably to an idealized woman who didn't exist outside of Jon's imagination. It seemed cruel.

In the last few days, Kate had felt embarrassed in her own body, fat and ungainly. Jon didn't want her. She couldn't imagine touching anyone else, making love with anyone other than Jon, but she knew Jon was imagining making love with Marnie Hawthorne and every time she reminded herself of Jon's gentle caresses just two nights before, her conviction of loss became stronger.

Why was he never at home? Why wouldn't he return her calls? This was the most damning evidence, that her half-dozen messages—at first chatty and then worried and then unattractively demanding—had gone unanswered. Nothing Jon might have been doing in the last two days could have prevented him from at least returning her calls.

She walked back inside the Case shop and retrieved her hamburger and drink, which Terry Wexler had scooted off of his brochures. Wexler was talking to a couple of sweaty, red-necked farmers, and he didn't look at her as she stepped away from the table. She didn't feel the least bit hungry, but she forced herself to eat: it was going to be a long afternoon in the field.

She had called her friends in Boston for advice, but their sympathy had only made her feel lonelier. She didn't rely on anyone any more except Jon, and she especially couldn't call the women she knew in Templeton—if she did, her story would feed the gossip mills and everyone in town would know that she could no longer "please her man." She felt sick.

She walked outside and wiped the sweat from her brow with the cool soda can. The sun shone strong and white, and only a single ridge of clouds crested the azure sky. She was reluctant to go back to the field, where she would get dirty and sticky, and the calluses on her hands would toughen. She imagined the beautiful Marnie Hawthorne in her fabulous mansion, lounging on a divan with her perfectly coiffured hair, her manicured nails shining on her soft pink hands. It seemed pitiless to Kate that Marnie was married, that Jon was willing to throw away their relationship for a woman he couldn't have—a tremendous and stupid waste.

"Daddy," she called. Her father turned away from his klatch of hard-faced men. "We need to get back."

Though other farmers had already eaten and left for their fields, Kate knew that calling her father this way embarrassed him, because everyone knew that he wouldn't be going back to work himself. He would be leaving for his armchair, and Kate sounded like his caretaker, or worse, his babysitter. The men around Mr. Benjamin became silent and waited for his reaction.

"Why don't you start the truck," he said. "I'll be there in a minute."

Kate made a goodbye gesture with her cola can, and the

farmers waved politely back with unsympathetic looks on their faces. A brief moment with Kate gone would give her father a chance to defend his manhood: he would make clichéd remarks about women and how they were the real bosses no matter what the men said, and by saying these things he would not feel completely emasculated by his daughter's impertinence.

Kate hated the fact that her father would not defend her or her mother. She knew that he loved them, but he wanted so desperately to be included in the community of farmers—a community that he only ever slandered in private—that he was willing to prostrate himself before the old boy's club and malign the only women in his life, the women who were the reason he still had a business.

She leaned against her father's truck and choked down the rest of her hamburger and chips. Traffic crawled past on Route 44, which here was Prairieville's Main Street, and she looked beyond it to the Prairieville Middle School across the way. A groundskeeper was trimming the hedge near the school's main entrance.

Kate took out her cell phone and dialed Jon's number. His answering machine picked up and Kate turned off her phone. She sighed and fidgeted, waiting glumly for her father to appear around the building.

13

Toffee in the Blood

A mile away from the Hawthorne Toffee Factory on West Main Street, Marnie sensed chocolate on the air, first as a tantalizing craving that made her mouth water, then as the sprightly, spindly aroma of pure sweetness, then as an invisible thickening, as the recognizably bitter smell of cocoa overwhelmed the lighter scents. Finally, as she came within sight of the factory, a salty undercurrent of melting butter blended with the cocoa to create a simultaneously acrid and sweet smell that enveloped the entire landscape, coloring everything around the Hawthorne Plant in a rich patina of candy.

The effect was remarkable. In front of the factory, a grassy field dotted with dandelions seemed delicious enough to eat. Across Main Street, the red and white marquee above the Hargis Dairy looked spun from pure sugar. Every object seemed positively mouthwatering and Marnie wondered how the factory workers could stand having their whole world transformed into a dense dream of toffee.

The factory was a sprawling collection of single-story brick buildings that took up a huge field on the south side of Main, at the western edge of town. The buildings were painted milky brown, the same shade as the chocolate that coated the Hawthorne Toffee Bar, but they otherwise did not announce themselves as a candy factory. There were no signs or banners attached to the buildings at all—only the look and smell of chocolate suggested the plant's purpose. The lone identifying marker was a city street sign: Templeton had christened the blacktopped road that led into the factory "Hawthorne Lane."

As Marnie turned onto her namesake street, she recalled the story of Hansel and Gretel, of the house made of sweets that had lured the children into the wicked witch's hands, and it occurred to her that this toffee factory was like the witch's house, so enticing and dreamlike, full of childish pleasures, but concealing a secret that would consume any child foolish enough to enter. It was as if the entire town had been persuaded by an irresistible craving to fall in thrall to the Mistress of Toffee, who was fattening them up for a feast.

I am the Mistress of Toffee, Marnie thought, not altogether fancifully.

She drove into the employee parking lot, full of candy colored cars swathed in the aroma of chocolate, and she was pleased that her entire fortune depended on the indulgence of a craving. She parked her car in a spot marked by a prominent brown sign with orange letters that read "Mrs. Hawthorne," a spot that had been reserved but unoccupied for more than ten years.

It was four in the afternoon, the hour Marnie had chosen for her tour. In addition to daily bags of irregular toffee bars, the plant manager had sent her numerous invitations to survey the facility and discuss its operations. Each invitation had conveyed carefully obsequious assurances that the entire facility and all of its employees were at Marnie's disposal, whenever she chose to visit.

Marnie's uncertainty about her inheritance had kept her from accepting the invitations—the idea of touring the facility as its ostensible owner had made her feel strange. But the longer she stayed in Templeton, the more assured she felt about her prospects there. Day by day, the world that opened to her as her grandmother's heir seemed more her own, a world she had missed her whole life without consciously feeling its loss.

Now that she had discovered it, she felt intimations of belonging, of a purpose she had never known before. Her life in London had been an easygoing, untroubled existence, with none of the pessimism or advantage attached to the life of an heiress; now that she had become a little bit familiar with her true heritage, she saw how narrow her outlook had been. The fact that she had been happy as an anonymous Londoner seemed beside the point: as heir to the gothic melodrama of the Hawthornes, she found new depths and textures in her heart, new desires, and the benign sunniness of her marriage and her quasi-artistic job seemed naive and boring. She could see how she had been shaped by what her grandmother had done, by the effect it had had on her father, and this knowledge gave Marnie a feeling of boldness that she felt as hard-pressed to understand as to resist.

Sleeping with Jon Ridgely also gave her a new sense of self-assurance. This forbidden romance, a previously unthinkable betrayal, had cast the other changes in her life in a less overwhelming light. Marnie knew that Graham would be crushed if he found out, but she was unwilling to waver from the course she was choosing. Being Dorothy Hawthorne's granddaughter gave her affair with Jon a feeling of inevitability. He seemed part and parcel of her inheritance, and the affair made her feel more at home in her new skin.

Marnie stepped out of her car and was accosted by the smell of chocolate. Her nose was not inured to the constant barrage of cocoa and sugar and butter: the smells were so insistent that she thought it might take days of constant exposure before she forgot about them, and even then the enticement of sugar and fat would surely continue as an unconscious craving. She expected to find a factory full of blotchy-skinned butter-saturated workers, compulsively munching candy despite their inability to smell or taste it any longer.

The glass and steel main door to the factory opened, and a short narrow-faced man in a shiny brown suit walked out to greet her. He had neatly parted salt-and-pepper hair, prominent ears with fleshy lobes, and thick red lips. His skin had an unpleasant pallor, but he was trim and moved with spry confidence.

"Hello, Ms. Hawthorne, my name is Jack Madison, the plant manager. It's a great pleasure to welcome you to Hawthorne Toffee."

"Thank you, Mr. Madison. I'm pleased to finally accept your invitation."

"You hardly need an invitation to visit your own plant." Madison laughed, a fawning guffaw. "And please call me Jack." He escorted her to the plant's entrance and held the door open.

Marnie stepped into a bright, airy reception area, which held several cushioned chairs, two large potted plants, and a table with an assortment of neatly fanned magazines. Presiding over the magazines was a large ceramic bowl overflowing with miniature toffee bars, each in a brown and orange wrapper.

"That's a very attractive dress, Ms. Hawthorne," Jack said, bowing slightly.

"Thank you. I'm hoping it will come back in style." Marnie had found the green frock she was wearing in a closet on the second floor of the mansion, still in its department store wrapping. A receipt indicated that her grandmother had ordered it in 1948, and it had apparently never been worn. Marnie was delighted to find that she and her grandmother were exactly the same size. She had accessorized the dress with an ornate silver necklace and antique diamond earrings from her grandmother's jewelry box, and she had found a pair of pumps to match: she was literally stepping into Dorothy's shoes.

"Judging by the way you look in it," Madison said, "I can't imagine how it went out of fashion."

"You're very sweet."

A freckly teenaged girl rose from behind the reception desk, and Jack introduced her as Erica Branch, a Lincoln Trail Junior College student who worked there part-time. "Many of our employees start right here answering the phones and greeting visitors, and they stay with us and work their way up," Jack said. "I myself started as a part-time tour guide thirty years ago."

Jack Madison, Marnie realized, had started working at the Hawthorne Toffee Plant—had started working for her, for all practical purposes—before Marnie was born. "From tour guide to plant manager?" she said. "That's an incredible accomplishment, Mr. Madison."

"Your family has always been great to work for, Ms. Hawthorne. They've inspired just this kind of loyalty."

There was an awkward moment in which Marnie felt that she was expected to say something, but she couldn't imagine what. She had no experience being a gracious boss or receiving unqualified flattery, so she said nothing and waited for Madison to fill the silence. He guffawed good-naturedly again and opened a door beyond the reception desk.

"Why don't we start by seeing the administrative offices," he said, "and then we'll go onto the production floor, if that's all right with you."

"You're the boss," Marnie said, enjoying the facile irony of this assertion. She reminded herself that she did not technically own Hawthorne Toffee yet, but she could not deny her delight in being treated like the owner.

Madison led her down a caramel-colored hallway lit with bright incandescent lights. On both sides were small rectangular offices, in which people sat at laptops or frowned over paperwork. The offices were smart and uncluttered, and each held state-of-the-art computers, stylishly minimalist desks and ergonomic chairs. As Madison introduced each administrator and described what they did, they said friendly hellos or raised coffee mugs in greeting, and Marnie felt genuinely welcomed—she felt no animosity here, as she did everywhere else in town. She met executive accountants and comptrollers and sales directors and distribution liaisons and technical directors: the management sector of the facility was larger and more expansive than she had ever imagined. There must have been fifty people in this wing alone, all managers of a team of other people somewhere else on the site or in far-flung places around the country and across the globe, and she began to understand what a vast enterprise an international candy company was. She could hardly take it in: outside was a grassy field of dandelions along a little Main Street in a town full of farmers, and inside was the corporate command center of a global manufacturing concern.

They arrived at Madison's office, and Jack directed Marnie to a seat across from his desk. His office was no larger than the ones they had passed: spatial egalitarianism held sway among the Hawthorne managers.

On the wall behind Madison's desk was a color television monitor: on the screen, a conveyor belt was shuttling toffee bars beneath a stainless steel funnel, which was drenching the bars in chocolate. Madison explained that he could view any area of the production line from his office. He clicked a remote control and the image on the monitor changed to show other bright, clean rooms full of steel machinery, giant vats and walk-in refrigerators.

"There's a security station at the back of the property that has a whole bank of these closed-circuit monitors," Madison said. "Same thing in the plant control room, so the guards and systems engineers can see every area at once. There's at least one camera in every production and storage module, and sometimes as many as three or four."

"For keeping tabs on the employees?"

"No, we don't have a Big Brother philosophy. Hawthorne employees are well compensated and highly motivated and there's no reason to suspect them of stealing or shirking." Madison clicked his remote control several times, more slowly, and he pointed at each image as he changed the view on the monitor. "You can see that the camera angles are designed to show the machinery more than the workers. There's a constant data stream coming from each machine, and the cameras are just one way we can troubleshoot quickly, to get visual confirmation of what the computers are telling us. Often, through a combination of video and digital information, a technician can make minor adjustments to the system to keep everything running smoothly, without having to go to the floor or stop production."

"So production is controlled remotely?"

"It's a combination. At every step along the way, there are people on the floor to oversee the process. Some things have to be done with human hands. There's no way around it, and it's better that way, to ensure the quality of the finished product. Candy tastes different if people are actually making it rather than machines, so we keep people materially involved in the production. That was your great-grandfather's way."

"And yet, this whole plant is dominated by machines, from the looks of it."

"Well," Madison put down his remote control and spread his hands apologetically. "You couldn't make as much candy as we do here without mechanization, and the computers allow us to fine-tune the works to an extent unimaginable using human perception alone. We can give the toffee bars a consistency that wouldn't be possible otherwise. I'm sure you know that every Hawthorne bar eaten anywhere in the world is produced right here in this plant—in that way, we keep production as local and human in scale as possible, but it wouldn't be feasible to have an operation this large if it weren't dominated by machines. The human touch remains very important, however."

"And that's the reason for all those irregulars you've been sending me? The human touch?"

"No, the irregular bars are the fault of the machines—it's the human beings that keep them in line." Madison pointed to the monitor once again, where a vast square of yellow toffee was passing under a series of robotic blades that cut it into candy bar-sized rectangles. "Through typical wear and use, the machines get out of adjustment, just the way parts on a car will, and the candy itself is constantly gumming up the works, leaving residues that affect the precision of certain parts—that's why we have people there on the floor every step of the way and people monitoring the machines by computer. For that matter, the computers have to be adjusted, too, according to the environmental variables in the plant, and we have a whole staff of systems information specialists to deal with that. No two days are alike and we're constantly making adjustments so that, despite changes in the weather or variability in the quality of cocoa or milk, every Hawthorne Toffee Bar tastes the same as every other Hawthorne Toffee Bar."

Since she had arrived in Templeton, Marnie had been picturing her great-grandfather Henry in his shop on the town square, mixing with a wooden spoon, blending with a whisk and cooking in his little kitchen—it had seemed romantic and quaint. She had never imagined what Henry's ambitions had become in practice. In her Grandmother Dorothy's rambling mansion, it was easy to believe that time had stopped; and in Templeton, which seemed so closely connected to farming and the earth, it had been impossible for her to conceive the complexities of managing such a big corporation. The toffee plant seemed out of place and time, remote from its beginnings and too advanced for its surroundings.

But then, where was all that refined petroleum from the Marathon Oil plant going? Marnie realized that the corn and grain and barley that the local farmers were growing was being shipped somewhere else as well, and all at once the remote quaintness of Templeton seemed like an artifact of her imagination. She thought of the Super K-Mart on the edge of town and the constant traffic of semi-trucks on Route 44. Yet, Templeton was quaint and remote and its people were salt-of-the-earth farmers. Both ideas—the quaintness of Templeton and its connection to the modern global economy—had to be held at once.

"I'm very impressed," Marnie said. "I had no idea how complicated making a candy bar could be."

Jack Madison smiled proudly. "Wait till you see the production line and the systems control center." He opened a drawer in his desk and took out a clipboard. "And then, I've arranged a get-together in the break room at five o'clock, so you can meet the floor employees informally—if you'd like."

"That sounds fine."

Marnie followed the plant manager out of his office, down a corridor to a locker room. Marnie donned a white lab coat, shoe coverings and a hair net. Jack put on a Hawthorne baseball cap and a personalized white smock, with his name over the left breast pocket. They stepped from the locker room into a cold, white-tiled kitchen.

Half a dozen men and women were working at long stainless steel tables, and half a dozen more were wheeling mobile bakers' racks to and fro. The racks were filled with metal setting trays, which were being transferred from the tables into a walk-in refrigerator. Madison introduced Marnie to everyone and then explained that this station was the first preparation area, where trays were wax-papered and buttered in order to hold the toffee that would be poured into them in the next room.

He led Marnie into the walk-in refrigerator, which held rack after rack of buttered trays, set alongside permanent shelves in the walls. The permanent shelves contained blocks of butter, marked with the Hargis Dairy label, from across the street.

They exited the refrigerator through a door on the opposite side, into a much larger, warmer room. Here, industrial-sized mixing blades were stirring vast amounts of butter, sugar and crushed nuts together in steel vats. The room was alive with whirring and clanking.

"You mean to tell me," Marnie shouted above the racket, "that all those people do—those people in that small area back there—all they do is put butter and wax paper on metal trays?"

"That's right. Then they put the trays into racks, and the racks are wheeled into the refrigerator, and from there they make their way into this room, the first toffee sector."

Here, the salty-sweet smell of butter was freshly overwhelming, and Marnie realized that, without consciously being aware of its disappearance, she had stopped noticing the smell of chocolate. In this room, thirty-five or forty people were feeding pre-measured ingredients into basins and chutes and then watching digital readouts, which reported the amounts of the ingredients. The chutes and basins then mechanically supplied the vast vats, where the ingredients were slowly heated, blended and extruded onto the trays from the first room.

Marnie was astounded by how narrow and specialized each person's task was—she thought she would go mad if she had to feed sugar into basins all day. In her job as Artistic Director at Bartel Records, there was a certain amount of mechanical repetition, but the tasks were never as strictly confined as these.

"Where do the nuts come from?" she shouted.

"Originally from Desert Diamond, a company in California." Madison pointed to a door on the opposite wall. "That's the dry ingredient prep room, where they're processed, and beyond that is the dry storage area, where we keep the granulated sugar, brown sugar, cocoa and so on."

Madison led her into the dry prep room, where men wearing heavy gloves were feeding whole nuts into processors and marking charts on the walls. Other men were portioning granulated sugar into containers of various sizes and labeling them. There were no women in this facility.

They passed through the dry prep room into a dark, cool warehouse, where giant burlap sacks were stacked on wooden pallets along the walls. Heavy metal carts were lined up near the shelves, waiting to carry the sacks away, and there was a loading dock at the back to receive supplies from the outside world. Two forklifts sat idle in the corner. Madison explained where each ingredient originated, the schedules of their deliveries and the number of tons of each item they used every month.

They returned from the dry storage area and passed through the first toffee room into a chocolate production sector, where cocoa, sugar, milk, butter and emulsifiers were turned into the milk chocolate that would eventually cover the toffee. Each successive preparation area was larger and more populated than the last, with bigger machines and more heat and hum.

After a detailed tour of each station, they arrived at the next-to-last production stage, where conveyor belts carried rectangular chunks of toffee beneath vats of melted chocolate—the place where the candy achieved its final form. Marnie watched as hundreds upon hundreds of toffee bars passed before her, and each bar was neatly and quickly covered in precisely the same amount of flowing milk chocolate. There was no wasted chocolate to speak of, and at each chocolate funnel a worker stood attentively, eyes following the progress of the bars with the utmost concentration.

Beyond the chocolate vats, the candies were flash-cooled by specially designed air compressors and then transferred by hand onto other conveyor belts. There were probably two hundred plastic-gloved people transferring tiny chocolate candies from one conveyor belt to another, and, as the workers moved the bars, they quickly inspected each one's texture and shape, discarding the irregulars into plastic containers and moving the acceptable bars on, where they were machine-packed in cardboard containers and then enclosed in the famous Hawthorne wrappers.

Jack Madison continued to recite the functions and statistics of each station, but Marnie had become swamped by the vast amount of detail. She just stared, mesmerized, her senses captivated by the chugging and humming of all the high-tech mechanisms, the precision of the employees and the baubly brightness of the machines.

In the next room, a slightly smaller area, workers took the wrapped candy bars from their conveyor belts and packaged them in cardboard cases for shipping. The toffee bars' last stop at the plant was a delivery dock, where teamsters loaded boxes of candies onto refrigerated diesel trucks and drove them away to retailers.

Marnie realized that she had just seen the making of a Hawthorne Toffee Bar from beginning to end, all in this one building. She asked Jack what purpose the other buildings on the lot served.

"This building is the production line proper," Madison said. "This is the only building where the toffee bars are actually made. In the other buildings, we have more extensive refrigerated storage areas for everything from raw ingredients to finished product, stations for printing and assembling our own packages and boxes, a truck garage—we own and maintain all our own trucks. There's also the computer control center: that's a wing attached to this building, but for all intents and purposes it's a separate structure. It was just added in the 1980s. There's a security post, and there's also a small dormitory, where swing workers or guards can sometimes sleep over if they're working heavy rotations. Henry used to practically live in the dorm when it was first built, and Calvin was known to stay over on occasion himself." Madison checked his watch. "I'll be happy to take you around the entire complex, or you're welcome to go by yourself, any time you want—but it's almost the end of the first shift, so maybe we could go to the break room to meet some of the other employees?"

Marnie followed Madison back through the production line, to the chocolate preparation area, then through a side door that opened into the break room. This was a large cafeteria-style space with metal picnic tables. There were snack machines along the walls, and the walls were covered with state regulatory notices, company announcements and Hawthorne promotional posters. About twenty-five people were already in the cafeteria and more were filing in from doors that led to other areas.

A few workers in white smocks diffidently approached Marnie and asked if she was enjoying her tour, and she chatted with them about their jobs, how long they'd been with Hawthorne and how they liked working there. She felt comfortable and supervisory: the Hawthorne workers treated her with an affable deference that she had not yet experienced in Templeton. She had seen none of these faces snarling at her around town, and within the confines of this plant they seemed not to care about her reputation, the complexities surrounding the Hawthorne family or the fact that she was an outsider. They appeared to like their jobs and hold no grudges against Marnie for anything her forebears might have done.

When a crowd of about a hundred and fifty had gathered, Madison called them to attention and made a short, complimentary speech introducing Marnie. He invited her to say a few words, and she felt inspired, looking across the cafeteria at *her* employees, everyone still garbed in their smocks and uniforms. For the first time since she had arrived in Templeton, she felt like fighting for every last thing her grandmother had left her.

"First of all," Marnie said. "I'd like to congratulate you all on your incredible willpower. Since I arrived in Templeton, Mr. Madison has been sending me bags of toffee, and I have to admit that I've finished every last morsel. I have a bag melting in my car at this very moment, and I'm afraid I'll double my body weight if I don't learn some self-control."

"Give it a month," a woman in the crowd said. "You won't be able to look at a candy bar."

"After a while," another woman chimed in, "you'll start craving vegetables!"

"That's a relief, I suppose," Marnie said. "Though I'm still in the greedy stage, so I'm going to enjoy it while it lasts." She turned to Madison. "So keep those candy bars coming."

"We'll send a case home with you," Madison smiled.

"I don't want to take up too much of your time," Marnie continued, "since I'm sure you're eager to get home. But I do want to thank you for your warm welcome and for the tour. It's been a pleasure meeting you all, and I'm sure we'll have time to get to know one another in the future. Thank you."

They applauded politely, and Jack Madison took Marnie's hand in a gesture of congratulations. Her platitudinous speech notwithstanding, Marnie sensed a rapport with the Hawthorne employees that went beyond their genuflecting. They seemed honestly not to mind that she might become their new boss.

14

A Crossroads

Jon knelt in the shade of the oak trees next to the Benjamins' field, cupping cool water into his hands from their stream. He drank in little swallows and then splashed water over the back of his neck. It was a muggy late afternoon: he had spent the entire day helping Kate and her mother clear sight lines and hoe weeds between terraced rows of crops, in preparation for the harvest.

Jon had worked in the Benjamins' field every summer since he and Kate had been dating. It was backbreaking and monotonous, and he could count on being utterly exhausted at the end of a day in the field. His shoulders would hurt, his hands would blister, and his head would feel buzzy and empty from the sun. He always wound up covered in plant clippings, bug bites and dirt. He marveled at Kate's physical stamina, working this way day in, day out for six months of every year—his life was soft and undemanding by comparison.

Though he dreaded the drudgery of hoeing, disking and trenching, it had become part of his life, just as the whole Benjamin family had, and he felt a special poignance in the work now. He knew that it might be his last summer with Kate, and being here reminded him why he loved her, how dedicated she was and how much unpleasantness she was willing to tolerate if she thought her persistence would be rewarded.

Because they grew such a wide variety of crops, the Benjamins' harvest was spread over a longer period than the harvests of other farmers. The work grew more urgent as different varieties ripened at different moments, and each required its own particular care. Though their field was small and each crop occupied only a few acres, they didn't have the luxury of sophisticated machinery or many hands to help them, and harvesting meant long days of sweat and strain.

Kate always went out of her way to include Jon in whatever she was doing. She asked his opinion about borderline plants; she let him check the corn moisture with a portable tester; she discussed the genetic irregularities of a new line of purple bell peppers with him. She tried to coach him in the subtler aspects of plant breeding, but he never developed an interest in the work, so he stuck to odd jobs and simple labor. He had enough wiry strength to handle the heavy lifting and moving that was difficult for the women and impossible any more for Mr. Benjamin; beyond that, he stayed out of the way and simply tried to help the Benjamins speed their work.

Jon finished refreshing himself at the stream, put his floppy hat back on and marched into the field. Kate was on her hands and knees at the end of a row of popping beans, and Mrs. Benjamin was off in the Indian corn at the far end of the field, invisible between rows of six-foot-tall stalks. Even Mr. Benjamin had come to the field this afternoon—he always helped with the lighter tasks at planting and harvesting. Today, he had brought his tool kit. He was lubing and oiling his prized Massey-Ferguson tractor and inspecting the mechanisms of the irrigator that pumped water from the stream into the field.

Though no one spoke as they tended their individual tasks, the imminent harvest brought a communal mood to the work, an air of expectation, and this hopeful atmosphere deepened Jon's pensiveness. Since he had fallen in love with Marnie, he no longer felt connected to the Benjamins' travails, and everything he had done with them over the years threatened to vanish into memory before his eyes. As fond as he still was of Kate, he couldn't help feeling that he had settled for this life with her, that it was nothing like the destiny he had imagined for himself. Marnie had awakened him to a larger moment in his life.

Mr. Benjamin called him from the tractor at the near edge of the pea patch, and Jon walked up a rise to meet him. "I'm gonna change the air and oil filters here," Mr. Benjamin said. "You can tighten the drive chain and grease the wear points." He unlatched the tractor's engine covering. "The grease gun's in the truck."

Jon nodded and walked to the pickup, which was parked on the dirt road at the edge of the field. He pushed aside the short strips of mesh fencing in the truck's bed and found the grease gun and a new tube of grease. He returned to the pea patch, where Mr. Benjamin was struggling to loosen a bolt on the tractor, his face stoplight red and pouring sweat.

"Can I give you a hand?"

"I got it." Mr. Benjamin grunted and strained. "Day's a long way off when I can't loosen a damn bolt."

"You want me to grease it up for you?"

"I said I got it."

Jon's relationship with Mr. Benjamin had always been bristly. Jon wasn't mechanically inclined and didn't take readily to the kind of work that came naturally to Kate's whole family, and Mr. Benjamin thought him unmanly because of it. Kate was much better with a welding iron or a wrench than Jon was, and Mr. Benjamin would usually enlist Kate before he sought Jon's help.

Though Jon had grown up in Templeton and been exposed to farm life from an early age, none of his family had been farmers and he hadn't been raised around crops or animals. His father had been a loan officer with the Lawford Federal

Credit Union and his mother had been a first grade teacher at Washington Elementary, and neither of them had cared much for the outdoors. (It was ironic that they had both died outside: his father of a massive stroke at the Lawford County Fair and his mother of a water moccasin bite near the Stoy reservoir.) Jon's childhood had been filled with books and music and clichés about growing up to be president. His parents had encouraged him in intellectual pursuits, and Jon had developed skills that were utterly useless in a barn.

Mr. Benjamin finally conquered the intransigent bolt and stared at Jon with self-satisfaction. Jon loaded the grease gun. He hated Mr. Benjamin's arrogant reprimands whenever he made mistakes; more than that, he hated the fact that Mr. Benjamin would snipe criticisms about him at Kate after he had left. Jon's continuing presence in the Benjamin household had never made Kate's life easy, and he knew that she had acted as his defender and champion for years. His heart felt tangled in the net of her efforts and he wondered if Marnie, or anyone else, could prove as devoted an advocate for him. But then, if Mr. Benjamin hadn't been such a hardhead, he wouldn't have needed Kate's staunch defense.

Kate seemed especially grateful for his presence in the field today, and she doted on him as much as her father allowed. Jon could see the anxiety in her eyes, and he hated himself for lying to her. She had become so much a part of him that he could no longer picture his life without her, yet her love and commitment had lost their allure next to Marnie's beauty and magnetism.

He set to work greasing the Massey's wear points. He could not stop thinking of Marnie, of the sound of her voice, the curve of her neck, the gentle roundness of her belly. He remembered how she had cut her grapefruit for breakfast, how she had held her teacup, and he imagined that his discovery of her everyday habits unlocked the secret world of Marnie Hawthorne, a new world where simple things reverberated with complexity and familiar things became strange.

Jon got down on his back and scooted underneath the tractor. He looked up at the rear axle and applied grease here and there, distractedly. A wasp hovered nearby, darted close to investigate the sweat on Jon's arms, then zipped away.

He recalled Jeremiah's advice, that he should act with caution when it came to the Hawthornes because the Hawthornes could make people do things they didn't necessarily want to do. Jon had not followed that advice, and now every word he said to Kate was a lie, and his presence in her family's field was also a kind of lie; he felt himself sinking into a quagmire of guilt and deception, and he was angry at Kate because of it, for reasons he could not understand.

He finished greasing the tractor's wear points, then got a pair of wrenches from Mr. Benjamin's tool box and tightened the drive chain. He imagined the slurs Mr. Benjamin would aim at him if his affair with Marnie ever came to light. He had always resented Mr. Benjamin's knee-jerk criticism, but now he was proving it all correct.

"How's the triticale this year?" Jon called up to Mr. Benjamin. "Ready for market?"

"Maybe," Mr. Benjamin said gruffly from under the tractor hood. "I'll plant another generation first, but it's about as regular as it's gonna get."

Mr. Benjamin's variety of triticale grew three times as large as the average with quadruple the yield, and he hoped to sell it as a more versatile and productive replacement for wheat: it was hardier, less labor-intensive and would grow in more diverse climates. In Mr. Benjamin's utopian vision, his superproductive triticale would eliminate hunger the world over. Jon had eaten triticale bread many times at the Benjamins' house and found it tasty. He saw no reason, outside of the plant's ungainly name, that it couldn't be successful.

It was one of the things he would miss about Kate and the Benjamins if his relationship with Kate ended—their unusual vision of the world. Kate loved to try new things. Her book collection included novels from Japan, memoirs from Africa and poetry from Brazil, and she was fond of all kinds of music, from European symphonies to Indian ragas. She would take Jon to St. Louis to attend Chinese operas or djembe festivals, and she was constantly getting him to try interesting foods he had never heard of before (like sorrel and cardoon). He would miss this eclecticism if he left Kate, and he would miss the openness to the weirdness of life that the Benjamins' strange crops represented. Kate didn't limit herself to the world she already knew, and yet her intellectual adventurousness did not engage him the way the simple fact of Marnie Hawthorne did.

Jon finished adjusting the tractor's drive chain, stood up and dropped the wrenches back into the tool box. The sun was shining brightly through a haze of thin, streaky clouds, and heavy beads of sweat trickled down Jon's neck without cooling him. The air was absolutely still.

"Looks like she's ready to roll," Jon said, patting the side of the Massey. "I've seen two-year-old tractors in worse shape than this."

"Nobody cares for their equipment any more," Mr. Benjamin said. "Most of these guys nowadays go to the dealer just to change their oil."

Jon had never had an actual conversation with Kate's father and did not know how to begin one. He abandoned Mr. Benjamin to his tractor and walked over to Kate, who was now kneeling to inspect the collapsed, forsaken-looking leaves of some potato plants.

For fun, Kate's mother had crossed some Kennebecs with some blue Peruvian russets and had planted a single row of the new variety. They had been ready to harvest for several weeks and some had already appeared on the Benjamins' dinner table; but potatoes could be left in the ground indefinitely after reaching maturity and these would probably remain here until all the other crops had been brought in.

"Looking for pests?" Jon said.

"No, it's long past time," said Kate. "Besides, we crossplanted this row with beans to keep the beetles out. Remember? I was just noticing how symmetrical these leaves are as they droop. Look. And the color striations. They're almost too pretty to be potatoes."

"They taste good, too."

"Well. . . that potato salad I made was pretty doctored-up. I think they're too bitter for the table, but they look nice in the ground. Mom will be happy with them."

Jon shaded his eyes against the afternoon sun. "I'm taking off," he said. "So I'll have enough time to shower."

He had told Kate that he would be working an evening shift at Ploughman's Grill that night, but this was a lie. He would actually be spending the evening with Marnie at the Hawthorne Mansion, and he fretted that Kate might call Ploughman's and discover the truth. This possibility—of being found out so easily—weighed on Jon's mind. Templeton was too small a place for an affair to go unnoticed (especially one with Marnie Hawthorne). He was certain that someone had seen him coming and going at the mansion by now, and Kate knew his schedule and habits too well for him to keep a secret like this for long: he would not be able to account for his time if he continued to spend it with Marnie. Something decisive would have to be done soon.

"You're still coming out to the house tonight, aren't you?"

Kate said.

"Yup. I'll come as soon as my shift ends. With any luck, it'll be a slow night and I can knock off early."

"Whenever you can. Mom rented a documentary about pandas, so we may only be half-conscious by the time you get there."

Kate had been pressing Jon to spend nights with her, and Jon was calling her on her cell phone three or four times a day now, to allay her fears. He tried to speak to her the same way he always had, but he no longer remembered what their conversations had sounded like before Marnie had arrived, and he could sense the worry and confusion in her voice, in her increasingly clingy and despondent invitations.

He shouted goodbye to Mrs. Benjamin, who thanked him for his help, and he nodded dutifully to Mr. Benjamin, who waggled a screwdriver at him. Kate took his arm and they walked along the tractor path near the oak trees.

"I argued my mom into letting me have tomorrow off," she said, "before we really start picking. I was wondering if you'd like to go to Terre Haute with me."

"What's in Terre Haute?"

"I'm going to buy a guitar. It's my winter project." Every winter, when there was little farm work to do, Kate pursued a new hobby. Last winter, she had taken tap dancing lessons from a woman in Hutsonville. The winter before that, she had brewed her own beer and tried to learn German. "You could help me pick out a good one."

"You can borrow my guitar any time you want."

"But I was hoping you could teach me some songs and we could play duets."

"We could still play duets—you could take my guitar, and I could play the banjo or the ukulele."

"I guess."

Jon's motorcycle was parked near the Benjamins' pickup. They walked up to it, and he unhooked his helmet from its holder and put the key in the ignition.

"I just thought it would be nice to get away for a day," Kate said. "For a break. You know how hard it gets once we start harvesting."

"I'll check with Maude, see if she has any articles she wants me to do tomorrow."

"Okay. Let me know—if you want to go, that is."

"Why not?" Jon said. "Maybe I'll buy a cheap mandolin. I've been meaning to, anyway."

Jon's grudging agreement momentarily buoyed Kate. "I plan to be finger-picking 'Orange Blossom Special' by spring," she said.

"You'll be teaching me, then." He kissed her on the lips. "I'd better get going."

As quickly as it had brightened, Kate's expression fell and assumed the preoccupied frown she wore all the time these days. Jon put his helmet on, swung his leg over his bike and grabbed the clutch. He hit the starter switch and, as he let the clutch out and started rolling down the dirt road, he turned to wave. Kate was standing with her arms crossed, looking down at the ground, and when she looked up and saw him waving, she forced a smile and a wave in return. Her sad bearing caused a lump in Jon's throat, and he wanted to turn around and ride back to her. He wanted to leap off his bike and take her in his arms and tell her he loved her.

But he didn't. He kept riding until Kate disappeared in the trail of dust in his rearview mirror.

* * * * *

By the time Jon clonked the heavy brass knocker against

the Hawthorne Mansion's front door, the heat of late summer had faded into a cool early autumn evening. He had raced home, showered and changed clothes, and now he waited expectantly at Marnie's door, freshly scrubbed, full of hope and trepidation.

He clonked on the door again. As usual, Marnie kept him waiting. She claimed she could never hear the thud of the knocker, but Jon thought she liked the control and suspense of making him stand on the porch like a beggar.

When the door opened, Marnie greeted him wearing a sheer white blouse emblazoned with yellow flowers, and a long violet skirt, slit up to her left knee. Her hair was piled on top of her head, like a Betty Grable pin-up poster. She wore antique pearl earrings, a strand of doubled pearls around her neck and a delicate diamond broach. She looked ravishing, but strangely formal and alien, as if she'd stepped off the pages of a 1940s *Vogue.* She smiled slyly and slipped out of the doorway, back into the darkness of the hall, beckoning Jon with her index finger. He swung the door closed behind him.

The wan light of the chandelier cast a spidery web of shadows across the entryway and Marnie walked slowly backwards, moving through dim pools of light, summoning him deeper into the house. Jon stood still, watching the curve of her hips as she set one foot behind the other in a calculatingly slinky line. His eyes followed the invitation of her body, her carefully tressed hair, her glossy lips, boldly rouged cheeks and thick black eyelashes, and he realized that the style of her make-up was from another time as well. He remembered Jeremiah's insistence that Marnie was a dead ringer for Dorothy, and he felt a paralyzing sense of déjà vu; in the baroque shadows of the Hawthorne Mansion, he might have stepped sixty years into the past.

But when he looked directly into Marnie's eyes, the uncanniness of the moment fell away: he wanted her, now, and nothing else mattered. He charged forward and took her in his arms, and they kissed, a rough openmouthed kiss, equal parts challenge and relief.

Jon pushed Marnie backwards toward the staircase. His hands found her slender waist and hips. He bit at her neck and nuzzled her ear, wallowing in the supple elasticity of her perfumed skin.

Her heel caught the edge of the first step, and she grabbed Jon around the shoulders. He fell forward onto her, in a pantomime tumble, his whole weight pressing down on her as they writhed against the stairs.

"Wait," Marnie whispered.

"For what?"

"I want to tell you something—"

"Tell me."

"—before we get carried away. Something important."

Jon's right hand found Marnie's erect nipple through her blouse and he circled it with the tips of his fingers. "Tell me." He kissed her and fondled her breast.

She hissed into his ear, "My husband will be here next week."

He froze. "What do you mean?"

"Just that."

He propped himself up on one elbow. Marnie kissed him lightly on the cheek and neck. She fluttered her eyelashes. "He's arriving next Tuesday."

Dismay spread through Jon's whole body. "What does this mean?" If Marnie's husband came to Templeton, there would be no way Jon could see her—their meetings were fraught with enough difficulty as it was, even with the mansion as their refuge. If Marnie's husband were here in this house, they would never have an opportunity to meet. "How long will he stay?"

"I don't know."

"Days? Weeks?"

"I don't know."

He felt panicked and desperately in love. He held Marnie's face between his hands and kissed her as if he might never kiss her again, but when he looked into her eyes, he could not find a reflection of his own anxiety. He realized in a rush of confusion that Marnie's husband was a problem for him but not for her, that he was powerless. Perhaps this meant the end of the affair—a romantic fling with him and then back to her married life when her husband arrived. She had announced her husband's coming so offhandedly, at the worst possible moment!

He inched Marnie's blouse up to expose her flesh. His mouth found her bare belly.

"Well," Marnie said. "Ooh." She sucked air through her teeth as he nibbled at her stomach.

"What does this mean?" he whispered again. He made patterns on her belly with his tongue, then bit her, trying to anchor himself to the taste of her skin. He unfastened the top button on the side of Marnie's skirt, pressed his chin into her soft flesh. She arched her back toward him and twisted, making little groans whose vibrations Jon felt through her belly. "What will we do?"

"I suggest... mmmm... I suggest you keep doing that."

"I mean about Graham."

"Ahh... so do I."

Jon stopped, annoyed. He had tormented himself all day about lying to Kate, and he thought this a poor moment for Marnie's cavalier attitude. He was risking everything important to him—Kate, his reputation, his whole future in Templeton—and Marnie was playing games.

"Look at me, Jon." Marnie cupped his chin in her hand.

She held his gaze for a long time before speaking. "I don't know what to do about Graham. I want to keep seeing you." She kissed him on the mouth. "I don't know what else to tell you, except that Graham isn't here right now, and we can't solve this problem tonight. But you need to know he's coming, and I don't know what it means."

This new complication made Marnie irresistible: she was so clearly not his, and that made Jon want her all the more. He felt unmoored, a body tethered to the growing hardness between his legs and a spirit transported through his shallow breath into the air around Marnie Hawthorne. He loved how willowy and lithe she was, and as she slid against him, he found the humid press of her skin the only answer to these problems.

He slipped one arm behind her shoulders and the other beneath her knees, and he lifted her into his arms. Marnie wrapped herself around him and kissed him with abandon, and he carried her up the stairs. Despite his weariness from the long day in the field, Jon found fresh strength in Marnie's body, in the urgent sense of loss he felt at the coming of her husband, and her weight felt light against his chest.

"You realize, of course," Marnie said, in a tone of joking easiness, "that my bedroom's two flights up."

"Don't think I can make it?" he said, trying to match her lighter tone.

His forced jocularity only made him more grave. When they reached the second floor landing, Jon laid Marnie down on the dingy Persian rug. The light from the chandelier below barely disturbed the gloomy shadows here, and Marnie's face assumed an otherworldly expression in the darkness. Jon felt a ghostly breath of stale air around him, a palpable feeling not so much that he had moved in just this way before, but that he was doing precisely what someone else had done before him, that something was being repeated through him, and he felt again the haunting fear of the Hawthorne Mansion from his childhood—a tremor of something unknown but morbid and somehow personal. Marnie parted her lips and stroked his cheek with her open hand and she seemed, in the half-light, only half real.

He tore at the remaining buttons of Marnie's skirt and dragged it and her underwear together down past her ankles. He unceremoniously pushed her thighs wide apart, grabbed her hips and descended between them. He lost himself in the soft wetness of the folds of her flesh and the tartness of her taste and the quavering of her sighs.

* * * * *

They lay silent in each other's arms on the landing, caressing each other, touching each other's hair, breathing the same air in and out. The grandfather clock in the dining room slowly chimed, and Jon counted the bells: eleven. He rolled his eyes back in despair. Ploughman's would have closed at nine and he was due at Kate's over an hour ago.

"Is that clock right?"

"No."

"Slow or fast?"

"Both." Marnie kissed him languidly and petted his hair away from his forehead.

"I need to go."

"Go?" She took his arm and pulled him closer. "Where," she whispered, "do you need to go?"

"Home."

"You don't need to go home."

"I have a story to finish for the paper," Jon lied. He had never told Marnie about Kate and didn't intend to. "For tomorrow."

"At this hour?"

"I shirked it earlier so I could come here. It's the Harvest Festival coming up in Newton." In fact, Jon had finished that article the day before, but he knew it would appear in the next day's *Constitution*, so he mentioned it by name. All these lies were giving him a headache.

"Will you come back later?"

"Probably not. I'm going to be late."

"I'll be up."

"All night?"

"All night. I'll wait for you."

"Mm. That's funny."

"What's funny?"

"I never thought you'd be the type to sit waiting for your man."

"I just want to fuck you some more."

Jon rubbed his cheek against hers. After a moment of pliance, Marnie resisted his pressure and they were suddenly locked in a taut struggle, pushing against one another with their faces, until the standoff moved down their bodies in a tremor, spontaneously, Jon pushing Marnie away and Marnie pulling him closer, and then Marnie pushing and Jon pulling, their bodies like magnets drawing each other in and pushing each other away, with real force and growing violence. It was an alien and disturbing confrontation that seemed to go on for minutes, pushing and pulling and grunting breathlessly.

Their lips met in a kiss like none Jon had tasted, a first kiss and a last woven together, their whole affair in a moment that seemed to ebb and flow and burn around them, not just in that instant but in the larger moment of Jon's life. He felt raw and tender and he thought of Henry Hawthorne on fire, tumbling down the steps of the Old Courthouse. The hallway seemed to spin around him and he felt giddy, felt himself slipping toward the stairs behind him and he held onto Marnie as if for his life. She seemed to whirl with him on a point, as the dizzy mansion spun and spun away from them, and he fell through the air, clutching onto her body, fearing the violent crash down the stairs.

When he summoned the courage to break their kiss, he found himself lying next to her, their bodies twined tightly together. The strange feeling of pushing and pulling, falling and spinning evaporated into thin air, but he was out of breath and sweating, and Marnie was panting, damp spirals of hair clinging to her cheek. He looked into her eyes for confirmation of the strange sensation he had just felt. The more time he spent in the Hawthorne Mansion, the more convinced he was that it was actually haunted, not by the ghost of a person but by something else, more subtle and dangerous—the ghost of an impulse, of love and death coupling, playing in his mind.

"I need to go," he said again. He got to his knees and began to dress.

Marnie kissed his bare thigh. "I can't believe you're going home to write about the Newton Harvest Festival when you could stay here with me."

"I can't believe it either."

Marnie luxuriated in her nakedness on the landing as she watched Jon dress. When he was ready to go, she stood up and led him down the stairs.

They stopped at the front door and kissed for a while longer and when Jon moved to leave, Marnie guided his hand to her bare ass and slid her foot up behind his knee. Jon broke their kiss and ran his fingers though Marnie's now-fallen blonde curls.

* * * * *

When he arrived at his apartment, he found a message from Kate on the answering machine, from nearly an hour before, and he was afraid that she had already called Ploughman's looking for him. It was too late to call Martina or Carl or anyone else from work, so there was no way to find out what Kate did or didn't know except to see her. He would have to go to her house blind and risk the consequences. He showered quickly and changed clothes.

He rode out Route 44 to County Road 12, staring hard at the wavering funnel of light his headlight threw in front of him, hearing only the steady growl of his engine. There was no traffic on the way and he held the throttle open, shivering violently now and again, the cool night air just chilly enough to make him tremble.

The Benjamins' house was dark when he killed the engine and coasted into the drive. Significantly, Kate had not left a porch light on for him, and he expected the worst. He parked near the house and let himself in through the side door—it was locked, which was unusual when Kate was expecting him, and he felt a wave of nausea as he used his key to click the deadbolt open. Perhaps the twisted convolutions of his conscience would end here and now. Perhaps Kate had caught him in this rather obvious lie.

He went in, closed the door behind him and listened for movements. Nothing stirred, and when he could make out objects in the dark, he walked up the stairs.

Kate's bedroom door was open a crack, and he closed it with a clack behind him. She stirred and turned over in bed. She had been sleeping, not waiting up in anger. She sat up to greet him, a silhouette with the starlight filtering gauzily through the window behind her.

"Hi," Jon whispered.

"Where have you been?"

"I had to finish a story." He took off his windbreaker and sat at the edge of her bed to remove his shoes. "Maude said I could have tomorrow off as long as I finished the article on Newton's Harvest Festival."

Kate yawned and stretched her neck. "I called the *Constitution*. No one answered."

"No, I didn't bother. I just wanted to get the work done."

"I called Ploughman's, too, but everyone was already gone."

"It was a slow night."

"You should have called. I was worried."

He finished taking his shoes and socks off, then stood up and removed his pants and shirt. He was still nervous: had the Ploughman's staff really gone home early, or had Kate actually spoken to someone? It was unlike her to be cagey, but perhaps she knew his secret and was baiting him.

"So you finished the article?" she said. "We can go to Terre Haute?"

"The day is yours."

"Good. Come to bed."

Jon slipped in-between the sheets and Kate snuggled up to him. She was wreathed in the comfortable smell of her own breath, in the warmth of the bed and the slowness of sleep. Because she exhausted herself with work every day, she could always sleep, no matter how uncertain or troubled other aspects of her life might be. Her anxieties appeared only in her nervous habit of grinding her teeth at night.

"When do you want to leave?" Jon asked.

"Doesn't matter. We can sleep till we wake up. I told my parents to leave us alone."

"Good."

Kate gave him a sleepy kiss. "I've missed you lately."

"I know." He was about to apologize and lie some more, until she made an entirely different kind of apology for him.

"I can't wait till we're done harvesting," she said, "and I can have a normal life again." She shifted into a drawling singsong. "I can sit on the swing and read and do nothing. We can go to the Flying Pig together and eat muffins and play chess and I don't know. . . that sounds nice, doesn't it? And we can play our guitars."

Jon normally loved Kate when she was half-asleep and dreamy, but tonight he was taut, restive and guilty, and he still had Marnie's smell in his nose and the feeling of her hands on his body. He wanted to get away.

"What's wrong?"

"Oh, you know. I shouldn't write so late."

"Did you drink coffee?" Kate said in a mock-scolding voice.

"I'm just tense." He pulled her closer. "I'll settle down."

Kate kissed him again, then sat up on her elbow and caressed his chest. "I know what'll relax you." She kissed his lips and chin and neck and kneaded his chest with her hands. Jon grew more tense as she licked his nipples, nibbled at his ribs and worked her way slowly down his belly.

She slipped his boxers down to his knees and stroked him with her hand and slid her mouth playfully all around him, and he soon grew erect in spite of himself. As Kate took him into and out of her mouth, he lay in her bed feeling lonelier and lonelier, more and more guilty.

He was thankful when he finally came. Kate kissed him and curled up beside him again and whispered, "I love you."

She drifted off to sleep, and he felt the rising and falling of her chest, once so comfortable and reassuring. His eyes would not stay closed. He lay awake and stared wide-eyed at the stark outlines of Kate's bedroom in the moonlight.

15

Old Affairs, New Desires

Jeremiah stood in front of his barber shop smoking his pipe, waiting for the taxi that would take him to the Hawthorne Mansion. He lifted his checkered golf cap, scratched his bald head and then pulled the cap low so the brim shaded his eyes from the sun, which was just setting over the Square. He felt autumn in the air as a vague hollowness, a brittleness in his bones.

He took the invitation from his pocket: a square of rough linen paper, artfully frayed at the edges and mottled with water marks. When the messenger had brought it, in a small envelope decorated with hand-painted purple flowers, Jeremiah had immediately recognized it as Dorothy's. In the invitation, Marnie wrote that she had found several old, unmailed letters addressed to Jeremiah, and that she would like to give him the letters. She had invited Jeremiah for drinks, and he had sent the messenger back with a note that he hoped, in its unornamented politeness, had not given away his eagerness to enter the mansion for the first time in two decades.

He cursed Kirk for being late. There was only one taxi in Templeton, driven by a man who had been injured in a Marathon Refinery accident and could find no other work. Jeremiah was one of Templeton Taxi's few regular customers and he was sympathetic to Kirk's disabilities, but today he was anxious and had no patience for the man's habitual tardiness.

He was little more than a mile from the Hawthorne estate, but he felt too enervated for the walk, and his frailty galled him. Marnie's youth filled him with fresh melancholy. He thought of all the nights he had spent staring at Dorothy's picture, refining his loneliness into a precise, consuming art. His obsession with Dorothy had long ago assumed an aspect of morbidity—he was ill with this love but he could not help returning to it, the way a sick dog returns to its own vomit. It was the only thing Jeremiah knew any more, bitter memories of a corrupt and regal passion, a garbled account of love in a dying language.

He lost patience with Kirk and started walking up the hill. He passed Jean's Jewelry Store without waving at Jean for the first time in thirty years. As he crossed the Square, a car horn honked and a man shouted his name. Kirk's taxi caught up to Jeremiah in front of Ploughman's Grill and Kirk waved frantically from the other side of the street. He made a U-turn across traffic, which prompted more honks and angry shouts, and he parked with his bumper sticking into the street.

Kirk limped out to help Jeremiah into the car. Jeremiah smelled scotch on his breath.

"You were supposed to meet me at quarter to six."

"You're lucky I saw you at all," Kirk said, inexplicably angry.

"Lucky!"

After much fussing, Kirk settled Jeremiah into the back seat, limped back to the driver's seat and headed off around the Square. He ran through the tail end of a yellow light and nearly clipped Sharon Kazee as she stepped into the crosswalk. Sharon loudly cursed him to hell.

"Where to?"

"Hawthorne estate."

"Oh ho ho," Kirk said, eyeing Jeremiah in the rearview mirror. He missed the turn he should have taken onto Cross Street.

"What does that mean, oh ho ho?" Kirk circled the Old Courthouse and turned east onto Main Street—the wrong direction. "God damn it, Kirk. Would you pay attention where you're going?"

"What're you so riled about, Jeremiah?"

"You're going the wrong way! And now I'm late. Do you know where the Hawthorne place is?"

"Of course."

"Well, go there, then."

Kirk flipped his blinker on, waited for traffic to clear and turned left onto Jefferson Street. "I'll just backtrack up Locust. No big deal."

Jeremiah stared out the window as they passed the Moose Lodge and Shirley's Hair and Nails. He took his pipe and lighter out and sucked flame into the bowl.

"No smoking in the cab, Jeremiah."

"No drinking and driving, Kirk."

"I don't have to drive you around, you know."

"I know, you do it out of the goodness of your heart."

"Jeremiah—"

"Just drive, Kirk. We'll be there in five minutes."

Kirk muttered to himself but kept driving. Jeremiah puffed furiously on his pipe, regretting doing so as he filled the cab with smoke. He didn't want to take his anxiety out on Kirk, but he couldn't harness it and he told himself that Kirk deserved it anyway.

They drove silently along Locust Lane, past Mick Frick's Dodge dealership and Templeton High School. Beyond the school's football field were several blocks of row houses and then an open field containing the helicopter pad of Lawford County Memorial Hospital—one of the few municipal projects of the last seventy years that Hawthorne money hadn't funded. Past the hospital, they came to the subdivision of Templeton's most well-heeled and highly respected citizens.

Jeremiah stopped puffing on his pipe and rolled down his window to look at the lovely yards, the old elm and walnut trees forming an arbor over the street. He remembered strolling these streets fifty years before, enjoying the thrill of his precarious affair with Dorothy; but that was before he knew about Dorothy and Calvin. Their affair had made his own insolence seem vapid and tame.

They turned onto Argus. The little children in this neighborhood gave the Hawthorne place a wide berth, and Jeremiah himself was one small reason for the sickly reputation that beautiful mansion had acquired. The Hawthornes had been so creative and strong for a time, but the rottenness at their core had found its way out quickly enough.

Kirk slowed the car. Even if you didn't know the address, you could pick out the Hawthorne place just by looking at the unkempt thickets surrounding it. It was the only house on the block with no neighbors, since its grounds took up several lots on either side, and the spinneys all around the mansion had grown tangled and dark with dense vines and unruly shrubs. They came upon the opening of the driveway, and Jeremiah lifted his hand to stop the car.

"This'll be fine, Kirk, I'll walk up the drive." He got out of the car and handed Kirk a twenty dollar bill. "I'm sorry about before."

"You want me to wait?"

"No, I'll phone if I need you again." He gave the car's roof a quick rap, and Kirk pulled away, leaving Jeremiah alone on the street.

The hedge guarding the front of the property blocked out the setting sun, and Jeremiah's heart beat fervidly in the still dusk. He walked up the curving drive, until the corner of the sprawling house greeted him around the shrubs. It was just as he remembered it: a splendid manor, Henry's tribute to his dead wife Charisse. Jeremiah had always thought the ghost of Charisse Hawthorne haunted it, since he was otherwise hard-pressed to understand how such a beautiful mansion could become such a sad and sagging hulk in so short a time.

His feet felt heavy and his steps were small and trembling. It was strange, how normal it all was, how solid and real. Any time in the last twenty years, he might have walked up this drive and stood on this porch, and doing so would merely have involved the unremarkable acts of walking and standing; but it had been impossible and would have remained impossible as long as Dorothy had been alive. He had been repelled by Dorothy's constant, pulsating self-hatred and the repulsive secrets that bound them together and held them apart.

Jeremiah rapped the brass knocker, then stepped away from the door. He fiddled nervously with his pipe, the one thing here that was familiar without being uncanny.

The door opened and Jeremiah stood face to face once again with Marnie Hawthorne. She resembled her grandmother more now than when he'd first seen her at Bertram's, and he found the likeness eerie. He felt a sharp rush that reminded him of falling in love.

"Mr. Grayson," Marnie said. "Thank you for coming."

"It's my pleasure. I'm sure everyone tells you how much you look like Dorothy, but I'll say it again. It's the highest compliment I can pay."

Marnie smiled. She stood aside and invited Jeremiah into the vestibule. "May I take your hat?" She hung his hat on the coat rack behind the door. "We'll sit on the back porch, overlooking the garden, if you don't mind the breeze. It's the most pleasant place in the house. And I'd be pleased if you smoked your pipe—it reminds me of my father."

She led him toward the back of the house and Jeremiah

realized that it was not just Marnie's face and manner that reminded him of Dorothy: it was her dress. She wore a black pantsuit whose cut and fabric had been stylish in Jeremiah's youth—the extremely high waist of the pants and the dramatic tapering of the jacket's lapels had fallen out of fashion so long ago that nowadays people might wear such an outfit to a costume party. Dorothy had been the first woman in Templeton to wear pantsuits to formal occasions, and now Marnie looked just as glamourous in what must have been Dorothy's clothing. The only striking difference between Dorothy and Marnie was the sound of their voices: Dorothy had spoken in a flat Illinois twang; Marnie's gracious lilt was melodic. She was a winning hostess who made effortless small talk about the town and the mansion, and Jeremiah was charmed.

On the patio, Marnie offered him a seat at the table and asked what he'd like to drink. Jeremiah requested a *cuba libre* and Marnie returned to the kitchen.

Some of Dorothy's stationery, sepia-colored from age, was lying on the table, and Jeremiah recognized her florid handwriting. He wanted to take the letters up immediately, to see what love or malice Dorothy might deliver to him from the grave; instead, he smoked his pipe and enjoyed the cheery burbling of the statue of Cupid in the fountain, where he had killed Robert Meese fifty years before.

He was surprised, as Jon had been before him, by how diametrically opposed the moods of the garden and the house were. The house and its coppice frontage had been in decline for years out of memory and Jeremiah, along with everyone else in town, had imagined the whole estate to be as dilapidated as the facade. Jon's brief description of this sunny garden in the *Constitution* had seemed an unlikely embellishment—Jeremiah hadn't been able to imagine such serenity hidden behind the wrecked manor. As it turned out, though, the becoming photographs of Marnie in the paper were not merely products of Marnie's brightness: they reflected the formality of the flower garden, which was crammed with order, and Jeremiah wondered who had been keeping up the grounds. The garden, and the apple orchard at the other end of the property, had always been Calvin's obsessions, and Jeremiah couldn't picture Dorothy digging in the dirt and pruning bushes. There was no way Marnie could have orchestrated such an abundance of beautiful blooms in the short time she had been there. This garden, unlike the rest of the mansion, had been tended meticulously for years.

"You know," Marnie said, when she returned with the drinks, "everyone else calls these rum-and-Cokes, but my father used to call them *cuba libres* as well. Didn't you wonder how I knew?" She handed him a glass.

"Fate reveals itself in small gestures," Jeremiah said. They clinked glasses and drank. Marnie lit a pair of citronella candles on stands near the patio door, then sat down opposite Jeremiah. They sipped their drinks as the orange and amber light of sunset played across the garden.

"I've made copies of these letters," Marnie said. "I hope you don't mind. You can have the originals, and the photograph."

"Photograph?"

"There was a picture of you attached to one of the letters." She flipped through the stationery sheets and held up a small rectangular photo.

Jeremiah squinted at it, trying to remember the occasion it had been taken. It was slightly out-of-focus, a picture of a man in a straw hat, holding a shovel, standing next to the gardener's shed in the Hawthorne apple orchard. The photographer had been fifteen or twenty feet away, so the man's whole body was in full view, but his face was blurry and indistinct. The brim of his hat fell over his brow, obscuring his eyes and nose in shadow. In fact, it did not really seem like Jeremiah—the man was about Jeremiah's height and build, but there was something about his bearing that Jeremiah found foreign. He turned it over, but there was no date or identification on the back.

"Would you like to see the letters now? Or would you rather wait till you can read them privately?"

"I suppose I should know what we're talking about," Jeremiah said. "You said in your invitation that you had some questions about them?"

"About you and my grandmother in general, if that's all right."

"To be honest with you, Ms. Hawthorne—"

"Marnie."

"Marnie." Jeremiah savored the sound of her name on his lips. "To be honest with you, Marnie, I'm happy to talk about your grandmother again. It's been a long time."

"You may not be, once you've read the letters. I know this might be presumptuous, but I'd like to talk frankly about your relationship. That is, it would be a great help to me if you were as candid as possible, Mr. Grayson. I don't want you to omit anything or sugarcoat the details to spare my feelings."

"In that case, you should call me Jeremiah, and maybe we should consider ourselves friends."

"I'm glad you feel this way, because I have some questions that are. . . well, I've read your letters to my grandmother. I think I know something about your relationship with her already, and my concerns are rather personal."

"No matter."

It hadn't occurred to him that Marnie might have read his own letters to Dorothy—but Dorothy had been a collector by nature and she must have kept every note he had ever sent her. He wondered if Dorothy had maintained their pact never to tell what had happened to Robert Meese, and he wondered if Marnie knew about Calvin's and Dorothy's affair.

She passed the letters across the table. There were four: three were handwritten on Dorothy's stationery and the fourth—the one with the photograph clipped to it—was typewritten on onionskin paper. He paged through them, at first just letting Dorothy's handwriting remind him of the complicated emotions of their affair, but the typewritten letter captured his attention most insistently. It was different from the others not only because it was typed but because it did not begin by addressing Jeremiah by name. He read it first and the style seemed uncharacteristic of Dorothy.

"This one here," he said. "It's not addressed to me."

"It was folded up together with that other one, and it carries exactly the same date, see? November 1, 1978. There are several like that—I mean, anonymous typewritten pages that are folded around handwritten letters. So I've just grouped them together. You think it was intended for someone else?"

"I don't know."

The typewritten letter was emotionally detached and concerned itself with practical details about the Hawthorne estate. Dorothy had always written about people or her feelings, never about objects or impersonal things. This letter even mentioned "Gravenstein apples," which Jeremiah found peculiar. Many people who grew up in Southern Illinois had heard of Gravensteins (they were the region's most common cooking apples), but not everyone could volunteer the name, and Jeremiah felt sure that the word had never crossed Dorothy's lips.

"Isn't that you," Marnie asked, "in the picture?"

"I guess it is." Jeremiah sipped his *cuba libre* and stared at the photograph, which he was certain was not of him. "It was a long time ago."

"I found another just like it. Taken much earlier, from the

looks of it, but otherwise almost the same."

"Could I see it?"

"Of course."

Marnie left the table and disappeared into the house. Jeremiah sat forward in his chair and tilted the photograph toward the light. The more he looked at it, the stronger his conviction grew that, not only was it not him, but it was Dorothy's brother. The clothes were right, his posture was right. There was only one thing wrong: if the picture was of Calvin, and if it had been taken on the date of the letter—November 1, 1978—then it was a picture of a dead man.

Jeremiah shivered. Was this evidence that Calvin had not disappeared into thin air after all, that he had remained alive and well after he had been declared legally dead?

This idea was not new—everyone in Lawford County had had it at one time or another—and it had been the prevailing theory for the first few years after Calvin's disappearance. Where was the body, after all? Anyone who suggested that he was actually dead was dismissed as naïve, because everyone could think of reasons why Calvin Hawthorne might want to disappear. He had been involved with some dubious horse breeders and gamblers—the same people who were eventually implicated in the disappearance of Helen Brach, the Brach's Candy heiress—and some said his supposed death was an attempt to avoid capture by the FBI. He was a notorious philanderer, and people suspected he had cuckolded the wrong husband, and he had disappeared to avoid the cuckold's revenge. The fact that Dorothy's son, Ronald, had left town only a few days before Calvin disappeared raised more suspicions, but no plausible theories emerged to connect the two. His disappearance remained the most inexplicable of all the unusual events surrounding the Hawthornes, but eventually gossip had died down and people had settled on the most reasonable conclusion: that Calvin really was dead and someone had rubbed him out for revenge or money and left no traces behind.

Jeremiah held up the photograph. It could easily have been taken in 1971 and gotten mixed up with some later papers—there was nothing in the picture that indicated a date, and there was no proof positive that this was Calvin. But Jeremiah knew intuitively, with every fiber of his being, that it was Dorothy's brother—his face obscured and his figure out of focus, but Calvin nevertheless. It certainly was not Jeremiah.

Marnie returned and handed him a second picture, this one much older, in black and white. It was indeed a photograph of Jeremiah, standing next to the gardener's shed in the apple orchard and striking a pose similar to the one in the other picture. Dorothy had taken it after a picnic in the orchard, it must have been 1952 or '53—Jeremiah remembered the day vividly, making love with Dorothy on a blanket that could be seen lying on the ground behind him. He was disturbed by his resemblance to Calvin in the photograph.

Marnie sat down. "Those aren't pictures of you?"

"I guess I just don't remember them."

He directed his attention to the other letters Marnie had given him. These were unmistakably Dorothy's work. Their dates indicated that they had been written years apart from one another—1971, 1974 and 1978—but they seemed to represent one long moment in time. None was complete and each ended not just in the middle of a sentiment but halfway through a sentence, as if Dorothy had spent her venom and given up. He felt stung by the flood of freshly tormented memories they inspired, and he recollected viscerally what a complex negotiation his affair with Dorothy had been, saturated with envy, anguish and disgust.

Dorothy's contempt was the only plain thing in the letters, and he was amazed now that he had continued their physical relationship after she had confessed her affair with Calvin. The tangle of love, sex and blame that their relationship became was byzantine in its confusion, and he wondered if he had mistaken pain and bitterness all these years for unrequited love. He thought love and disappointment must share the same chamber in the heart.

He evaluated the onionskin letter in light of these others. It was so different in attitude and content that he was convinced that Dorothy had not written it, that it had not been intended for him; but the only other person he could think of who might have written about Gravenstein apples, whose papers could easily have become confused with Dorothy's, was Calvin, and the implication that Calvin might have written it in 1978 was too momentous for Jeremiah to wrap his mind around. These papers must have been mixed up with later ones, the dates confused, the photograph taken years earlier. He set the letters on the table and finished off his drink.

"Perhaps I shouldn't have shown them to you."

"There's nothing in these letters that I didn't already know," he said. "I'd just forgotten what it was really like. I had made it all into something else, in my mind."

"About that—what it was really like, I mean. I understand a lot of what my grandmother writes in those letters, and—as I said, I've read your own letters to her, so I know a little bit about your relationship. But there's something that isn't clear to me at all."

"You mean her relationship with Calvin?"

"That I understand." Marnie fixed him a knowing look. "Well, I don't understand it, but I know what happened. And I know why my father left town."

"Oh." Jeremiah rubbed his head. "I guess there's not much you don't know, is there?"

"There's a lot of talk in these letters about my grandfather, and it has an elliptical quality for me. It seems that Robert played a significant role in your relationship with my grandmother, long after he was dead."

"That's true, but—wait. You said there's a lot of talk in these letters about your grandfather?"

"Yes."

"I'm not sure I understand."

Marnie looked confused. "Well, there are three long passages about him in the letters you just read, and he seems central to your relationship with my grandmother. Your letters mention him, too, quite often."

"Mention your grandfather?"

"That's right."

Jeremiah held up his hand. "I don't think I'm following you. When you say 'my grandfather,' who do you mean?"

Marnie hesitated. "Robert Meese."

"Ah-ha." This, Jeremiah thought, *was* dangerous. Now he was really unsure what Marnie knew, and it made him feel wobbly inside. "May I have another drink please?"

They stared at one another, and Jeremiah felt transported back in time. Looking into Marnie's eyes was just like looking into Dorothy's and inspired the same old longings. He wanted to come closer to Marnie, to hold her face in his hands and have her see him for everything he was, and for the first time in recent memory his body responded to his erotic imagination. The citronella candles had begun to cast some light of their own as the evening shadows deepened, and they guttered black smoke and radiated a strong sweet acid scent, which even Jeremiah could smell and which intensified his desire.

Marnie took Jeremiah's glass, and the way she moved when she stood up reminded him of Dorothy. He almost reached for her arm as she passed. He wanted to smell her and feel her body and travel through time with her, and he realized that it was nothing as simple as sex that he wanted—it was redemption. He wanted Marnie to hold him against her breast, to receive his confession and assure him that everything would be all right. Marnie could make everything all right.

She returned with a bucket of ice and bottles of cola and rum. She poured Jeremiah another strong *cuba libre* and sat down to finish her own drink. He noted the patience in her bearing, in the simplicity of her actions.

"Robert Meese wasn't your grandfather," he said. "Calvin Hawthorne was." He studied Marnie's face for some reaction, but other than the light of recognition slowly dawning in her eyes, her expression remained composed and sober. She did not fluster easily, another trait she shared with Dorothy. "That's why your father left Templeton."

"So my father was—?"

"It seems obvious, doesn't it? Once you know that Calvin and Dorothy were lovers?"

"And that's why he left Templeton?" she said, half to herself.

"That's why."

"It wasn't just the affair he found out about. He discovered that his true father was. . . is that right? Or is there still something else I haven't figured out?"

"Your father was a bastard with one set of grandparents."

"There's no need to gloat about it," Marnie snapped.

Her sudden change took Jeremiah aback. She became scolding and haughty, which reminded Jeremiah all too well of Dorothy's wild temper. But as quickly as she had snapped at him, she regained herself. She held her hands momentarily in front of her and looked down at her lap, and when she looked up again, calm had returned to her eyes.

"What I meant was," Marnie said, more softly, "did my father really leave Templeton because he found out Calvin was his father, or is there more to the story than that?"

They were almost completely in darkness now, and Jeremiah sat still in the wavering shadows of the candles. He sipped his drink and listened to the crickets and the water splashing in the fountain, watched fireflies blinking low over the lawn as he tried to decide how he would begin his confession.

"Did Calvin kill Robert Meese?" Marnie asked. "Is that why my father left Templeton?"

Not an unreasonable conclusion, Jeremiah thought. It would be a tidy explanation: Calvin and Robert had been rivals, after all, and their hatred had reached a fever pitch once Ronald was born. Calvin might have killed Robert, and when Ronald discovered the incest and the murder, he could have chosen to flee instead of going to the police. It was logical enough. Jeremiah could absolve himself of all blame simply by saying yes.

"No," he said, "Calvin didn't kill Robert. It's funny, people rarely suggest that. Usually, they think Henry did it, because Henry had a difficult relationship with Robert. Henry handpicked Robert for Dorothy, but Robert was always chafing against Henry's authority. It got so they fought all the time, at the factory, at home. And people usually think that's why Henry killed himself. You know—he kills Robert, the guilt eats him up inside, day after day, month after month, till he just can't take it any more."

"Why is everyone so certain that Robert was murdered in the first place?" Marnie said. "He got drunk, fell into the fountain and hit his head. Isn't that right? That's the police version."

"Well, it's not very sexy, falling down and hitting your head. It's sexier to be murdered, especially when you've married into money, and the man with the money grows to hate you. You see?" Jeremiah could no longer see Marnie's face distinctly in the flickering yellow candlelight. "Anyway," he continued, "it's mostly because of Henry's suicide, that's all. People want a story to make sense of the events, and that's a story that does, in a way."

Jeremiah found it hard to believe that everything around him was not his—the manor and the garden and Marnie herself. He had spent most of his life thinking about things that might have happened, but Marnie's beauty shimmered before him as evidence of all that had. If he had married Dorothy, all of this would have belonged to him. He finished his second drink and poured himself another.

"But why doesn't it make sense," Marnie said, "that Robert really did just get drunk and fall? We can't all have sexy deaths, can we?" Jeremiah felt this last remark as a jibe at him, mocking his age and frailty, and it made him hate Marnie with the same corrosive despair that he felt for Dorothy. "And why did you go on talking about Robert at such length in your letters?" Marnie continued. "Twenty-five years after his death, my grandmother spends half a page writing to you about him and not really saying anything. And your letters do the same."

Jeremiah sighed. "I always felt that I should have married your grandmother, but I left for the war and while I was gone she married Robert. I saw him as the obstacle to my happiness."

"But that doesn't—"

"Robert was just as angry about Calvin and Dorothy as I was—much more so, actually. I mean, your wife is sleeping with her brother. . ."

"So he knew?"

"Dorothy confessed everything to him. To both of us. That's why Robert was drinking and stumbling around in the garden the night he was killed. They were fighting about Calvin, and about the baby—about your father. He was a healthy baby, as normal as any other, but he had Calvin's eyes and Dorothy told Robert the child was Calvin's. She said it because it was true, of course, but more than that, she wanted to hurt him. And it did."

"But that still doesn't explain—" Marnie hesitated. "Did she kill Robert Meese? If he didn't fall and die on his own, somebody must have killed him. Do you know what happened?"

"Could you turn on some lights?" Jeremiah asked. "Or could we go inside? I'd like to see your face."

Marnie went back into the house. Soon, a harsh white light above Jeremiah's head came on. She sat back down at the table.

Jeremiah felt his lust for her rise again. She was so lovely, even in this unflattering light. It was torturous and stupid, this feeble desire. It was painful that she was wearing Dorothy's clothes, and he thought how easy it would be for her to erase his anguish, how completely he could lose himself in her body; but it would be impossible for her to have a sexual feeling about him. All the jealousy he had once felt for Calvin flipped to Jon. He hated them both. He wanted to tell Marnie that he knew about her affair with Jon, that everyone in town knew. Suddenly, he was in no mood to confess, or to help her.

He thought that he should take his guilt and loneliness home with him, where he had kept them for so many years, that he should let the troubles of the Hawthornes pass to another generation—to Jon Ridgely if he wanted them. He decided he should give Marnie whatever neat ending she needed to tie the loose ends together and be done with it. Why should he care if Marnie Hawthorne slept with Jon Ridgely? What did Robert Meese matter to him now? What satisfaction could he ever hope for again?

"You're right," he finally said. "I may be the only person in the world who knows this, and it's a secret I swore I'd take to my grave. Dorothy took it to her grave, I have to hand it to her. But now that she's dead, it doesn't matter any more." He paused for effect. "Dorothy killed Robert Meese." He paused again. "They were fighting, like I said. He was drunk." He watched the effect this lie had on Marnie, and he wanted more than ever to hold her, to make love to Dorothy one last time. "She pushed him and he hit his head."

Marnie sat silent for a long time. Jeremiah wondered what all of this meant to her.

"Do you know this for sure?"

"She came to me the night it happened," he lied. "I guess she trusted me more than she trusted Calvin. She came to my house before she called the police."

"And you told her to say it was an accident."

"We discussed many things that night, but what she did was her doing. I said the police would probably let her off, call it self-defense, but she didn't want to take the chance."

"And Henry's suicide?" Marnie asked, almost clinically. "Do you know about that as well?"

"No one does," he said. "I imagine Henry found out about Dorothy and Calvin. You know, between his toffee and his family—that was all Henry ever had. His children were the last legacy of his wife, so when he found out what his children had done, what Charisse's legacy had actually become..." Jeremiah was exhausting himself, just being here in Marnie's presence, saying these things out loud.

His mind wandered back to the letters on the table—particularly to the anomalous fourth letter and the picture, which bothered him more and more. As evidence, it wasn't much: an unsigned typewritten letter and a blurry undated photograph, but the feeling that Calvin had remained alive after his disappearance, had remained here, muddied Jeremiah's imagination. His envy swerved uncontrollably between Jon and Calvin, both having their way with the Hawthorne women.

"I think I'm going to leave now, Marnie," he said. "I feel very tired."

"Oh. All right."

"I need to call a cab."

"I can drive you home, if you'd like."

He imagined Marnie driving him home, coming into his house for a drink, sitting across from him in his living room. He would invite her into his bed. He wondered if beauty was as ghastly a burden for the beautiful as it was for their admirers. "I appreciate it," he said, "but I've got a guy who drives me."

Marnie pulled her cell phone out of her pants pocket—an unmistakable sign that it was no longer the 1940s. Jeremiah called Kirk and arranged for him to come back to the mansion.

"Thank you," Jeremiah said, handing the phone back. "He'll be a little while."

"There's no hurry. We could wait out front, in the parlor, if you'd like, so we can see him."

"That's fine."

"And perhaps I could ask you some more questions while we wait."

"All right. And I have something to ask you, too."

"Anything."

"How about another *cuba libre*, before you put that bottle away?"

Marnie smiled. "I thought you had something serious to ask me."

"That's serious enough."

Marnie poured them both another drink. Jeremiah rose to his feet. As he turned toward the house, his right knee gave and he stumbled sideways into Marnie. He grabbed her shoulder for support and she let out a cry and dropped the plastic soda bottle. She grabbed him under the arms and helped him stand upright.

He clutched at Marnie's shoulders and leaned into her, finally steadying himself, and they stood holding each other in an uncomfortable embrace. Jeremiah looked into her eyes with a mixture of embarrassment and greed.

"I'm sorry," he said. "I'm so sorry." They were close enough to kiss. "I'm afraid I'm just. . ." He felt out-of-control drunk for the first time in ages.

"Are you all right?"

"Fine. Fine." He apologized about the soda, which had splattered Marnie's pants and shoes. The bottle had rolled under the glass table.

"It doesn't matter," she said.

Though his legs felt solid underneath him again, Jeremiah continued to support himself against Marnie's shoulders. He felt a bottomless pit of lust and mortification open in his stomach.

"Why don't I help you inside?" she said.

She turned and put Jeremiah's arm around her shoulder. He grabbed the letters and photograph from the table, and they walked together inside. He leaned on her all the way through the kitchen and the wine pantry, reveling in the feeling of her softness, hugging her body to his. She didn't resist and Jeremiah felt ashamed.

Marnie helped him sit down in one of the high-backed leather chairs in the parlor. "Thank you," he said. I'm sorry to trouble you. It's just. . ." Jeremiah felt tears in his eyes. He had become maudlin, and he fought the tears with a fierceness that made him feel vulnerable.

Marnie sat down in the chair opposite his. She perched on the very edge of her seat and put a sympathetic hand on

Jeremiah's knee. "Anything you need?"

Jeremiah couldn't believe that Marnie was touching him in this way, and he sobbed involuntarily. He brought his hand to his face, to hide his drunkenness, and pressed his thumb and forefinger into the corners of his eyes. He sniveled and wiped his eyes on his sleeve. When he finally stopped crying, he felt utterly exposed to Marnie, and sad and relieved because of it.

"Please," he said. "I'm going to ask you a favor, and there's no reason you should grant it. And if you say no, I'm going to feel old and foolish."

"Perhaps you shouldn't ask, then."

"But you could say yes. So I will ask, I hope you understand, just because you remind me so much of your grandmother. I know this is a very personal, an intimate request, but I don't mean it as personally as it might seem. I'm not sure if that makes sense."

Marnie sat up straight and removed her hand from his knee. Jeremiah fidgeted, working up his courage.

"I was wondering," he said, "if I could touch your face."

Marnie's expression remained unchanged, a perfect poker face. He had never once thought her icy or calculating; on the contrary, she seemed unusually sympathetic, but she was one of the most unflappable people he had ever met. Was it possible, he thought, that she was nonplussed by everything he said because she understood him, really understood him? That she didn't believe his lies? That she took pity on him?

Marnie asked, "Why do you still love her so much?"

His eyes misted again and his chest welled with another sob, which he suppressed with great difficulty. "I don't know." A single tear found its way down his cheek, and he wiped it away aggressively and pressed the others that were brimming up back into his eyes.

"All right," Marnie said. She stood up, brought an upholstered footstool from across the room and set it down in front of Jeremiah's chair. She sat down on the stool, facing him, and tilted forward, as if she were sitting at a department store make-up counter. "It's all right, if that's what you really want."

Jeremiah did not hesitate. He wiped his hands on his pantlegs and slid forward in the chair. He brought both hands up and ever so slowly, gently, with the very tips of his fingers, he touched Marnie's cheeks.

Her skin was smooth and cool, just as he'd imagined. He traced a line down her left cheek to her jaw and followed it to her lower lip. Marnie looked into his eyes without blinking, and he could see the authority and detachment growing in her. He felt weak and elated. He loved the feeling of her flesh, and he held her face in both hands for just a moment, then traced the line of her jaw again, down to her neck. The touch of her skin was like magic, like forgetting, and as long as he looked into her eyes and touched her, all thought dropped away. It was a satisfying self-annihilation, but after the briefest time, the new conceit in Marnie's eyes disappeared and she grew visibly uncomfortable. He pulled his hands back and looked away.

"Thank you," he said.

They heard Kirk's car pull into the driveway outside. He honked his horn, and Jeremiah said sadly, "I guess it's time."

Marnie stood and pushed the footstool out of the way. Jeremiah labored out of his seat and Marnie offered him her arm. He collected the letters and the photograph, leaned against her and shuffled toward the door.

In the foyer, Marnie handed Jeremiah his hat. "Thank you for coming, Jeremiah. I feel I've barely scratched the surface of my grandmother's life."

"I feel that way, too."

He felt small and lonely. She opened the front door, and he walked to Kirk's car. Kirk hobbled out and opened the back door for him—Jeremiah couldn't decide which of them was more decrepit.

He got in and looked out at Marnie through the rear window—she was barely visible, framed in the shadows of the doorway. He waved. They rolled slowly down the drive, and Marnie stood watching them go, cool and collected, seeming now so much a part of the Hawthorne Mansion.

16

AN EQUAL AND OPPOSITE REACTION

Kate sat in the recliner in her parents' living room, wishing she could enjoy the afternoon breeze blowing through the open window. Instead, she was staring through the window screen, worrying, as her father stormed out to meet the white pickup truck that had just pulled into their driveway.

The bright red logo on the truck's door identified it as a Marathon Oil truck, which could mean only one thing: they were coming to make another offer on the oil rights to the Benjamin land. Kate's father was fuming. One of these days, she felt sure, he was going to give himself another heart attack. He was always angry, and though Kate often believed his anger justified, she wished he could let it go.

The Benjamin land occupied a potentially lucrative drilling site. The Mathers, whose field encircled the Benjamins' plot, had sold their oil rights earlier in the year, which made Marathon's pursuit of the Benjamins more urgent. The big oil companies typically wouldn't drill an area until they had secured a square mile of land, six hundred forty acres, and if Mr. Benjamin didn't lease them his rights, they would have to break protocol in order to work the Mathers field. Marathon hated breaking protocol. They had made half a dozen offers in the last six months, each more lucrative than the last, but Mr. Benjamin was steadfast in his refusal.

The standard deal was straightforward: Marathon would pay a certain amount of money up front for drilling rights, and the company would incur all the costs of digging the wells, building the pumps and exploiting the find. If they found enough crude to process, the owner of the land would receive twelve-and-a-half percent of the market price per barrel for as long as the well was productive—if they found significant quantities of oil on your land, you'd have income for years or generations to come, and that was how many farmers in Lawford County subsisted when harvests were poor or crop prices fell.

"What's your father so worked up about?" Mrs. Benjamin called from the kitchen.

"It's the oil-lease guy," Kate yelled back. Through the screen in the living room window, she could hear the Marathon representative greeting her father with talk about the weather—textbook farm etiquette.

Kate leaned against the window sill and wished she could make the oil guy go away, wished she could make the whole house go away. She did not want lunch, nor did she want to go back to the field. She was fed up with everything: the harvest and her parents and especially Jon Ridgely, the thought of whom made her heartsick. This limbo was maddening. She wanted reassurance or violence or anything at all besides the dull weariness of working in the field and waiting for Jon to call and wondering what Jon was doing.

"You can save the small talk," Kate's father was saying outside.

"Let me tell you the new offer we've put together, then."

Gossip about Jon's affair with Marnie Hawthorne was all over town. Kate's friends had called her and timidly asked how Jon was doing, trying to squirrel out some telling detail, which Kate resented. She made her friends confess every rumor they'd heard, and they delivered their gossip with a healthy dose of self-righteous indignation, in order to cover their own prurient interest. Mrs. Benjamin had heard the rumors around town, and Mr. Benjamin had taken every opportunity to join the chorus of condemnation. Jon had been so distant and cagey lately that Kate could no longer defend him—it was just assumed around town that he and Marnie were having an affair, and Kate felt weak in the face of it.

On their recent trip to Terre Haute, Kate had tried to discuss Marnie and the rumors. She had given Jon every opportunity to reassure her, and while he had affirmed his love and fidelity in words, his actions told another story. His gaze shrank and shifted when he looked at her, he seemed perpetually distracted and his complaints of overwork rang false. Ploughman's Grill was no busier than usual, and his stories for the *Constitution* had become, for some reason, less frequent as the court date for adjudicating Dorothy Hawthorne's will drew near. There was nowhere he was plausibly going all the time—unless he was having an affair. Kate now found it difficult to believe otherwise, no matter how much she wanted to, and Jon would not address the issue in any real way. He dismissed her worries, glibly or seriously or petulantly, but with such little care that, even if the rumors weren't true, she felt offended.

Kate did not want her relationship with Jon to end, but she could not go on like this. She felt ill, watching four years of love and devotion fall apart so shabbily.

"We're gonna give you four hundred dollars an acre," the Marathon man said. "That's eight thousand dollars, and I've got the check made out right here." He held out a check. "That's well above market price, Mr. Benjamin—well above."

"I don't see why my plot matters to you people," Kate's father said. "You're gonna drill up Mathers' corn field, anyway, so why don't you just go ahead with it? Why do you keep bothering me?"

"We're not trying to bother you, Mr. Benjamin, we're trying to make you some money. And we have a system of doing things that helps minimize the risks. That's all we're trying to do."

"Minimize the risks to you."

"And maximize the profits to you."

This oil talk bored Kate. They had been drilling Lawford County for more than half a century, and the untapped crude remaining in the ground, after so much exploration, couldn't amount to much; but Marathon wouldn't rest until they had squeezed every last drop from the earth. She heard her mother singing off-key in the kitchen, and she wanted to scream.

She had felt so lonely these last few weeks, as Jon had slipped silently away, that everything else in her life had begun to seem empty. She recognized with horror that she had slowly, unconsciously, organized her whole life around Jon—and more horrifying still, she had been happy to do it! Jon was her center. Without that center, her life with her parents, the pleasures she took in Templeton and her old childhood friendships seemed paltry. She couldn't decide which upset her more: Jon's unfaithfulness or her absolute dependence on him in the first place.

"And what if you drill an empty well?" Mr. Benjamin said outside. "What then?"

"You'll still have the money for the rights."

"Just like the Rheinhards? That was a nice piece of work."

The previous year, Marathon had drilled the Rheinhard farm, several miles away on Squirrel Hill Lane, and had found nothing but sulfates and brine. They had abandoned the project and left a forty-square-yard hole in the ground, with all of the dirt still heaped to the side.

"Is anybody going to fill that hole? How much do you think that'll cost?"

"We'll fill it in," the Marathon man said. "These things just take time. Surveying, drilling, restoring—it all takes time."

"And what about the water? You're going to clean that up too?"

"Lunch is ready," Kate's mother sang. "Would you call your father and tell him to stop fooling around with those idiots?"

Kate yelled through the window screen. "Lunch, daddy! Come inside and eat." The Marathon representative waved at Kate. She turned away from the window and slouched into the kitchen.

She felt like breaking a plate; instead, she helped herself to the food her mother had prepared and then sat down at the table. She ate angrily, enjoying the pacifying effect of great mouthfuls of bratwurst and potato salad.

"I wish he'd stop talking to those people," her mother said. "It only gets his blood pressure up."

"He can't agree to disagree."

Going to the fields, coming back to the house, talking to her parents; going to the fields, coming back to the house, sleeping; getting up in the morning and going out first thing to the fields and always, always coming back to this stupid house on this stupid country road five miles from the nearest stupid town. The land, the seed contracts, the oil rights, her parents, Jon Ridgely—Kate hated it all. Driving into town, which had so recently seemed so enjoyable, now felt like a slow ride to purgatory, where they punished her with pitying stares.

Kate's father came in. "They're up to four hundred an acre."

"Sit down and eat."

"You know what they want, don't you?"

Kate couldn't believe they were going to have this conversation again, but there was no stopping her father once he got started. She got up and served herself another huge helping of potato salad.

"They want to use our land as a sluice," Mr. Benjamin continued. The oil drillers used fresh water to prime their wells—they typically dug a football-field-sized hole next to the drill site and filled it with water. "They're going to redirect the flow of our stream and use it to prime their damn wells. They'll ruin the field and the stream and nobody'll ever plant there again."

"Here, let me fix you a plate," Mrs. Benjamin said.

"And they drill right through the water table," Kate's father went on. "The solvents they use to break up the crude and the minerals—where do you think they end up? Why does our water look so rusty since they drilled Squirrel Hill Lane? The mercury and the lead from the wells, that's why! And why does it smell so clammy? From the benzene and formaldehyde they use! It's all going right into our water and right into the crops and right onto our tables!" Kate's mother set a plateful of food in front of Kate's father, but he ignored it. "It's worse than pesticide! And these guys think a few thousand dollars can pay for that!"

"You won't convince the Ullreys," Mrs. Benjamin said. The Ullreys had recently sold their oil rights, and two of their wells had struck huge reserves. Now they were adding a wing to their house and driving a new sport utility vehicle.

"The Ullreys might as well eat that oil they're pumping, because their corn's gonna taste like benzene from now on. They're mortgaging the whole county's future—the future of the land—so they can have a luxury car they don't need in the first place."

Kate slammed her fork down on the table. "Shut up! Will you please just shut up!" Her parents stared at her. "We know, daddy, all right, we already agree with you, so will you please stop lecturing us!" She burst into tears.

"Kate, honey." Her mother put her arm around Kate's shoulders. Kate leaned into her mother's breast and cried.

"What is it?"

"I'm sorry, Katie," her father said.

Kate snuffled. "No. It's not you, daddy."

"Then what is it?"

Kate sobbed into her mother's bosom for a moment before she could gather herself to speak. When she finally did, she yelled. "That bitch is ruining my life."

"What bitch, dear?" asked her mother.

"Marnie Hawthorne."

"Oh," Mr. Benjamin said. "I thought you meant Jon."

Kate stamped her foot under the table. "That isn't funny."

"But you said—"

"What was I supposed to say?! That Mrs. Sanford was right? That Connie Carter was right? That my boyfriend is a liar and a cheat?"

"You don't know that for sure," Mrs. Benjamin said. Unlike her husband, she had grown fond of Jon and wanted to think the best of him. "You can't trust gossip—that's why they call it gossip. Remember last year when they said the dairy was closing? And there was no truth to it at all."

"No," Kate said, pushing her mother away. "They sold out to a bigger dairy."

"See?"

"Very comforting, mom. I swear, sometimes—" She pushed her plate away in disgust.

"Why don't you ask Jon about it?"

"What do you think I've been doing?" Kate yelled. "Don't you pay any attention?"

"And what does he say?"

"God! What do you think he says? He says it's just gossip." She wiped her eyes with her napkin. "But if you hear the same rumor from twenty different people. . ."

"Maybe it's just because he's writing all those stories in

the paper," Mrs. Benjamin said. "You know, it might give people the wrong idea, like, 'how does he know all those insider things, unless he's having an affair?'"

"Nice daydream, mom, but where's he been disappearing to? Why won't he return my calls?"

"He calls you five times a day. How many times have I told you to stop yakking on that cell phone and get back to work?"

"But he's never at home."

Mr. Benjamin broke in. "You know who I'd talk to? I'd talk to the bitch."

Kate almost never agreed with her father's ideas about relationships, and this suggestion struck her as unusually cranky and hopeless. Still, there was something about it that appealed to her.

"You know, dad," Kate said. "You might actually be onto something." If two people were having an affair and you didn't think one of them was telling the truth about it, it might be reasonable to ask the other. If not productive, it might at least be cathartic.

"You realize, don't you," Mrs. Benjamin said, "that your dad watches soap operas all day while we're gone?"

"I don't hear you suggesting anything better," Mr. Benjamin said.

"I just don't think confronting Marnie Hawthorne is such a good idea."

"Why not? At least she'd be getting somewhere, instead of moping around here all the time."

"But what good would it do?"

"She'll find out one way or another, and then she'll know where she stands and what she should do."

"But Marnie Hawthorne is a married woman. If she were having an affair, she wouldn't admit it. If I were having an affair, I wouldn't admit it."

"If you even thought of having an affair, it'd be written all over your face."

"Oh, would it? And you'd know?"

"I'd know, believe me."

"Maybe you don't know everything you think you know."

"All right!" Kate yelled. "You two are unbelievable. Nobody's having any affairs in this house. Let's just eat."

They continued eating and Kate's parents managed to stay silent for a few minutes, before her father started fuming about the Marathon representative again. Kate had a whole afternoon of work ahead separating and collecting the corn, and the clouds in the south were threatening rain. There would be no time to do anything dramatic now, but she let this new idea pip around in her brain.

She could confront Marnie Hawthorne. She wasn't sure what she might gain by doing so; just considering it meant that she had accepted the fact that Jon could no longer be trusted. Approaching Marnie Hawthorne could not fix that, but Kate had felt sapped for so long that even a useless act seemed like an improvement. As she finished her bratwurst, she resolved to drive into town that evening, perhaps right up to the Hawthorne Mansion, and test the possibilities.

* * * * *

At sundown, Kate and her mother returned from the field and pulled their pickup into the drive. It had been a typically grueling day, but Kate emptied the truck quickly, with practiced efficiency. She ran upstairs and took a quick shower. As she dried herself, she stared at her reflection in the steamy bathroom mirror, torn between the desire to primp and the need to move quickly before common sense took hold and she lost her nerve. She thought how plain she probably looked next to Marnie Hawthorne; but then, she wasn't trying to win a beauty contest. She tied her hair back in a ponytail, threw on some old jeans and a t-shirt and dashed out to her car, without saying goodbye to her parents.

She took Harvey Road to Squirrel Hill Lane, the back way into Templeton. She lacked the bravado to drive right down Main Street to the Hawthorne Mansion for everyone to see, and she hated Jon for making her so self-conscious every time she went to town.

Lightning flashed to the south. The wind was blowing briskly and she hoped their crops would be spared the coming storm. Besides Jon, her family's farm was the only thing that mattered, and she wondered if that would be enough if her relationship with Jon failed. The winter vacation she had been longing for now loomed like a vast empty space.

As she cruised past Shinglerock Creek on Beech Lane, she had grave misgivings about her present course: confronting Marnie Hawthorne could yield results worse than uncertainty. She might find Jon at the Hawthorne Mansion, and she wasn't sure how she would handle such a thing. Badly, she imagined. Her secret hope was still to exonerate Jon and then find out what was really driving them apart. She had every confidence that, short of Jon's actually cheating on her, any other problem could be resolved.

She felt pathetic.

As she passed the hospital, traffic increased and her pulse quickened. Turn around, she told herself. Keep your dignity, at least. She couldn't believe Jon was doing this to her. She was so infuriated and hurt that she couldn't even feel her anger any more. Surely, this can't be me, she thought, driving into town to check up on my boyfriend again, going to a strange house to accuse a strange woman of stealing my man. Surely, I'm not humiliating myself like this.

She turned into the so-called wealthy section of Templeton. Kate had always been baffled by the pretensions of this hick town's supposed elite. It wasn't hard to amass more money than a few dirt farmers. Nobody outside of Southern Illinois had ever heard of Templeton, yet the people who lived in this district acted as if the world owed them something for their meager success. Only the Hawthornes had the kind of money that mattered in the wider world, and the Hawthornes were crazy enough to stay in this backwoods. The rest of these thick-necked country socialites were as trapped here as the farmers they despised—without the Hawthornes' golden toffee bars to fuel the economy, all the oil money and trust funds in Lawford County wouldn't amount to a hill of beans.

It was pitch dark by the time Kate reached Poplar, and she was relieved to approach the Hawthorne Mansion under the cover of night. She couldn't believe how angry she was. The closer she got to Marnie, the angrier she felt, and she realized that it wasn't evidence one way or another that she wanted tonight—she wanted to hurt Jon, to make him feel what she had been feeling. She suddenly understood that she was secretly hoping that Jon really would be there, that she could witness their affair with her own eyes, so she could unleash her fury.

This is a bad idea, she told herself. She didn't want to be involved in some squalid scene. If she met Marnie under these circumstances, she would feel like a tremendous fool, but if she turned around right now and drove home, she would feel utterly empty and defeated. If she went to Jon's apartment, she would feel lonely and rejected whether he was there or not. She had nowhere to go, no good options. Perhaps this is the true legacy of the Hawthornes, she thought, that no one can interact with them without melodrama.

She parked at the edge of the Hawthorne property and got out of her car. The air was heavy with rain, and a cool wind swirled around her, whipping the branches of the trees overhead into a whirr of scratchy noise. She felt disembodied.

She strode up the driveway, gawking at the shadowy form of the mansion. She had passed this estate many times, had heard and told legends about it many times, but she had never come here, and from the looks of it she didn't want to be here now. She couldn't keep her eyes on the house—it was too derelict and pompous. Instead, she stared at the gravel directly in front of her, walked past the dark compact car in the drive and marched up the brick walkway to the porch. Before she had a chance to reconsider, she clonked the brass knocker against the door.

Her heart was pounding. She felt fever coursing through her blood. She had no idea what she was about to do.

The door was flung open and Kate found herself standing in front of a man. He was tall and stocky, blonde, with a mustache. He wore a tan sweater and white corduroy pants. He seemed ready to rush out, his lips already parted in a greeting, but he came up short and looked at her uncomprehendingly.

"Hello?" the man finally said. "May I help?" He had a patrician English accent.

Kate stammered, softly, "M-May I speak to Marnie Hawthorne please?"

"Are you a friend of hers?"

"Sort of."

They looked at one another. Kate felt peculiar and out of place.

"She's not here, I'm afraid," the man said.

Kate realized: an Englishman, at the Hawthorne Mansion! "Are you her husband?"

"Yes, that's right. Oh, forgive me." The man held out his hand. "Graham Harris."

Confused, Kate shook Graham's hand. "Kate Benjamin,"

she said and then mentally kicked herself for giving her name.

"Won't you come in? I'm afraid I've forgotten my manners."

"No, that's all right, thank you. I just wanted a quick word with your—with Marnie."

"Is there a message?"

"No, I don't guess so." Kate wanted to go, but she stood still. She hadn't imagined meeting Marnie's husband. She opened her mouth to say—she didn't know what—and then closed it again, but her mind went racing ahead without her and she said, half-consciously, "I thought you were in England."

Graham put his hands in his pockets and shrugged. "Say, um—I don't remember Marnie mentioning you—are you from the toffee plant?"

"Yes."

"So she's not there now, obviously, if you're looking for her here?"

"No," Kate said. "I just had a message for her—from the toffee plant—but it can wait till morning. Thank you." Without quite being in control of her own body, she turned and walked quickly down the driveway.

"I'll tell her you stopped by?" Graham called.

Kate continued marching until she was completely off the property. She got into her car, turned the ignition and raced down Poplar Street.

Nothing like gumming up the works, she thought uncertainly, her anger now thin and objectless. She wasn't sure what this new development meant. As she reached Main Street, she pulled out her cell phone and dialed Jon's number. His answering machine picked up.

She drove toward downtown, thoughtlessly, almost involuntarily. She turned onto Sycamore Lane, heading with increasing bleakness toward Jon's apartment. She could not quite admit to herself the new alarm that was creeping over her. The prospect of discovering Marnie at Jon's apartment frightened her much more than the possibility of finding Jon at the Hawthorne Mansion. A flutter ran through her chest.

Kate skirted the edges of Deerfield Park, careening past the city pool and fairgrounds, squealing her tires around every corner. As she turned onto Cross Street, her headlights swept across the soccer fields and she saw a couple walking arm and arm in the dark. Their backs were to her. The woman was small and blonde, with curly hair, and the man was taller and darker. Her heart leapt into her throat. They turned severely away from the street and walked faster, farther into the park.

Kate accelerated past the Blue Cup Café and skidded to a stop in front of Fendick's Glass and Mirror. She leapt out and ran to Jon's landing. A white sedan was parked at the foot of the stairs, next to Jon's truck. His motorcycle was there, too.

It was him. It had to be him. Jon was walking in the park with Marnie.

Everything around her slowed—her mind was moving so frantically fast that the rest of the world seemed petrified, and her thoughts slipped by more felt than known, like river snakes in the slipstream, slithering invisibly through the murk. She felt dumb.

With extraordinary effort, she turned and forced her leaden legs to carry her back to her car. She got in. She didn't know what to do. The idea of confronting Marnie, of unleashing her rage at Jon, froze into a cold steel ball in her chest.

She started the car and drove without purpose to the Square, then around the Courthouse. She headed west on Main. As she passed Ploughman's, she slowed out of habit and looked in through the picture windows: Martina was there, as usual, wiping off a table. Jon was walking in the park with

Marnie.

She was too shocked to cry. She had never, deep in her heart, believed that Jon could do this to her and her disbelief had lulled her into a purgatory of anticipation—she had become so used to dreading this moment, expecting it as part of the future, that its arrival in the present stunned her. A car horn honked, and she realized that she had slowed almost to a stop on Main Street. She speeded up, took the next right turn and pulled to the curb.

The reality of Jon's betrayal corkscrewed up and down in her chest. She had to force herself to breathe, but she could only sip air. She sat, she wasn't sure how long, as the wind kicked up stronger and the smell of rain sieved into the car.

When she finally looked beyond the dashboard at the world outside, she realized that she was facing north on Argus Street, pointing toward the Hawthorne Mansion. She stomped on the accelerator and squealed her tires again, whipped into the Hawthorne driveway and skidded to a stop right next to Graham's car, kicking loose gravel against it. She leapt out, left the engine running and rushed up to the front door, pounding on it first with the knocker and then with her fists.

Graham appeared. "Hello again," he said warily.

Wind thrashed the hedges in front of the house, and Kate shouted above the violent gusts. She spoke quickly, so she wouldn't lose her nerve.

"I lied before. I don't work for Hawthorne Toffee. I came to talk to your wife because she's having an affair with my boyfriend." Graham squinted, and he leaned forward as if he couldn't quite understand what Kate was saying. "His name is Jon Ridgely. She's with him right now. He lives at 214 South Cross Street, above Fendick's Glass shop." A tremendous sob shook Kate's shoulders and she burst into tears. "It's just off the Square. I know this doesn't make any sense to you, but it's true." Graham took a step toward her, his mouth open and his brow furrowed. "Jon Ridgely. He works for the newspaper. They've been having an affair for—" Graham extended his hand as if to touch her but then dropped it again to his side. "They're having an affair," she gasped between sobs. "Everyone knows it. Jon—" Kate couldn't look at Graham's face any more. "Jon Ridgely."

She stood still, caught between sobs, the world a heavy, hazy blur. Graham said something she didn't really hear and took another step toward her, but she couldn't bear to talk to him any more and she didn't want him to look at her. She turned and sprinted for her car.

Even before she closed the driver's side door, she jammed the transmission into gear and pumped the accelerator. Gravel flew up behind her—she heard it ricocheting off of Graham's car again. Her foot slipped off the gas pedal, the spinning tires caught and the car darted forward. She barely missed an elm tree at the edge of the drive. Her car fishtailed into Poplar Street.

Half a mile away, swerving out of control, she realized that she was going to have an accident if she didn't stop. She slammed on her brakes and skidded to a halt sideways in the middle of the street. She sat there, trying to come back into her body.

Her throat felt like plastic. She slumped forward with her head on the steering wheel and cried. She let the tears flow freely down her face and into her mouth and onto the steering wheel.

She stayed there a long time, sobbing, inwardly frantic, forgetting entirely where she was, not really caring. She didn't even notice when the storm finally arrived, and rain swept over her car and washed down the street in dirty streams.

17

A Loss of Equanimity

Marnie didn't know what to think when she pulled into her driveway at three in the morning and found a maroon-colored car there. Her instincts were clouded by dreaminess, wine and the languor of lovemaking—she was feeling drowsily satisfied and this dark car didn't make sense.

She had spent the whole evening with Jon, walking in the park, making love, drinking champagne, making love again, and then lying in Jon's bed listening to the thunder and rain. The storm had swept through violently and then settled into a pattering, deliciously seductive drizzle, the perfect accompaniment to Jon's ardent declarations. It was like being in a fairy tale, and Marnie did not want to wake up; but as she sat in her car, staring at the maroon compact in her driveway, she realized that all was not well. She fluttered back into real time.

It occurred to her vaguely that she might be in danger and she clicked the car's automatic door lock. She peered all around, into the thick mist left by the storm, but she saw nothing unusual aside from the strange car itself.

Parking a car in the driveway was very unburglar-like, and there was nothing menacing in the air, just a feeling that things were cockeyed. It did not occur to her that Graham might be there. He was the most methodical man Marnie had ever known, not given to deviating the slightest jot from a plan, and he wasn't due to arrive until early the next week.

Marnie got out of her sedan and walked cautiously to the other car, which glistened wet in the darkness. It had Missouri license plates and the bracket around the rear plate advertised the same company she had rented her sedan from. Her heart sank. She rummaged in her purse for her cell phone, turned it on and found three messages from Graham.

Graham organized his fun, budgeted his money, watched the clock—his consistency made him a good recording engineer and a good husband, and it made his sudden appearance here not just inconvenient but alarming. Marnie could think of no reason for Graham to have flown four thousand miles, then driven two and a half hours through strange country to arrive on her doorstep without telling her he was coming. Under normal circumstances, he would have planned the date weeks in advance and asked her to meet his plane in St. Louis (in fact, that was what he had done). There was no way he could have completed work on the album he'd been mastering. He must have left the project unfinished—still more uncharacteristic behavior. Graham's phone messages said only that he wanted to surprise her, but his tone was somber and by the third message he sounded more distraught than disappointed that she wasn't at home.

Marnie had known this moment would come eventually, the moment when her actual life would meet the fantasy she had been living, a fantasy that, until now, had seemed more or less safe. She had imagined being in complete command when the day came—meeting Graham at the airport with gifts and kisses, carefully orchestrating her affair with Jon, but now she realized that her confidence had depended on a previously unconscious illusion of control.

She walked to the front door, wishing she could be happy that Graham was here, but she simply didn't want to see him, didn't want to wake from her dream yet. She wanted to go on being the quixotic and alluring Hawthorne heiress, not the common middle-class wife, and she realized with a start that those two things had become mutually exclusive in her imagination.

She wondered if she had given Graham cause to suspect her affair. In addition to his steadiness, Graham was also the least jealous person Marnie knew, so it seemed unlikely that he had come all this way in a fit of lover's pique. And yet, here he was.

She went inside. The house was dark and silent. "Graham," she called. She turned the chandelier's dimmer switch to high. There was no sign of her husband.

She walked into the parlor and switched on a table lamp. Graham's suitcases—a single wardrobe bag and a large satchel—rested in a chair across the room. His luggage sucked all the old morbidity out of the parlor and replaced it with a different kind of deadness, the inertia of normal life, and this token of her ordinariness made Marnie aware that she had become accustomed to lolling around this extravagant gothic mansion, reinventing herself in its image.

"Graham!"

She walked through the wine closet into the kitchen. She flipped on the light and saw more evidence of Graham's presence—he had fixed himself tea and eaten some toffee. A wisp of air brushed her cheek, and she looked toward the breakfast nook, where the door to the veranda was open.

She would have to gather herself into a credible reproduction of Graham's wife, fast. This might not be easy, she thought, coming home at three in the morning tousled and smelling of sex.

She walked onto the veranda apprehensively, but Graham was not there. She watched the garden. The back yard was lit by the diffuse gray glow of moonlight, filtering through the parting storm clouds and lingering mist.

She couldn't think what to do. She was about to go upstairs

to check the bedrooms when a shadow crossed the fountain. As she watched, it became the recognizable silhouette of her husband, which then disappeared into a farther section of the garden.

Marnie's heart thumped and she came wide awake. Tears welled in her eyes, the conviction of shame so strong and sudden that she had to catch her breath.

She wondered how dire the situation actually was. She had been out late. That wasn't such a crime. Perhaps she had been to St. Louis, maybe to a show she had attended on the spur of the moment. She had been lonely, she had gone off to St. Louis to escape this stifling little town, they must have passed each other on the highway, how funny! She was only feeling guilty because she was guilty—she didn't necessarily appear guilty. Why shouldn't she be delighted to see him? She could explain this misunderstanding away. She could make fun of him: see, this is why you hate surprises, because they never turn out the way you think. She took a deep breath, shook the guilt and cobwebs out of her head and smiled a bright, welcoming smile for practice. But her explanations sounded lifeless in her mind and she could feel her eyes giving her away.

She stepped outside and eased the veranda door closed silently behind her. Her face and arms felt wet all over again in the cool mist. She shivered, which made her feel vulnerable and out of control. She walked stealthily toward the garden, unable to convince even herself of her innocence and delight.

As she rounded the first hedge, she saw Graham's profile again. He was kneeling, hunched-over, perhaps fifteen yards away, inspecting the blooms on a rose bush. His attitude was so peculiar that Marnie lost her forced, unconvincing jauntiness as she walked up the path.

Graham did not move to greet her. Marnie drew closer, and he continued to gaze straight ahead at the roses.

"Graham?"

His knees were creating divots in the mud of the flower bed, and his corduroy pants were stained up and down with muck, where he had apparently been wiping his hands. Graham loved to garden, but he was also fastidiously neat and unused to such carelessness.

She put her hand out to touch his shoulder, but he flinched and drew away. He was soaking wet and must have been waiting here in the garden for hours.

"What are you doing out here?"

"Where have you been?"

"I went to St. Louis. I went shopping and saw a show." Marnie cringed—the lie had come out too fast and too easily. "When did you get in? Why didn't you tell me you were coming? I would have picked you up."

Everything else Marnie could think to say sounded false in her head, so she said nothing, and this made things worse. Graham's refusal to look at her made her feel doubly accused, and she wanted to drop to her knees and throw her arms around his shoulders. Her conscience began giving her reasons to confess, so quickly and eagerly that she was amazed at her lack of nerve. She wanted to go back, to erase everything she had done in Templeton, to begin again exactly as they had left off in London.

Graham pointed to a rose bush. "You see these?" he said gravely. "Do you know what they are?"

"No, Graham. I don't. Roses."

"They're hybrid tea roses." For a long time, he said nothing more, but Marnie felt that he was gathering himself for something important. "That's the kind you get at the florist. It's hard to see in this light, but I think this is an English variety called Princess of Wales. It's very popular." He paused. "See those over there?" He pointed to some shrubs a few yards away. "I think those are First Kiss. I could be wrong, there are so many different roses, but. . . these two are very common. You see them everywhere." His voice sounded dead. "Most of the varieties here I've never seen before."

"Graham?"

Graham loved to visit manor gardens, and he read gardening books and watched gardening television shows. His great dream was to own a house in the country, and the Hawthorne garden was the thing that had truly excited him about Marnie's letters from Templeton.

"The gardener could even be making his own hybrids." He said everything flatly, as if reciting. "Those near that gate are pink. See? And these over here are yellow and red. That's one way to tell what they are."

"Graham."

"I can't believe you didn't tell me about this."

"I told you all about the garden," said Marnie quickly, trying to pretend that his real meaning did not exist—she convinced herself that it didn't exist, in a flash. How could he possibly know about Jon? He didn't know. "What's wrong, Graham?"

"Closer to the fountain," Graham went on obstinately, "there are some white roses." His tone was so formal and affectless that he sounded as if he were making an official presentation, as if the flowers were evidence against Marnie. "There are more white ones near that trellis, but this gardener likes pinks and rubies—the white ones are different. The blooms are tighter." Finally, Graham looked up at her.

"Why don't we go inside?" she said. She battled her conscience, swinging between the impulse to confess and the contrary need to elaborate on her flimsy alibi.

"There's a scheme to the gradations," he said. "It's hard to make out in this light, but the pinker pinks are over there and the salmons are over here and the yellows. . ."

Marnie finally understood that Graham was furious. The incongruity between what he said and his meaning gave her a frightening feeling of isolation: his anger seemed impotent as he channeled it through the flowers, and this made Marnie feel strangely helpless herself. She wondered what he knew.

"There's something else, something you should have noticed," he went on stubbornly. He stood up and wiped his muddy hands on his pants. His blonde hair hung lank against his head. "It's hard to make out at first, but you begin to see it as you put your hands in the soil."

"Tell me what's wrong, Graham." Marnie heard a quiver in her voice and then the quiver moved down into her chest, and she trembled. At first, the little shudders resembled shivers, as if she were merely chilled from the rain, but they grew more unsteady and rapid. "Please, Graham, it's late and I'm freezing. Why don't we go in?"

Graham didn't move.

"I'll make you a cup of tea and you can tell me about your flight. Really, let's go in, you can tell me all about the roses in the morning." She touched his arm and her quivering suddenly stopped. "I'm so glad to see you!" she said spontaneously.

She was overwhelmed by the relief she felt at touching him, a relief she hadn't known she'd needed. She really was glad to see his lovely round face and his heavy mustache, and she felt a deep ache in her chest for what she had done. He scrutinized her coldly. When she tried to embrace him, he stepped back, and she felt sick. Unbidden, an image appeared in her mind, of lying next to him in bed, at home in Kensington, the drama of her brief life in Templeton only a dream, the prospect of coffee and eggs with Graham and a Sunday paper the true reality.

"Kate stopped in for a visit," he said.

"Kate?" Marnie looked at him quizzically. "Kate who?"

"Kate Benjamin. Jon Ridgely's girlfriend."

Jon's name sounded strange enough coming out of Graham's mouth, but coupled with the word "girlfriend" it became almost foreign. "Jon Ridgely's girlfriend?"

"Doesn't ring any bells?"

"I'm afraid it doesn't, Graham." Her shock at learning, in this way, that Jon had a girlfriend made it easier for Marnie to act naïve—she became genuinely confused.

"She came to tell me about the affair you've been having."

"Affair?"

Despite Marnie's longing to confess or to forget that she ever knew Jon Ridgely, Graham's demeanor made both things impossible. His mind was set, and Marnie would have to find a way to placate him right now, in order to give herself the opportunity of denials or confessions later. She was shaken by the idea that Jon had a girlfriend at all, a girlfriend he'd apparently been lying to her about. She felt betrayed. She had thought Jon an open book, a puppy in love for her to play with, and she was confused by the spike of jealousy she felt.

She strained to figure out how to handle her husband. To hide her uncertainty, she took a more aggressive tack.

"If that's what brought you out here in this muck—! I'm afraid you're ruining a perfectly good pair of pants for nothing." She reached out to touch his arm again, but Graham pulled back. "Come inside and put some dry clothes on and we can get to the bottom of this."

"I think I'm already at the bottom."

Marnie said, "Honestly, Graham, I've never heard of this Kate person."

"And Jon Ridgely?"

Marnie shook her head solemnly no. "Please, let's go inside."

"You've never heard of Jon Ridgely?"

Marnie looked into Graham's eyes and saw that he knew something he wasn't telling her. "Of course I've heard of him," she said. "He's a reporter for the local paper. He interviewed me when I first arrived—I'm sure I told you about it."

"No. You didn't."

"Well, I didn't think much of it."

"No?"

"No, I really didn't."

"Did you think much of this?"

He stuck his muddy hand into his shirt pocket and withdrew a sodden piece of paper, folded into a rectangle. He handed it to her. It was soiled and delicate as tissue, frayed at the creases, as if he had been opening it and refolding it over and over in the rain. Marnie unfolded the paper and saw Jon's handwriting.

"Was that part of his newspaper article?"

It was a love note Jon had left one night. After Marnie had escorted him out of the mansion, she had returned to bed to find the note on her pillow, and she was certain that she had then crumpled it up and thrown it away—she remembered throwing it away. But here she was holding it in her hand.

Graham's lips were pursed, as if he were about to say something, but no words came. Marnie couldn't have moved if she'd wanted to, as the indignation and hopelessness coiled tighter and tighter around them both with each passing second. Finally, when it seemed as if they might be trapped like that all night, Graham moved; he swayed toward her, and this released Marnie to reach out to him. She touched his face, and he fiercely slapped her arm away. She was so stunned by that slap that she didn't even react when he backhanded her across the cheek. Her neck snapped back and she staggered. She had never been hit before, and her shock hurt almost as much as the blow. Before she could turn to face him again, he pushed her with such force that both her feet came off the ground and she landed with a thud on her hip. Her head hit the ground and she bit her tongue.

She lay perfectly still, eyes closed, fearing what Graham might do next, but she soon realized that he was not hovering over her. She opened her eyes. He was striding quickly toward the house. She sat up. He opened the veranda door without looking back.

Marnie felt rooted to the spot, her cheek and tongue aching. Only a few moments passed before she heard a car door slamming from the front of the mansion and an engine starting. Not knowing exactly what she was doing or why, she picked herself up and bolted toward the house.

She kicked her sandals off in mid-stride, stumbled, then regained her balance and sprinted toward the side of the mansion—she didn't have time to wend her way through the house. Her feet flew up behind her. She ran faster than she thought possible, rounding the corner and rushing helter-skelter through the darkness. A thorn pierced the ball of her right foot and she cried out and ran faster.

As she came to the hedge guarding the front, she heard Graham's tires crunching gravel. She flung the gate open and darted through, her bare feet smarting against the rocks of the driveway.

The tail lights of Graham's car rounded the bend in the drive. "Graham!" she screamed.

By the time she reached Poplar, his car was already a block away, veering in a wide arc onto Argus Street. She heard the engine wind tighter, and he disappeared into the night.

She stopped and stood in the middle of the street, heaving and panting. Her lungs and throat ached from the cool air, and she finally just doubled over and sat down, feeling her heart pound against her chest.

"Fuck," she said, quietly. She bent her head between her knees.

18

One Predictable Consequence

Jon was walking down Cross Street at eight in the morning, feeling unusually bright and alert. The previous night's storm had left the streets strewn with leaves and branches, and the morning air breathed a wet sigh of relief. The bronze doe at the head of Deerfield Park glistened in the sun. The morning was alive with the calls of scavenging birds: Jon watched them hopping and darting through the park as he strolled along sipping coffee from a plastic mug.

Maude, the *Constitution*'s editor-in-chief, had asked Jon to come in early this morning. It was only two days before the first probate hearing about the Hawthorne will, and Jon figured Maude wanted to brainstorm about the op-ed pieces and sidebars they would need to bulk out their coverage. He had already written up interviews with Josephine Longmore and Susan Meese that had not yet appeared in the paper, and he had a call in to Mack Fuller requesting a post-hearing interview—he could fill half the paper at a few hours' notice.

The whole county would be following the hearing. There were so many different potential outcomes of the competing claims that Jon hesitated to speculate about them. The will was more than ten years old, so the claimants would have trouble proving Dorothy's incompetence: she had written the document before she'd retired as CEO of Hawthorne Enterprises, and her mental incapacity at that time was by no means a foregone conclusion. Dorothy's relatives would have to make a claim based on her eventual deterioration, and the lawyers

Jon had interviewed had told him it would be nearly impossible to make such a case. But he also knew that the Fullers and Longmores had prepared for this day for many years, and it was hard to predict what private, damning information they might reveal about Dorothy.

In addition to the consequences the hearing might have for Templeton, it would have a direct effect on Jon himself. The claims against the will might be enforced or dismissed, or the judge might require a potentially lengthy inquest—the outcome could determine whether Marnie stayed in Templeton or not, whether she shuttled between Templeton and London over a period of years, or left and never came back. If this hearing proved the first volley in a war that lasted years, it was impossible to say what she might do, and though Jon tried to resolve himself to the temporary nature of their affair, every day he invented new reasons for hope.

He came to the Templeton Free Press building, on the corner of Cross Street and Ash. The Free Press Company occupied the entire first floor of a three-story brick transfer house. In addition to the Templeton *Constitution*, the company printed the Lawford County *Courier* (a monthly farm report), the *Handy Shopper* (a free advertising weekly) and yearbooks for the local schools.

"Morning, Allison," Jon said jauntily, as he walked into the lobby. The receptionist was setting doughnuts out next to the coffeemaker. "Nice storm last night."

Allison's eyes were puffy and bloodshot. "You might want to ratchet that pep down a notch. Maude's waiting for you."

"Bad mood?"

"Not good."

Jon selected a chocolate longjohn from the tray and topped off his coffee. He pushed through a swinging metal door into the news room.

The news room was a long, low space crowded with file cabinets and wooden desks. Most of the writing staff would not come in till later in the morning; now, only the copy editor was there, watching tv. Perched on wall mounts in the corners of the room, small color televisions transmitted satellite news reports, and a few computer monitors sat dormant on the desks—this was the extent of the *Constitution*'s concession to modern technology. There were still more manual typewriters in the office than laptops, and Maude believed digital speed was no substitute for solid reporting. She believed in "The Story" above all else, and she was fond of recounting the days when she wrote the entire newspaper by herself every day. She defied anyone to write cleaner copy than she did hunting and pecking on her old Underwood upright.

Jon greedily scarfed his doughnut. He washed it down with coffee and knocked on Maude's door.

"Come!"

The editor-in-chief had both elbows on her desk, a telephone receiver cradled between her shoulder and ear. She was twirling a lock of her short, bottle blonde hair with her left index finger. "Uh-huh," she said into the phone. "Uh-huh. All right. That's right. As soon as you can." She hung up and waved Jon into a seat. "You're late."

Maude's gaze was direct and piercing. In her late fifties, her face had become jowly, but she was still attractive, with deep smile lines around her eyes and mouth, which made her toughness seem all the more robust and disarming. She always wore smartly cut, dark skirt-suits, no matter what the season or temperature—she had a whole closet full of them, blue and brown and black, because she believed that no matter how hard a woman worked or what position she attained, she always had to dress for business or men would not take her seriously. She smoked cigarettes morning, noon and night. Today, a deep frown wrinkled her brow and Jon felt the tension in the air as soon as he sat down.

"Jon, we have a problem." She opened a file folder on her desk and handed him a sheet of paper. "You recognize this?"

It was a bill from Nellie's Restaurant. He checked the date and the itemized charges: it was from the evening he had met Marnie there, their first real date.

"Sure. I took Marnie Hawthorne there, to interview her about her grandmother."

"Mm-hm. I haven't seen that story yet?"

"I have some more people to talk to."

"I spoke with Nellie. She said you left the restaurant in a hurry that night."

"That's right. Marnie remembered some papers she had, some of her grandmother's letters she wanted to show me."

Maude appraised him coldly. "Look, Jon, you're a good writer. You've always been reliable for me—one of my best employees. But I can't have this."

"Have what?"

"Scuttlebutt is you're having an affair with Marnie Hawthorne. Anything to it?"

"No."

"Nothing to it at all?"

"No."

"And this?" She motioned for Jon to give her Nellie's bill back. "This was just a working dinner? In Palestine? And the fact that you left there with the Hawthorne girl in her car and didn't pick up your truck until the next morning—that doesn't mean anything?"

"It was late when I finished talking to her. I walked home that night from the Hawthorne Mansion."

"Nellie says Marnie dropped you off the next morning."

"That's right. She gave me a ride back."

"She picked you up at your apartment the next morning and drove you back to Palestine? Because that was more convenient than taking your truck home in the first place, when you left the restaurant? You know, Jon, people have seen you coming and going at the Hawthorne place."

Jon shrugged. "If I spent time getting to know Josephine Longmore, no one would say a word. It's just because Marnie's the heir, it makes tongues wag. You know how people are."

"That's right, Jon, I know how people are." She looked past Jon's head at the office wall. "See, I'm pissed off enough without your lying to me."

"I'm not lying to you."

"No?"

"No."

Maude took a cigarette from a pack on her desk and lit it. "You must really be in love." She exhaled smoke through her nose and shook her head. "Look, whatever else I feel about your fooling around with Marnie, I have my own reputation to protect. I have to sell papers and I can't have someone writing articles for me if he's personally involved with his subjects. See what I mean? It's a conflict of interest, all the more glaring in a story like this. It hurts my credibility. Not to mention the scandal, which I don't need attached to my business."

"So what are you saying, Maude? You're saying I'm not credible on the Hawthorne story any more?" Maude did not answer. "But the judge has called a hearing for the day after tomorrow! You can't take me off the story now."

"I'm not taking you off the story, Jon. I'm firing you."

He sat back in his chair. He couldn't believe his ears.

"It'll be hard to replace you. You know the town, you know how to write, you're fast. People used to trust you, and that's hard to come by, but nobody trusts you any more, not as a reporter, probably not for anything else. You wouldn't believe the calls I've been getting, the letters. People canceling their subscriptions, boycotting my advertisers." She gave Jon an opportunity to react, but he said nothing. "I've tried to reserve judgment, to let you work through this yourself, because you've always come through for me before. You may waver, but then you right yourself, or you come to me and ask for help, but this time—you just cross one line after another with Marnie Hawthorne and you don't care who you offend. I can't trust you any more, and I may be the last ally you've got—outside of Kate." She added this last comment with such irony and hostility that Jon felt like crawling into a hole.

"What does that mean?"

Maude took another drag on her cigarette. "You know, sometimes I can't decide if you're as simple as you pretend to be or if you're so convinced by your own incredible ideas of yourself that you think everyone else shares them." She blew smoke. "The bottom line is, if you're compromised, then I'm compromised. I'm giving you two weeks' severance pay. It'll be in the mail on the next pay cycle. And you can have till the end of the day to clean out your desk."

"No," Jon said. "You can't fire me because of some rumors. You can't fire somebody because of something you think might have happened, something somebody decided must have happened, with no evidence. You're a journalist! I just told you I'm not having an affair with Marnie Hawthorne. Besides, controversy is good, it means people are talking about the paper."

"No, controversial reporting is good. What you're doing, you're making yourself the story."

"Still, you can't fire me for an unsubstantiated rumor."

"Can I fire you for abusing your expense account, then? Do I have permission to do that?"

Jon had known that, by seeing Marnie, he was risking his relationship with Kate, but it had never occurred to him that he was risking his job at the paper as well. He could see the depth of his arrogance in Maude's hard disappointed eyes, and he felt childish.

"I don't know what to say."

"I'm sorry, Jon."

He felt deflated and saw no point in arguing any more. Maude was unassailable.

"Let me give you some advice, Jon, while you can still use it. Fooling around with the Hawthornes is no way to win points in Templeton. You already know what everyone thinks of that family, the good and the bad, and most of it's bad. And I'll tell you right now, whatever comes of your relationship with Marnie, no one is ever going to accept her. She's too pretty for the women and she's too rich and powerful for the men—there are only reasons to hate her, and everyone's going to hate the people she loves, out of envy if nothing else. You're only setting people against you. And if that weren't enough, you're running around on Kate, which makes the whole thing despicable. Kate's a good girl—she doesn't deserve to be treated like this. You're digging your own grave, right in front of everybody's eyes, and you act like you've never even touched the shovel." She stubbed out her cigarette while holding Jon's gaze with a look equal parts pity and disgust.

"But it's not too late, Jon. That's why I wanted to talk to you this morning—because I've always liked you, and you can still fix this. We all make mistakes, but you'd better screw your head back on, right now. This can be a hard town to live in if people decide they don't like you. People liked your mom and dad, and they've liked you for the most part, but you're spending their good will fast, and once it's gone, you can't get it back."

Jon had stopped listening. He was having trouble understanding that he had been fired and, much worse, that the whole town knew he was having an affair with Marnie. He thought he had taken adequate precautions, and now he felt profoundly embarrassed and weak. People all over town must have been pointing and talking about him behind his back, his secret affair an open topic at every bar and restaurant, every beauty salon.

"Get your stuff, Jon. I've got work to do."

He stood up slowly. He hesitated at the door, hoping for a word from Maude to call him back, but she remained silent. He left her office and stood frozen in the news room.

The copy editor looked up at him. The television news blared. He would not be coming here any more. He abandoned the things in his desk—the suddenly useless style manual and thesaurus, the junk office supplies. Did Kate know? Who knew? He wended his way between the desks and out the side door.

19

Claims Against The Will

Jeremiah shuffled down the main corridor of the Lawford County Court Annex on the northwestern edge of Templeton. The hallway was crowded with people chattering in expectation—preliminary rulings about the Hawthorne case would probably be handed down before lunch.

This corridor, Jeremiah thought indignantly, gave the impression of a long, open public bathroom. The walls were finished with beige ceramic tiles, the floor was a scuffed ashen gray and the ceiling managed to be ugly in spite of its attempt at undetectable blandness. There was no past in this building because no memories could stick to architecture this antiseptic, and Jeremiah believed the designers had intended just that. The whole complex reeked of veneered pressboard and drywall, and it would age badly since it was never intended to be anything but new. The idea of progress that these buildings represented—these strip mall offices and big box shopping centers and cookie-cutter municipal parks—was not improvement on the past so much as obliteration of it. Progress, to the people who built such structures, was an ideal of perpetual replacement, and if the past needed to be replaced, then it must necessarily have been a failure in some way, and no one wanted to be reminded of failure. He wished these proceedings were being conducted in the Old Courthouse downtown, where the importance of the past was unmistakable, in the design of the clock tower, in the patterns across the cornices, in the austerity of the staircases. The Old Courthouse had aged well because it had been intended to last.

Jeremiah stopped to drink from a stainless steel drinking fountain. "Excuse me, sir?" a female voice said. Jeremiah turned and found a woman in a dark blue pantsuit holding a photograph out to him. "I think you dropped this."

He took the photograph—it was the out-of-focus picture Marnie had given him. He stared at the woman. It seemed strange that the picture had escaped his sweater pocket, since he had been so protective and careful of it.

"Are you all right, sir?"

"I'm fine," he said irritably. The woman continued to probe his face until Jeremiah dismissed her with a roll of his eyes and a scoff.

A knot of people had gathered outside the probate hearing room, drinking sodas and eating candy bars. Some were claimants to other estates that were being settled, but most were idlers and gossips with an interest in the Hawthorne case. They had spent the whole morning listening to the judge rule on small family properties, sorting out estates with no wills, allocating assets to pay creditors and so on. It was all routine and the people on hand to see the fireworks surrounding the Hawthorne estate had grown bored; but the cases were moving along, and expectations were mounting again as the morning recess ended. Jeremiah stepped back into the probate room.

There was no judge's bench, jury box or witness stand, none of the accouterments usually associated with trials. It looked instead like a hotel conference hall, with yellow plastic chairs for the claimants and fold-out tables at the front for the judges and clerks. On these tables rested reams of papers and files, divided into neat groups, and an absurdly large black cassette recorder with two microphones. One of the microphones faced the judge's seat and another pointed toward the other end of the table, where a wooden chair served as the witness stand. It seemed more like a PTA meeting than a legal hearing.

The claimants to the Hawthorne estate were already back from the recess. Josephine Longmore, a prim seventy-five-year-old in an elegant black dress, was unconsciously pursing and unpursing her lips, fidgeting with her handbag. Mack Fuller, a mottled white octogenarian, whose tiny brown eyes were incapable of filling the sunken craters of his sockets, sat leaning forward against a cane. Susan Meese, the youngest of the claimants at sixty-nine, whispered ostentatiously to her two sour-faced daughters. Alexandra Bergren, the executor of the will, kept to herself in one corner of the room: she held a shabby leather satchel in her lap and wore a vintage green skirt-suit whose style had never been fashionable.

Marnie and Graham (whose unexpected presence was causing a stir in Templeton) were accompanied by a man in an impeccably tailored gray suit who carried an expensive-looking briefcase. Jeremiah had never seen this attorney before and thought that, for the price of his suit coat, most local lawyers could have furnished their entire offices. The attorney sat between Marnie and Graham and occasionally one or the other leaned close to speak with him, but the couple never spoke to each other and their body language and faces revealed some private strain. Marnie looked unwell—pale and distracted, with dark circles under her eyes.

Jon Ridgely had not turned up. Everyone knew that Jon had been fired from the *Constitution* and young Jake Ziegler, fresh from Eastern Illinois University, had been sent in his place; but Jeremiah half-expected Jon to show up anyway, to create a scene with Graham.

The tension in the room was palpable, but the morning session had so far been orderly and the Hawthorne claimants had all been polite to each other. After all, probate on the Hawthorne estate would not be closing today—Illinois law allowed six months to file claims before a will was finally executed. It was something of a mystery, as far as Jeremiah could gather, why the judge had convened the parties now, since the estate was still in probate. This circumstance made everyone edgy, uncertain what to expect.

Jeremiah sat down in a plastic chair at the back of the room and continued worrying about the mysterious typewritten letter and the photograph he had received from Marnie. He had been mulling his insubstantial clues in quiet agitation, but there seemed no way to investigate them—he could not prove when the provocative letter had been written or by whom, and he could not say for certain who the man in the photograph was. Instead, he pursued another oddity he had observed at the mansion, which he considered more concrete and telling. Dorothy had never cared a whit for nature, and Jeremiah knew that it took real effort to maintain a garden as magnificent as the Hawthorne rose garden. He speculated that whoever had mentioned Gravenstein apples in that letter might also have been capable of the beautiful order of the garden, especially if that person was Calvin Hawthorne.

Once this possibility had suggested itself, Jeremiah started thinking like a detective. He made phone calls—he knew every professional gardener in town capable of such handiwork—but no one had any idea who was maintaining the Hawthorne grounds. He had telephoned Marnie, and she had said that no landscaping service had ever come to the house and that she had never thought much about it. She had seemed oblivious to Jeremiah's implications and she'd hung up on him the moment her husband's voice had sounded in the background.

Jeremiah had then widened his search, calling everyone he could think of in a three county area: horticulture shops, garden supply stores and farm equipment salesmen. If someone wanted to have a garden as well turned out as the Hawthorne rose garden, he would have to buy supplies, fertilizer, pesticides; no matter his skill, he would require outside help. But no shops had sold the Hawthornes anything for years and no yellow-page landscapers had worked on the grounds. Before Jon's interview with Marnie had been published in the *Constitution*, no one had even been aware of the garden's existence.

This absence of knowledge was nettlesome. Jeremiah imagined that someone was tending that garden secretly somehow, and who would want to do such a thing? Most gardeners with such splendid botanicals would want to show them off.

"Pardon me," a voice at Jeremiah's elbow said. He turned in his seat. A man he didn't recognize was staring at him. "Are you all right?"

"What?"

"I'm sorry to bother you, but—are you feeling well?"

"Fine, fine," Jeremiah snapped. "Why do you ask?"

"No reason, I guess." He held his hands up in apology. "I was just going to offer you my handkerchief."

Jeremiah thought he might have a nose bleed, so he reached up and felt the end of his nose. When he brought his fingers down, they were wet, not with blood but with sweat. He touched his forehead. He was sweating profusely, all over. "Oh," he said, confused and embarrassed. "I guess it was warmer outside than I thought." He took the man's handkerchief and wiped his brow.

"Can I get you some water?"

"No. Thank you." Why was he sweating so much? He took a few deep breaths. The man hovered over him for a moment and then eased away, and Jeremiah immediately forgot about him and returned to his private anxieties.

He imagined that Calvin, after disappearing, might have exiled himself not to some remote foreign land, but into the heart of the Hawthorne Mansion itself. He might simply have never left that house after his supposed death in 1971. Dorothy's own voluntary seclusion for the last ten years of her life seemed to argue in favor of this idea, and he imagined them holing up there together, living out their incestuous dreams of love in utter solitude. There was ultimately no logic to this theory—why would a man fake his own death so he could secretly occupy a house he already owned?—but, in a perverse and inexplicable way, the very illogic of it seemed to Jeremiah to make it more plausible.

Calvin had remained steadfastly absent—no one ever saw him again after 1971, a fact that supported the official version that his disappearance was ultimately fatal. There were many miles of isolated Illinois forest where accidents could happen or bodies could be hidden, and Jeremiah was almost certainly the last person in Lawford County entertaining any notions at all about Calvin Hawthorne. But, Jeremiah thought, he was also the only person with a photo of Calvin from 1978.

The judge sauntered back into the courtroom. He wore a black suit but no judicial robes, and he stood at the front of the room talking informally to one of his clerks.

Despite the presence of so many interested spectators, the judge seemed exaggeratedly casual, as if to show that his office would not be swayed by the perceived importance of individual cases. He spoke to the clerk in this casual manner for what seemed a long time, and the crowd became silent without being asked. At last, the clerk turned on the tape recorder and a bailiff called the session to order. Everyone stood up, waited for the judge to take his place and then sat down again. The court reporter hovered tensed and ready over her stenograph machine.

The Hawthorne crowd was frustrated for another forty-five minutes, as the judge sorted two feuding brothers' claims to their dead mother's property outside Honey Creek. Jeremiah made a special point of observing Marnie and her husband. Graham's face remained grim but unperturbed, and Jeremiah noticed that Graham looked like Robert Meese, a fact he hadn't perceived earlier. It was like seeing Dorothy and Robert in their youth, and Jeremiah mopped his brow and thought there was one coincidence too many here—this resemblance, the photograph, the letter. He felt as if some larger plan were unfolding before him, in a pattern that depended on him to see it. After so many years of sitting in the wings of the Hawthorne drama, pining away alone, he felt that fate had placed him at center stage once again, only he wasn't sure what the play was any more.

The judge handed down a ruling in the Honey Creek case, and after a moment of paper filing and water sipping, he announced that he would consider matters arising from the will of Dorothy Elizabeth Hawthorne. He began by calling a roll of the claimants, asked their counselors to identify themselves and instructed them all to stand and raise their right hands. He administered an oath of honesty to the whole group at once.

"As you all know," the judge drawled in a thick Southern Illinois twang, "Illinois probate lasts six months, but in the event that the validity of a will is challenged, as in this case, the court may be obliged to hold hearings to determine if the challenges are valid. This particular meeting is not such a hearing. I've called you all here before the expiration of probate for a special purpose—namely, I'd like to save the county some time and money."

Jeremiah felt a puzzled restlessness sift through the courtroom. The judge had offered routine preambles before every other case, none of which sounded like this.

"I remind you," the judge continued, "that you are all under oath, and you will be held accountable for the things you say in this courtroom, but there will be no hearing as such, though I may entertain some discussion. I may. I've called you here today because I wish to dissuade reckless litigation and unsubstantiable claims regarding this will, and to clarify for the claimants, and their attorneys, what will and will not constitute legitimate claims."

The judge gave them a superior, folksy smile, challenging the attorneys to dispute his authority.

"The last will and testament of Dorothy Elizabeth Hawthorne," he continued, "provides that all properties, stocks, bonds, certificates of title, business incorporations and so on, including all material wealth and obligations proceeding from these possessions, should be transferred to her granddaughter, Marnie Alma Hawthorne, of London, England. I have three challenges to the will before me, based on the incompetence of Dorothy Hawthorne at the time of the document's creation. I also have one request for a state-appointed supervisor to administer the will until its execution."

The clerks, who in previous cases had remained busy, passing folders back and forth and whispering behind the judge's back, now sat silent and watchful, belying the atmosphere of routine that the judge had tried to create.

"In the motion filed on behalf of Susan Meese, requesting a court-appointed supervisor to administer Dorothy Hawthorne's estate, the motion is denied."

Susan Meese's mouth dropped open. Extravagant outrage blossomed on her face.

"Before her death, Mrs. Hawthorne duly appointed Alexandra Bergren of Hutsonville as her executor, and this court has reviewed Ms. Bergren's actions and found her capable and conscientious. Ms. Bergren has been accountable to this court beyond fault." The judge smiled at Alexandra Bergren, who mouthed a demure thank-you. "The court finds no cause to appoint an independent supervisor.

"As to the matter of the competence of Dorothy Hawthorne at the time of the making of this will—and this is why I have asked you all here today, because it occurred to me that some of you might not appreciate the full import of my words if they were merely written on the page. I'm speaking now specifically to you, Mr. Hanover, and you, Mr. Reid, and you, Ms. Coleman," the judge stared down each of the attorneys as he named them. "I will not have the time of this court wasted with frivolous contentions."

The mood had been growing more incredulous as the judge spoke, but now the courtroom deflated completely, like the drooping of a collapsed circus tent after the show: the judge had brought Dorothy's relatives here simply to dash their hopes. Jeremiah was as dumbfounded as everyone else. It hardly seemed possible that the liens and claims and accusations that had gripped the county's imagination for weeks on end could simply be waved away.

"The burden of proof falls to anyone claiming irregularity in properly prepared and filed documents. Though I have three different claims of Dorothy Hawthorne's incompetence before me, they are substantially identical, so I will discuss all three of them now in general, leaving aside for the moment their particular merits. Each challenge asserts Dorothy Hawthorne's incompetence at the time she signed this will—to wit, November 1, 1991—yet the proofs offered in each date from after the creation of the instrument and include no evidence, as such."

The judge seemed to be enjoying his work this morning. He looked at Marnie to see the effect of this apparently good news, but she stared disconsolately before her, as indifferent to the judge's pronouncements in her own case as she had been to all the others. Graham remained stoic as well.

Though not much was known about Graham, it was rumored that he had spent several nights at the Templeton Country Inn when he had first arrived in town, which had raised speculations at the barber shop that Marnie had thrown Graham over for Jon. However, Graham had since moved into the mansion and Jon had not been seen there for many days, so there was considerable doubt about what was going on. Whoever ended up with Marnie might also end up with the Hawthorne money, and it was thought that Graham, as Marnie's husband, might already be entitled to half of downtown Templeton, whether Marnie left him or not. Most galling to Jeremiah's customers was the prospect that their sons and daughters might eventually wind up working for Jon Ridgely.

Jeremiah felt a prickling at the back of his neck, and he looked over his shoulder. He saw a face peering in at the narrow sliver of glass in the courtroom door. He squinted—the glass was tinted, and the hallway seemed dark through it. It looked like an old man was looking in, but Jeremiah could see only his nose and part of his cheek. The face lingered for a moment and then moved away, and a chill shook Jeremiah's body.

He reached into his pocket for the mysterious photograph, comparing the blurry face there with the fleeting glimpse of the face he had just seen in the window. He suppressed the impulse to leap up and dash for the door—an old man was lurking in the hall outside!

"In the first instance," the judge addressed the assembly again, "regarding claims of the decedent's incompetence, I would like to say that the rulings of this court are not capricious. These claims have been evaluated with due diligence."

Jeremiah sat petrified, his heart thudding wildly. Was Calvin Hawthorne at that moment monitoring the progress of his sister's will? Was Jeremiah just a few feet away from the man who had caused him so many years of unhappiness?

"That is," the judge said, "I am not dismissing these claims impulsively or carelessly. However, I am dismissing them. The statements given in their support deal almost exclusively with developments after the drafting of this will, but whatever may have become of Dorothy Hawthorne later in her life is not germane. This is her only and last will and testament, so her competence at the time of its creation is all that matters. I'm disappointed that the attorneys here today did not learn that in law school."

Jeremiah felt lightheaded. Surely, Calvin would not be so brazen as to show up in such a public place, after being invisible for decades. But what if it was him, and here Jeremiah sat—here they all sat—Calvin's dupes?

"Now, as to claims of undue influence," the judge continued. "Marnie Hawthorne is Dorothy Hawthorne's sole direct descendent, so that even without a will, the laws of the State of Illinois would indicate her as the heir. The fact that other, more distant relatives were excluded entirely does not strike this court as unusual. Simply being related to someone in some distant manner does not entitle you to their belongings.

"The court recognizes that the assets belonging to the estate of Dorothy Hawthorne are important not only to Mrs. Hawthorne's family but to civic communities throughout this county. However, this circumstance will not cause the court to entertain wild and insupportable motions. Each of you will receive written statements with attention to your particular claims, but I brought you here so I can see your faces when I ask you if you understand my rulings—so we'll have no misunderstandings."

The judge then asked each attorney in turn, including Marnie's, if he or she understood the rulings. Each answered in the affirmative and the judge cut Mack Fuller's attorney off when he attempted to raise a point of order.

Jeremiah looked over his shoulder again at the courtroom door, but the face that had been there did not reappear. He looked at the photograph, which he had unconsciously crumpled in his hand.

When everyone had been cowed into silence by the judge's peremptory declarations, the judge looked up at the clock. "It seems prudent to me to go to lunch now, because I don't wish to hold any of you in contempt, and I'm persuaded by the looks on some of your faces that this would become necessary." The judge affirmed that penalties existed for failing to follow state and county guidelines for claims and that the attorneys should remember this when filing in the future. "Next up after lunch will be Simmons," the judge concluded. "Let's take an hour."

He banged his gavel and suddenly the clerks and court reporter were gathering up their things and making for the door. The bailiff instructed everyone to stand, and the judge ambled, with studied, inflammatory ease, out of the courtroom, accompanied by the bailiff, who pointedly monitored the audience.

When the judge passed into the hall, everyone seemed instantly released from his authority. Fifty voices filled the courtroom at once. Jake Ziegler, the *Constitution*'s young reporter, dashed out of the room, and Jeremiah baby-stepped past the chattering, gesticulating people glutting his aisle. He hurried as fast as his old legs would carry him into the hall, but there was no sign of the old man. He saw Ziegler rushing outside, cell phone to his ear, and he saw clerks and other county workers with name tags clipped to their shirts, but no one who looked like Calvin Hawthorne. Jeremiah's knees felt weak. He went back into the hearing room.

Everyone was yelling. He picked out Marnie, who remained withdrawn and unresponsive under a vituperative attack from Susan Meese. Marnie's lawyer was threatening Mrs. Meese with legal action if she didn't restrain herself, but Marnie just stared vacantly at her husband, whose face had grown red with anger. Soon, Marnie's lawyer put an end to these confrontations by ushering Marnie and Graham toward the door.

Jeremiah reached out to Marnie, but she was engulfed in such a cloud of anger and disorder that she didn't see him. He touched her arm, but her attorney pushed Jeremiah's outstretched hand away, and they were out the door.

As soon as Marnie and Graham had left, Dorothy Longmore and Susan Meese turned their anger on each other and Mack Fuller began waving his cane in a provocative manner. Jeremiah stepped into the hall just in time to see Marnie disappearing past the security guards through the main exit. He followed in her footsteps, at a much slower pace, searching the crowded hallway for any sign of the face he had seen at the door.

The judge's rulings would come as a shocking development, and the whole town would be full of beans by the time Jeremiah got back to the barber shop. Marnie, it seemed, would now almost certainly inherit the whole estate. Jeremiah did not believe, however, that courts of law would have the final say in matters concerning the Hawthornes.

He called Kirk from a pay phone. As he arranged for taxi service downtown, Susan Meese burst out of the courtroom yelling to no one in particular that attorneys were a dime a dozen and we would see who had the last laugh. Jeremiah hung up and followed the excited crowd—people were comparing their already embellished postmortems of the hearing, tall tales they would tell their friends in town.

Outside, the Hawthorne mob receded into parked cars. Jeremiah sat down on a concrete bench. The sun was trying to shine through a layer of high clouds. The warm, gentle breeze seemed quite cold to Jeremiah, and he wrapped himself tighter into his sweater. As he did so, he noticed that the stranger's handkerchief was now completely soaked in his own sweat. He dropped it onto the bench, shivered violently, and reached into his pocket for his flask.

20

KATE BENJAMIN WRITES A LETTER TO JON RIDGELY

Dear Jon,

I've written this letter a dozen times in my head and started it a dozen more on paper, but I still don't know what to say to you. I sometimes think I don't know what words mean any more, since they no longer connect to anything in the world. The words we used to say to each other, for example.

I try to comfort myself with lists—I make lists of things I know are real. Things like my father's varieties, triticale and potatoes and corn. I can see the crops I've planted and I can touch them, and when I find myself thinking of you, which is all the time, I reel off the names of my father's clients in my head, what seeds they've bought and the new varieties we're harvesting. It's grounding and concrete, these simple facts, and I've now memorized my father's entire account book. But heaven help me when the harvest is over.

I feel small confiding this in you, but you've been my best friend for so long that I hardly know who else to tell. It's funny, the one person who might really understand how I'm coping with this pain is the person who caused it in the first place, and I just feel so hopeless.

I wish I could hate you, the way my father wants me to, but I don't think it's in me. I'm just trying to understand. I thought we valued the same things, I thought I knew what those things were, and that's what hurts the most—I see now that I had no idea what was important to you, that I fabricated a whole idea of us based on a mistake. I thought we'd made something together that only we could make and that meant so much to me. It made me feel exceptional. You made me feel exceptional. But I guess I was wrong. I guess I'm not exceptional and neither are you.

You always told me I was beautiful, and I wonder now if you ever really believed it. I never thought so, anyway, but I thought we understood each other at a different level, I thought our love was built on something else—but saying that over and over isn't going to make it less a mistake. Maybe you did think I was beautiful. And smart. And funny. All those things you said. Or maybe you were just settling for me and you secretly wanted something else all along, something like rich and powerful—I suppose even beauty takes its chances in a world where money is the most important thing.

I don't know what to think any more. I look at everything in my life and think—is this right? Is this real? Or am I as blind about this as I was about you? Cherie came by the other night and we sat on the porch and drank lemonade, and I thought. . . do I really know Cherie? . . . I felt so alone.

Of course, everyone else thinks they know you all the better now that you've "shown your true colors," as they say. My father says the most awful things about you and he thinks I'm foolish and naïve when I argue with him. He thinks it's unhealthy for me to stand up for you still. But he doesn't understand that when he says those things about you he's really saying them about me because I believed in you, and now I have to rise to your defense in order to defend myself, to show that I wasn't a fool to have loved you. It's difficult because it's so obvious what a fool I really was, and then I go to my room and lie on my bed and call you all the same names that my father just called you.

But I can't be angry, if you want to know the truth—I wish I could, but all my anger just floods into the emptiness I feel and disappears. I'm trying to see things the way they really are for a change.

I don't know why I'm telling you this. It must bore you that I'm saying how much you've hurt me.

I heard that you got fired from the paper. I don't know what you could have been thinking, parading Marnie Hawthorne around like that with the whole town watching. Looking back, what you were doing was so obvious that I guess no one could really believe it. I know I didn't want to believe it. I still don't.

It's about time for my parents to wake up and for me to go into the field. This is the first time in my life I can remember having insomnia, and I can't concentrate on anything. That's one reason I'm finally sending you one of these letters, to push these thoughts out of my head.

I miss you. I miss the Jon I thought I knew and I wish everything could go back the way it was. The guitar I bought in Terre Haute is standing in the corner like a substitute you, and I can't look at it without crying and thinking of the emptiness of what we won't do together. I still can't believe you would do this, that there won't be an us. But I'm not the one you wanted, I guess.

I hear my mother downstairs making coffee. It's going to be a long day.

I don't suppose I'll write to you again. It's so hard to know that we won't talk any more. I wish I could pretend that you're going to miss me as much as I'll miss you, but I'm trying to stop lying to myself, especially on your behalf. I will allow myself this one last little lie, though: I'll sign this letter

Love,
Kate

21

The Apple Orchard

Milky white light suffused the sky. Thick dew blanketed the ground. It was just before dawn, and Jon stood outside the black iron fence at the northwestern corner of the Hawthorne estate, the farthest point on the grounds from the mansion.

Outside the fence, the land sloped gently down into a grassy dell, where Jon's footsteps formed a matted trail; beyond the dell, a stand of sycamores and oaks hid a row of houses huddled on Hampton Street. To the north, several hundred yards of hilly thickets choked with ash trees, wild shrubs and poison ivy stretched toward Baker Road. Just here, Jon was invisible to the sleeping streets.

Inside the fence stood the unruly Hawthorne apple orchard, whose gnarled trees crowded close to one another in irregular patterns. There were no rows as such—the grove was organized in clusters rather than lines, which gave it a feeling of natural, chaotic profusion, an order that impersonated the teeming bedlam of the natural world. It was impossible to see more than twenty feet in any direction: the view was a tangle of contorted trunks, crooked limbs and branches heavily laden with fruit.

Jon's hands slipped on the cold, wet metal fence as he hoisted himself over it. He plopped down inside the orchard and tried to take a measure of things. A thick mat of leaves covered the earth and he stepped gingerly, mindful of fallen apples and hidden tree roots.

He was unsure where he was going. After several days of

begging into Marnie's cell phone voice mail, he had finally coaxed her into returning his calls, and then into a rendezvous, and for some reason she had chosen this time and place. Her instructions had been short and cryptic—"the apple orchard at dawn tomorrow"—and she had hung up before he could respond.

Things had not been going well for Jon. Since his dismissal from the *Constitution*, a fog of ill will had enveloped him. Every interaction—from buying gas to mailing bills and grocery shopping—was now fraught with thinly veiled hostility. He still had his job at Ploughman's, but he felt that his boss was one feeble excuse away from firing him, and he was tempted to quit just to avoid the humiliation. This animosity had probably been building for a while, but he had remained blissfully and stupidly unaware of it, believing that his affair with Marnie was a secret.

On top of the disdain he felt from everyone else, Kate would not answer her cell phone and Kate's father had made it clear that Jon was no longer welcome to call the Benjamin house. He regretted the way he'd handled things, and he wanted desperately, selfishly to explain himself. He wanted Kate's approval, but he knew there was no way to make things right with her and there was no going back. Kate's letter, which he read many times, made him feel sorry and empty.

To make matters worse, Marnie had almost completely disappeared since her husband had arrived. She rarely answered her cell phone and was sullen and uncommunicative when she did; and while Jon understood that Graham's presence made her situation difficult, he felt that something else was happening, that Marnie regretted their affair.

His tennis shoes smushed the damp leaves, and he felt twigs spring and roll under his weight. The orchard seemed to grow larger by the moment: he knew logically that it could not extend more than an acre or two in any direction, but he felt slightly unhinged, lost within a dark mass of woody arms. Even the fence he had just jumped was already hidden behind dense leaves and branches. The orchard's layout, and its eerie stillness, encouraged panic and claustrophobia.

There were many different kinds of apple trees here, some whose low branches Jon had to duck and skirt, others whose lowest fruits he could barely reach on tiptoes. He thought of Kate and how interested she would be in the design of the orchard, how she might console herself by examining the traits of different varieties of apples.

Despite its abundance, the orchard was eerily clean. There was no rotting fruit on the ground, no crabby husks or withered skins among the mulching leaves, and the trees seemed well-trimmed: it was as if someone had pruned the branches and gleaned the apples from the orchard floor but left all the ripe fruit hanging on the boughs, and this oddity amplified Jon's disquiet.

"Marnie," he hissed into the heavy morning air.

When Marnie had suggested the apple orchard, Jon had thought it romantic and exciting. As a schoolboy, he had heard the usual rumors—that the orchard was inhabited by ghosts and nameless little beasts that vanished the instant you glimpsed them. The Edgar Allan Poe creepiness associated with the mansion had been transformed into scary Washington Irving-style legends for the outlying grounds, and Templeton's young people gave the orchard as wide a berth as they gave the mansion itself.

"Marnie," he hissed again.

It made Jon crazy to think of Marnie in Graham's arms, but it could not be otherwise, he told himself, not yet. She was married, after all, and he intended to break up her marriage, which was no petty enterprise. He had to proceed with caution and could not demand or insist for fear of driving Marnie away. She would lean toward the established order, since change would be much more difficult than stasis. The situation was delicate but not impossible, and he reminded himself to be patient and wait for the opportune moment.

The orchard suddenly opened into a clearing, and Jon stopped under the eaves, observing it suspiciously, as if the clearing might have been a trap set there specifically for him. In the middle of the clearing stood a wooden shed, old and weathered, with a flat, slanted roof and slatboard walls that furred and bowed. A large wooden bucket next to the shed was filled to the brim with red, green and yellow apples, which looked fresh, and he wondered who had picked them. Perhaps Marnie herself had been coming here as a kind of therapy, an escape from Graham, and perhaps that was why she had chosen this spot for a meeting. The fallen leaves in the clearing were trampled and trodden, as if they had been mashed underfoot many times.

A shiver ran up his spine. The trees seemed abnormally alive here, as if hidden eyes were observing and noting. He told himself that his head was just filled with old legends and tall tales, but the feeling of being watched did not go away.

"Marnie?"

The shed's door faced him. Above its latch handle was a hinged metal plate with a ring for a padlock, but the clasp was empty—no lock secured the door. Jon stepped out from beneath the trees and approached it. His heart was racing. As he reached the middle of the clearing, he turned and looked all around him, but nothing stirred. He put his hand on the latch, lifted it and pulled the door toward him.

The door opened silently, without a squeak from its old hinges, and a moldy draft breathed out at him. Darkness clung to the inside of the shed. He made out a jumble of indefinite shapes, but his eyes could not find the outlines of identifiable things. He stopped breathing, and as he crossed the shed's threshold he recoiled inside. Someone was in there.

"Marnie?"

He felt a stinging whack across the face. He cried out and lurched back into the clearing. Marnie charged out after him.

He raised his arms to defend himself, too late, and she smacked his ear. He staggered, and she raised her hand to strike him again, face pale and eyes fierce. Jon found his bearings and stood his ground, and they froze, facing one another, Jon with his arms out to ward off the slap Marnie was about to deliver.

"Marnie! What's wrong?"

He took a cautious step toward her, palms out in a gesture of peace, and he slowly reached for Marnie's uplifted right arm. She allowed him to clutch her wrist and then caught him square across the cheek with her left hand. He grabbed her in a bear hug and held her tight against his body.

"Stop it."

She struggled for a moment, and then all the energy seemed to drain out of her and she wilted in his arms. "What's the matter?" She wrapped her arms around Jon's waist and buried her head in his shoulder and pushed feebly against him. "Marnie," he said into her ear. "Tell me what's wrong."

He was practically holding her up. He smelled her hair and felt her breath against his neck. She sniffled, and he was as disarmed by her sudden submission as he had been by her attack. He rubbed her back and made shushing noises into her ear.

She let Jon console her for a long while, until she pulled back just enough to look into his eyes. "Kate Benjamin," she spit. She slapped his arms away and walked in a semicircle back toward the shed. "You could have at least told me."

"That I was seeing Kate?"

"That you were seeing Kate!" she yelled.

"I couldn't have." He opened his arms wide. "How could I have told you?"

"You could have stopped seeing her."

"I have. It took time to—for us to—settle things. Surely you know how that is." Marnie turned and stared at him hatefully. "Anyway," he said, "that's over. It's over."

"Hardly. She paid Graham a visit."

"Kate went to see Graham?" Even repeating it didn't make the idea real in Jon's mind. It seemed very unlike Kate—but then, his own betrayal of Kate had probably seemed just as unlikely to her. All bets were now off. "What happened?"

"Nothing! Except Graham knows everything now. He knows everything."

She raised her right hand above her head and let it fall heavily against her thigh. She stared at Jon, defying him to say something useful, and he noticed something new about Marnie. As she paced slowly in front of him, her body seemed heavy, and her face looked drawn and strange. For the first time since he'd met her, she did not seem graceful.

"You admitted it?"

"I had no choice. He found one of your notes."

"My notes?"

She sighed aggressively, as if she were explaining the most obvious thing in the world to an obtuse child. "I was careless. I don't know what happened, I guess I didn't double-check." She raised her voice. "I left one of your notes in the bedroom and he found it. Understand?"

Jon imagined Marnie lying in bed, reading one of his love notes and laying it fondly on her nightstand before she went to sleep, leaving it there as a keepsake: despite her present anger, he felt gratified and in love.

"So now he knows," Jon said. "Now they both know." He said it reassuringly, as if they had jumped a necessary hurdle.

"And so—what?" she said with condescending fury. "Now they both know—and what?"

Jon recognized with a shock that she had never intended to tell Graham about him, that she had never considered leaving Graham. "Well," he said flatly, turning on her, "now they both know."

He felt cornered and alone. His options were disappearing as fast as he could think of them. He walked away and squatted down at the edge of the clearing, picked up a leaf and tore at it. He couldn't believe what he was hearing. He shredded the leaf down to its stem and then twirled it between his thumb and forefinger, until a new idea occurred to him.

Perhaps Marnie was merely confused, and the shock and turmoil of confronting Graham had frightened her. She was taking her fear and anguish out on him. He thought about his own conflicted feelings for Kate and then multiplied them by marriage, and he realized that Marnie was terrified of leaving her husband. Forsaking her marriage must surely have seemed a crushing failure, but she was standing here, with him, not sitting with Graham trying to work their difficulties out.

Jon collected his dashed hopes and took them back to her. There is no way of knowing what will happen, he thought, so I must remain steadfast in my love.

When Marnie saw the conciliatory look on his face, she seemed confused and a little put off, but she allowed Jon to embrace her. He held her and rocked her gently, stroking her hair, offering her the consolation he needed himself.

He felt Marnie soften into his body again, and he kissed her head and nuzzled his cheek into her hair. He was terrified that, at any moment, she would pull away and say something angry and final and run off through the apple trees, but he continued to stroke her and rock her. He wished that that moment—holding Marnie in the middle of the Hawthorne apple orchard, with an electric and almost unbearable tension passing between them—would never end. He felt the strain of it deep in his heart: she controlled his entire future.

He stopped rocking her and they stood holding each other. Beyond the trees, the sun had risen and dew was steaming off the earth. Jon smelled the heady odor of decaying leaves mixed with the solid woody promise of apple bark. Nothing had been settled, but he felt calmer and clearer now, as if Marnie's bond to him had been reaffirmed. He looked at her face.

She seemed drained and hurt and, for the first time, vulnerable. She felt very dear to him just then, in the crisp morning light, and he wished he knew that she was sharing this moment with him, the desperation and anger he had felt only moments before evaporating into the fragrant air.

They stared into each other's eyes until the distance between them disappeared and they seemed to share a single openness, tense and demanding, which felt at every moment that it would break and leave them with nothing. They continued to stare until the tension melted away again, and they were left with the candidness of their unblinking eyes. Jon kissed her lips and whispered, "I love you, Marnie."

It was the first time either of them had said it, and saying it seemed a benediction, an end to the moment and a return to their problems. She kissed him and caressed his cheek.

"I need to get back," she said. "Graham will miss me." Neither moved for a long time, as the weight of Graham's expectation fell over them.

"What happens now?"

"I have no idea," she said. "At this point, it's not really up to me."

"Not entirely, you mean." She looked at him with something like pity. "When will we see each other again?"

She shrugged. "I'll call you. This isn't easy for me."

"For me, either." He looked at her significantly, trying to convey how much he himself had risked, how much he was losing for her, and she nodded and cast her eyes down in a sign of understanding.

"I'll call you," she said.

She turned and headed into the orchard, toward the mansion. Jon stood in the clearing and watched her disappear through the trees.

22

No Good Reason

Marnie walked across the gently rolling meadow between the apple orchard and the rose garden, taking long inattentive strides, her mind a jumble of half-formed notions. The calf-high grass shushed and snapped against her pantlegs, lending her contemplations a steady rhythm. The grass was wet enough with dew to darken her pant cuffs and dampen her socks, but Marnie was barely aware of the ground beneath her feet. She nearly stepped into the stream that trickled through the meadow—she came up short in the soft mud on its banks. Her sneakers sank into the muck and she jumped awkwardly to the other side.

She had left Graham fast asleep in his bed, but she was sure he would be awake by now, and she wanted to get back before he missed her. They were barely speaking and were sleeping on different floors, but they had nevertheless been with each other continuously for days, rarely leaving the mansion and never going out without the other. The tension between them was breaking Marnie down. She could think of nothing to say that wasn't an explanation or a plea for forgiveness, but Graham refused to entertain her apologies, instead filling the void between them with forced banalities or ambiguous suggestions of violence. Marnie had begun to feel like a prisoner in her own mansion.

Graham occupied himself with the business of Hawthorne Enterprises. Where Marnie had done almost nothing to prepare herself for her inheritance—either to challenge the liens against her grandmother's property or to assume control of her grandmother's holdings—Graham had immediately and thoroughly organized all the court documents and developed a plan for monitoring probate and managing the transfer of property. It was entirely due to him that they had had legal representation at the probate hearing. He had been efficient to a fault, managing Marnie's affairs far better than she had herself, and Marnie felt his helpfulness as a rebuke. He had always been more practical than Marnie, but now he was so forcefully well-organized that the barest hint of emotion from Marnie was smothered under a heavy blanket of order.

The first hedge surrounding the rose garden loomed atop the next hill and Marnie felt as if she had lost her hold on reality: for no good reason, she had betrayed a lovely man, who had never been anything but affectionate and kind to her; and now she had two men to manage, one desperate and lovelorn, the other hurt and bewildered, and both unpredictable. It was as if Dorothy had cast a spell on her from beyond the grave, and now she was forced to repeat her grandmother's mistakes.

She entered the long arbor that led to the fountain. There was something about being in the orchard, in the garden, in the old dilapidated mansion itself, that felt curiously like home to Marnie and gave her a sense of self-possession. She viewed herself differently here than she ever had before and, even with her marriage in jeopardy, she liked being the imperious Hawthorne Toffee heiress. The money, the power, the air of inscrutability—she was fascinated by herself in relation to this town and to the huge fortune her family had built on tiny toffee bars. The judge at the probate hearing had been more right than he had known, Marnie thought: she was indeed the natural heir of the Hawthornes, especially her grandmother.

She passed through a second small gate and came to the rose garden, where the splashing statue of Cupid in the fountain seemed to mock her. Since Graham had arrived, she had begun to hate that fountain and the perfect order that bloomed all around it, since it seemed to take Graham's side. The disorder of the mansion suited her much more than the regimented beauty of the garden.

She had never intended to choose Jon over Graham, and she felt hopeless and exasperated that Graham characterized her affair that way. She felt that this dalliance with Jon was attached in an indirect way to the bizarre experience of inheriting a candy dynasty, that it was nothing to be taken so seriously. Theirs had not been the kind of marriage that suffered dalliances, however, and she could hardly blame Graham for being disappointed and furious, but she wished he could see the whole thing for an instant through her eyes.

Marnie came to the veranda, wiped her shoes on the mat and went inside. The vigilance and circumspection that she had once found so admirable in Graham would not incline him to forgiveness.

She filled the tea kettle, turned on the stove and got breakfast settings out of the cupboard. At least, she thought dryly, she was eating decently with Graham in the house, three regular meals a day, as systematic as an army mess hall. The toffee bars that she had at first eaten with such abandon were now collecting in the refrigerator.

The kettle whistled. "Graham," Marnie shouted.

Graham's bedroom was on the second floor, but he often roused himself in the morning by looking at old Hawthorne stock portfolios in the main dining room. Marnie could sometimes find him there after a sleepless night, making graphs of company performances. She would interrupt him with breakfast in the middle of his careful sense-making, and he would scold her with the figures. He would compound this appalling display by studying the graphs over his meal, and the whole charade made Marnie feel bleak and lonely.

This morning, he wasn't on the main floor, and she was relieved that he was not yet up and about; she debated whether to go upstairs to wake him or eat a light breakfast alone and give him one more thing to hold against her. She tired of this battle of wills, but she knew that if she didn't hold up her end of the fight—if she showed any sign of weakness in the face of Graham's relentless everyday routines—she would lose him. She trudged upstairs.

Graham had selected a bedroom at the end of the hall on the second floor, a corner room with a view of the garden. His room was filled with awards: all around the queen-sized bed were cases filled with trophies, ribbons, plaques, medals and certificates. Most were from Dorothy's and Calvin's school days, but there were also civic awards to Henry and a few honor roll citations given to Marnie's father. Marnie found the room unsettling—all those mementos of the proud achievements of the dead—but Graham had been captivated by the preoccupations of the Hawthornes that he could infer from them. Marnie would sometimes find him, after his morning shower, carelessly handling a trophy as he stared out the window.

She walked down the hall from the landing. Graham's bedroom door was ajar, and she rapped on it lightly before pushing it open.

He was sitting on the edge of the bed, his hands planted firmly on either side of him, staring at the floorboards between his feet. Behind him, in the middle of the bed, were his suitcase and wardrobe bag. He was neatly dressed, freshly shaven, his blonde hair pomaded and his mustache trimmed.

"Out for a walk?"

"I couldn't sleep." Marnie leaned against one of the trophy cabinets. Graham looked at her with swollen eyes: he had been crying. "You're packed?" she said.

"It's increasingly clear I'm in your way here."

"Not true, Graham." She sat down beside him. "You're not in my way and you shouldn't leave."

"I don't see how I can stay."

"Just like this. Just like we're doing. Why don't you talk to me?"

He said nothing. She touched his hand.

"Please don't leave, Graham. I don't know what I can say, but I wish you'd at least let me try to say it. Your leaving solves nothing."

"My coming didn't help. I can barely look at you, Marnie. It hurts me to look at you."

They were silent for a long while. Marnie rubbed Graham's arm and leaned her head on his shoulder, but this felt all wrong and she sat up straight again and sighed.

"What if I went with you?"

"What about your boyfriend?"

Marnie's heart sank. It was a question that had no answer. Trying to define Jon as anything other than her boyfriend would only retrench the argument against her; but she felt intuitively that Graham would interpret a non-answer to this wounded question as a sign of her loyalty to Jon, and that was unacceptable as well.

"He won't be in London," she finally said. She knew she shouldn't have said it as soon as the words left her mouth. She could think of nothing to say that wouldn't muddle things further.

Her aplomb in dealing with Jon and everyone else in Templeton had been possible only because she had another life—a real life, a real career, a real marriage to Graham. She had never had to take anything in Templeton seriously because she had a life in reserve that she did take seriously, and she saw with sudden clarity that, without that other existence to support her, without Graham, the life of the Hawthorne heiress that she was creating in Templeton would not be possible either—not in the same way.

"I'm coming with you," she said.

Graham shifted his weight and looked out the window. "I don't want you in our place in Kensington any more. I'm going to wait until the will clears probate, and then I'm going to file for divorce."

"But. . . Graham—"

"I can't tell you what to do, but I'd rather be alone. I'd rather not have you there."

"Is that what you really want?"

He suddenly yelled. "How should I know what I want? You think I wanted you to sleep with another man? Why don't you tell me what you want, Marnie, since that's the only thing that really matters."

"Graham—"

"How dare you ask what I want!"

He raised his hand as if to strike her, and Marnie shrank away toward the foot of the bed. She felt hopeless and didn't know if it would be better if they said these bitter things, if Graham screamed at her and she agreed and agreed and begged his forgiveness, or if he really should leave until he could stand to look at her again. She could hardly stay in Templeton without him—Graham's mind would be filled with thoughts of her and Jon together. She would have to go with him if she wanted to save her marriage.

Graham exhaled a long, controlled breath, closed his eyes and bowed his head. "I don't know what I'm supposed to do," he said. His voice was flat and dead. "But there's obviously nothing for me here, and I can't. . ." He shook his head. "I can't. . ." His upper lip trembled. "I'm not saying. . . I don't know what I'm saying."

"Graham—"

"Look, the estate will clear probate soon enough, and then we can do something about you and me. This limbo won't last."

"Oh, who cares about the estate?" she said. Graham looked at her uncomprehendingly. "I'm sorry, Graham. I didn't mean to—"

"I know," he said, "you've told me."

"I'm so sorry."

They sat for a while in silence. It felt to Marnie that they had been encased in amber.

"Do you have a plane ticket?"

"I'll buy one in St. Louis."

"I started tea," she said. "You should eat something."

He shook his head. "Not like this."

They sat for several more minutes in silence. Marnie feared that her inability to act decisively now might prove costly in the future, in more ways than one. But this thought, instead of giving her some direction, made her less able to act, for fear of doing something decisively wrong.

Graham finally stood up. When he turned to get his suitcase, Marnie leapt up and put her body between him and his bag. Before he could object, she wrapped him in a hug and held on tight, until he put his arms around her.

"I wish you wouldn't leave. I wish you'd let me come with you."

He leaned around Marnie to pick up his luggage. He swept the suitcase between them and walked resolutely into the hall. Marnie trotted after him.

"Will you call me when you get to St. Louis? Or at least when you get to London, so I'll know you're all right?"

"You're concerned for my welfare?" he scoffed.

They walked down the stairs in silence. When they reached the entry hall, Graham set his luggage down, retrieved his windbreaker from the coat rack and put it on. He opened the front door and then stopped, hovering for a moment with his hand over his suitcase. He took Marnie in his arms and kissed the top of her head. "I love you, Marnie."

"Don't go, Graham. Please don't go."

He picked up his suitcase and strode purposefully to his car. Methodically, he unlocked the doors and stowed his baggage, without looking back. He got in, started the car and eased it down the driveway.

When he got to the curve, he sat for awhile with his foot on the brake. Marnie thought he might come back, but as soon as that idea occurred to her, the car's brake lights winked out and he drove around the bend, out of sight.

She could not bring herself to move from the doorway, but continued to stare at the empty drive long after he had left. I am the Mistress of Toffee, she told herself.

23

The Ghost of Calvin Hawthorne

Among the scissors, electric clippers and glass jars filled with combs that Jeremiah kept on the shelves behind each of his barber chairs, several unremarkable cologne decanters hid in plain sight. They were filled with white rum, and Jeremiah had taken to drinking when his shop was empty. Now, at two o'clock in the afternoon, with the kids in school and the farmers in their fields, he unscrewed the lid of a cologne bottle and took a slow drink.

Jeremiah had not been completely sober since his visit to Marnie at the mansion. As with practiced alcoholics, he managed to appear reasonably self-controlled most of the time, but the alcohol twisted his thoughts and feelings into smaller and smaller knots. The extraordinary amount of rum he was now consuming could not make him sleep: he sometimes entered a catatonic stupor, but mostly his mind raced through the night, through the day, through the same bleak tunnels over and over.

As a rule, he had never touched alcohol while he was working, but since he had become obsessed with the idea that Calvin Hawthorne was still alive, he drank throughout the day, trying to calm his whirling, churning thoughts. He felt it a personal insult that Calvin had been alive through all these long years.

If you were rich enough and clever enough, you could do anything you wanted and then hide the evidence, pay people off, bribe the highest officials. Everyone had a price and in

Templeton, Jeremiah thought, the price might not be very high. But you couldn't hide everything. No one simply disappeared from the face of the earth, and he couldn't believe how blind everyone had been to Calvin's perverse hoax. He was convinced that there were reasons for Calvin to go into hiding, that they had to do with Calvin's and Dorothy's love affair—but he could not fathom the depths of their twisted minds nor understand the contorted logic that had led them to such inexplicable behavior.

He took another long drink of rum from the cologne bottle and caught his reflection in the mirror. After decades of not really seeing himself in his barber shop mirrors, he suddenly could not stop looking into his own eyes, searching for something. He stared at himself now, his eyes unnaturally wide, unblinking. He drank again and then wrenched himself away and sat down in the barber chair next to the Main Street window.

In order to test his hypothesis about Calvin, he had employed Kirk as an operative—had sent him to park his car as inconspicuously as possible near the Hawthorne estate and watch, to see who came and went. He had instructed Kirk to change locations every day or two, so that he could watch from different vantage points, but so far Kirk had seen nothing unusual.

Jeremiah realized that Kirk was probably spending all the money he gave him on scotch and then sitting in his car drinking and sleeping, not watching at all. Moreover, there was a large section of Hawthorne property that couldn't be seen from the roads, because of the trees and hedges that had been planted specifically for that purpose. So it did not discourage him that Kirk reported no dark-clad strangers sneaking onto the property in the middle of the night, nor even an ordinary groundskeeper in the middle of the day—but that didn't mean they weren't there. Something was going on, something far more devious, inexplicable and difficult to detect than Jeremiah could imagine, but he was determined to get to the bottom of it. He saw now, finally, what Calvin Hawthorne was up to. He couldn't articulate it, but he saw it.

Someone in Templeton knew something they weren't telling—perhaps even Marnie herself. It was such an open thing, a garden, so practical and real and obvious—so why didn't anyone know anything about it? It made no sense at all. Marnie must know, Jeremiah thought, who was tending that garden. Why wouldn't she tell him? He didn't understand how it all fit together, but it had Calvin's fingerprints all over it, and he had the letter and the photograph to prove it.

He unscrewed the cap from a cologne bottle and drank. Suddenly, Jon Ridgely darted past the window. Jeremiah nearly dropped his decanter as Jon burst into the shop.

He had a helter-skelter look in his eyes. His beard was scraggly and his unkempt hair made him look ragged. His clothes were lank and looked slept-in, and he moved unnaturally quickly, with short, skittish gestures. If he hadn't seemed so forlorn, he might have looked dangerous. He dipped his shoulders and clasped his hands in a gesture of supplication. "I need to speak with you, Jeremiah. I need your advice."

"All right. Why don't you sit down?" He motioned Jon toward one of the seats across from the barber chairs.

Jon sat on the very edge. His words came out in a manic rush, tumbling over one another. "You were right, about getting involved with the Hawthornes. About everything. But I couldn't... I mean, no matter what... I didn't have a choice—you know what I mean?"

"Well," Jeremiah said deliberately, "why don't you settle down. If you want to talk, then let's talk, but there's time for everything. There's nothing but time."

He flipped the Open sign to Closed and pulled down the

shade, then went to the picture window and twisted the blinds, shutting out the view of Main Street. "Now, just sit calm a minute." He walked to the back of his shop.

"Jeremiah! I don't have a minute!"

Jeremiah waved him quiet. "Let's have a drink." He opened a supply cabinet and withdrew two ceramic shaving mugs.

"I don't want a drink!" Jon's leg bounced energetically.

"I can hardly talk to you like this," Jeremiah answered. "Look at yourself—your eyes are crazy and your leg's about to run away by itself. Here." He held a hand mirror up to Jon's face. "Have you seen yourself?" Jon brushed it aside. Jeremiah peeked at his own reflection: by comparison to Jon, he actually looked composed. He put the mirror back on the shelf and immediately wanted to look at himself again, so he stared at the wall mirror as he selected a cologne bottle from the shelf. Everything's fine, he told his reflection.

He unscrewed the decanter, poured rum into both their mugs and gave one to Jon. "Mud in your eye." He drank and Jon followed suit.

"Obviously," Jon said, "I need to talk about Marnie."

"Things going bad since her husband came to town?"

"Don't mock me."

"I'm not mocking you."

"Well don't."

"I said I'm not." Jeremiah smiled. He was on the verge of figuring out the real secret of the Hawthornes, tying together all the loose ends, and Jon was still worrying about a tiny piece of the puzzle. Jon was a fool, as big a fool as Jeremiah himself had once been.

"I was there at the courthouse for the probate hearing," Jeremiah went on, "and I saw the two of them together, Marnie and Graham."

"You saw them? How did they look?"

"Like a married couple—like they were fighting." He paused to study Jon's face. "What does Graham know?"

"Everything. Everything's a mess." Jon finished off his drink and poured himself another. "I'm losing her."

Jon could contain himself no longer and he launched into a wild, rambling account of his meeting with Marnie in the apple orchard. He told the story in patchwork, skipping backward and forward to his first meeting with Marnie, to his relationship with Kate, to how inevitable falling in love with Marnie had seemed. Everything in his life had begun to revolve around the Hawthornes, and he told how thrilling their affair had been at first and how worried he was that he had been a mere trifling for Marnie, that she might stay with Graham, that he had thrown everything away for nothing.

Jeremiah puffed on his pipe and listened keenly. While he heard the wretched details of Jon's affair, he was transported back to the time when he himself had said the same things and felt the same futility of love. He knew what Jon was going through because he had gone through it for so long himself, and he felt a new prick of hatred for Calvin. Why hadn't he seen it before? Calvin and Dorothy, alone there in that mansion, rejected by their own father, by their own son, forced to flee into themselves, cut off from the whole world because of their wretched love.

Jon's tale circled obsessively back to its beginning, to his rendezvous with Marnie at the old gardener's shed in the orchard. Jeremiah thought it remarkable that Marnie had chosen that place, since Dorothy had chosen the exact same place to meet him fifty years before. He wondered what it was about that apple orchard that had drawn Dorothy there, that drew Marnie now. It was secluded enough and close enough to the mansion to be convenient, but it struck Jeremiah as an incredible coincidence, the past repeating itself so literally—such an incredible coincidence that it probably wasn't coincidental at all.

He interrupted Jon's tale of heartache and asked him to elaborate instead on the apple orchard itself, and he sat up and took notice when Jon explained the strange feeling of being observed in the clearing. He described how peculiar the whole orchard was, how there were no fallen apples at all, that the ground had been picked clean. To Jon, this was merely one odd detail among many, but to Jeremiah it was yet another sign.

"But that has nothing to do with anything, Jeremiah! Aren't you listening?"

"I'm listening. What's more, I'm hearing."

"I don't know what to do, and I don't know who else to turn to, but I didn't come here to talk about fucking apples! Don't you understand? Everybody else just thinks. . . well, you, at least, should know what I'm going through. I know you had an affair with Dorothy—that's why I came. I know everything."

"You don't know anything. I tried to help you before, kid. I told you to stay away from her, didn't I?"

"Yeah, all right. You were right. But what do I do now?"

The gardener's shed. Jeremiah remembered the cot he and Dorothy had set up there, the kerosene heater and the oil lamps and the makeshift table. He had slept there many nights after making love with Dorothy, and there was no reason someone couldn't be sleeping there still, living there.

Everything fell into place: Calvin Hawthorne had become a phantom, and that was why the mansion felt so creepy and haunted—because it *was* haunted. Calvin and Dorothy had become ghosts together, living ghosts. Only now everything was at an end—Dorothy was dead, and what could a living ghost do with a real one? How could Calvin live out his death after his ghost lover had died? To Jeremiah, it suddenly made perfect sense.

"Are you listening to me?"

"I'm sorry, kid, I was thinking about something you said."

"Well?"

"You want my advice?"

"Yes, Jeremiah, Jesus!"

"Well, I'm not going to give you any. Know what I'm going to do instead?"

"What?"

"I'm going to solve your problem. And mine, too."

"What? How? What do you mean?"

"I'm going to solve the whole god damn problem of the Hawthornes. It's about time somebody did it."

"What are you talking about?"

Jeremiah leaned forward, punctuating his words by poking the stem of his pipe in the air. "I'm going to kill Calvin Hawthorne."

"But—" Jon sat back, for the first time completely still. "You're what?"

"I'm going to find him and kill him."

"Calvin Hawthorne . . . has been dead for thirty years, Jeremiah."

Jeremiah stood up. He was overcome by a heavy coughing fit, and he hacked and gagged and cleared his throat. His chest heaved and shuddered. He staggered to the sink at the back of the shop and sputtered several times, spitting up phlegm.

He looked at his own phlegm in the basin, and it formed a pattern so disturbing and terrible that he couldn't stand the sight of it, and for a time—he wasn't sure how long—he was caught, unable to look away. It was happening to him more and more—he saw patterns in sidewalk cracks, in fractured bathroom tiles, in the hair on his barber shop floor. The patterns nauseated him, invited him, and it was harder and harder to look away.

Jon walked toward him, and his movements shook him out of the spell. He turned on the faucet to wash the spit down the drain.

"Jeremiah, are you all right?"

"Never better. You want my advice, kid?" He walked toward the front door. "Get as far away from Marnie Hawthorne as you can get. There's nothing left for you here, anyway. Just get the hell away. That's my advice. Now I've got something to do." He motioned Jon toward the door.

"You don't look well, Jeremiah."

"Marnie's nothing but trouble. Dorothy, too. You only see part of it, but I know what it's like to be in love with those Hawthorne women. Not any more, though. I'm going to save everybody a lot of worry. Myself most of all."

"By killing Calvin Hawthorne?"

"That's right."

"How do you think you're going to do that, Jeremiah?" Jon said, in a mollifying tone.

"Don't patronize me! Go fuck Marnie, if that's what you want—that's what you're so gung-ho for. That's the advice you want, isn't it? Go have your little affair. I'm done with it."

"Done with what?"

Jeremiah scoffed—what could Jon possibly know about anything? He was so young and stupid. Marnie had him wrapped around her finger, the way Dorothy had once done to Jeremiah, all the while sleeping with Calvin. But he would settle the score at last. He should have killed Calvin Hawthorne long ago, when Dorothy had first confessed her sickening affair with him. But Calvin would get what he deserved.

He ushered Jon through the front door, and they both squinted into the bright afternoon sun. "Is that your truck?" Jeremiah pointed at Jon's truck, parked on the Square near the

Old Courthouse.

"Yeah."

"I'll tell you what you do. You get in that truck and start driving. North, south, east, west, it doesn't matter. Just drive. And when you run out of gas, put in more gas. And when you run out of money, you stay there, wherever you are, and you forget about this place, forget about Marnie Hawthorne. You forget about the name Hawthorne. And you tear up your photographs of Marnie and think about something else from now on."

"But, Jeremiah—"

Jeremiah started walking up the hill toward the Square. Jon caught him by the arm.

"You're not making sense."

"I've never made more sense."

"Why don't we sit down for a minute? All right? Why don't you just sit down and rest for a minute."

"Get away from me." Jeremiah was shouting and people on the street were looking at them. "I'm doing you a favor, kid, but if you want Marnie Hawthorne so bad, just go to her. Go to her right now. Go fuck her right in front of her husband. That's what you're doing anyway."

"Jeremiah!" Jon looked frantically at the people all around, staring at him.

"That's what you want, isn't it?" Jeremiah yanked his arm out of Jon's grip and walked away. "Now leave me alone."

Jeremiah reached the Square, turned toward his house and walked as fast as his old legs would carry him.

24

THE END OF THE SEASON

Kate chugged along Squirrel Hill Lane on her father's weathered Massey-Ferguson, exhilarated and exhausted. It was four in the afternoon and she and her mother had just finished disking, their last task after the harvest. The disker attachment—its blades locked at a thirty-five degree angle above the road—clanked and rattled behind the old tractor. Kate's mother followed her in their truck, hazard lights flashing so no reckless farm boys would rear-end Kate as she guided the tractor back to the garage for the winter.

It had been a long season, and Kate now felt every aching muscle, every bruise, bite and scratch of the summer. Autumn was late this year, but it had finally arrived in earnest—a crisp breeze blew in her face, and the corn and wheat and soybean fields had all been picked clean. She was sad to be leaving Templeton for the winter—she would miss watching the snow float down in its silent blessing of the empty fields.

She had made arrangements to spend the winter in Boston, with friends from college—she would sub-let a room in Cambridge, though for what purpose she wasn't sure. She only knew that she didn't want to spend a season alone in her parents' house, listening to them argue about nothing, hearing the gossip about Jon and the Hawthornes. She refused to go into Templeton any more—she did her shopping in Prairieville, met her friends at her parents' house rather than the Flying Pig—and this circumscribed life wore on her. It would be a relief to be somewhere far away, with friends she could trust.

A car honked behind her. Sarah Winslow's blue hatchback passed her mother and pulled alongside the tractor. Sarah ran a vegetable market in Honey Creek.

"Hey there!" Sarah called, leaning into the passenger seat to look Kate in the face. "You about finished?"

"Just did," Kate shouted.

"Good yield?"

"Pretty good. Steady rain for a change. Probably means a mild winter."

"Let's hope so. Say, I heard you were going to Boston."

How had Sarah Winslow, of all people, found out that she was leaving town? Kate had told only Cherie and Joanna—Joanna could have told her mother, who might have told Suzanne at the ceramics shop, and then someone from the ceramics shop might have mentioned it to Sarah while buying vegetables. Or Cherie might have told Andrea at the Flying Pig, who would almost certainly have told Dana Frost, the manicurist at the Lady's Oasis Salon, where Sarah got her hair done. Actually, Kate thought, the path was pretty short, either way.

"I'm leaving in a couple weeks," she said. "As soon as we balance the books and whatnot."

"You should come over before you go," Sarah said. "Dan and some of the guys go for beers at the Elks after they get the crops in, and we use it as a ladies' night. At my house, Friday or Saturday."

"That sounds nice," she lied. "Call me and let me know."

"All right, see you then." Sarah sped off with a wave.

Kate stared out at the Fowler's barley fields, now empty but for gleanings and churned rows of clodded dirt. The whole town pitied her. It was disgusting, and all the relief and satisfaction of piloting the tractor home for the winter disappeared.

She was weary of thinking of Jon, letting him rob her of these simple pleasures. She was trying to remain above it all, to avoid becoming implicated in her own disgrace any more than she already was, but the idea that Jon could betray her and never acknowledge her suffering seemed unfair. She had to completely re-imagine her future because of him, and he was out cavorting with Marnie Hawthorne, with all that money on the horizon, all those possibilities. And what did Kate have? If she left the farm, her parents' business would fail; if she stayed, she would have months, if not years, of humiliation to live down.

She came into view of their house, her ponytail flopping in a stiff, chilly crosswind. The giant hickory trees out front welcomed her, and she spied her father sitting on the porch. Her mother honked her horn.

Kate reminded herself that Jon had called quite a few times after he'd received her letter, but this was not Kate's idea of being responsible. She did not want explanations or mea culpas, and she did not wish to forgive him. She wasn't sure what she wanted, but she knew she wanted it on her own terms—this skulking and moping and slinking out of town so that Jon could enjoy his affair in peace seemed the most ignominious kind of defeat.

"Hey, hey!" Mr. Benjamin called. He ran to meet Kate as she pulled into the driveway.

She killed the engine as her mother drove in behind her. "Hi, daddy." She jumped down from the seat, and her father gave her a big hug. Mr. Benjamin was truly affectionate only at the end of the harvest, a quirk Kate found comical and endearing.

"Good year this year," Mr. Benjamin said, beaming. "A very good year."

"I'll put everything away," Kate said.

"We can do that later. Come inside—I have a surprise for you."

Kate looked at her mother knowingly, and her mother rubbed her hands in mock greed. Kate's father always prepared an elaborate treat for them at the end of the harvest, with desserts and champagne and gifts. It was almost like Christmas.

"You should at least let us shower first, daddy. We're like giant dust bunnies."

"Don't worry about that. I've arranged everything. Just come inside."

"Better humor him, honey," her mother said. "We'll never hear the end of it."

Mr. Benjamin held the kitchen door open, and they trooped inside, not bothering to take their boots off. Kate smelled the sweet earthy flatness of pie crust, and the thick inviting bitterness of coffee. The dining room table was laid with a rust-colored tablecloth, and Mr. Benjamin had scattered acorns, ears of Indian corn and miniature pumpkins across the table, in the center of which orange and yellow candles burned in a silver candelabra. There was a fresh-baked apple pie, and two small boxes in crinkly gold wrapping paper.

Kate stood and admired the table, so carefully prepared, and felt like crying. "Daddy, this is so sweet." The fact that her father laid out a similar spread every year made it no less moving, especially now that Kate wanted comfort so badly.

"But that's not all," Mr. Benjamin said. "This year, I have a special treat. Wait here. Take off your shoes."

Mr. Benjamin rushed upstairs, and Kate and her mother sat down at the table and removed their boots. Kate looked at her wrapped gift—for once, it didn't feel like a book.

"Your father," Mrs. Benjamin said lovingly. "You know how much he appreciates your being here with us, don't you?"

"I know."

"We both do."

"I know, mom."

Mr. Benjamin clomped downstairs, held up his finger for them to wait and then hurried toward the master bedroom. After a minute, he came back into the kitchen.

"My dear," he said to his wife, "if you'll be so kind as to wait here. Katie." He held out his arm and Kate took it. "If you'll allow me."

She smiled, her first genuine smile in weeks. Even at harvest times in the past, her father had never been so gallant or dramatic. He led her upstairs, past her bedroom and down the hall. She heard water running. She smelled vanilla. Her father stepped aside and motioned her into the bathroom.

Kate put her hand to her mouth. The shade was drawn to darken the window and scented candles were burning everywhere, on the counters, on top of the hamper, on the floor around the bath. The faucet was steaming and plomping as it filled the tub, and red rose petals floated in the water. On a little wicker table next to the tub was a bowl of chocolate-dipped strawberries, a bottle of champagne in a cooler, a fluted glass and a vase filled with long-stemmed roses and baby's breath.

"What—possessed you?"

"Is that any way to show gratitude?" He beamed at her. "Now I have another harvest treat to deliver." He kissed her on the cheek and walked away down the hall.

"Thank you, daddy."

"There's dinner when you're finished and you saw the pie and the gifts for later. Take your time." He disappeared down the stairs.

Kate shut the bathroom door and picked a strawberry out of the bowl. The chocolate was sweating. She popped it into her mouth.

She poured a glass of champagne and undressed as the bath filled. When she had shed her grubby work clothes and freed her hair from its band, she sat on the edge of the tub, sipping champagne and lolling her free hand in the hot water. She emptied her first glass and dipped one foot cautiously in the tub, then the other foot, and then she sat down all at once, smarting pleasantly from the heat. She rubbed her wet hands into her cheeks, feeling the soothing effects of the warmth along the whole length of her body.

She lay there, moving gently with the water, thinking how affectionate her father could be. She breathed in the vanilla and dallied with the floating rose petals, and it occurred to her that this was the kind of display a boyfriend should make, not a father. She slipped down in the tub, dipping her head under the water, and came up with her hair in her face.

She poured herself another glass of champagne, plucked a rose petal from the water and tore it with her teeth. The silky wetness felt good against her lips and she ate a corner of the petal and drank deeply of the champagne. The bubbles tickled her nose.

As she thought of all the loving gestures her boyfriend would never make for her, she made a resolution. Yes, she would go to Boston, but before she did she would drive into Templeton one last time and talk to Jon. She wasn't sure what she could say or what she wanted to hear, but she wanted to recapture a little of the dignity he had stolen from her. She wanted him, at least once before it was all over, to meet her on her terms. She dipped her head under water and swept the hair away from her face.

25

A Farewell

It had been a busy night at Ploughman's—at eleven o'clock, Martina was still mopping the kitchen and Jon was refilling salt and pepper shakers in the dining room. They had the music turned up—an Ink Spots album reverberated off the walls, the high volume and old speakers muddying the four-part harmonies.

Jon was finding it harder and harder to get anything done: harder to sleep, harder to work, harder to make sense of anything. His life now revolved around his distance from Marnie at any given moment. She formed the background and foreground of every waking action, and her absence there at the diner or in his apartment only made her presence stronger in Jon's thoughts.

His relationships with his co-workers had turned flinty. His regular customers, who had once enjoyed Jon's offhanded repartee, would no longer indulge his banter. Every moment at work had become a test of endurance. He could no longer distinguish between the actual disdain of those around him and the contempt his paranoid imagination created, so that every encounter became a new occasion for hostility and suspicion.

He was spending as much time as he could at the Hawthorne Mansion, since that was the only place he now felt welcome, but Marnie seemed cold since Graham's departure. She was spending more time at the toffee plant and had become obsessed with the operations of Hawthorne Enterprises. When Jon and Marnie were together, Jon felt like an observer, and his displays of affection had grown grander and more desperate, increasingly obvious pleas for attention. He knew that the suddenness of Graham's disappearance troubled Marnie, and there was nothing he could do about it but wait and hope she stayed.

He finished filling the salt shakers, screwed on their lids and then started on the pepper. His most tedious tasks at Ploughman's gave his mind the best opportunities to wander and the most cause for despair.

He had resolved to keep his mouth shut and his head down, but he knew that as long as he continued to see Marnie, the silent uproar around him would continue. He was living like a refugee in his own home town, watching, dreading, not talking to people on the street. Worse yet, he was now dipping into his savings—he didn't earn enough at Ploughman's to pay his bills. This state of affairs could not last. Something would have to change, in his work, in his relationship with Marnie, something. . . but he was in no position to force a change, so he had to wait and watch. It was maddening, but at least he was actually with Marnie, as her lover, and at least their love still had a chance.

He went around the room setting the bottles back on their tables, wiping the booths with a wet cloth. He thought about Jeremiah's bitter ranting: Jon had returned to Jeremiah's barber shop twice since their last confrontation, but the shop was always closed and no one had seen Jeremiah for days. He wondered if Jeremiah had finally gone mad—he had looked and sounded awful, raving about killing Calvin Hawthorne, as if he no longer knew what year it was, as if he had lost all touch with reality. Jon wondered if his love for Marnie would devour his mind the way Jeremiah's love for Dorothy had consumed him. He already felt out of control, and he imagined himself fifty years in the future, in Jeremiah's place: if he lost Marnie, he didn't know what he would do.

Martina wheeled the water bucket into the dining area and mopped the aisles. They worked to the slow rhythms of the loud music, barely looking at one another.

Martina was especially disappointed in Jon. She had looked up to him as a surrogate older brother, confiding in him, asking his help with boyfriends and schoolwork, and she felt personally betrayed on Kate's behalf. He felt Martina's resentment around him like a toxic cloud. She never talked to him any more, and he missed their easiness together and her respect.

They worked toward one another, mopping and wiping, until they met near the cash register. He clumsily hopped around her and stepped onto the wet floor she had just cleaned. His tennis shoes left a dirty trail and Martina sighed pointedly and shook her head.

He walked behind the counter and turned off the neon beer signs and the stereo, and when the music stopped, only the dull metallic clank of Martina's loose mophead broke the silence. Martina kept her eyes steadfastly on the floor. Jon wiped the nozzles of the soda machine. He had grown to hate closing.

When all of their tasks were finished and Martina had emptied the dirty mop water down the kitchen floor drain, Jon escorted her out onto Main Street. He walked her silently down the hill from the Square to the parking lot behind the restaurant. "Good night," he said. Martina said good night without looking at him, then got into her car, started it and quickly drove away. He watched her until she turned on Spring Street, out of sight. He sighed, his breath steaming lightly in the damp night air.

He climbed the hill to the Square. He could see cars parked in front of the Elks' Lodge farther east on Main Street, but the

Square itself was empty and quiet. He crossed to the Courthouse, stopped and looked up at the clock tower silhouetted against the sky. The half-moon glowed cold overhead, and stars twinkled dimly around it.

He was glad work was over, but now he faced something far more difficult—a night alone in his apartment. Despite his relationship with Marnie, he had never felt so alone and anxious, and they struggled constantly over how much time they would spend together. Jon wanted to spend every night at the mansion, but Marnie resisted and guarded her privacy. In order to resolve the stalemate, Jon invented ostensibly useful projects to do, to give him excuses to be at the mansion when he and Marnie weren't doing anything together as a couple. He would fix fallen rain gutters, mend collapsed trellises, tinker with the mechanisms of the grandfather clock, using skills that he had learned working with the Benjamins, and the more routine and ordinary his activities, the more smoothly their relationship went. He felt bonds of familiarity growing between them, but Marnie's lack of resolve about Graham pained him, and he felt insecure and anonymous when they made love. He didn't know what Marnie wanted. He didn't think she knew, either.

When he wasn't with her, he wondered constantly if he should call her or go to the mansion or wait for her to call, and this pressure caused him to act diffident whenever they actually were together. Before Graham had come to Templeton, Jon had never known a woman so insatiably passionate about him; after Graham had left, he had never known such scrupulous sexual ceremony, where so little risk was involved. Marnie had withdrawn some part of herself, or it had left with Graham, and Jon would make love to Marnie's body while she explored the depths of her own mind, independent of him. Jon told himself that she could not remain this way, that either she would have to offer herself to him body and soul, or she would have to refuse him her body; and so he continued to love her and hope.

He started walking again, past the Old Courthouse toward Cross Street, when he heard his name. His heart raced. It was Kate. He turned and saw her coming toward him, out of the shadows near the steps of the Courthouse. His mouth turned dry.

"Can I talk to you?" she said. Her voice was oddly honeyed and sad.

"Sure," he croaked. He cleared his throat and the sound echoed against the Courthouse bricks.

He approached hesitantly and stood several feet away from her, waiting for permission to come closer. Kate motioned with her hand toward a bench near the steps, and they sat down without looking at each other. A minute passed like an hour. Her calm presence was almost unendurable.

"How have you been?" Jon said. The words felt like marbles in his mouth.

"All right."

"I got your letter."

Kate nodded.

They were silent again. Jon struggled not to blurt out how sorry he was. Any other conversation seemed pointless, but saying he was sorry seemed empty, so he said nothing. He forced himself to look Kate in the face. She was trying not to cry. He had mistaken her unhappiness for composure.

"I tried to call you," he said.

"I know. I didn't want to talk to you."

"And now?"

She sighed heavily, not quite a sob. Their eyes met. "What happened, Jon?"

He wanted to look away but couldn't. "I don't know." He

could think of no satisfactory explanation. "I'd never felt like that before."

"Like you felt with Marnie?"

"Like I feel with Marnie."

Kate looked away. "Didn't you love me?"

"Of course."

"But not like you love Marnie?"

Her tone now felt like a condemnation, but what she said was true. He remembered how comfortable and contented his relationship with Kate had been, especially compared with the anguish he was enduring with Marnie, and he tried to relive the moment when that contented love had first seemed wanting. But that instant eluded him. It seemed like the wrong question.

"Were you just waiting for something better to come along? All that time?"

"No."

"It's just that it did come along."

"No, Kate, that's not it."

An old El Camino chortled rhythmically up Cross Street toward them, and they watched it and waited. When it reached the Square, it caught them in its headlights and then turned and wheeled around the Courthouse, out of sight. Its brakes whined, and then it idled for a while at a red light, until it drove away, leaving them once again in silence.

"You can be honest with me," she said. "There's no point in hiding anything now. I'm just trying to understand. You know? I don't want to think of the last four years as a complete waste of time."

"It wasn't."

"Tell me why."

Jon thought in a panoramic way of everything he and Kate had been through, the ups and downs of their early relationship, the slow intermingling of their dreams and everyday lives. In some ways, they had been natural allies—unlike many of Templeton's residents, they had left town and come back, so they knew for certain that they had other options elsewhere. That knowledge had given their decision to remain here a secret strength, a perceived superiority that they could draw on in difficult times; and it had let them imagine futures together beyond Templeton, which gave their stability an undercurrent of untapped promise. And yet, as soon as Jon thought of Marnie, everything he had shared with Kate hardened into discrete, recountable details, and the complexities of their relationship simplified into reasons.

"At least we didn't get married," Kate said sadly. "At least we didn't have children."

As she said this, her voice wounded Jon, cut through all the motives and possibilities and defenses he had erected against her. Losing Kate suddenly seemed real in a way it hadn't before. He realized that he now had no one to be weak in front of, and the dreams he had shared with Kate, the dreams whose worth they had taken for granted, would have to become arguments with Marnie, to be negotiated and justified. The desperation he felt with Marnie would have to be turned into new dreams, and Jon looked at Kate and felt profoundly alone.

"Are you happier now?" she asked.

It was a hopeless accusation. Jon's choices were no longer a question of happiness, and he couldn't say for certain if he had been happy before he'd met Marnie or if he would have been happy had he stayed with Kate. There were no such equations to be done.

"You think you'll stay in Templeton?" Kate asked. "You and Marnie?"

"I don't know what's going to happen."

"I don't think I will."

"No? Where will you go?"

"I'm going to Boston, to see Faith and Ritu, and I'll see how things look from there."

Jon tried to imagine Templeton without Kate, and he thought of Mr. and Mrs. Benjamin alone out on Harvey Road. "What about your parents' farm?"

She shrugged. "It's just a matter of time, anyway. The only new contracts we've had in years are with organic co-ops, who can't pay, or small foreign farmers, and it's just a matter of time for them, too. Besides, my parents aren't getting younger, and I can't operate that farm alone." She looked sidelong at Jon, another accusation. They had talked about taking over the Benjamins' farm together, enduring the six months of heavy labor every year in order to travel the other six months; but that would not happen now. "Anyway," she said, "nothing has to be decided now."

They were silent for a long while. Jon felt the chill around him growing denser.

"When do you leave?"

"As soon as we get the books in order, and. . . I'm not sure." Kate put her hands in the pockets of her jacket and hunched forward. She looked intently at Jon and held his gaze when he finally looked back. He felt trapped in the dejection in her eyes. "I guess that's why I wanted to see you." She shook her head. "No," she said, almost to herself, "I wanted to see you because I wanted you to feel guilty. I wanted you to feel responsible. But I guess it doesn't matter now." She stood up, and Jon jumped up next to her.

"I do feel responsible," he said.

"It doesn't change anything, though, does it? So you feel responsible. . ." She shrugged again. "So what?" She started walking.

"Wait."

Jon sensed the finality of the moment. The bond of rejection and silence that had tied him to Kate these last few weeks would unravel when she walked away, when she left Templeton. She had come to say goodbye, and though he had rejected her, he did not want her to leave.

She stopped, but Jon could think of nothing to say. He didn't want to revive their relationship—he just wanted Kate to stay, just for a few moments, but he could give her no reason to do so.

They stood facing one another in front of the Courthouse until it became clear that neither had anything to say, and Kate started walking again. Jon watched her until she passed Bertram's Drug Store and left the Square. He put his head down and turned toward Cross Street.

26

A Shot In The Dark

Jeremiah sat on an upturned wooden bucket outside the gardener's shed in the Hawthorne apple orchard. He was smoking his pipe, shivering, trying without success to enjoy the afternoon sunshine. After two nights in the shed, he felt achy and downcast; his clothes were rumpled and stale, his face unshaven for the first time in many years. He had not really slept. The shed provided little protection against midnight breezes, which crept between the slats of the walls, and the chill morning dew had settled into his bones.

He had stuffed his old army backpack full, haphazardly: canned food, bottles of rum, grime-caked camping supplies from his garage. He wore his army issue Colt .45 on his hip—he had cleaned and oiled this gun once a month for the last fifty-five years, ever since he had left the service, as a meditation on the past. He had never imagined that one day such constant care might seem like preparation. Because he had been a mop-up soldier in a supply unit during the late stages of the war, always following the action, he had never fired on an enemy, and his Colt retained a measure of romance that it might otherwise have lost in use. When he held it, he imagined only the sound of its report and its violent recoil, not the weird mangling of flesh that would follow.

He had walked here in the middle of the night, and at first it had felt like old times, just the way he remembered it—sneaking into the garden, on a secret errand that he alone knew. But things had changed: the vigor of his youth was barely a memory, and he had struggled under the weight of his pack as he'd clambered out of the dell below the orchard. The iron fence around the property had nearly defeated him—with the specter of a broken hip and a useless death balancing on his shoulders, he had swung over it and lowered himself with great difficulty to the ground. He had nearly impaled himself on the *fleurs de lis* atop the posts and had twisted his ankle, but what his muscles lacked, his will made up, and he had recovered and tramped through the gnarled trees to the shed. Arriving there again after so many years had brought his memories of Dorothy home with fresh force and filled him with a sense of destiny and purpose.

He had cleared a space inside the gardener's shed and spread his bedroll on the floor. There was no sign of occupation, no cot or personal effects that someone might leave behind in the course of coming and going. There were only gardening supplies, but Jeremiah believed it significant that the rakes, clippers, hoes, trowels, shovels and other implements were all neatly arranged, clean and in good condition, as if someone had been using them. There were no spider webs, and the floor seemed freshly swept. Jeremiah walked all around it, got down on his hands and knees and peered at the baseboards, kicked it and stamped around the inside, examined every inch for wires or electric switches, but there were none. It was just an ordinary shed, but one that had been used recently and often. Whoever had been using it would surely return—Jeremiah only had to wait long enough, and in this he was happy. If Calvin Hawthorne hadn't been here, someone else certainly had, and knowing who it was might take him a long way in the right direction. Something was going on here that no one was talking about.

He finished his bowl of tobacco and wiped blood from the stem of his pipe. He had developed a painful canker on the inside of his lip, and it would tear and seep, making it difficult to drink or smoke without pain; and in the moments when he could resolve himself to this indignity, he would suddenly break into a soaking sweat and his teeth would chatter, his tongue would swell and he would involuntarily chew up his cheeks. The fevers made him feel shrunken and weak; there were times, especially at night, when he thought he had come here to die, when his obsession with Calvin seemed an empty, hopeless excuse for his own end. He took a long drink of rum.

He stood up from his bucket and walked around the edge of the clearing, fingering his gun in its holster. He drew it, held it at arm's length and sighted a tree trunk, feeling the balance and gravity of it. The ache of arthritis in his hand radiated all the way up his arm, and he brought the gun down, wondering if he would be capable of using it when the time came. He examined its sandblasted gray-blue metal and the brown grips screwed into its handle, and as he slid his index finger onto the trigger, as he felt the gun nestle smoothly into his palm, a calming dispassion settled over him.

He imagined Calvin at the end of the barrel. He imagined bringing the gun to his own temple. He was overcome with a violent coughing fit, and he spit bloody phlegm and wiped a trail of saliva away from his lower lip.

* * * * *

In addition to the orderliness of the shed, the apple trees all around it were well-groomed, and no apples littered the ground, as Jon had reported. The grove was nowhere near wild, the way an orchard untended for thirty years should have been. It was still carefully pruned, and it surely produced a vast wealth of apples. It was just the kind of secret Calvin would have loved: an open one, hidden in plain sight, too obvious to be discovered.

Jeremiah tried to entertain alternatives to his theory of Calvin Hawthorne, explanations for the abundance of the orchard and the immaculate state of the rose garden, but he could think of no hypothesis that satisfied the way a death hoax did. Despite its irrational elements, his theory was not only satisfactory but necessary: if he accepted simpler, safer explanations, he felt miserable and small. The Hawthorne story, without its most spectacular, inexplicable puzzles, could not justify the life Jeremiah had lived in its shadow. He had to maintain the romance of the orchard, the romance of the Hawthornes themselves, or his own life would become meaningless.

Jeremiah found the clearing around the shed dreamlike, though the dream had changed since his youth. The fairy tale had grown more sinister: the way the laden branches hung over the perfectly circular clearing invited him in but also forbade him to leave. It was still the enchanted garden where his love for Dorothy had bloomed, but it felt smaller now. At night, the clearing was like a bright island in dark waters, the moonlight silvering its edges, all its colors reduced to cold blues and grays. The sleepless, painful, rum-soaked nights waiting to kill Calvin Hawthorne convinced him that he belonged here, that this was his final destination. After years of doing nothing but thinking, he was finally acting, though he couldn't tell if he had been released from an evil spell or captured by one.

His appetite had disappeared—though he had all the apples he could ever want, they felt like wood pulp against his tongue. The canned peaches and kippers he'd brought from home made him feel foolish. Eating became a painful burden. Instead, he drank, and every time he took a drink, he toasted Dorothy.

He remembered Dorothy as the beautiful woman she always was, as the kind woman she had rarely been, the passionate lover, the fun-loving coquette of her youth, the strong-willed head of Hawthorne Toffee. He remembered his original love for her, in its naive first moments, and he remembered all of the pain and bitterness that had overlaid it, which would now come to an end. Jeremiah found a measure of fondness in his memories of Dorothy, and he was glad she was dead, so that he could think of her in this way, without her animosity blazing back at him.

Underneath everything else, he had really loved her, with a love beyond reason, and he did not feel sorry for it. His love was true. Everything could have been different.

He put the gun back on his hip and returned to the shed to have another drink of rum.

* * * * *

Just after nightfall of the third day, Jeremiah was gripped with another bout of fever, and he sat in the shed shivering and clinching his teeth. When the fever passed, he felt lonely and exhausted. His brittle bones told him it would be another chilly night, and the rum was no consolation. He decided to make a night patrol, to fight his weariness with action, instead of sitting there freezing and suffering—perhaps, he was simply standing guard on the wrong spot.

He took his last bottle of rum, which was almost empty, grabbed the flashlight from his backpack and wrapped a blanket around his shoulders. He set off walking through the orchard.

Almost as soon as he left the clearing, he grew disoriented—the apple trees did not permit travel in a direct line, and he weaved around them this way and that, trying to walk as due east as possible, but he quickly became unsure of his bearings.

The orchard was small enough to blunder through, whether you knew your exact course or not, and he soon emerged into the meadow, a little south of where he wanted to be. He clicked the flashlight off and hung it from his belt. He looked up at the stars, drank a swig of rum and headed in the direction of the rose garden.

It was a long way across the meadow, and he walked slowly, taking care not to step into a hole. He continued to drink as he walked, trying to stay warm, and though he was painfully aware of how exposed he was to watchful eyes, he could also see by the light of the moon that he was alone in the open field, and he knew he could not be seen from the surrounding streets. If Calvin were somehow tracking his movements, there was nothing he could do about it anyway.

He came to the creek that crossed the meadow. It was too wide to step across, and he tested the ground on its muddy banks for a hop. When he found a spot hard enough, he bounded gawkily across, and as soon as he touched the ground on the other side, the muscles of his lower back seized. He buckled and almost fell. He stood for a while, hunched over, breathing through gritted teeth, massaging his back. The pain shot in pulses down the backs of his legs, and this pain inspired others throughout his body, in his hips and knees and chest. He drank rum and continued walking.

He came to the first hedge. He was careful to move quietly, so as not to alert Marnie or Jon or anyone else who might be near. He wound his way among the hedges and down the paths and came to the opening of the rose garden itself.

He looked at the fountain and the rose bushes and the house beyond. There were lights on inside the mansion, and Jeremiah wondered what it would be like to be sitting in the parlor at that moment, what it would have been like sitting quietly with Dorothy, as her husband. But the idea passed as quickly as it had come, a reflex more than a desire, and he turned instead to the garden right in front of him.

Jeremiah had been obsessed with this garden for weeks—with the idea of Calvin kneeling here openly, secretly, troweling the flower beds—but now that he was standing here once again, his obsession with Calvin mysteriously disappeared. He listened to the splashing water of the fountain and enjoyed the beauty of the carefully ordered flowers in the moonlight, as if they had been laid out especially for him. Just being there, alone and covertly, gave him a measure of tranquility that he had lacked for years, but the feeling confused him. He reminded himself consciously of his hatred for Calvin, but in his heart he felt nothing. He didn't have the energy for hatred now.

He turned and retraced his steps down the garden path, underneath the arbor and back into the meadow. He felt weary down to his soul.

By the time he reached the stream again, he was too dissipated to negotiate the leap, and he didn't care any more. His body felt ragged. He placed his left foot in the water, found a foothold and stepped across. It was only after he had crossed the stream and walked farther through the meadow that the cold registered against his ankle, and he regretted stepping into the water. He wanted to lie down and cry. His back hurt, his mouth throbbed, his ankle was turning numb. All of his hatred had vanished into the rose garden, and he dropped all pretense of vigilance. When he arrived at the edge of the apple orchard again, he drank off the rest of the rum, dottered slightly and threw the bottle to the ground. He felt the pistol in its holster and wished he had the nerve to shoot himself.

He bumped and stumbled his way through the trees. Again, he lost his bearings, and he became unsure which direction the shed lay in, which direction he was facing. The orchard's maze-like design infuriated him. He shivered violently. After bumbling along for a while, he remembered his flashlight and unhooked it from his belt; but shining it into the dark revealed only a tortured mass of limbs, trunks and leaves in every direction. The knobby, contorted shapes frightened Jeremiah, so he turned the light off.

After what seemed a long time and a lot of tramping, he still had not reached the clearing, or the fence, or the meadow. He pressed forward, weaving around trees, becoming more and more lost. At some point, he thought, the orchard had to end—it wasn't large enough to get really lost in—and he trudged on. His sopping wet left foot had become frigid, and he felt like pulling out his gun and shooting randomly into the trees. Violence seemed the only recourse for every problem.

He was sweating under the blanket around his shoulders, sweating and shivering at the same time, and he felt on the verge of vomiting. He shrugged the blanket off at the base of a tree and squinted into the darkness, fighting his need to wretch. He panted and wiped his lips. Off through the trees, he saw a light.

He caught his breath. All the pains in his body seemed to fall away. He blinked and stood up straight—a light! Moving toward him!

He watched the light bobbing and turning through the tangle of trunks and branches: it was too big and white to be anything but a flashlight. Jeremiah's heart pounded. Yes, he thought, he had been right all along. He hurried forward to meet it.

Tracking the light was no easy matter. Though it had appeared to be approaching him, he now saw that its path was uncertain. He lost it in the trees, and when he picked it up again, it was in a different place than he expected, shining in a different direction. He wasn't sure where it was heading, where it was coming from, and as he traced its path, he realized that it might not be Calvin, after all.

He thought of Marnie and Jon meeting at the gardener's shed; Marnie's husband; the people in the houses down in the dell below the orchard; whoever had been collecting the apples. There were many people who might have been holding that light, and Jeremiah decided to sneak up, as close as he could, and find out for certain who he was dealing with. There should be no mistakes.

But no, none of those people would be here now. No one picked apples at night. Marnie was in her mansion and Jon was probably with her. Marnie's husband was gone, and even if he came back, he wouldn't come here. Whoever was holding that light had no legitimate reason for being there. It was Calvin Hawthorne. It was obviously Calvin Hawthorne, he told himself, and the purity of this idea was incontrovertible. He drew his revolver. Calvin would not get away, not this time: his secret had been discovered. Jeremiah would finally be vindicated. He would put an end to his suffering.

The light disappeared. Jeremiah crept forward and came unexpectedly to the edge of the clearing, in the heart of the orchard. He stopped and held his breath, and then he saw the light bobbing through the slats of the shed. Whoever was holding that light was inside the shed! Judging from the height and angle of the beam, he was inspecting Jeremiah's things.

Jeremiah cocked the Colt's hammer. He stole forward, out from beneath the eaves, trying to remain steady, but he could feel the adrenaline and rum coursing through his chest. He gripped the gun tighter to stop his trembling.

Calvin was cornered in the shed, and in a muddled flash Jeremiah debated whether to call out and let Calvin come to him or fling the door open and shoot him like a duck in a barrel. Should he say he had a gun? Should he confront him and gloat before he killed him? It had to be Calvin Hawthorne, he told himself. It was clear.

He was almost at the shed door, and the light inside stayed steady at waist level. He could hear the person inside fumbling with something. Whoever it was had found Jeremiah's things and knew that he was not alone in the orchard—he imagined that the person was selecting a shovel or a hoe to use as a weapon, to set an ambush for him inside. Jeremiah was not safe just because he had a gun. He was sweating cold sweat and his heart was racing. He decided to fling open the door and fire. He took another step toward the shed, when the light suddenly swung around and the door burst open.

The light beamed directly into Jeremiah's eyes. He leveled his gun.

"Who's there?" Jeremiah cried. "Who is it?" The light remained fixed directly on his face. "Who's there?" he cried again. He adjusted his slippery, sweaty grip on the pistol. The stranger didn't move or speak.

"Calvin?"

No answer.

"Calvin Hawthorne?"

The light changed position, and Jeremiah sensed motion in the dark. He saw the outline of a dark object above his head.

He pulled the trigger, and the shot cracked through the night. The fierce recoil jerked the gun out of Jeremiah's hand. He lost his balance. His right knee gave and he fell sideways to the ground. He landed hard on his shoulder and lost his breath.

He lay crumpled and waited for a blow, the shot still ringing in his ears. Nothing moved. After a few unbearable moments, he lifted his head and saw the stranger's flashlight fallen to the ground; it was casting its beam across the leafy floor of the glade twenty feet away.

He sat up and coughed and labored for breath. He had no

idea where his gun had fallen.

"Calvin?" No answer.

Jeremiah struggled to his feet, barely breathing, testing the air for movement. The night now seemed aggressively silent.

He felt on his belt for his own flashlight, but it was no longer there. "Can you hear me?" he said. "Calvin Hawthorne?"

He walked warily to the stranger's flashlight. His right shoulder felt wrong, and he couldn't breathe except in painful gasps. He knelt and picked up the light with his left hand. Whoever was in the clearing with him was not moving. He swept the light across the shed: a man's body lay on the ground in front of the door. He walked closer and saw that the man's chest was covered with blood.

He guided the light up the stranger's body. A noisy throbbing pounded his head, and he could think of nothing but the name Calvin Hawthorne, over and over. Calvin Hawthorne. He froze, unable to bring himself to shine the light on the man's face, staring instead at his bleeding chest, which did not rise and fall.

He aimed the light a foot farther up. He closed his eyes and tried to steady himself, to talk to himself, to still the chaos jumbling his mind. Calvin Hawthorne, he said to himself. He had it coming.

When he finally summoned his courage and opened his eyes, his heart swelled with triumph. He had just killed a dead man. Calvin Hawthorne. He had been right all along.

27

Nothing More To Say

Templeton Police Headquarters was a freestanding, single-story brick building half a mile north of the Square. Its colonnaded walkway and architraved front entrance were its only nods toward martial grandeur; otherwise, it was an unassuming, almost quaint building, with a pair of benches on the front porch and an ornamental fence along the sidewalk. To the side of the building, a high chain-link fence topped with razor wire guarded the parking lot, where three squad cars and a golf cart sat waiting for action.

Jon rode his motorcycle up, parked in front of the building and plugged the meter. He strode up the front walk and went inside.

The main room was a large, open office with linoleum-tiled floors and tan wallpaper. Photographs of Templeton's mayor, Illinois' governor, and the President of the United States hung on the walls in heavy gold frames. Scanners and radios blinked and squawked around the room—the air was filled with staccato bursts of white noise and tinny voices.

Two large desks faced each other from either side of the office, and an army of file cabinets lined the walls, with overflowing In and Out baskets on top of them. Three wooden doors with frosted glass windows led off in different directions, and a pair of ceiling fans spun slowly overhead, barely moving the stiflingly warm air.

A woman seated at one of the desks greeted Jon as he came in. She wore the blue Templeton Police uniform, except that her badge and walkie-talkie rested on the desk in front of her. Jon identified himself and said that he had called earlier about visiting Jeremiah Grayson.

The policewoman waved him to a seat in front of her desk and punched an intercom button on her phone. "Chief," she said. "Jon Ridgely here to visit Jeremiah Grayson."

Jon waited, sweating uncomfortably in the overheated room, while the policewoman stared at him without making small talk: they just looked at each other in silence. Jon felt guilty of something he couldn't remember doing.

One of the interior doors opened and Chief Rusty Miller walked briskly through. He stood six feet two inches tall and was muscular and broad across the shoulders, and he moved with short, precise steps, always of an exactly equal measure. He was forty-five years old, had waxed salt-and-pepper hair and smelled strongly of Old Spice. He was popular in Templeton for his mixture of small shrewdness and simple credulity, and though he was affable in a jokey, chin-chucking way, he always seemed to be evaluating the probability of your statements, even if you were just talking about the weather. This habit had made him the butt of endless jokes and imitations, which somehow made him more popular. His attitude since the night of Calvin's shooting had been especially severe and suspicious—murders were rare in Templeton, especially the murders of men who were already dead, and the case made him feel important.

"You came to see Grayson?" the chief said.

"I did."

"What do you want to see him about?"

Chief Miller had questioned Marnie personally on many occasions since the shooting, and Jon had twice given sworn statements to detectives. The chief knew everything about Jon's encounters with Jeremiah; he knew practically every move Jon had made in the last few months, and he was aware of Jon's affair with Marnie and the marital complications that accompanied it. There was no reason for Jon to feel guarded with the chief, since he already knew everything, yet something in the chief's demeanor made Jon want to lie.

He had come purely out of curiosity. He wanted to speak to Jeremiah about the circumstances of that fatal night, to find out what he knew and what he believed and how it had all happened, first hand, instead of reading the blood-and-thunder accounts in the *Constitution*. These were the same reasons anyone in town might have wanted to speak to Jeremiah, but Jon felt personally connected to the events, both through Marnie and through his conversations with Jeremiah himself.

"I just want to visit him," he finally said.

"Social visit?"

"I guess."

The chief shifted his weight to one leg and scrutinized Jon. "All right, we'll see if he wants to talk to you. Come with me."

Chief Miller led Jon down a short hallway into a small room with no windows. It seemed to Jon like an interrogation room, bare except for a long conference table and four chairs. The chief searched Jon bodily, told him to have a seat and excused himself.

No one was sure yet what crime Jeremiah would be charged with—he had confessed to killing Calvin, but no one could predict if the charge would be second degree murder or manslaughter; for that matter, a homicide charge was not certain. If the authorities believed that Jeremiah's story was true—that Calvin had attacked him—then the severity of the charge might be mitigated. Jeremiah's admitted drunkenness at the time complicated matters, and he was still awaiting evaluation by a state psychiatrist, whose report might change the substance of the charges. Moreover, there were bureaucratic problems surrounding the charges, since the dead man had been dead already at the time of his death, and he would have to be readmitted into the company of the living before he was officially declared deceased. Jeremiah had also admitted killing Robert Meese fifty years before, though he claimed self-defense in that case as well. No one was sure how to proceed.

Jon heard feet in the hall outside the interrogation room. The door opened with a sharp metallic clack and Chief Miller came in alone.

"Sorry," Miller said. "He says he has nothing more to say to you."

"Oh."

"As long as you're here, do you mind if I ask you a few questions?"

Jon sighed. "I've given two statements. I don't know any more than I've told you already."

"Just the same. I have some different kinds of questions to ask you."

"Different kinds. . . ?"

"We're pursuing a number of leads, and you may know something that might help us, something you might never think to say because it doesn't seem related on the surface. You've been helpful, but there are still a few things we'd like to clear up." Chief Miller looked at him without blinking. "Surely you have a few minutes?"

"Obviously," Jon conceded.

"I promise it'll be painless. I'll be right back."

The chief turned and left the room, closing the door behind him. Jon heard a door open and close in the hall. He put his elbows on the table, and rested his chin against his knuckles. He was certain he knew nothing that would help the police; at this point, he could barely help himself.

28

The New Head Of Hawthorne Enterprises

Marnie sat at the writing desk in her grandmother's parlor, sipping tea, pondering a stack of accounting spreadsheets from Hawthorne Toffee. She had been mulling figures and jotting notes all afternoon, as she did every afternoon now, trying to learn the procedures of her family's business.

Making toffee was a complicated affair. There were many suppliers, distributors, wholesalers, unions and government agencies to consider, and the sheer multiplicity of the business made it difficult for her to track. It was the perfect way to avoid thinking about Calvin or dealing with the police, who had practically taken up residence at the Hawthorne Mansion.

She spent almost every morning at the plant, observing, working, interning herself position by position. Jack Madison, the plant's manager, gave her private tutorials, demonstrating equipment, including her in negotiations and conferences, suggesting books to read and people to call. Hawthorne Toffee was still the only place in Templeton where she didn't feel reviled, and her incrementally broadening understanding of the business pleased her and gave her solace. She felt it was the one area of her life whose complexities she could master, while everything else seemed to spin out of control.

The police had been at the mansion every day since the killing. They interrogated Marnie and combed the house and the grounds and sat in their patrol cars on Poplar Street and watched. A twenty-four hour sentry had been established at the "crime scene"—the apple orchard—and blue-uniformed men came and went at all hours. Marnie had told them that she knew nothing about the shooting, or the victim, and she had recounted many times everything that had happened when Jeremiah had visited her at the mansion. But the police still watched her and waited, and detectives came around daily to ask new sets of questions: no one believed how materially insubstantial the connection between Jeremiah and Calvin really was, and they were constantly looking for links. Marnie thought it quite enough that they had both loved the same woman, but then, she thought, she was probably more romantic than the police. They wanted information with a police code already attached to it.

No one believed, either, that Marnie could have been completely unaware of the tunnel underneath the property, or, more importantly, the fact that she had been sharing the estate with Calvin. No matter how much she proclaimed her own amazement, detectives persisted in trying to catch her in a slip, to get her to admit that she knew about Calvin and what he had been doing there, dead to the world for more than thirty years.

Alexandra Bergren had been asked to turn over the Hawthorne account books, so they could be evaluated for evidence of Calvin's involvement in Hawthorne Enterprises, a key component to some of the new claims filed against Dorothy's will. Ms. Bergren had refused to do so without a subpoena, temporarily forestalling the investigation, and then once she did hand over the books, no trace of Calvin could be discovered. Either his support had been wholly subsumed into Dorothy's household budget, or they had hidden his existence through a trail of corporations and accounts so byzantine that even federal investigators were stumped.

In addition to the police, Jake Ziegler had been calling Marnie relentlessly, and the *Constitution*'s journalism since the shooting had become so yellow that Marnie no longer spoke to them. Reporters from other papers had been snooping around as well, and the story had gained notoriety beyond the borders of Illinois.

What surprised Marnie most about these new developments was her own sang-froid, which returned as soon as she learned of the killing. She had long ago accepted that her family's past was tangled and tawdry, and the new revelations were so unbelievable that they returned her to the attitude she had originally had about her grandmother, when she'd first come to Templeton. Though she did not quite admit it to herself, she enjoyed the melodrama and intrigue of it all: her grandparents' lives had ended unhappily, but they—and Jeremiah—had dared to be something other than ordinary.

Marnie's secret enjoyment did not make her days any easier. Her inheritance was thrown into doubt once again, and she had run out of money. She had reached the credit limit on her charge cards, and Graham had withdrawn all the funds from their joint accounts. She had filed papers with Lawford County Superior Court for an advance against her inheritance, but it was a lengthy bureaucratic process, complicated by the new claims against the estate. Marnie was almost certain to inherit the lion's share of the money as the Hawthornes' sole direct descendant, but the holdings might now be tied up in litigation indefinitely, since Calvin had survived Dorothy as the legal heir and his wishes about the disposition of the estate were unknown. Marnie was reduced to borrowing grocery money from Jon. Until the will cleared probate, she was effectively broke, and this new dependence on others galled her.

To add to this injury, Graham would not answer her letters or return her phone calls. She had written him all about Calvin and Jeremiah, but Graham remained silent, and Marnie felt his absence as a special insult in the face of these new revelations. In part, she was learning the intricacies of Hawthorne Toffee to please Graham, to show him that he had been right about that much all along—she had used his meticulous organizational scheme as a foundation for her own ever-expanding files, and she felt that her crash course in the candy business was homework that Graham had assigned her, a path back into his good graces. Whether or not he would be pleased that she was now taking her inheritance so seriously was difficult to determine—it was impossible to impress him if he wouldn't pay attention—but if he contacted her again, she wanted to demonstrate how competent and efficient she had become, to show that she really did care about the things he cared about.

Her atonements, however, did not extend to ending her relationship with Jon. She was aware of the contradiction of trying to impress Graham with her responsibility and simultaneously continuing her affair with Jon, but she could not bring herself to stop seeing him. If she broke up with Jon and Graham decided to leave her for good, she would be completely alone, and she couldn't tolerate that. Besides, she liked Jon's ingenuousness and his romantic spirit; she liked how devoted and earnest he was, and she liked making love with him, in a way that she had never enjoyed making love with Graham. She was stuck in-between, unable to commit to either one, unable to let either go. She wrote letters to Graham professing her love and recounting her progress at the toffee plant, and she prepared candlelight dinners for Jon and invited him into her bed.

Whenever she was overwhelmed by the jumbled, inconsistent, competing emotions of her heart, whenever the police and the *Constitution* drove her to distraction, she called Jack Madison's business contacts and picked their brains about the candy market, or she went down to the factory and wandered the grounds, or she memorized market protocols, as she was doing this afternoon. Hawthorne Enterprises was large enough to absorb her attention day after day, and she could always find new, emotionally neutral things to think about in her family's portfolio. The business became her sanctuary.

She got up from her desk, went into the kitchen and turned on the burner under the tea kettle. Jon would arrive soon and they would drive to Terre Haute to look at new curtains for the library and parlor. Marnie was not enthusiastic about redecorating, but Jon had insisted on helping her renovate the place. Once the decrepitude of the inside of the mansion had been exposed to the public, it had lost much of its romance in Marnie's mind, and refurbishing suddenly seemed in order; still, she balked at throwing anything out, and she remained fascinated by her grandmother's clothing and jewelry. There wasn't enough money at the moment for real renovation, but Jon liked to propose changes to this room or that and to shop for materials. It seemed a harmless enough distraction, and it placated Jon—sometimes, his anxiety about their relationship, about Graham, drove Marnie crazy, and it was good for them to have something ostensibly normal to do together, so he wasn't always walking on eggshells. She imagined them in some chintzy fabric showroom in Terre Haute, speaking to the salesman as if they were newlyweds fixing up their first home, and the idea did not displease her.

She thought about being with Graham. She thought about being with Jon. She came to no conclusions.

The kettle whistled, and she fixed a cup of tea. She took it to the back porch and sat down with her feet up on the chair opposite. She shivered and watched the afternoon shadows lengthen across the garden.

Except for her daily excursions to the toffee plant, she took no pleasure in anything in Templeton except her grandmother's estate. Strolling the quaint town square and downtown shops now seemed like an exercise in amateur theater, and she could certainly not sit in front of the Courthouse with her sketchpad and charcoals, trying to capture the old clocktower—not after the discovery of Calvin's handiwork. If she wanted to draw now, she would have to do so in the privacy of her own home, away from prying eyes, just as Calvin had done.

She finished her tea and walked out into the garden. The more she knew about Hawthorne Enterprises, the clearer her idea of the role she might play in it. She would be required to do nothing—she was replacing her grandmother, who had done nothing for the last ten years, and the business and charitable foundations worked marvelously without her; but she began to see how she might take over some small duties of oversight, giving herself something essential to do that still left plenty of free time. She might start her own foundations, fund some pet projects and work part of the year at the toffee plant, just for the pleasure of playing the role.

The idea of staying in Templeton stole upon her unconsciously, but it also felt natural. Being head of the toffee factory pleased her enormously, despite the animosity of the town, and the old dilapidated house felt more and more like home: it satisfied some mischief in her soul. She thought she might spend a few months of every year in Templeton, then sneak away to a paradise of her own making, which she could construct in Auckland or Lisbon or London. Of course, how much money she would have was in doubt—the new claims against the will had to be settled, and Graham might follow through on his threat to divorce her and take half—but if every judgment went against her, there would still be enough money left over to last a lifetime.

Marnie's grandmother had spent practically nothing—Dorothy had been content to earn money and hoard it, and Marnie vowed not to make this same mistake. As long as people kept eating toffee bars, she saw no limit to her earning potential, no matter that the actual money, for the moment, remained unavailable. For now, her reality was this garden and this house and borrowing cash for groceries, but there were far bigger things on the horizon.

She lingered near the rose bushes where Graham had been kneeling when she'd first found him here. That night seemed ages past, and the afternoon she'd spent with Jeremiah on the veranda seemed wistfully long ago, and Jon's first visit felt like another life.

The splashing of the water in Cupid's fountain drew her. She loved looking at the play of the strong afternoon sunshine on the cascading waters, being caught in the cold spray of a sudden gust of wind. She stood at the edge of the fountain and peered into the water and noticed for the first time that there was no algae in the marble basin. She dipped a finger into the fountain and tasted it—it was chlorinated, but not heavily, and she suddenly noticed that the water level was always exactly the same, had always been the same since she'd arrived, despite the fact that she had never filled it. She walked around it, inspecting the base, thinking that it must have an automatic sensor, that an irrigation pipe must run underneath it somehow, but she saw no evidence of it. She put her hands on her hips and stared at Cupid's face, which stared inscrutably back.

Calvin. It should have been obvious all along.

"Hello!"

Jon walked around the side of the house. "You didn't answer the door," he said, "so I let myself in the gate." He was wearing his black double-breasted suit, the same suit he'd been wearing when she'd first met him. He took Marnie into his arms and kissed her affectionately.

"What are you dressed for?"

"Our trip to Terre Haute. I have a little diversion planned

for us, if you're up for it." He kissed her again. "How's your Lindy?"

"Lindy?"

"Foxtrot?"

"What are you talking about?"

"I assume you can waltz."

He led her through some waltz steps and dipped her over the edge of the fountain. Water splashed their faces and Marnie squealed and laughed. "Don't drop me." Jon lifted her up and led her through a twirl and another half-dip. "I haven't danced in years," she said.

"There's a place in Terre Haute that hosts Big Band dancing every Thursday night. They play Swing records, and you can dance the night away. Till eight-thirty, at least."

"So the fabric warehouse was just a ruse?"

"We can do both."

"Do I have to dress?"

"Of course. It'll take our minds off. . . all this." He waved in the direction of Poplar Street, where Marnie knew a patrol car was monitoring them. "It'll be fun."

She looked at Jon's face: with the golden afternoon sun deepening the laugh lines around his eyes, lending his pale skin a high, healthy glow, she felt a genuine, reassuring affection for him, so different from the imperious uncertainty she had grown accustomed to. For the first time, for just an instant, she looked at him and didn't think of Graham. As soon as she recognized this feeling, she withdrew from it and nervously sealed her heart against it, but it did not go away.

"Actually, it sounds nice."

"Good. Come on, let's dress you up."

He escorted Marnie into the house and Marnie started genuinely looking forward to the evening ahead, to losing herself in something other than furtive secrets. She realized with a start just how unassailable she had become since moving into her grandmother's mansion, just how harried her new emotional life was. Calvin's secret and Jeremiah's crime had tormented her days, and the dim revulsion and attraction of her family had colored her life. She remembered what it was like to have fun, to have no worries whatsoever, and as she walked arm in arm with Jon, she stopped inventing alternate versions of her life and took a moment simply to live it.

* * * * *

The Wabash Senior Center in downtown Terre Haute looked like a Soviet apartment building: a beige concrete-block high-rise that went straight up and down, all right angles, cracking bricks and cheap-looking windows. It was an assisted-living care home with a large community room on the ground floor. Every Thursday evening, the space was turned into a ballroom and all the seniors came down to dance and listen to the music of their youth. The public was invited for two dollars per person. In deference to the age of the participants, most of the dances were in waltz time, but there were occasional brassy numbers, jitterbugs and stomps.

Jon and Marnie were the youngest dancers by forty years and easily the best-dressed. Marnie, in a full-length crimson dress—one of Dorothy's old formals—would not have looked out of place when this music was new, and Jon seemed perfectly at home beside her. Some of the oldest people there greeted Jon by name.

As they danced, a few still-spry old men occasionally cut in, and Jon went off to dance with their dates—Marnie enjoyed watching him charm the older ladies, and the men flirted scandalously with Marnie—but mostly she and Jon waltzed together, and Marnie was impressed by his dancing. As they swayed cheek to cheek to Glenn Miller's "Tuxedo Junction," Marnie astonished herself by truly enjoying the evening, the simple movements of her body against Jon's.

"How do you know about this place?" she asked.

"I used to come here quite a bit."

"With Kate?"

"Yes, with Kate. That's why they're all looking at you so funny."

"I suppose I suffer by comparison," she said, brazenly fishing for compliments.

"Not even a little."

She kissed him, petted his hair and pulled him closer. "Tuxedo Junction" ended and the faster "Song of India" snaked across the room. Jon led her through some quick three-step maneuvers and twirled her. She had become so used to Jon's earnest meekness and emotional beggary that following his lead was a revelation—he seemed forceful and masculine while dancing, and she liked this new side of him.

The song ended and everyone clapped. The DJ announced that all proceeds from the sale of punch would go toward the billiards fund, so why didn't everyone wet their whistles? Jon and Marnie smiled at each other as if this were their own private joke, and then the slow brass of "I Had The Craziest Dream" began, and they came together for another cheek-to-cheek waltz.

By the time they bought cups of punch and sat down, the evening was almost over. Marnie sipped the strawberry Kool-Aid and looked around the senior center, its bulletin boards cluttered with announcements and its fold-out chairs along the walls filled with people chatting and laughing. Two women in wheelchairs were swaying to the music, and a few nurses in unflattering green uniforms stood leaning against door frames, chewing gum and looking bored.

The DJ announced the last song of the evening. Jon bowed gallantly and asked for the dance. Rosemary Clooney's version of "People Will Say We're In Love" came through the speakers, and they sashayed to the center of the floor. Jon held her close and sang softly with the music, pronouncing every word as if he had written the lyric himself.

When the song ended, he squeezed her tight and gave her a warm kiss on the cheek. They said goodbye to their fellow dancers and walked out into the night, where Jon's truck awaited them.

"Thank you," Marnie said.

"It's my pleasure." He opened her door for her, then got into the driver's seat and turned the ignition.

"I mean," Marnie said, more intently, "thank you." She was feeling especially in his debt tonight, and she hoped he would understand this feeling from her tone, because she was sure she couldn't explain it.

He laughed with delight. He slid his hand to the back of her neck and pulled her toward him, and they kissed.

He put the truck into gear and they drove toward Indiana Route 40, which would lead them across the Wabash River to Templeton. It would be an hour's drive through heavily wooded countryside before they came to Marnie's front door, and Marnie sat back in her seat and relaxed, ready to enjoy the ride.

A night out waltzing to the Big Bands, she thought, staring at the darkness beyond the passenger side window. A nice, social evening that Henry might have approved. She adjusted the long skirts of her grandmother's flowing red dress.

29

ANOTHER FAREWELL

Mrs. Benjamin sat at her kitchen table, reading a copy of the Templeton *Constitution*. "That Jeremiah Grayson. I always suspected he'd do something like this some day."

"Why?" Mr. Benjamin said. He was sitting next to her, sipping coffee, looking through the dining room window at the empty field across Harvey Road.

"I could tell by the way he looked at me. You could always see there was something strange going on behind those eyes."

"When did Jeremiah Grayson ever look at you?"

"I used to see him down at Bertram's. He sat at that lunch counter every day."

"He won't be sitting at any lunch counters now. Besides, what he did hardly compares to what those crazy Hawthornes did in the first place. That tunnel? I can't believe those lunatics were the richest and most influential people in the county. And now it's Marnie, who's hardly any better."

Mrs. Benjamin continued reading the paper and shaking her head. They had finished an early breakfast and were waiting for Kate to come downstairs. Her car was packed for her trip to Boston, and she was in her bedroom, getting the last of her things in order.

"There's always something unusual happening with those Hawthornes," Mrs. Benjamin said.

"And none of it good."

It was the fourth week since the shooting and the newspaper had been filled with nothing but tasteless, sensationalized stories. Jake Ziegler was enjoying minor celebrity status—his articles were full of bluster and hyperbole about Dorothy and Calvin, Jeremiah and Dorothy, and the morbid love triangle that had developed among the three of them. He had written an imaginative re-creation of the days leading up to the shooting, a caricature of Jeremiah's obsession with Calvin Hawthorne, and his stories were full of sly implications about Marnie's love life.

The *Constitution* had run a long biographical profile of Jon, with pictures of the scene of the shooting and the Hawthorne Mansion, linking him to the events by association. There were man-on-the-street interviews expressing how simultaneously taken aback and unimpressed everyone was about this latest strangeness associated with the Hawthornes. The interviewees always affected a superior coldness, as if Calvin's reappearance should have been expected all along, and his death was met in print with cold-blooded irony. Privately, Templeton's residents admitted that the weirdness of the incest and the vast collection of oil paintings of Dorothy were the first genuinely shocking things they had encountered in years. Calvin's resurrection and murder, his relationship with his reclusive sister and the chaos that these events had caused in the succession of the Hawthorne Toffee dynasty were sufficiently macabre and titillating that reporters from the Chicago *Tribune* and St. Louis *Post-Dispatch* had taken rooms at the Templeton Country Inn, and the New York *Times* was carrying stories about it off the wires.

"What does the heiress say?" Mr. Benjamin asked.

"Nothing, at least not in today's paper."

"She's hiding something. She had to know about it. I'll bet she's just like Dorothy."

"She can't be just like Dorothy—she doesn't have any brothers or sisters."

"But there's Jon and her husband, and who knows who else," Mr. Benjamin said under his breath, so Kate wouldn't hear. "That's almost as bad."

"Marjorie Sweet said she drove by the Hawthorne place the other day, on her way to the store, just to see how things looked, and the police followed her! Followed her to the IGA, wrote down her license plate number, as if she'd done something wrong, just because she stopped to look at the mansion. The whole thing is just. . ." Mrs. Benjamin shook her head. She put the paper down, got up from the table and poured herself another cup of coffee.

"I wonder if Jon had anything to do with all this," Mr. Benjamin said. "Like the papers suggest."

"Of course not. How could he? Besides, I talked to Elizabeth Healy—you know, Martina's mother, down at Ploughman's—and she said Jon was just as shocked as everyone else was."

Mr. Benjamin looked at her ironically. "I'll bet he was."

They heard Kate tromping down the stairs, and she appeared in the dining room with a heavy gym bag in one hand and her guitar in the other. She wore blue jeans and a white cable-knit sweater, and her newly shorn hair was combed toward her face—she'd had most of her hair cut off and restyled the previous day at the Lady's Oasis Salon. Her cheeks were freshly scrubbed and ruddy, with no makeup, and she set her things down, spread her arms wide and smiled at her parents.

"This is it," she said. She felt herself beaming. Her giddiness at leaving bordered on euphoria.

"You decided to take your guitar?" her mother asked.

"Ritu's boyfriend said he'd give me some tips. Anyway, what good is having it if I don't play it?"

"Okay, now, do you have enough money?"

"Daddy, you've asked me a dozen times."

Mr. Benjamin pulled out his wallet. "All the same," he took out forty dollars, "you can never have enough money on the road." He stuffed the bills into Kate's hand. "You'll thank me for it in Ohio." He kissed her cheek.

"All right, Daddy. Come on, help me put my stuff in the car."

Mr. Benjamin picked up the guitar and Kate slung her bag over her shoulder, and they all walked out to the driveway. Frost lay on the ground in sparkling white patches, and the night's cold lingered in the morning air. As she stepped out of the house, Kate's breath appeared and disappeared before her in wispy clouds—a perfect morning, she thought. She opened her Toyota's back door and tossed her bag in, then took the guitar from her father and set it gently across the seat.

Her mother was stoically fighting back tears and her father was looking at the ground. She went first to her mother and gave her a long hug.

"I'll miss you," Kate said.

"You be careful, and call us along the way."

"I will."

Next she hugged her father, who said nothing, but kissed her on the cheek once more. She walked around her car, said "I love you guys," and got in. Her parents stood in the driveway, arms around each other's waists, waving as she backed into the road.

She waved one last time and headed off toward Route 44. A quarter of a mile down the road, she looked in her rearview mirror and her parents were still there. They had walked down the driveway and were standing with their arms high above their heads, waving. They stayed and continued to wave until Kate saw them only as tiny specks in the mirror.

* * * * *

For the first thirty miles outside of Templeton, she continued to feel elated; but when she reached Interstate 70 and accelerated to highway cruising speed, she relaxed into a feeling of calm. The terrain became less familiar and seemed alive with possibilities.

The recent news, about Jeremiah and the killing of Calvin Hawthorne, had made Kate feel more distant than ever from Jon, and she no longer envied Marnie or felt jealous of Jon's new life. He had found himself more trouble with Marnie Hawthorne than Kate could have invented in a lifetime, and she felt that he deserved it. If that was what he wanted, he could have it.

The stands of dwarf willows and sycamores at the side of the highway gave way to rolling meadows and empty, stubbled corn fields. Kate would have plenty of time to reacquaint herself with Boston and find new nooks and niches she had missed in the past. She could start anew, if she liked, completely from scratch, and part of her begged to do just that. If she didn't return to her parents' farm, it would fail and her parents would be terribly disappointed, but she was not sure she wanted to share their dreams any more. She was not sure what her own dreams were any more. She would find out this winter just how much the farm meant to her, whether it called her back in the spring or not.

She had enough money to stay in Boston till March without working. She thought she might take a part-time job anyway, or she could see if there were positions available in her old department at Wellesley. The possibilities of Boston brought her unexpected euphoria back, and she told herself that, if nothing else, she could take day cruises out of Boston Harbor and go skiing in Vermont, relax for the winter and have fun. It would be such a pleasure to do things completely unconnected to Jon, to be with people who wouldn't speak his name, to walk down streets where even his ghost would not appear.

She tilted her seat back, set her cruise control and activated her cell phone. She dialed Ritu's number in Boston and told her she was on her way.

30

The Living And The Dead

Jeremiah lay on a thin mattress atop a metal platform screwed into the wall of his cell in the Templeton City Jail. The jail was actually the basement of Police Headquarters, and its qualities reminded Jeremiah more of a vegetable cellar than a prison. It consisted of one large room that smelled of fungus, with six-by-ten cells in two of the corners. Usually, these cells were occupied by drunks or vagrants; serious offenders waited here to be transferred to county, state or federal facilities, but there were almost never any serious offenders. A third corner contained a tiny bathroom stall with no door: a policeman escorted prisoners to the toilet and watched them relieve themselves whenever the need arose. The floor was concrete, and every object—the walls, the ceiling, the bars of the cells, the toilet—was painted the same dispiriting gray. Humming fluorescent lights overhead cast a light blue glow, intensifying the claustrophobic effect.

Near the stairs was a gray metal desk with a telephone and an intercom receiver, and behind it was a rolling office chair. A young policeman sat there, chewing gum and reading a magazine, his feet up on the desk. Jeremiah was the lone prisoner—the cell opposite his stood empty—and the policeman glanced at him occasionally and popped his gum.

An ancient furnace squatted in the middle of the basement and roared to life occasionally, with a whooshing sound that filled the room. Jeremiah took comfort in the yeasty heat, which warmed his bones and eased the aches in his joints.

He had spent his first two weeks in custody in Lawford County Memorial Hospital, receiving intravenous fluids, racked by pain and fever, sweating, vomiting bile and then retching when he could no longer vomit. The Serax the doctor had prescribed for his alcohol withdrawals had made everything seem slower and less threatening, and his thoughts had eventually stopped revolving exclusively around rum, which had gripped his mind for what seemed an endless stretch of brittle days and sleepless nights. When the sores in his mouth had healed and he could finally keep food down, the hospital had released him and he had been transferred to the jail, where the police had been feeding him three square meals a day, so that he felt physically better than he had in years. He was gaining weight. He still longed for his pipe, which he had lost in the apple orchard, but that was a craving that didn't grip his whole being the way the alcohol had. As he lay on the uncomfortable prison mattress, he was actually able to relax, and there were moments when he thought of neither Dorothy nor Calvin.

After he had killed Calvin Hawthorne, he had been too feeble and triumphant to think. He had stood over the body for a long time, released, and yet unable to believe that he had shot Calvin, that he had been right after all. He had paced in circles, around the shed, around the body, around the edges of the clearing in the apple orchard, trying to understand what had happened, feeling with his whole body the final severing of his ties to the Hawthornes. In the moment, he had remained baffled about the details—how Calvin had come into the orchard, what he was doing there, why he had faked his death in the first place—but his relief was boundless, and it seemed that a tangible weight had been removed from his heart.

As he'd stood over the body, Jeremiah had considered putting a bullet through his own head and ending the matter once and for all, but with Dorothy dead and Calvin's secret now uncovered, he no longer felt the impulse toward self-destruction, and there were too many questions he still wanted answered. His physical exhaustion ebbed when he imagined presenting the corpse to the town, and he found the strength to carry his gun and the dead man's flashlight past the Hawthorne Mansion and right down Main Street. He had walked all the way to the front door of police headquarters, turned over his gun, proudly confessed everything and then collapsed.

Jeremiah was taken to the hospital, and a patrolman was dispatched to investigate the apple orchard. The discovery of Calvin's body, like the pop of a starter's gun, had set the whole town running in an endless, breathless circle. Jake Ziegler, the *Constitution*'s cub reporter, had heard the dispatches on his police radio scanner, and he'd arrived at the orchard before the medical examiner's van: a story with garish photographs had run in a special edition the next morning, and every lunch counter and beauty salon in the county buzzed with the news.

The shock of finding Calvin Hawthorne alive after so many years and then dead again would have been enough to set Templeton on its ear for weeks, but what the ensuing police investigation revealed was beyond the most lurid gossip's daydreams; even Jeremiah had not imagined a tunnel leading from the gardener's shed to a bunker-like compound underneath the mansion itself. Police had needed a week to find the tunnel opening—it was cleverly hidden beneath a false foundation below the shed—and another week to break into it, since its inner door was guarded by specially encrypted, coded electronic locks, governing a reinforced steel swingarm gate. Experts from the Bureau of Alcohol, Tobacco and Firearms had been called from Chicago to crack the codes, and when they had broken in, even those cynical veterans had been dumbfounded at the scope of the chambers they had found.

The tunnel itself was no crude escape route: it looked like a corridor connecting terminals in an airport. Judging by the photographs in the *Constitution*, Jeremiah thought it better designed than the new Lawford County Court Complex: it was floored with cut stone in-laid with geometrically patterned colored glass. The tunnel led to an apartment consisting of three large rooms, directly beneath the rose garden. There was a regal bedroom with a king-sized bed; a home spa with a sauna, a whirlpool and a steamroom; and a cavernous main room with motion picture projectors, darkroom equipment, a short-wave radio receiver and board games from the 1950s. Most astonishing were the oil paintings, charcoal sketches, photographs and 8-millimeter films: there were thousands of them, all with only one subject—Dorothy Hawthorne.

Calvin's underground labyrinth was a shrine to Dorothy, and his images composed a visual record of her entire life. There were snapshots of her as a little girl, black-and-white films from the 1940s and '50s, and countless boudoir photos. There were also hundreds of sketches and oil paintings, some technically accomplished, imitating well-known Renaissance nudes and Flemish portraiture. Only one canvas remained unfinished—a depiction of Dorothy as a young woman, standing in the rose garden.

The item that drew the most attention was a color 8-millimeter film that police had found loaded in a projector, ready to run. In a single riveting sequence, Dorothy aged thirty years: she sat in a black leather armchair wearing a frilly pink blouse, looking directly into the camera, and withered away right before your eyes. Investigators had determined, according to the number of individual frames of film in the reel, that she had posed once a week for the last three decades of her life, in exactly the same spot, in exactly the same clothes, right to the very end, and Calvin had exposed only a frame of film each time, creating a stunningly rapid time lapse—the movie hurtled the fifty-year-old Dorothy through old age to deterioration and death in less than two minutes.

The main room of Calvin's bunker opened onto another tunnel that led to the basement of the mansion. It ended in a secret door, the basement side of which was hidden behind false paneling, which itself was blocked by a clot of steel pipes with no real function. This door, too, was guarded by sophisticated electronic code-encrypted locks that took several days to crack.

Once both entrances to Calvin's underground compound had been penetrated, the police spent the next two weeks combing every square inch of the mansion and grounds, looking for more secret passages and hidden rooms, but so far their searches had proved fruitless. Unlike the gothic castles in nineteenth-century romance novels, the Hawthorne Mansion contained only one elaborate secret.

Jeremiah lifted himself up on one elbow, swung his legs out from his mattress, and stood up. "Hey," he shouted at his guard. The policeman looked up from his magazine. "I need to use the bathroom."

"Again?"

"I can prove it."

"All right."

The young man walked to the cell and unlocked the door. He escorted Jeremiah to the bathroom, then stood and watched him lower his trousers and pee. Jeremiah found it insufferably undignified.

He finished and zipped his pants. The Templeton Police Department didn't have jail uniforms, so the police had gone to Jeremiah's house and brought clothes from his own closet. It was like having a valet service—they even did his laundry while they decided what charges to press against him.

He went back to the cell, enjoying the brief walk. They let him out for exercise only once a day—and then only to the parking lot next to the police station—with shackles on his arms and legs. It was absurd: all these strapping young bucks, who could twist him into a pretzel without breaking a sweat, and they insisted that he be manacled.

The policeman locked him back in his cell and returned to his magazine, and Jeremiah lay down again on his narrow mattress. He stared up at the ceiling.

Being confined, physically unable to participate in the world around him, relaxed his mind. He was able to think about Calvin and Dorothy without descending into regret and hatred.

Though their confrontation had been wordless, Jeremiah knew that Calvin knew that Jeremiah had discovered his secret, that it had been Jeremiah who had killed him. Jeremiah still did not understand Calvin's and Dorothy's motives, but he felt nevertheless justified: by killing Calvin, he had restored Dorothy's honor. Moreover, the whole town had to admit that Jeremiah had been right, and the tawdriness of the rest of the affair, the waste of his own life, no longer vexed him.

He could think charitably of Dorothy again, and he could blame everything on Calvin: the underground shrine fixed Calvin's guilt in Jeremiah's mind. He imagined Dorothy a prisoner of Calvin's unspeakable fetishes, and Jeremiah's simple fondness for her unexpectedly returned. He remembered her now with a sadness untainted by anger, and her life became tragic in his imagination.

For the first time since her death, for the first time in his memory, he thought of his own life without bitterness. He realized that, in a way, he had gotten what he had always wanted: he had spent his entire life bound up in his love for Dorothy Hawthorne, thinking about her, shaping his life around her, and though it was not the way he wished his love had been expressed, she had nevertheless been the love of his life, his center and focus. The time he had spent with her long ago had filled him with joy, and when that joy had turned to horror, it had flooded his heart with passion.

He still mourned the loss of Dorothy's love, and he wished they could have lived together happily ever after, but love was not always so rosy or obvious, not with a woman as complicated as Dorothy. For reasons beyond his comprehension, Dorothy had loved her own brother, and Jeremiah felt sorry for it, sorry for her; and though she would have scorned his forgiveness in life, he forgave her in death. "I forgive you, Dorothy," he had said to himself, and as soon as he had said this, something in his heart had uncoiled and released. He felt lighter and younger than he had in ages.

He sat up on his elbow. He was locked in a tiny cell in a dingy gray basement. He would probably spend the rest of his life confined in places much worse than this, with violent and unsavory characters, but he didn't care any more. He didn't have to. He was free.

31

How The Doubts Lingered

It was after noon when Jon rode his motorcycle into the driveway of the Hawthorne Mansion. He parked it behind his own truck—Marnie had returned her rental car when her money had run out, and she was now using Jon's pickup. He locked his helmet to the side of his bike. For the first time in weeks, neither police detectives nor reporters were lurking about, and he wondered what new wild goose chase they had invented to take themselves away from their posts on Poplar Street.

Some robins and red-winged blackbirds fluttered in the trees overhead, picking at the last autumn fruit before heading south, and he stood a moment and stared—he had never seen birds in these trees before. Earlier in the week, he had spied a squirrel timidly sniffing around the driveway—they were the first animals he had ever seen in front of the house, as if Dorothy's black spell over the mansion—or Calvin's—had weakened enough to let some life return. A rook cawed at him and flapped away.

He shivered. In spite of the cold, he took a moment to admire his own craftsmanship: the newly hung storm shutters next to the French windows; the mended trellises against the walls, where freshly-trimmed vines climbed the side of the house; the hooded black footlamps along the walk leading to the porch, which he had paid for out of his dwindling savings. The repairs and improvements might not have been the most expert—compared to Kate or Mr. Benjamin, Jon was still ham-fisted—but he congratulated himself nevertheless. The mansion was beginning to show signs of respectability again, and Jon thought that, with all the unpleasantness surrounding Calvin and Dorothy behind them, with Calvin's black secrets out in the open and the death and macabre fascination of the Hawthornes finally put to rest, Marnie could live the life that Henry had always envisioned for the Hawthornes: one of prosperity and happiness.

He knocked on the front door and waited. His next project, if Marnie approved, would be to install an electric doorbell.

Marnie opened the door, wearing a fetching old-fashioned yellow blouse with frilly white cuffs. Jon slid his arms around her waist and gave her a slow, wet kiss.

"You're freezing!" she said. "Come get warm."

The smell of Marnie's cooking filled the house. "What are you fixing?"

"Ratatouille." She led him into the kitchen. "I found eggplant at the market, and it seemed a shame not to use it. I have red wine, too, if you'd like some."

She poured two glasses of wine and announced that they had a few minutes until lunch. They went out to the veranda, where a portable gas heater bathed them in warmth. They sat down at the glass table.

"What did Jeremiah have to say?"

"Nothing. He still won't see me."

Marnie and Jon had both continued to make trips to the jail, but Jeremiah's refusal to see them remained steadfast. They were beginning to understand that they, like everyone else, would learn nothing more from him till he took the witness stand.

"I was interrogated by the chief again." Chief Miller took their unsuccessful visits to the jail as proof that Jon and Marnie were trying to conceal something, or to keep Jeremiah quiet. His increasingly absurd questioning had become as off-putting as Jeremiah's silence, and Jon vowed privately that this visit had been his last.

"What did he ask you this time?"

"He's got it in his head that I was facilitating Calvin's secret life somehow, that I was being paid off for helping him come and go. I think he's just amazed that someone could pull off a ruse so elaborate so completely, and he'll ask everyone in the county till he finds out how Calvin did it. They still haven't found the contractors who did the original work on the tunnel, and I have to admit that's a hard thing to keep secret."

"Between Calvin and Dorothy," Marnie said, "Calvin was certainly the more devious—the one who knew how to use money to get what he wanted."

"Devious is one way of putting it. Stark raving mad is another." Jon sipped his wine. "Calvin and Dorothy both were."

"Why do you think they did it?"

"Love."

"But why become hermits in a town they owned? Why fake your own death when you have nothing to hide?"

"He was in love with his own sister!" said Jon. "That's something to hide. And remember, he faked his death at exactly the same time your dad discovered that Calvin was his father. I'm sure Calvin and Dorothy thought your dad would publicize everything—they'd be found out and they'd both have to leave Templeton forever. Maybe exile seemed like a fate worse than death."

"He really loved my grandmother, that much I do believe. The care he took in painting those portraits is amazing."

"I don't know if I'd call that love. What about the naked photographs? He started taking them when she was just a young girl."

"You mean she started posing for them when she was a girl. And she kept doing it till her dying day." Marnie looked at a tiny piece of cork floating in her wine glass. "Why is Calvin worse than Jeremiah? They both loved Dorothy, and she loved them. I don't think it's fair to sit in judgment of them without knowing the complexities of their relationships. I mean, who did they hurt?"

Jon looked at her uneasily. "Dorothy, for one. Just because she posed for those pictures didn't mean she wanted to."

"My grandmother was a lot of things, but I don't think 'victim' was one of them. Ask Jeremiah. She made her own choices."

"Maybe. I have to agree with this much, at least: we don't know the internal complexities of Calvin's and Dorothy's relationship. But I think we can say certain things are wrong without knowing every single detail."

"Were Romeo and Juliet right? Their love was forbidden, too."

"Romeo and Juliet weren't brother and sister. And they ended up dead anyway."

"I guess you're not very romantic, after all," Marnie said, "are you?"

He leaned over and kissed her. "More than you imagine."

"To inspire that kind of love and devotion," she went on dreamily. "Two men sacrificed their whole lives to Dorothy Hawthorne."

"Three men—don't forget Robert Meese."

"She must have been the most remarkable woman. . ."

Marnie wore Dorothy's clothing exclusively now, and she spoke of her grandmother in increasingly reverential terms. Jon thought Marnie was having her own romance with Dorothy Hawthorne, and he thought it lucky that the two had never met.

A timer buzzed harshly from the kitchen.

"Love," Marnie said, "is a mysterious perversion."

"It's not a perversion. It's only mysterious."

They went into the kitchen and dished out the ratatouille and sliced some bread. Marnie brought butter, silverware and the wine bottle to the veranda.

They ate in silence, listening to the splashing of the fountain and the rustling of the breeze through the hedges. The hedges were looking ragged, and the grass around the back of the property was becoming long and crabby. Jon wondered how Calvin had managed for so long after Dorothy's death without getting caught. The more he thought about it, the more incredible it became—not that Jeremiah had finally found Calvin out, but that no one else had done so before.

They finished their meal, and Jon cleared the dishes and put them in the sink. He returned to the veranda and kissed Marnie on the forehead.

"You have plans for this afternoon?" he asked.

"Dreary dull—laundry, I think, and my bedroom's a sty. I hardly know what to do with myself, now that the police aren't here day and night. You?"

"I think I'll trim those hedges. And tonight the last drive-in movie of the year is playing."

"What's on?"

"They always show 'Halloween' and 'Friday the 13th' as a double feature before they shut down for the winter. It's fun. Most of us know the dialogue by heart, and people get up in front of the screen and spoof the scenes."

"Let's see how we feel about it later."

Marnie kissed him, then left him on the veranda. He slouched comfortably down in his chair and thought for a while about Jeremiah and Calvin and Dorothy, about love and all of its varied expressions. His relationship with Marnie could have gone as badly as Jeremiah's had gone with Dorothy—for a while, he thought, it had been touch and go, but Marnie was settling down, and she now allowed herself to depend on him in tangible ways. They were building a bond of trust.

He thought of Marnie upstairs doing household chores. She had prepared a nice lunch, and now she would spend the afternoon puttering inside while he worked in the yard. It was so domestic and normal that he finally felt they were in a real relationship. He sipped his wine and, for the first time since he'd met Marnie, did not feel insecure.

32

MARNIE HAWTHORNE WRITES A LETTER TO HER HUSBAND

Marnie stood at the threshold of her bedroom on the third floor of the Hawthorne Mansion, looking at the riot of clothing on the floor, the drinking glasses on the nightstand, the necklaces and earrings strewn haphazardly across the dresser. Between the constant clamor of the police investigation, the renewed claims against her grandmother's estate and her attempts to distract herself with Hawthorne Enterprises, she hadn't had the energy or peace of mind lately to pick up after herself.

Contrary to what she had told Jon, however, she had not retired to her bedroom to catch up on ordinary household chores. She had come to read, once again, the letter that had arrived by express mail while Jon was at work the previous day. It was from Graham, the first communication she'd received from him since he'd left Templeton.

She lifted her mattress. Underneath, she found the red and white international express envelope she had hidden there. She opened it and withdrew the letter—a single sheet of slate-gray stationery—and sat down on the bed to read it.

There were two handwritten paragraphs, the first declaring Graham's continuing revulsion at her infidelity, the second professing his abiding love and the hope that they might overcome these difficulties and be together again. Marnie read the letter several times through, her feelings profoundly mixed. She did not wish to return to London—she loved her husband,

Marnie Writes a Letter

but she did not want to go back to the life they'd led, and she could no longer imagine the new life they might create together. Her life with Graham had stopped; and yet, she told herself, that was only because she had stopped it.

She did not wish to give Graham up, but she had come to enjoy being with Jon. She felt that she belonged to the Hawthornes—to her grandmother more than anyone else—but it was difficult to define what that meant in everyday life.

She walked with Graham's letter in hand to the window. Outside, the sun was casting pale white light across the rose garden, and the arbors around it shimmered in the breeze. Jon was standing in front of the first row of hedges, a pair of clippers in one hand, the other hand on his hip.

Staying here with Jon, leaving him behind: each alternative offered a measure of hope and a measure of cold despair.

Jon dropped his clippers to the grass and walked unhurriedly from the hedges into the rose garden. At the first little bed, he knelt and reached for a rosebush, bending its branches toward him; he pawed the soil, scooping up a handful of dark loam. He stared at it for a long time before tossing it unceremoniously back.

He stood up again and looked at the house. His gaze tilted up and his eyes found Marnie staring down at him. He waved.

With a small adjustment of her arm, Marnie slid Graham's letter behind her thigh, and with her other hand she waved back, and with that simple movement she found the answer she had been looking for. She suddenly saw no need for anything at all to change. She could find many plausible reasons to split her time between London and Templeton, between Graham and Jon, indefinitely.

She turned away from the window, sat down at her grandmother's vanity and took up a sheet of Dorothy's stationery.

"My dearest Graham," she wrote. "I cannot tell you how relieved and happy I am to hear from you. I've been such a fool, and the fact that you're speaking to me again fills my heart with gratitude. I've been so confused by my grandmother's death and this inheritance, by all the changes happening so fast—I've handled myself so poorly! I have much to redeem, and I'll try to earn your forgiveness every day."

She continued writing in this vein for two pages, promising her undying devotion, swearing that the temporary madness of her newfound wealth had passed. She ended the letter by suggesting that she return to London, and she asked Graham if he would allow her back into their house. "It would be the greatest gift you could give me, and more than I deserve."

She folded the letter into an envelope, sealed it and hid it among the loose papers on the vanity. She would find an excuse to go into town later and post it, while Jon was working in the garden.

Many married women had lovers, she thought. It was the stuff romance was made of.

She caught her reflection in the vanity mirror. In her grandmother's high-necked yellow blouse, she was the spitting image of Dorothy Hawthorne.

Printed in the United States
88958LV00001B/7-42/A

9 781933 975009